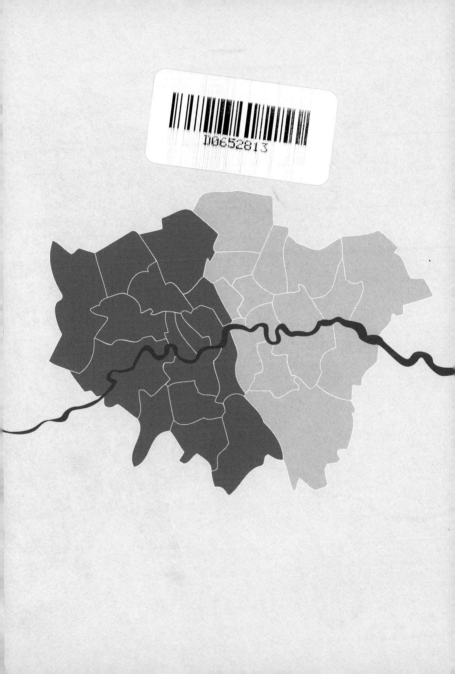

D0652813

33 boroughs shorts
WEST

GLASSHOUSE
BOOKS

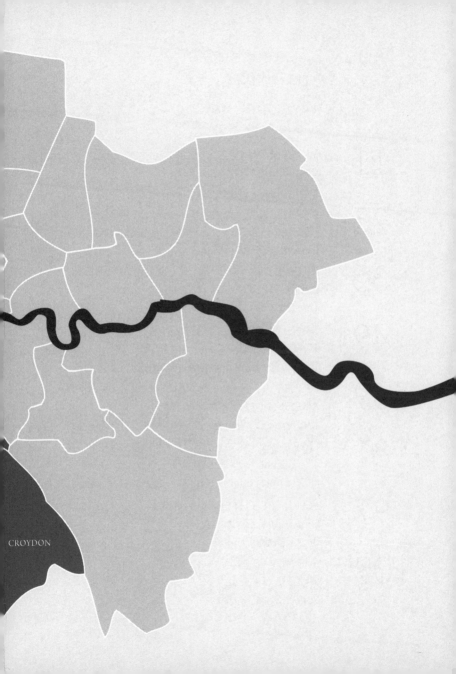
CROYDON

Contents

WESTMINSTER

Run. Thought. Life.

Run. Thought. Life.

Catherine Hetherington

I am thinking about life, I am thinking about my knees. A camel. Am I doing well enough, have I achieved enough, am I getting too old, how old is too old? Lady with a buggy, is that success, or is it the lady with the Gucci handbag? Keep going. I am thinking about my knees again. I am doing OK, surely? I am not 30, well 6 months away. That is plenty of time, yes I am older than the Sugababes and I haven't had a number one single, but I am still younger than my boss. Keep going. Man with girlfriend, where is my boyfriend, does he really like me? Is he thinking of me right now too, if he's not, what is he thinking of? Is it someone else, does he wish he was with someone else? What if I am something to pass the time, is her boyfriend passing the time? I had given him my heart to hold, to take care of and sometimes he just drops it on the floor, he would stuff it in his pocket and it would fall out. One day I worry he won't notice he doesn't have it anymore, it would lie there alone in the street battered, second hand, irreparably damaged. The couple. Love. What does that look like, how do you know when it's right? My parents, they weren't but that doesn't mean that love isn't forever. But what is love? Is it about the right time and place or is it about the right person? Who is the right person, maybe it's him, or it could be him over there. I need to stop. I start walking for a while. When I run it's not just my legs but my mind that races too.

***

START

The Marylebone sky is a perfect blue, a watercolour blue that is soft focus and hazy on the eyes. The warm red mansion blocks, the distinguished gentlemen of London housing, comfort the street with an embrace from both sides. There are days for running, and there are days for not. Today is a running day, I wake up in the morning as if I have just had a double espresso. My limbs are ready, they feel alive. I feel a sense of awake in every part of me. I have woken up in single figures, I have woken up with an energy. I love these Saturdays. I leap out of bed and my feet move straight into my trainers.

Then she left the house.

A challenge of gross proportions, but somehow it's possible. There are 10 million people all around, as she steps out of the door and outside of herself she could almost fall over them, but she was completely alone. They sit outside the café downstairs, under its blue awning, a royal blue, very appropriate for the opulence of Marylebone which stares in the face of the high rises of north London and goads them. She could almost imagine an uprising one day when the tower blocks of Mornington Crescent would pull themselves up and thunder down Hampstead Road and straight into Regent's Park and defiantly refuse to be moved.

So she started, towards Regent's Park, a park of small dogs, show dogs and show money. People like her, running nowhere vainly trying to look like someone else, trying to forget things, no-one going anywhere, all engaged in a lonely futile pursuit. She began slowly, listening to Four Tet, this would be a long one, she didn't want to listen to Daft Punk too soon, she would go too fast and her heart would try to burst from her chest.

Towards The Globe, where one football fan shouts to another, 'I'll 'ave another lar-ga'. A dirty pub, with sticky floors. There's a publican's map of the world on its cracking exterior, which adds a fault line to the whole of South America, crumbling but dressed idiosyncratically in fairy lights. Marylebone was ruined by the dirty clogged artery of Marylebone Road. If only you could create a paper fold in the map from Dorset Street to Regent's Park, Baker Street station wouldn't be missed, although its Sherlock Holmes tiles may be. It was a Saturday and she was greeted by riot vans at the top of Chiltern Street, and towards The Globe by a sea of blue, Chelsea FC fans amassing to warm up. Mild hooliganism, like running, needed a warm up. There could be no more distance in usage and attendees in two identically named buildings than The Globe and The Globe.

Into Regent's Park and she saw the zoo, the free zoo that is. The better one in fact, free of both the cost of paying and the moral questions of whether one should support zoos. She ran past the camels and llamas, and remembered Chile, seeing real llamas and indeed many camelids. Why so content to be in a city that replicates other places but lacks all authenticity, where everything is available at a price? There is contained exploration banded by prices and snobbery. Imagine being able to run, run out of London, out of zone one, through zone two and beyond, to run with these animals in the wild.

She ran past a man, sitting on a bench. She still felt alone, sad, and focused on that sadness; to lose it would mean a struggle to regain it. She didn't know what he was thinking, that he, one of four brothers once, had lost two already and another was dying in two weeks. Even knowing this might not have pulled her from her own sadness. Too many tube journeys avoiding the eyes of strangers and developing and honing her distrust for other humans had slowly scraped away her compassion, her ability to see others for what they were. We were/are all the same.

To Hyde Park, first navigating Oxford Street. Oxford Street is London's answer to waterboarding. She was once asked in a job interview, 'What do you find annoying?' Would it have been OK to answer, 'Oxford Street'?

The fact that there aren't traffic lanes for people, the fact that people dawdle, then stop, just stop suddenly in the middle of it all. Don't they understand the person behind them, well at least one of the throng, is from London, therefore is hurrying, hurrying to be somewhere. Not thinking about stopping. In London there is no slow. Speakers' Corner was coming into view, audibly first, then she could see it. Why it was Speakers' Corner who knows, there was no time to learn these things when you were here. One day when she was old, like a withered empty balloon who had given its air to the city, she would learn these things. For now she was running, past the people on the street canvassing, telling the lost masses of their moral obligations. 'Don't shop at X they support the war in Palestine, don't shop in Y they promote landfills, don't shop in Z they test on animals'. She was always being told what to think; life was like a prolonged Michael Moore film. Could she do it all by herself? She had seen a play once that was about characters being 'on headphones', being told what to think, how to act and what to say. Sometimes this was an appealing prospect.

Finally into Hyde Park, so open and yet fenced in by the city. Faster. Towards Hyde Park Corner, the lake, the café, more people. Everyone with dogs; who knew you had to bring a small dog, preferably cat-sized to come to the park? She had obviously missed the instructions. She overheard 'I was so nervous in my driving lesson I almost had a heart attack, I sweated so much I had to go home and change my bra and pants'. She smiled, those moments were when London was a stage, and she a voyeur into everyone's life, stealing moments of their joy, happiness, sadness and pain.

Towards the Royal Albert Hall, where listening to Rachmaninoff's third had dwarfed any achievement she may reach in a lifetime. A soft, beautiful and reflective piece, where the instruments danced with one another, the strings coaxing the piano forward only to then run in retreat at the solid, strong and certain advancing piano. A building befitting of its usage, contrary to many in the city. Past the grandeur and through into

Kensington Gardens and round the statue of Peter Pan, a reminder of age, of life. Squirrels darted across the path, like dolphins on land as they arced smoothly from one tourist's snack to another. She was sure this was a high calibre park for squirrels, the Ivy for a squirrel. Clapham Common is more like a late night kebab shop.

Past an old lady on a bench clad in furs, wrinkled in the way she would be after a long bath. Reading the *Daily Mail*, her prop, with a cigarette held like a pencil, looking emptily at the pages. Remaining completely static but for the arm from the elbow down, which acts as a hinge, and allows the cigarette to enter her mouth. The rest of her is still, the cigarette perpendicular to her face. She surveys the park with her hands on the paper, like someone slowly observing whether it is safe to cross a road. It's hard to be out there in amongst everyone else, truly on your own, better to take friends in the form of nicotine and printed pages, looking purposeful.

Towards Kensington Palace and more reminders of the opulence of the city. Why had she had to contribute a charity donation to the 'royal' parks when running the half marathon? Surely if these parks are royal then they can be paid for by the aforesaid royals (OK, so it was only two pounds but this more of a principle). The polarised options of life in London were both unfathomable and unattainable. Gangs of youths in Stockwell, toting knives and fighting and treating the streets like their property, to Louis Vuitton-toting ladies with dyed blonde hair – each strand sitting regally, higher than the last – wearing giant sunglasses and engulfing coats. They both reflected a fear, a sense of not belonging, of being somewhere in the middle, but going in neither direction.

Past another pond, where deck chairs sit idly waiting for residents, with their green and white striping buffeted in the wind, they billow out like a deck chair beer gut. And to the road at the north of the park, the stretch that extends to the horizon, or so it seems. To the Italian fountain, where she sometimes met her friend for running. An anomaly, as this was her solo pursuit. She was always alone although sometimes she inhabited this place from within a crowd, telling jokes about stolen cheese (nacho cheese … 'nat yo cheese') and anecdotes of her day. Stories of her success and failures for all to admire, open and honest, yet a closed book as the darkness of her feelings within were pushed away from all to see. Sometimes she would cry in the toilets at work, annoyingly this was often disrupted by other toilet users, one was never truly alone in London despite how hard you may try. She thought again of her friend, they would run together, gossiping of colleagues, boyfriends, husbands, diets, creating a manifesto for the modern woman, yet to be shared with a wider audience. The friend was an 8/10 on the friend scale, it was nice to order life in such a way. She lost only a few marks on the newness of their friendship, which meant that as yet she was unable to share the sadnesses she carried like an albatross with her. She didn't know why she carried them, people had worse lives, the man on the bench, the helpless lady she didn't know, old and alone creeping through the park with heavy bags, but she couldn't run fast enough to avoid the chase of sadness.

She saw the Odeon emerge from the green, a giant 'O' through leaves of orange and brown, a lighthouse at the corner of the park warning those of approaching Oxford Street. She wondered if her expectations were all wrong, if films set us up to fail by relentlessly delivering the happy ending. Where was it? Whose was it? Should we all be encouraged to covet the same thing?

Around Marble Arch. How does a traffic island become deserving of an 1850s solid marble arch? She remembered a time, which seemed so long ago, when she was in Vientiane and visited the Laotian version of the Arc de Triomphe. The government of the day had been given concrete by the Americans to make a runway. Instead they built a monument. She thought of things we are told we need versus those we want. Are either right in the end? She was tired.

Up Edgware Road, Lebanese Lane. She ran to eat essentially. If her body were more obedient this bizarre process of donning lycra and pushing her limbs into moving co-ordinately and faster than they ever desired would be less frequent or absent altogether. They say it's like meditation, when you find the rhythm and your body moves on its own, you are free. She had these moments, releases, and would sometimes run back to where it happened for a hope of a replay, but her conscious would be tricking her to think she could control it to happen again. Tired, pump the arms, keep going.

Turning across the grid system she started to run towards Marylebone High Street. Like Tesco Express orienteering, she turned her run into interval training as she ran across the smog of Baker Street. She saw billboards in bus stops, showing her the idea of beauty, the things she 'needed'. She felt proud that no amount of marketing would steal her sense of self and replace it with an off-the-shelf other. She thought of her flatmate, an ad account director, the balance of intelligence, person-ability and balls. A phrase she had stolen from a colleague. She wished there was a less hetronormatively loaded way of describing the guts the flatmate had, to do the right thing, be herself and yet all the time be human. Not one of those who lose themselves to a perceived appropriate corporate identity, someone who is important, sharp, brief, pinstriped, humourless, the same as all others.

Along Marylebone High Street, a village in central London. Part of the zone one jigsaw that makes a confused incoherent picture, if you were the child assembling this you would throw the puzzle away. Running along the tree-lined street, the endless row of coffee shops broken by whiteness, shops with little in them, although this is not the point. They softly gaze at you, tempting you to admire their windows full of unaffordable items. She looked passers-by in the eye and wondered how do you have this money, where did it come from, will I ever have this? She passes a lady

17

who murmurs of how the weekend nanny wants time off, but neither her weekday nor weeknight nannies will cover it, 'some people are so inconsiderate'. The fear of spending time with those made in your own image, when it is something you run from by cloaking yourself in costly garments and sojourns to Harley Street. She thought of her own mother, a saintly woman even in the biblical sense, a lady so patient, intelligent kind and gentle, who thought everyone was great at something, had time for everybody, who had an inner reserve and strength. She felt sad for times she had made her mother cry, even though these were distant from who she was now, she wished she could go back and not be that teenager who needed to win arguments and be right every time. It had taken time but realised the more she knew, the less she knew. The wise woman is the one who knows she knows nothing at all.

She wanted to stop at one of the cafes but had no money, could she barter her iPhone for a coffee, did she want to, or did she want to listen to Daft Punk for the sprint finish home or did she want a skinny dry half-half caramel macchiato with one pump of vanilla? London made everyone demanding, it would seem ridiculous to request this anywhere else but to not request this in London would be the ridiculous part. Waiting was a thing of the past, the before London time, coffee in moments, food in minutes, a train in two minutes. Life was fast.

She was not ready to go home, she kept running away from something and towards something else. She was slower now, her steps in time with her deliberate breaths, her body obediently moving. Her body was ready to go home but her mind was not, today only more questions and even fewer answers had surfaced. She tried to run from it or to it, she was never sure what. She wanted to be the person who said every day was the happiest of their life, but she didn't know what that meant. Happiness was elusive in so much that it was undefined.

18

Weary she thought to the beginning, of the girl and boy, the couple temporarily in love. With every stride part of her died, as she tried and tired to fit. To become one of those girls who hung on his every word, didn't question life, who found him funny, who was happy to pretend he was indeed the cleverest not just of the pairing but of them all. So people threw themselves under carts and fought for this moment, that we could realise we are cleverer, better, and then we hide it, as if it were the contents of Pandora's Box.

STOP

And so it ended as all things do. She stood and watched life pass by. She had lost the race with herself, but it was OK to stop, her heart told her, as she felt her veins in her neck pulse as though hitting her rhythmically from the outside. Like a time-lapse film everything glided by in slow motion, people, cyclists. It was as though she were invisible. In the compound stillness she observed life; she had found an inner quiet, sanguine at least for that moment. Her mind was still.

CAMDEN
Dukwane's Deliverance

Dukwane's Deliverance

Neil Ramsorrun

When the alarm bell went at 3.45pm, Dukwane stuffed his books into his bag and raced out of the classroom. He charged out onto York Way and sprinted home as quickly as he could.

'Is it here yet?' he asked, bursting through the front door and gasping for breath.

Through the wall, Dukwane could hear his dad in the other room, cursing at the election on the telly. 'Bloody Eton fool. What he gonna do?'

'Is it here, dad?'

'You home already son?'

He ran through to the kitchen where his mother was busying herself over a pot of oxtail stew. Before she could say anything, he spotted it on the kitchen table: a crisp white envelope marked with the official stamp of King's College, Cambridge University. Dukwane tore it open, and in his haste to read what was inside, dropped the letter to the floor.

'Listen son, it's not the end of the world if you don't get in, remember that.'

He grabbed at the letter and with a deep breath, began to read.

'Screw that, I got in!' He hugged his mother, lifting her up off the floor so her slippers fell to the ground. Waving the letter above his head, he ran through to the front room, ignoring his dad's gestures for him to get out of the way of the telly.

'I did it dad, I got in!'

'Damn tory foolishness.'

'You won't be saying that when it's me up there, dad, just you watch.'

'Son, if you make it up there, I'll eat my pork pie hat.'

'Then you'd better get used to the taste of hat. If Barack can do it, so can I.'

'You an' bloody Barack. He ain't even a real black man.'

They smiled at each other. As he looked at his father sat there, his bottom shirt button open and exposing his belly overhanging his trousers, he felt a sense of sadness, but also a determination to be more.

'I'm going to work.'

'OK son. Don't forget to pass by the grocery store on your way back – you've got the list of what we need?'

'Yes dad, don't worry.'

His mother came in, wooden spoon in hand. 'Well done darling, you know we're proud of you. Be careful you don't go by the canal, it'll be dark soon.'

He kissed his mother and reassured her not to worry. As he stepped out onto York Way, the sun was setting over King's Cross in the distance, a crimson candyfloss sky broken by a dozen cranes all busy building his city. Beyond the clock tower of St. Pancras Station he could just make out the London Eye and the buildings of Westminster in miniature, legoland dimensions. Somewhere over there, the new Prime Minister had just been sworn in. He'd watched the press conferences on the BBC and wondered what it must feel like to be the Big Man. He could walk to Big Ben in 40 minutes from his house, and could almost see it from his street, but he couldn't really say he felt part of any of it. Yet.

As he rounded the corner from Camden Road to Kentish Town Road, the red neon hen of Holy Fried Chicken was blinking and beckoning him in for another shift of grease and banter. 'Three months till uni, six shifts a week, only 72 shifts to go,' he thought as he put on his HFC cap. 'Shit.'

'What you saying D? Where'd you go after school?' Jermaine was compiling a Number 6 Meal: chicken burger, with fries and a drink – the healthy man's alternative to the fried chicken meals. 'Me and Andre hung out with Keisha – man, that girl is baaad.' He held out his hands, as though he were fondling two freakishly large pieces of fruit. 'You missed out, know what I'm saying?'

'Melones hugos! Nice,' said Dukwane in what he imagined was a Spanish accent. 'That's all you think about.'

'Pretty much, except when I'm thinking about ass. You should try it. £2.99, boss.'

It was the usual banter – girls, who'd done what with them, who'd still not done anything with them. At some point there'd be a game of Fantasy Woman where they'd take it in turns to build their ideal lady out of their favourite celebrity body parts. In between rounds, Dukwane told him all about Cambridge and that he'd be moving there in a few months after they finished school.

'It's gonna be weird you know. Not seeing you any more,' said Jermaine.

'I know, but you can come visit. And I'll be back here in the holidays.'

'Yeah, but it's not the same. As this. But it's good though. This is your chance to do something. Aren't you afraid of not fitting in?'

'What do you mean?'

'Well, they're all loaded, and white. I heard you get the cane from your teachers if you don't do your work. And the older guys are gay and make the younger ones do weird shit.'

Dukwane explained that that wasn't quite how it worked, and that he was determined to be as good as any of the other students there, regardless of how rich they were.

It was 10.30pm and Jermaine's shift was coming to an end. Dukwane did the last hour and a half by himself as it quietened down towards the end of the evening in the week. As he poured his umpteenth coke of the evening, he thought about how the clientele changed at that point in the night.

Early on it was mostly young kids from the estates picking up their evening meals: just chicken and chips, as much as they could get for under £2.00. But after 11pm the young professionals with the post-pissup munchies came in – ordinarily they'd be eating organic at Pret and Eat, but after a few pints they wanted chicken with beans, coleslaw and bottled water so they didn't feel too bad in the morning.

He wiped down the aluminium work surfaces and scraped the last few yellowing bits of lettuce into the bin before turning off the heat lamp above the empty chicken cage.

'71 shifts to go,' he thought, as he stepped outside to lower the shutters and set the alarm.

Just turned midnight and Camden changed again. For 10 minutes the streets around the tube station were a steady stream of anxious faces running to make the last train. Then all that's left are the late night revellers heading to the World's End and Electric Ballroom: the goths, the wannabe Winehouses and the men with shopping trollies but no shopping.

Ten past midnight. Dukwane pulled the shutters down and clamped them shut. The road fell silent for what seemed like the first time that night. He glanced at his shopping list and headed towards the Turkish store. Another day gone, he wouldn't be in bed until one.

As he crossed the road, the silence was pierced by the sound of footsteps from the alleyway to his right. Dukwane's first instinct was to cross back. Too late. A youth maybe thirteen or fourteen ran straight into him. They both fell to the pavement, Dukwane catching the panic in his eyes. The others chasing had caught up.

It happens in four, maybe five, seconds. Dukwane gets up first, his hands raised to try and calm the gang of four, instinctively he places his body between the kid and his pursuers. He recognises one of them – Danny's younger brother – and they recognise him. He glances back and sees the kid scrambling away, the gang rush at him, steel glinting under streetlamps. He hears the sound after he feels it. Almost like the release of air, his body no longer in his control, falling to the pavement again. He feels the blood but cannot lift his head to see it. All he can see is the blur of neon fading.

***

'Dukwane?'

'He probably can't hear you Mrs. Williams, the morphine is quite strong,' said the nurse. There were tears still in his mother's eyes as they waited for the doctor to arrive.

Beneath the morphine cloud, Dukwane was vaguely conscious for a moment. He could make out noises – some familiar voices, like his mother's – and lights softly focused. His body throbbed, but he couldn't tell where he was, or why he wasn't able to see or hear properly. He needed to sleep.

'Mr and Mrs Williams? I'm Doctor Rasheed.' They looked at him, and then at each other, their hands clasped tightly as though the harder they gripped, the better the news would be.

'Dukwane has been badly injured. The knife severed part of his spinal cord and we fear that he may not be able to walk again. We'll be relieving the morphine dose soon, so he should regain consciousness enough for you to be able to talk to him.'

The doctor went on, describing the next bleak chapter in Dukwane's life: the tests they needed to do to confirm how bad things were, the likely therapy and rehabilitation he would need to go through. Hunched over the bed, his mother wept and asked the Lord Jesus to make him better as his father sat in shock.

***

'Damn, D, you look like shit.' Jermaine was staring down at him like he was examining some alien object.

'Say something, man. You OK?' He reached over and grabbed the jug of water from on top of the bedside cabinet and poured himself a glass with a shaky hand.

Dukwane opened his eyes slowly, knowing that speaking was going to hurt. 'You know who it was? It was those psychos from Phoenix Court. I recognised one of them, Danny's younger brother,' Dukwane said.

'Yeah, yeah, I know who you mean. His sister's well ugly.'

'They were laying into this kid. They were gonna kill him.'

'You did the right thing you know. Stepping up.'

'Did I? Look at me now. I can't even walk.'

Jermaine looked down at the hospital linoleum, rubbing one trainer over the other. Dukwane pointed out that the kid didn't even stick around to help him.

'Yeah but still man, you always do the right thing – that's you,' said Jermaine.

'I don't want to be me. This is not how it's supposed to be. I was going to be someone, and now I'm a cripple.'

'You can still do the things you were going to do,' said Jerrmaine.

'How? You said yourself that it would be hard enough to fit in anyway. What about now? How many black kids in wheelchairs do you think there are at King's? I give up man, there's no point.'

They sat in silence for a few moments before Jermaine spoke up again.

'Maybe there's something we can do.' He leant closer to Dukwane, and whispered. 'Revenge.'

'What you talking about?'

'It's not right, D. They can't just go around stabbing people. No one cares about us. The police won't do shit, your dad's useless. It's down to you and me. You know the Bengalis my cousin Frankie hangs out with?

Frankie says they're into some real heavy shit. He was telling me how one time they did this guy in because he stole their parking space.'

'So what you saying? We have them killed?'

'No man, I'm not saying we go that far. But we could give them what they gave you.'

Jermaine spelled out a plan and Dukwane listened, not wanting to talk any more, and imagining how it would feel to get his own back.

'I'll talk to Frankie, see what he says. I'll swing by tomorrow before school. Think about it,' said Jermaine as he left to start his mission.

Dukwane turned on the TV console above his bed. £3.50 per day to watch the BBC. He switched it off again and plumped his pillows as he settled down for the night to reflect on what Jermaine had said. He could just about make out the faces on the screen in the bed next to him: the new Prime Minister giving another speech.

'In terms of the future, we have some deep and pressing problems. A huge deficit, deep social problems and a political system in need of reform.'

'Too right,' muttered Dukwane to himself, feeling a twinge in his lower back. He closed his eyes and tried to listen, the sound quickly fading as he fell asleep.

In the background, deep, further than he could see, he heard applause. It was the rarest form of applause: grateful and full of wonder. He smiled and opened his eyes, he could feel a gentle breath upon him.

'They were clapping for you, you know.'

The man was seated to Dukwane's right side, an unmistakeable voice, a straight back and crisp suit.

'I can't believe it,' Dukwane said. 'Is it really you?'

The man nodded, his face thinner and darker than he had imagined.

'This isn't an hallucination?' Dukwane continued.

'Between what we say and what we feel inside, we find truth. The rest is hard to say and of no consequence. What is important is how you feel now Dukwane?'

He knew his name. Dukwane muttered that he was OK, still not sure what was happening.

'And how do you feel about what happened to you?'

'I … I feel angry, I mean what did I do to deserve this? What am I going to do with my life now?'

'You are going to do what you always wanted to do. Do you hear?'

There was a deep resonance in the man's voice - he could have asked for anything and Dukwane would have done it.

'One of my forebears said that a house divided in itself cannot stand. You are that house, Dukwane, and your choices are your own, but you must choose wisely.'

'What choice? How am I going to go to university now?'

'Same way you were going to before. By your wits and guile and sheer persistence. This is what makes us rise above other men, it is how we face adversity, how we challenge those who hold us back, how we make real our dreams. Tell me about your dreams.'

'I want to study then get involved in politics, be more like you.'

Dukwane heard footsteps approaching. A nurse pulled the curtain back, both of them startled. He looked over to his right to see that his guest had departed.

For the next few hours, he lay awake going over and over the two conversations he had had that evening and thinking about what to say to Jermaine in the morning. His old dreams flickered one last time as he thought about what his life might have been like, and then he looked down at his legs and tried to imagine how different things were going to be from now. 'But I'm still the same person as I was before,' he thought.

***

The next morning, Dukwane had no trouble waking early. By the time Jermaine arrived at 8.15, he had already eaten breakfast and read the newspaper from cover to cover.

'Yo, D. I spoke to Frankie.' Dukwane looked at him, wishing he could get up and walk out. 'He says he'll hook us up with the Bengalis any time.'

'Listen man. I've been thinking. You know what you said about me always doing the right thing? Well, that was so true. I can't do this.'

'Fair enough, D. I was only trying to help. You seemed so angry with them.'

'I know man, I am. But everything that happens, happens for a reason. And I think this was meant to make me stronger in some way.'

'So what are you gonna do?'

'I'm gonna call King's.'

BARNET

The Outsider

The Outsider

Jemma Wayne

The Wheelbarrow Man was the one they saw most often. Always near the graveyard, which is why they concocted tales and explanations that involved a dead wife, or the decomposed bones of the already-buried, or, as they grew older, a mountain of Rizla-ready leaves. The mythical contents of the wheelbarrow were pinned down by a piece of grey tarp, and the man was bearded so heavily that it was impossible to guess his age, while his all-weather raincoat – worn whatever the weather - hid everything but a pair of muddified Doc Martin boots, so their theories were based on speculation more than scrutiny, but were the better for it. It was a conscious fictionalisation, a pubescent flirting with fantasy, still, they tried always to reach the graveyard together, in case he was there. Or else to sprint through it.

During the first months, they ran the whole Four together. Gaby had been training with Mr Lombardini for a year already when Laura arrived, a gangly 14-year-old fresh from the Barnet Schools Champs, and she immediately became Laura's guide into the floodlit hierarchy of Copthall's famous Shaftesbury Harriers. Gaby had seemed unfathomably cool to Laura, fluent in a language she had not yet heard, versed already in its etiquettes. Her shock of red hair had been pinned flat by a black fleece headband that covered her ears, she wore proper lycra running tights and a jumper that had special loops at the ends of the sleeves to hook ones hands through, and she possessed two pairs of spikes, both of which she kept in a blue spike bag with the key to change the pins in a zipped compartment on the outside. Between runs she drank Isostar instead of water, and she timed not only the speed of their sprints, but also the rest they had between them on a grey Baby G watch. She knew to look for Mr Lombardini's arm on the other side of the track to signal they start, shouting 'Go' to Laura each time that she missed it, and to put her own arm up when they reached their finishing point, and to shout 'track' at slower runners blocking their lane, and to walk on either the grass in the middle, unless the javelin throwers were out, or along the very outside lane, so as not to get screamed at oneself by muscle-toned men in tights with frightening bulges. That first night, Laura had rolled up her amateur tracksuit bottoms, and un-tucked her baggy Naf Naf T-shirt, and copied the way that Gaby rolled her socks under the heels of her feet so they weren't showing. She noticed their matching necklaces, but they didn't mention their star-dangling Jewishness; it had not at the time seemed a thing to define or bind them.

It was three months before Laura started beating Gaby. At first, she would slow down towards the end of their sprints so they could still finish together, but then Mr Lombardini gave her a lecture on always pushing through the line, not stopping short of it, and it was the first time he had spoken more than a sentence to her, so Laura listened. Gaby had explained at the very start that Mr Lombardini reserved his words, coated in passionate Italian tonalities, for his favourites only, and that his favourites were always his daughter Maria, and whoever else was the rising flavour of the month. Talent only begot attention. 'I'm the best runner at my school,' Gaby had shrugged. 'But my school is crappy.'

Gaby went to a Jewish high school that she hated. Being neither beautiful, nor religious, nor slutty, nor into boys or bitching or hanging out at Edgware Station on a Saturday night, she said she didn't care that no-one liked her at school and preferred to play sports, but they barely scraped together a netball team so she did athletics because she could do it on her own. At Copthall however, Gaby was the worst runner in Mr Lombardini's group. Above her were three different cliques of ability even before the dizzying heights of Maria who was so good that she sometimes did her sessions with the boys and whose current training partner was Natasha, the tallest, prettiest and blackest girl Laura had ever met; the only black girl Laura had ever met. Properly. There was a mixed race girl in her class, but her skin was barely darker than Laura's after the efforts of a summer.

Maria's attentions strictly followed those of her father. In the beginning, she only entertained Natasha, laughing loudly, smoothing their hair down in the toilets, joking easily with the boys, ignoring the young and the new and the untalented. But when one night in her fourth month at Copthall, Mr Lombardini set Laura a session with the girls in the group above Gaby, Maria smiled at her when they were stretching, and the next week she waved hello. Natasha still glared at her only, but Laura couldn't help but watch in awe as the two of them did their strides and jumps and swung their muscular legs one by one onto the fence around the track. 'Never seen a nigger before?' Natasha threw at her one day, catching her watching.

'Fuck off Natasha,' Gaby spat back, fearless, but Laura said nothing.

On Sundays, instead of the track, the whole group met at the entrance to the stadium, stretched on the grass and then began the gruelling Shaftesbury Four – a four-mile slog, as the name suggested, that started at the track and wound its way down the pulsating Great North Way, around the tamer residential roads with their quiet semis and their parked Hondas, through the muddy graveyard, up the hill over the train tracks, and back past the football pitches over the slow humps that returned them to the stadium. Mr Lombardini set them off at staggered intervals, Gaby starting first, the rest following in specified increments, a game of cat and mouse. Gaby didn't seem to mind always being the mouse the rest of them were chasing, or as Laura improved, begrudge the growing gaps between them. Occasionally, she mock-grimaced when Laura caught her early, rounding the corner at the ancient Mill pub where, if nobody else was around, they took a shortcut through the car park. But afterwards, they always warmed down together, dissecting the days since they'd seen each other last, and comparing where they'd spotted the Wheelbarrow Man.

Sometimes, they saw the Waving Man too, at the bus stop on Page Street, grinning inanely and shouting, 'Hello, hello!' to all who passed him. Once, when they were taking the hill together, Gaby waved back and the Waving Man was so overcome with shock and excitement at this rare slice of human reaction that he seemed to lift from his spot and for a moment looked as though he would dart after them, and they had to run faster to contain their giggles. Very occasionally, the Walking Man would cross their path. Wearing only shorts and trainers, his bare back hunched over almost to his knees, he would appear arms swinging by the busy road and they would have to run wide to avoid him. But they thought it sad, these two men, mental suffering driving them to the point of two dimensions, and didn't dwell on them. It was only the Wheelbarrow Man, who they could not explain or understand, who disturbed their stride. In the early spring, if he was crouching amongst the headstones, his dark green coat would camouflage him with the burgeoning daffodils so that when he stood he startled them, and once made Gaby fall and gash her knee so deeply that Laura had to practically carry her to the main road and flag down a car to call an ambulance, which took Gaby to hospital for six careful stitches that kept her off training for three weeks. But by April, when the place was a flood of yellow trumpets, they saw him well in advance, standing scarecrow, or filling his wheelbarrow with those un-guessable goods.

'Body parts, probably,' said Maria one Sunday, a year after Laura had joined the group, by which time she was doing the occasional session with Maria and Natasha, who still barely spoke to her and elbowed her as they were rounding bends. Laura had offered up the Wheelbarrow Man in an effort to make conversation, carefully toning down the sharpness of her accent and remembering to drop the letters off the ends of her words, and Maria found the idea of their pariah-like character hilarious. 'Or rope to tie up his victims. God, I saw the freakiest Yid by the Hendon roundabout today. He was one of those black-hatted fucks and had these bits of hair that looked like rope, and rope hanging from his pants. Probably uses it to tie up all his money. Hey, maybe the Wheelbarrow Man's a Jew and he's heaving around all his cash.'

'Laura and I are Jewish,' said Gaby, but Laura said nothing.

It was the first time that Laura had experienced prejudice first hand, not repeated to her via history books, or news clips, or grandparents who could still remember it being sewn forcibly onto sleeves. 'You don't look Jewish,' Maria had told her the following session, as if in conciliation, but Laura didn't know how to answer such softly-couched enmity, and so merely smiled and tucked it away as they lined up to start another 300m, along with the rest of the suffocating facts of her existence too confusing for her to sort. It was not the tangible elements of her life that made her feel like running, but something elusive, that somehow was everywhere. Natasha sulked off when Laura finished before her.

After training on Sundays, Gaby and Laura would get on the 113 bus and go for bagels in Golders Green. The mix of Hebrew and Yiddish and English that flew across Carmelli's take-away counters somehow salted the conversation like the expertly rolled dough, and this is where truths were unpicked, differences unravelled, similarities weighed. Lighter and heavier than their gold necklaces.

Gaby was proud to be an outsider. It was an intention as well as an unavoidable state and she said provocative things to prove it. She lived in the leafy suburb of Mill Hill with her mother who was onto her second nose job, and in Hendon with her father who was onto his second wife, and an elder brother who was at Leeds University and rarely home. Her father insisted on traditional Friday night dinners with candles and challah and kosher wine, and synagogue on Saturday mornings, but this was with his new family - two perfectly bronzed boys and a baby girl who shared Gaby's red hair – so usually Gaby would pretend that her mum wanted her home, or that she didn't believe in participating in such archaic irrelevance. A few years later, when Gaby quite suddenly grew into her hair and her features and became beautiful, and popular, and wore short skirts with whore boots, and had boyfriends who she cheated on, she would spend Friday nights at Chinawhites or other clubs where they no longer asked her for ID, and told both of her parents that the other one wanted her.

Unlike Gaby, Laura was an outsider more because of a particular sensation that convinced her of it, rather than a consequence of desire or circumstance. An only child, she lived with her dentist-lawyer parents in a large house on the border of Golders Green and Hampstead Garden Suburb. As a teenager, this meant little to her other than the benefit of being in suburban-sized surrounds, yet still a walkable distance to buzzing Golders High Street, with it's all-night falafel take-aways and Chinese all-you-can-eats, and the Woolworths with pick-a-mix, and the giant Blockbuster, and the cafes from which she could watch every colour and class of person, the likes of whom she never saw at her private girls' school nor tended to spot in the Mercedes-littered suburb. But in later life, depending on who she was talking to about her childhood, Laura picked one of these two geographies methodically, to illicit reaction; it was helpful shorthand sometimes to watch the response to the twin crosses of 'rich' or 'Jew'. Not that they were either particularly. Neither of her parents believed in god though they made her go to synagogue every week for a year before her batmitzvah - where she had her first kiss in the toilets with the rabbi's son who was shorter than she was but had curtains in his hair and a dimple in his chin. Her mother kept two sets of crockery to separate milk and meat, but when they were out she was allowed to eat cheeseburgers at McDonald's. And their house was big, but they only went on holiday once a year, never skiing like the girls Laura met later at university, and she didn't have a trust fund, only £10 pocket money a week, which was enough at the time to buy tickets and snacks at the Odeon. They were middling. Comfortable. Not one thing nor the other but cut-up pieces of competing flavours, like the ingredients her mother grabbed from the cupboard and threw into the knish she made on Friday nights. Not British, wholly. Not Jewish, only. And not excessive about anything, except history. This however was something that seemed to emanate from every gold-leafed book and framed certificate, and faded war-time photograph that adorned their home, and followed her through the streets where the grocer asked after her grandmother, and there was a 'Jewish Interest' section in the bookshop, and the shops bore Hebrew writing, and in December the council erected not only twinkling Christmas trees but also giant menroahs, and during Purim even the orthodox kids with their curls and their otherness wore fancy dress and looked like everyone else who took part in the Halloween-esque celebration that only she and those with equal measures of history were privy to. And made them different.

As a child, she didn't notice the abnormality of it all. But perhaps the dichotomy cut without permit into her soul, because it was suffocating sometimes, being both an insider and out, seeking both freedom and belonging, defined unconsciously but always by an inherited, self-proclaimed, connected, disparate otherness that in her bubble-wrapped borough she could sense but not see. Perhaps it was this that prompted her to start running. And to make friends with other types of teens, like Maria, and even Natasha eventually. Perhaps it was this that made both Gaby and Laura create a close-knit community of two, culminating in a moment when they were 17 - a week after exams had finished, at a party where the boys were goading them, their respective red and jet-black hair already mingling on drunken, giggling shoulders - when they threw their arms dramatically around each other's necks, and kissed.

'I love you Lor,' whispered Gaby, but Laura said nothing.

A week later, Laura went away for the summer. In August, when they got their exam results, they spoke on the phone and congratulated each other on their places at university, but by the time Laura returned home Gaby had already left for her gap year in Israel. Laura got ready for Oxford. She continued to train at Copthall, but Maria had shin splints and was no longer running, and Natasha was working by then, and Mr Lombardini had started delegating the leading of sessions to one of the boys, so she ran the Four with the younger girls who watched her stretching, and was usually alone through the graveyard where the grass was overgrown, and the daffodils were resting, and occasionally, she caught sight of a man with a wheelbarrow. Who irrationally frightened her still. At the very end of the summer, Mr Lombardini came to watch her race in the Southern's and punched his hand in the air when she pushed all the way through the line and took Maria's title. 'I always knew,' he told her in passionate, lilting vowels that took up all of his attention. 'Keep running at Oxford.'

At Oxford however, Laura didn't sign up for the track team. She ignored too invitations from the Jewish Society and instead joined the debate team and the student union. She wrote for the paper and went salsa dancing, she got a boyfriend and learnt how to ski, and that Christmas she didn't return to Golders Green or Hampstead Garden Suburb, but to a new house in Cornwall where her parents had moved and where there was no local menorah in the high street but Christmas trees only, and where everything felt cleaner and clearer and less complicated. When Gaby called and told her that she too had met a boy, and that she was not returning to take up her place at university but was staying in Israel where she was getting married and living on a kibbutz, it felt to Laura like merely an extreme change in a catalogue of changes, and barely noticed nor pondered the absence of Gaby from her life.

She got married herself, eight years later, to a man who was not Jewish and didn't know how to salt the bread on a Friday night nor noticed the lack of candles, but who shared her love of politics and bought a flat with her from which it was a short commute to Westminster. Together they held dinner parties with friends who were as ambitious and engaged and eclectic as they were, they took weekend breaks to Europe, they rode bikes, they joined book clubs, they studied the contours of their perfectly matched frames; and at night Laura lay in his arms and wondered how inside them, while so perfectly wrapped, she could still feel like an outsider.

Gaby called in the March of 2008. She was back in London visiting her parents and they arranged to meet in Golders Green, though not at Carmelli's because they wanted to sit properly now, and catch up on a decade, and had more than £10 to spend. Over the phone, except for the new, almost American twang, Gaby had sounded exactly like herself, and as Laura drove through the streets she had once pounded and loved and hated, and never visited, time flickered, like Shabbat candles.

But the woman sitting at a table with six children looked nothing like Gaby. She wore a skirt down to the floor, a long-sleeved, high-necked shirt, and a tea-cosy hat, from underneath which it wasn't possible to spot even a tendril of red hair. Had she not stood up and called out to her, Laura would have walked right by. 'You look exactly the same,' Gaby laughed, embracing her while Laura stood, trying to work out if this tactile closeness was allowed, now, and Gaby's six children stared.

Over lunch, Gaby broke off now and then to referee a dispute between her kids. Before each of them ate she reminded them to say their bracha, and she washed her hands and said her own. But, amidst stories about her rabbi husband, and her tiny, kibbutz community, slivers of the old Gaby slipped from beneath her careful shrouds, and it struck Laura that not so much had changed. Except everything.

'It's not like we thought,' Gaby said meaningfully, cutting into their conversation as though reading Laura's silent scepticism. 'It's the truth, you know. And I'm content now. Inside it.' She took a slurp of her soup and grinned devilishly. 'My dad is still furious.'

And as if to make her point, to him, to the world, when Gaby and her brood started down the road, they faded seamlessly into the uniquely Jewish high street where their religiousness was both ordinary and other. And familiar and absurd. And unexpectedly made Laura feel like running.

The Wheelbarrow Man was older and more fragile. His Doc Martins were as robust as always, his raincoat as dark, his beard as heavy, the grey tarp as ever present and opaque. But he seemed thinner somehow, and he cast less of a shadow across the graves. The daffodils were early and Laura spotted him at once. She stopped running and cut across the grass.

'Excuse me.'

The Wheelbarrow Man didn't take his eyes off the horizon.

'Excuse me,' Laura tapped him lightly on the arm.

Now he turned slowly, as though it had been years since he'd moved from this outpost. Laura panted a little, not as fit as before.

'Excuse me. Sorry. Can I ask? What's in your wheelbarrow?'

The Wheelbarrow Man smiled, his face cracking into deep, time-trodden creases. And he laughed as he said, 'Where's your red-haired friend?'

'You noticed us?'

'You two were always sprinting away.'

Now Laura laughed, and smiled back at him, seeing suddenly and for the first time the girls that they were, hurtling by with matching necklaces they didn't then understand and that for too long Laura had left languishing in her jewellery box. 'What's in the wheelbarrow?' she asked again.

Slowly, he lifted the grey tarp. 'Daffodils,' said the Wheelbarrow Man.

And Laura smiled again, but said nothing.

KENSINGTON & CHELSEA

The Truth About the Dishwashers

The Truth About the Dishwashers

Tena Štivičić

Helena ran her hand across the leather surface of the desk.

'It's an early Victorian mahogany pedestal partner desk, very well preserved,' the shop assistant said, his low voice appropriate to the exclusivity of the item.

'Mhm,' Helena said. A neutral reply.

Silvija stood a couple of steps behind looking bemused. The price, when turned into her currency of Croatian kuna didn't make sense to her as no desk could cost that much. Unless it came from a museum, in which case she felt that that's where it should remain. She found her daughter's unperturbed face still more surprising; it was as though she was stroking a particularly finely assembled Ikea piece.

The desk was, in fact, out of Helena's price range at the moment. She could imagine it in Andrew's study and thought it would work really well with the eclectic style, but it wasn't the right time. Doing up a new house had sucked in most of what they had put aside. Which is how things inevitably go. The right house at the right address is worth the risk. Nevertheless, her years of living in London, even before she met Andrew when her lifestyle drastically changed, had taught her that one always keeps a neutral face when discussing prices. Outrage quickly discloses far too much about one's background.

Helena and her mother descended a few floors to the Harrods food hall. Silvija stood mesmerised. She watched her daughter gliding round the counters laden with choice. Silvija kept falling behind. Each time she lost sight of Helena it brought on a slight sensation of panic. Why did she feel so intimidated? Yes, maybe twenty years ago, before capitalism extended its tentacles to the virgin ex-socialist territories and conquered them without a drop of blood, but now... Now when there is much choice even in Croatia and she usually feels a sense of superiority over the hysterics surrounding the 'having' and the 'owning' and the 'needing' of stuff...

She was holding a bag of pea shoots that said £3.59. She estimated that came to around 30 kuna and decided it couldn't be right. She should probably carry a calculator.

'What would you like to eat?' Helena's voice snapped her out of her calculations. Silvija looked around. She realised that each counter in this massive room was a restaurant of its own. There was an oyster bar and a Fromagerie, there was a place called the Iberico Ham house, a sea grill and a Caviar House and something called Dim Sum. Her mind stopped. It was all alien. Who eats oysters in the middle of the day in a department store? She couldn't think. She wanted a sandwich but was embarrassed to ask. It would almost be sabotage asking for a sandwich in a place like this.

'How about sushi?' Helena suggested. Sushi was something she would want her mother to learn to appreciate.

A few minutes later Helena made a disproportionately 'yummy' sound in response to what looked to Silvija like a plate of plain, steamed green beans.

'They're very nice. Edamame. And very, very healthy. Try them. Like this.' She showed her mother how to suck the beans out and discard the skin. They were tasty, it had to be said, but Silvija would still have preferred them with some roast chicken and mashed potatoes.

Helena looked at her mother from the corner of her eye as they ate. She's not enjoying it, Helena thought, even though it was mostly California rolls she was having, which really is the easiest way into sushi. Maybe they shouldn't have gone straight for sushi. Some nice smoked salmon and champagne might have been a better idea.

'Shall we have a glass of champagne upstairs?'

The idea caught Silvija by surprise. Just as she was starting to think that maybe raw fish and cold rice were not a completely misguided concept, champagne came rushing from left field.

'I don't know. What are we celebrating?' The moment she said it she felt like she ought to be more enthusiastic.

'Your visit. My new house. Your first sushi. Doesn't matter. It's what women do here. They shop and then they go up to the bar to reward themselves for a good days work with a glass of champers,' Helena said, not without irony, which she thought her mum would appreciate. She hadn't completely lost her sense of humour, even if she did begin to find some of her mother's jokes inappropriate.

They found a seat at a small table in the champagne bar. Helena held the menu in one hand and her Blackberry in the other and seemed to manage reading from both at the same time.

'Don't you think it's curious how the tent-ladies are lined up at the bar in the ice-cream parlour?' Silvija said. 'What's that about? Some sort of infantilisation thing?'

'You can't say that. You can't call them tent-ladies,' Helena protested patiently when the question sunk in.

'I thought it would make you laugh.'

'It's not funny.'

'It is a little. If you think about it. What are they shopping for here? Clothes? Jewelry? Underwear? Where do they wear it?'

'They wear it for their husbands.'

'You're right. It's certainly not funny.'

'It's different from … us. Doesn't mean to say it's wrong.' Helena could hear her own voice sounding unconvincing. Her views on such matters used to be much more pronounced. She just didn't seem to have the time anymore. She wished they could leisurely chat about everyday things, just a bit of relaxing, inconsequential chatter. Her mother discovered feminism quite late in the day and failed to install it in her family life, but she was a fierce opponent in theoretical debates. She also came from a place that was not too familiar with PC and found any kind of difference, in skin, habit or dress hilariously funny.

'How do they eat the ice cream?' Silvija insisted.

'I'm sorry?'

'Well, you've seen them. Three, four at the counter, all with large ice-cream sundaes. How do they eat it? I mean, practically speaking. Is there a flap in the cloth?'

'Oh, for god's sake, mum.'

There were times when Silvija protested at that tone, one third annoyance, one third contempt and remaining third split between guilt and embarrassment. Yes, many times. But not this time, she decided. Maybe, after all, she didn't know best. Not here, in this alien world through which her daughter seemed to navigate so well.

They drank their champagne in silence. Helena was beginning to wonder if having her mother over was going to prove to be a mistake. There have been moments in her London life which she thought of as small feats. Dotted with regular drops into doubt and despair, the curve of her life has been on a steady rise for a few years now. She would sometimes like to share it with people back home. She would sometimes like to show off in front of people back home. Her girlfriends, her dad before he died, and her mother. A night like tomorrow, when she will be cooking for twelve of Andrew's most important partners and clients including Sir Phillip, whom even self-assured Andrew felt tongue-tied around.

'It is one of those dinner parties a person's professional fate might depend on,' Andrew said the night before in a sort of half-jocular manner. Helena could see her mother squinting and knew subtext was being read into that statement, subtext that was not going to bode well for Andrew. 'How much are you, Andrew, contributing to this fate-determining night?' or something along those lines. There was a corner in Helena's mind that defied the idea of a dinner party having that much weight. But she knew it was a coded world she lived in. And if sometimes, often even, she did not understand the codes, she knew that contesting them or worse still, making fun of them, was not the right course of action.

In any case, a night like that, hosting a dinner party, success glistening across their long dinner table, that was what she wanted her mother to see. But sitting here after only a day of being together, Helena could already feel the draining effects of their disagreements. How on earth was she going to manage to cook for twelve in a new house and not lose her nerve?

'You are cooking?' Silvija regretted saying the words the very second they came out of her mouth.

'I can cook.'

Of course Silvija didn't mean it like that. When they last spent some time together Helena had cooked her parents a Vietnamese-inspired meal and apart from the questionable use of peanuts, Silvija was very impressed. Not only did it taste good, she had also very assertively used a number of ingredients Silvija had never heard of, like lemongrass and cardamom. And then a few other she had heard of, mostly from TV cooking shows and Jamie Oliver's cook book and had tried to used on a couple of occasions but had given up on, after a particularly disastrous attempt at roast fennel with ginger. She would never forget the bewildered expression on her husband's face when he tasted it. So she went back to her good old fashion continental cuisine.

It wasn't that she didn't have faith in her daughter's cooking. But the lifestyle she caught a glimpse of in the day and a half she'd spent here led her to believe that catering would certainly be involved. Rent-a-chef or some such nonsense that surely existed in this silly world of surplus.

She had not expected her manicured, pedicured, groomed beyond all reasonable expectation daughter to cook for twelve, in fact, counting her, thirteen people.

Silvija thought of herself when she was that age. The straw-like feel that henna used to give her hair. The smell of expired make up – make-up doesn't expire these days, she'd noticed. They both had good skin and good, white teeth. Silvija would like to have been slimmer though and Helena seems to have rid herself of the few extra pounds she carried as a very young woman. She was now as slender as a willow. And she was going to cook dinner to impress twelve unimpressionable people.

'I'm sorry about the sushi,' said Helena in the taxi on the way back. 'It's an acquired taste I guess. You used to like trying new things.'

'It's funny', said Silvija thoughtfully looking out at the magnificent architecture, 'you don't notice when that goes. The thirst for trying new things. You simply discover one day that you prefer not to bother.'

As they turned into a side street behind the Natural History Museum she was struck with how overwhelming beauty can be followed immediately by how bumpy the ride was and what dreadful suspension the famous black cabs had.

'But I like the idea of having tried something you like so much.'

The kitchen was shiny and dark. Granite comes highly recommended in the kitchen world, Andrew explained last night when Silvija's first response to seeing the fabulous new kitchen was that it was rather dark. These, apparently, were the best kitchens in the world. Silvija thought that 'the best in the world' was a term one could use to describe one's mum's pie. Or a particularly fine cup of coffee. She thought it much too pompous to use with a straight face.

'How do we know that they're the best kitchens in the world?', she asked, as Helena started the espresso machine, 'Has it been put to a vote?'

Helena sighed. She got out of the habit of talking to her mother. This was not the way they talked around here, she thought. They nod, they make the 'mhm' sounds a lot, they say excited 'ohs' a lot, they admire other people's achievements, and a Poggenpohl kitchen is a fucking achievement. Well … in a manner of speaking. It was annoyingly Croatian to be sarcastic about it. These people had no respect for equanimity.

'They just are,' she said resolutely.

Her mother looked away, through the window, where rain was starting to wash over another London day. Sitting on that chair was quite a balancing act. Another impression she shared last night and didn't get a laugh.

'What are you cooking?'

'Sarma,' said Helena smiling mysteriously.

'Sarma?!'

'Sarma.

'I don't understand.'

Helena was silent. She vaguely felt like sulking though she wasn't sure if it would have been justified. Is it acceptable to sulk about things someone *might* say or indeed, things someone was thinking?

'You are going to serve all these important people a staple peasant dish?'

Between sulking and proudly presenting a cunning plan, Helena decided to let the sulking rest for a while. After all, there is always plenty of time for sulking in life. She smiled a wide sassy smile.

'It's going to be very, very cool. Do you know they sometimes hire the best chefs in the world to cook for, say, the Oscars, and then they serve fish and chips?'

She elaborated on how people can get tired of the fancy, complicated food that you never fill up on and that sounds like you need a degree to understand.

'You know, these people actually get to a stage where they go to a two hundred pound-a-head dinner and come out saying: "If I'm honest, I'm just not that impressed."'

The impersonation gave a cheeky spring to her voice. Silvija smiled. That sounded more like her daughter.

'So, we'll sort of be subverting the rule, thereby making it very chic,' she continued proudly. 'I could slave over tuna carpaccio and it wouldn't be like the one at Claridges. And for all the gadgets you see around here I am not actually sure how you achieve a frothy cauliflower purée.'

'I don't think I ever heard of frothy cauliflower purée and I'm not entirely sure it should be allowed.'

'I'm sure you're not. Anyway, what we are counting on is the surprise effect. And another thing we have over them is the simple knowledge of how important it is to end an evening feeling comfortably stuffed with food. This is something they don't realise, as eating for pleasure is a relatively new concept to the British.'

Her mother laughed out loud for the first time since she got there. They set out to make sarma: sauerkraut leaves stuffed with rice, minced meat and herbs, because sarma is always best the next day. The air around them suddenly felt lighter.

Silvija watched as her daughter moved around the kitchen. She lightly touched a button on the front of the dishwasher; the door popped down elegantly and the inside rack came sliding out without so much as a sound. The edges of the dishwasher were lined with some undetermined soft material almost invisible at first glance. Silvija reached out to feel it.

'Do you remember our dishwasher? The one in our old flat?' Helena asked.

It was a small flat, with small rooms and very narrow corridors. They always had far too many things and her mother was forever inventing new storage space. Behind the long curtains, underneath the windowsills. On top of wardrobes, under the beds. Their kitchen was a slightly widened extension to the narrow corridor with no windows. The light came from the adjacent dining room. Well, and the electricity. It's not like they didn't have electricity.

Dishwashers were a bit of a luxury in a socialist country. Not out of reach. But not standard equipment. Helena's family had one because they were doing well enough to treat themselves to a little bit of luxury. It broke down very soon, a few days after the warranty expired. The spare parts turned out be more of a luxury than the wretched thing in the first place, so they never quite made it to the priority list. And then the power cuts came and they had to invest in a generator and so on ... The dishwasher eventually proved to be a useful storage unit and for the next several years acted as one.

Helena could remember sitting on a stool in the kitchen, late at night, when the TV programme was over and her father had gone to bed. She had bouts of insomnia when she was a girl and her mother would let her sit in the kitchen and sometimes even eat her favourite desert, 'winter ice-cream', a cone filled with sickly sweet white filling and dipped in chocolate. She would lick her 'ice-cream' and watch her mother doing the dishes in the sink, wiping them dry and storing them away in the dishwasher. And she could to this day remember her mother's weary face, her feet in skin-coloured tights, worn and washed a thousand times, and the way she'd swear silently when she hit her shin on the edge of the open dishwasher door.

'Don't you remember how frustrated you were with that dishwasher. Every night when you washed the dishes and it was just standing there, useless ...'

Silvija looked lost in thought, remembering the same image. The tiny kitchen, about a tenth of the size of this one and her tiny daughter curled up on a chair. She nodded vaguely.

She couldn't help herself but scrutinize Helena and her environment. Her mind was constantly and inadvertently substituting X with what she saw and Y with what came out of Helena's mouth and she couldn't work out what the result was supposed to be. What was more mesmerizing than anything else was the authority with which Helena moved around this world, how she spoke to the staff, how she handled all the sophisticated technology in the house, how she had the world worked out. At her age, Silvija remembered herself as a timid person with no-one to talk to about the increasing number of dilemmas. And yet, this woman who looks at a twenty-one thousand pound Victorian desk as if she was about to declare it fake, pricks up her ears to the sound of the front door opening. Immediately, she goes for the fridge and pours a glass of cold white wine to hand to her husband the moment he steps into the kitchen. He kisses her and smiles, has a sip of wine with his eyes closed. He sits down and sighs, 'a long day,' as she rubs his back.

'Why does he call you Helena?' Silvija asked, stressing the first syllable as opposed to the second which is the Croatian pronunciation of the name.

'That's how it's pronounced in English.'

'It's not how your name is pronounced.'

'I don't mind.'

'It's not a question of you minding, it's a question of your husband getting your name right. It's a question of minimal effort. '

Helena sighed. Where did her mother get these … objections? Were those glasses she wore a special kind, infra-red for things to complain about?

'When are you planning to go back to work?'

'I don't know.'

'But you are planning to go back to work, aren't you?'

'I don't know mum, probably. I'm not sure. I've taken some time because of the move and doing the house up and all that and, to be honest, there is quite a lot to do.'

'The house is pretty much finished.'

Helena could feel her blood pressure rising. 'Yes, but I mean, there is quite a lot to do every day. And the work in the City is ... relentless. And if I'm going to have a baby at some point ...'

'You're going to be a mother and a housewife?'

Helena slammed a pot on the counter a little louder than she had intended to. Surely that was not the answer to hearing one might become a grandmother soon.

'Mum, what ... what is wrong? What's with the questions? I feel like you're trying to catch me out.'

'I'm trying to understand your choices.'

'Why are you so suspicious? And negative? Why don't you like this? How can you see this,' her arms went sweeping through the air, 'all this and ... and ... and me ... and ... not be proud and ... happy with how well I've done?! I don't get it!'

She suddenly found herself ranting about 'this country' and how closed off it was and how difficult it was to get past a certain invisible bar, how Mars was a more feasible destination than upscale London if one was a foreigner. And here she was, about to entertain all these important people at her own table and feed them bloody sarma. How can she not be proud?!

'Who are you competing with?', Silvija asked.

'What?!' Why can't her mother just follow the line of conversation?!

'I suppose your ambitions have changed dramatically. And you never told me about it.' Silvija paused to think about the phrasing. 'When you left ... into this complete unknown I was so scared. Every day I had to give myself a pep-talk, that you will be fine and safe and that you're going to make a great future for yourself. And you have. And I am happy. I guess I never expected that you would take his big step only to become a housewife.'

'Only to become a housewife' rang in Helena's head. She thought of a time, years ago, when she stood on a platform at Gatwick for an hour waiting for the *second* Capital Connect. A couple of young local girls had given her directions, no doubt finding it rather amusing. She often thought of that incident. It was quite funny, in retrospect, but the feeling of being made a fool of in a strange world, standing alone on the platform waiting for a train that would never arrive and the way the conductor laughed when she asked when the *second* Capital Connect was due – it stayed with her for years.

'I like it,' she said finally, with a rush of stage fright.

Silvija shook her head almost involuntarily.

'I like it. There. The job was stressful. My colleagues were like animals. They were backstabbing and false. I like doing up the house and cooking and searching for beautiful pieces of furniture and art. I like taking care of my husband.'

'He makes you nervous.'

'He doesn't make me nervous!'

'He comes in, you tense up. I have never seen you that anxious about somebody's opinion.'

'Really? You mean a lifetime of being anxious about your opinion doesn't count?'

Even at fifty-nine Silvija still couldn't crack that riddle. How does one raise a child and not get ambushed by resentment at some unforeseen turn?

***

Silence descended on the Poggenpohl. The granite seemed to Silvija as silent as a grave. She had a pointy nose, her daughter, the same pointy nose she had from the day she was born. Somehow, the pointy nose of her little girl and her small frame didn't make sense in this massive, shiny kitchen that was the best in the world. She looked at Helena's hands submerged in the bowl of sarma stuffing and her eyebrows knitted in tight frustration. She was probably wishing she had never invited her in the first place.

A long minute of regret and stubbornness passed. 'I … I should go to bed,' Silvija said, though, 'Honey, I love you so much,' and 'I'm sorry, I don't mean to judge you,' were also in the mix.

Helena nodded with her eyes firmly on the stuffing.

Silvija got up and slowly went for the door. 'I was frustrated because I was unhappy with your dad and saw no way out. I doubt very much that a functional dishwasher would have made that much difference.'

A couple hours later when Helena came to bed, Andrew was asleep. People generally didn't look nearly as attractive asleep as they did in films, she thought. Of course, in films they weren't actually asleep.

This man with his funny wheeze who always sleeps in the corpse position did in fact make her nervous. She didn't know why that was. She suspected there were layers of complicated explanations, but she knew she somehow, for reasons unknown, blamed her mother for it. She climbed into bed and tried to fall asleep. 'Unhappy'. Her mother had been unhappy. She always remembered her childhood as happy and her parents' marriage as a fairly peaceful one. For hours she couldn't fall asleep. A nagging image taking shape for the first time in her mind would not leave her alone. Her mother, a woman.

***

Silvija looked out the window to inspect the morning sky. What strange weather they have here. It looked like it wasn't going to rain although it desperately wanted to.

After a breakfast of scrambled eggs, smoked salmon and wheat-free toast, Silvija suggested that it might be a better idea if she didn't attend the dinner party. It wasn't any sort of a protest, she assured Helena. It was simply to make things easier. Her English wasn't great and she would be the thirteenth person and so on, it might prove altogether simpler if she went for a walk or to the theatre.

A wave of not entirely unfamiliar but almost forgotten and definitely stronger-than-ever emotion came over Helena when she heard her mother's suggestion. Her chest tightened. A cartoonish landscape opened in her head. Two cliffs separated by a canyon. She imagined a group of snooty, babbling businessmen and their wives squashed together on one edge. She imagined them clanking their glasses and adjusting their spectacles and her husband in the middle, handsome and a little tired, topping up their drinks. The cliff was dangerously close to giving. And on the other side was her mother, the only blood relative she had. She stood alone, smiling reassuringly, wanting to make things easy for her.

Helena hugged her mother, she embraced her tightly and her eyes filled with tears. She was immediately cross with herself for being so overly dramatic. After all there was no cliff and no canyon and it was all so annoyingly overstated in her head, as if her strongest Croatian gene had fought its way up to the surface and was now gasping for air. 'I really need more excitement in my life than swanky kitchen appliances can provide,' she thought for a fleeting second.

Silvija didn't understand quite what came over her daughter but accepted the hug almost instantly. The moment she heard a sniffing sound coming from the pointy nasal area, her eyes welled up as well, but she managed to control herself.

'Mum, would you make pancakes for desert? With cream and cottage cheese? We might as well go all the way!'

Towards the end of the evening it was safe to say that the party was going to be remembered as a great success. In the history of the dish, no sarma had even been served on such fancy plates and with such haute cuisine flare. It was initially met with reservation but eventually went down a treat. After pancakes, a couple of guests had discretely loosened their belts. Silvija and Helena shared a conspiratorial smile.

Fairly early on in the evening, just as Andrew was starting to fret about the ice still remaining unbroken between him and Sir Phillip, it transpired that Sir Phillip was a passionate German speaker. As was Silvija.

The two of them chatted away for most of the night, ending up on the balcony with a cognac and a cigarette. He was the last to leave the party sporting a funny glow that comes from a mix of alcohol and unexpected joy of human bonding.

Silvija went to bed curiously happy. However suspect this world seemed to her, her daughter pulling off a dinner party like that with such grace or at least apparent grace did make her feel immensely proud. The fact that the two of them had bonded over cooking made her feel slightly too much like a poster for conservative values but she thought she'd take whatever she could get for the moment. And she had to admit it – apart from a touch of nervousness around Sir Phillip, Andrew was a seductively confident and generous host.

At the beginning of the evening Silvija had hoped just to pull through without making everyone feel self-conscious or locking them in simplistic conversations in basic English. She never expected to have a good time. What's more, she had showed someone a good time. She had a smile on her face as she took her makeup off. Had she just flirted a little with a Sir?

***

'Sir Phillip is taking your mother for a day trip to Oxford on Tuesday,' Andrew said taking his shirt off in the bedroom.

'Is he now?'

'It was a tremendous dinner, sweetie,' he kissed Helena on the cheek, 'but I fear our future now depends on your mother's chastity. Or lack of it, as it were.' He went to bed and turned the light off straight away. They were both exhausted.

'Andy?'

'Yes?'

'My name is Hel-é-na.'

'Sorry, what?'

'Not Helena, Helena,' she said stressing the second syllable, 'I would appreciate it if you tried to call me that. Helena.'

'Where is this coming from?'

'Nowhere. Just something I would like. Would you do that?'

Andrew looked at her intensely for a second or two and then shrugged.

'Sure.'

BRENT
The Samosa Whisperer

The Samosa Whisperer

Nikesh Shukla

It's the fourth restaurant along the Ealing Road that welcomes Prakash's strange request. They're having a slow day. The chef is going through an existential crisis, having had all his cooking outsourced to a local catering company that delivers every menu item in plastic containers every morning, and all his extensive years of training under Chef Rajput Ali Lal of the Veeraswami in London's fashionable West End is now wasted on reheating other people's food. The manager is off work, sick with food poisoning. He ate at home last night for the first time in two years. The prawns were out of date.

Prakash is wearing jeans, a T-shirt with Spiderman on it, black trainers and a light coat and hasn't shaved in four days. He hasn't got a man bag with him. The only thing he carries is the folder. The chef, Ram saab, is sitting at the back of the restaurant listening to the new Arctic Monkeys album loudly, glad to be out from under the strict Bollywood regime that rules with an iron melody when the manager is on the premises. The waiters are smoking in the kitchen, at the back near the extractor fan. It's warm enough for them to smoke outside but tiny rebellions alleviate the repetitiveness of their normal working day.

Ealing Road is blocked as usual. It's Sunday and the cash and carries are full of masis and kakis and faibas stocking up on the week's aubergines, okras and potatoes. Fresh coriander is smelt and picked at, noses and fingers unshy to the merchandise. The men are sat outside cafes, chewing betelnut juice and spitting it out on the poor pavement, blotches of

Pollock-esque dirt lining the pavement like a gauntlet. Bhangra throbs from passing cars, houseproud with sub-woofers that betray loud thuds into the streets. Inside, one can only assume, it sounds amazing. Children run around, unafraid of broken Britain. Boys smile at clusters of girls dressed in black. Clusters of girls deconstruct the failings of all the local potential husbands. When Prakash gets home he will notice a reddish tint to the soles of his trainers, where they have trod on fresh betelnut splurts. He will be annoyed.

Ram saab listens to Prakash's odd request with a smile, bemused at first, charmed at the end. He categorically decides that he will help this man. The waiters can handle the reheating. He barely needs to be here; he is but a token nod to past culinary glories – what a decadent idea, an actual chef who can cook things instead of press START on a microwave. What a novelty. This is broken Brent, he snorts to himself. The Gujaratis have really taken over every possible business. There's even a Gujarati family business dedicated to recycling the plastic containers all the pre-prepared food arrives in. He will help this man, yes. It's a slow day and the manager has missed a trick. This is the only restaurant that doesn't offer a vegetarian Gujarati buffet. It's the only empty restaurant on Ealing Road. Sunday lunch in Brent is observed with all you can eat buffets. They are a cash cow. Even Hindus like cash cows, he snorts to himself. In his head, he constantly tells himself, he is hilarious. Ram saab thinks about stand-up comedy being a possible out for him. It's a shame he works nights anyway.

Prakash shows Ram saab the book, and the page in question. Ram saab looks down the page, oscillating his head from side to side in agreement with the recipe and the instructions. Prakash smiles at Ram saab's nods of enthusiasm. He may well have found his chef.

'When did your grandmother die?' Ram saab asks Prakash.

'Three months ago. To this day.'

'Three months to the day. Fresh, like fish from the sea. Let me see, let me think, let me do. I will help you.' Ram saab sometimes talks in rhyme when he's excited.

'Thank you so much,' Prakash says. His mask slips for a second and he looks glum. 'I miss her so much.'

'When did she write this recipe for you?'

'Six months ago. For a wedding present, my faiba collected all the family recipes in this book so I could make them. I've been working through them.'

'How often have you attempted this particular recipe?'

'Once a week since my grandmother died. I cannot get it right. Neither can my wife. It doesn't ever taste like grandmother's samosas. Never.'

Ram saab ponders this. It is indeed a sad situation for Prakash to be in. This is a challenge. He has to make a samosa like Prakash's grandmother made it. This impersonation will be his greatest feat: to cook something with a taste so ingrained in a man's DNA because of family history that only a chef like him can accomplish the mimicry. This is the challenge he has been waiting for.

'I accept the challenge.'

'It's not a challenge. I just wanted you to help me decipher some of the writing.'

'No. You will come into my kitchen and we will prepare the samosas. They will be just like your grandmother's. You will cry when you taste the first bite and you will want to see her again because it will taste like she is in the room. We will not rest until we have achieved that. Or until the restaurant closes. Whichever comes first.'

Ram saab asks Prakash if these are Punjabi or Gujarati samosas. Prakash isn't aware there's a difference. Ram saab is horrified. There is a massive difference, he explains. The first major difference is the shape. The Punjabi samosa is more pasty-shaped, more 3-D than its Gujarati counterpart, which is a triangular. He makes a dirty joke comparing the

71

shape to female private parts. He laughs, much like someone who has never seen any female private parts, Prakash thinks, but then dismisses the thought. He only wants to think good things. This could be what he needs to taste his grandmother's food again. He's moved at Ram saab's enthusiasm for the project.

He follows him into the kitchen. Ram saab takes out a sharp knife that has hitherto only been used to pierce the film on top of the cartons of food he has to reheat. He takes out the chopping board that he last used to make a papier-mache moon for a fancy dress outfit. He takes out the garlic press, the grater and some frozen peas. He finds some pastry. Lastly, he fills a big wok with a litre or so of sunflower oil and puts it on to simmer, to slowly heat up, as per the instructions. Ram saab notes that not only could Prakash's grandmother not write legibly, but she couldn't spell either. Her written Gujarati is worse than my written Russian, he thinks. He knows this is an exaggeration. He looks at the first step. It's the hard bit, preparing the pastry and he starts to do what he needs to. Prakash is watching intently, and filming the process on his mobile phone. Ram saab instructs the camera as he goes, imagining himself on a cooking show. The camera represents his loving and adoring audience. Prakash is some celebrity brought into the studio to promote their new film or CD and is being shown how to make an authentic Gujarati dish. Ram saab imagines the story he will tell, how this was his grandmother's recipe and he learnt to perfect it so he would be reminded of her whenever he ate the samosas, a perfect memory of her through her food.

Ram saab stops his narration and video fantasy and stares at the recipe, bringing it up to his face for confirmation. She has suggested three tablespoons of garam masala instead of the usual four. She is a maverick he thinks. Should he follow her recipe or should he do as his great teacher did? If he chooses option a, he is preserving the family recipe, written down for the first time ever. If he chooses option b, he is mutating it and evolving it.

Prakash spots his hesitation and asks what's wrong.

'Well, your grandmother has asked for three tablespoons of garam masala. Personally, I would put in four. And I'm the best samosa maker in the whole of Brent.' He points up to a photograph where he's holding a three-foot samosa in his hands, a red sash round him declaring 'MR SAMOSA, BRENT 1998.'

'That's fine,' Prakash says, anxious. 'But I would really prefer if you followed my grandmother's recipe. I'm not trying to make the best samosa. I want to make her samosa.'

'I understand,' Ram saab says. This is turning out to be quite a challenge, especially now he has to go against everything he believes in. He should have asked for payment. Damn this rut. Damn Ealing Road. Damn Wembley. Damn Gujarati samosas. He puts in three tablespoons of garam masala. The third spoon is heavy with the ground spice and he tips it in quickly so Prakash won't spot his subversive act.

Prakash notes the heft of the spoon and assumes that the recipe calls for generous portions. His grandmother always used to try and teach him how to make things and would insist that, with Indian foods, you had to learn by doing. He looks towards the restaurant. From the kitchen vantage point, it's still empty while the foot traffic outside ebbs and flows like a forceful tide. He looks at Ram saab, who is in his element. He stares intently at the page, tracing each word with his index finger, his nail yellow from years of turmeric use. Prakash remembers sitting on his grandmother's footstool in the kitchen and watching her make the samosas. The moment the oil had heated up to the point of bubbling was when he would start salivating expectantly. She would always let him drop one or two samosas into the wok before shielding him from any oil spatter. He would wait patiently. She would never let him have the first one. She insisted that the virgin oil hadn't soaked up the spices enough. The second and third were his. The first would form the base of a large pile. Prakash blinks and notices his hand has slipped, causing the camera to not catch all of the action. He asks Ram saab where he's from and how long he's lived in the UK but Ram saab waves him off. He is concentrating.

Ram saab cannot believe this woman's methods. They are insane. The first samosa is the freshest, he insists in his head. But, as he steals a look at Prakash, he realises that this isn't so much about what the perfect samosa is, it's about the perfect one for him. He feels sorry for this guy.

The mixture is fried in oil and placed in a bowl next to him as he extracts shapes from filo pastry, slowly dolloping an exact tablespoon of innards on to them, folding in the right creases and leaving to one side. Prakash's phone has run out of memory so he's watching intently. The kitchen is silent except for the hum of microwaves around them. Two couples have arrived for food, and the waiters are heating up their order for them. This is the busiest it's been since opening at 9am. The trade secret, the food being prepared off-site, it's all an elaborate disappointment once the veil of curry houses is pulled back from its purdah. Prakash realises. Maybe he will never eat in an Indian restaurant again. Where's the love and tenderness that goes into the cooking? He can see Ram saab lifting up the first samosa. Ram saab is ready.

'I will only make five samosas from this mixture. If it is the right one, we will make more.' Prakash nods. Ram saab looks at the simmering wok and cranks the heat up a bit. The wok takes about fives minutes of awkward silence before it starts to boil. When the first bubble plops at the top, Prakash licks his lips in anticipation. That smell has hit his nose. He is Pavlov's dog. He has to sit down and watch, his hands clasped. He has a specific memory of one samosa he ate. It was the week after his grandfather had died and his grandmother had stopped wearing the white mourning saree. She was back on her feet keeping busy. He hadn't even been hungry, instead being 10 years old and clingy, followed her around the house, checking up on her to shield him from his own hurt. She eventually found the best way to get rid of him. She heated up the wok of oil and pulled out some pre-prepared frozen ones.

They tasted of life before his grandfather had died. They tasted electric.

It was a wonder he hadn't put on any weight.

Ram saab pulls his face closer to the bubbling wok and decides it is ready. He plunges the first samosa in, and heated bubbles caress it as it fizzes in the wok, cooking quickly. Prakash gasps, Ram saab smirks. He likes being able to shock and awe eaters once more. He remembers the first samosas he ever made, aged 11, to appease his father for getting bad marks at school and to impress a girl he loved, who loved food more than men. He considered himself a chubby chaser and loved feeding girls the deep-fried delights he cooked up in the kitchen. He remembers the way his dad smiled and wiped the grease from his fingers on to the school report, fudging the grades, making the illegible handwritten character assassinations meaningless. He remembers how the girl, Basanti, let him kiss her after her second samosa. He could taste the flakes of pastry in his mouth. To this day, samosa flakes arouse him in some form or another.

Prakash remembers the day his grandmother died. He had promised to take her to bingo, a pastime they both loved seeing as it didn't involve conversation or language skills of any kind, seeing as the bingo caller now used an electronic number generator. They had got into an argument with his mother and their neighbour about the correct rules for a syndicate. He maintained that the syndicate was legion and all were equal within in, whereas his mother and their neighbour sought to assert, having had the winning houses, that they got a larger percentage of the winnings as they had possessed winning tickets. He was appalled at their behaviour. His grandmother sat quietly in the corner clutching her chest. He had assumed she had cramp from all the felt-pen rubbing on the bingo sheets. By the time they tried to usher her out of the car at her house, she had died, quietly in the front seat, sitting on Prakash's new Kanye West CD, while he attempted to railroad his mother into giving him back his equal share, now that the neighbour had gone her own way home.

Ram saab lifts the first one out of the wok and places it down on the cutting board to cool. He places another samosa into the fizzle of the oil and watches it brown. Prakash picks up the first samosa and throws it in the bin. Ram saab understands now. The first one isn't the right one. This is all starting to make sense to him. Maybe, he wonders, it doesn't matter so much whether the samosa tastes exactly like the grandmother's recipe. Maybe it's the process that Prakash wants. He saw how the smell of the sizzling oil made him weak at the knees. Ram saab thinks back to a year after his mother's death when he had defrosted some of her old okra shaak and reheated it. The smell filled the kitchen with the smell of his mother and his eyes with the water of tears. For a pregnant second mother and son were reunited. It's not about the samosa, he realises. It's about the process. It's about the smells. It's about the journey. This oral history he is glancing down at, this will live on for generations as the most priceless artefact in Prakash's house. Ram saab then wonders whether he should be getting paid for this.

They both stare into space, awkward with each other. Ram saab sums up how much he can charge this man for his involvement, factoring in time, cost of ingredients and amenties like gas and electricity, minus how much enjoyment the last two hours have given him. Actually, he thinks, if he's to do that sum properly, he might end up owing Prakash something. Prakash is wondering how much to offer this great chef that wouldn't make him think that Prakash thinks he's a cheap Wembley Gujarati chef, and how much will make him think Prakash is grateful. Neither comes to an agreed figure in their head.

Ram saab lifts out the second samosa, the perfect samosa and places it on the cutting board. It's the right shade of beige. It's crisp and glistens with the remains of the oil. Prakash smiles, counting to sixty in his head before reaching down to try it. He picks it up. It smells exactly like grandmother's samosa. He smiles at Ram saab as they both ingest the aroma, loudly through their thick nasal hairs. Prakash lifts the samosa to his salivating mouth. It smells of her and he is transported back to a montage of memories: hiding in her saree away from arguing parents; her teaching him how to write his name in Gujarati; him reading comics while she watched Neighbours; hours of bingo; mountains of samosas – each one tasting like those moments, like that brilliant amazing time when they would spend entire summers together while his mum and dad worked. His teeth crunch through the hot flaky pastry and a thousand sensations dance into his mouth like a triumphant procession lead by elephants, trumpets blaring, men dancing in concentric circles, women looking demure under their sarees. The filling hits the back of his throat as he chews and in his head, he can see his grandmother walking through the thick crowds of jubilation and he chases her and runs towards her, putting a hand on her shoulder and spinning her around as the sun beats down upon them. She spins around. He swallows. He smiles. It is one. This is it. This is the meaning of life, he shouts in his brain.

'How was it?' asks Ram saab, sweating anxiously, using a knife to dislodge cumin seeds from under his nails.

Outside, the Ealing Road carries on bustling as if nothing short of a miracle has just happened here.

HARROW

Maybe It's Because I'm a Londoner, That I Live in London

Maybe It's Because I'm a Londoner, That I Live in London

Tim Scott

1

I liked this part of the walk. You finally leave the buildings behind and slip down the narrow lane through the trees.

I nodded to a man coming the other way. He was wearing a trilby and looking pretty smug about it. Maybe he even got some kind of Arts Council grant for wearing the hat to keep the tradition alive. I carried on down the path, letting my feet slap on the tarmac. Was it possible to get a grant for wearing a hat? I couldn't properly decide. Towards my right the sun was setting. I stopped and looked out over the tennis courts and the fields beyond. It was almost as though someone had poured oil on the horizon and set the sky alight. A little further around I could see the running track, and I just made out a tiny figure standing on the far straight. There was something not quite right about this but I couldn't decide what it was.

'This way! No Mr Beagle!' said a voice and I turned to see a woman hauling along a small brown and white dog. 'He's part cocker spaniel,' she said to me as though this was an answer to a question I was about to ask and passed busily on before I had time to settle on a reply. I remembered I had seen her before yanking the same dog up Church Hill though this was the first time she had said anything to me.

The lane led down the hill and was lined with trees that peeled bark. After walking on a little way I looked back, but there was no one there and the stillness of the evening seemed to ratchet up a notch or two. I reached the bottom of Football Lane and turned right, past the empty tennis courts and I stopped to enjoy the grainy haze of the evening dusk, which seemed almost a palpable thing as it hung in the air.

Silence.

I headed in the direction of the woods, intending to skirt past the lake and complete my little circuit back up to Crown Street. But I saw a grey shape on the running track. In the heavy twilight my brain had trouble turning the ragbag of crumpled edges into anything that made sense and so, out of curiosity I drew closer. Eventually I trotted down a little set of steps to the dusty path that ran around the whole of the track in a wide curving oval.

From the path the pile of edges was now on my level and it looked bigger and slightly sinister, rising as it did in a hump at one end, but I still couldn't determine whether it was simply a tarpaulin or some rubbish that had been dumped. I stepped onto the running track, which had a spring to it and as I walked towards the strange shape I had the weird sensation I was treading on slightly melted tar. My thoughts surged for a moment and I stopped. I felt slightly dizzy and a little nauseas. I blinked. Christ – the past always had the ability to mug me like this. Why was I thinking about Joanne? Why did my thoughts always return to her in moments of stress as though she was some kind of pre-set in my brain?

Joanne would have loved seeing this sunset in Harrow. She didn't take long to fall in love with the area. Always commenting on the names and giggling because they sounded to her like they had come out of the Hobbit. 'Pinner Green,' she'd say pointing to a sign as we passed.

'Nowhere is called Pinner Green in real life.' Or, 'Look! Hatch End. That's where Mr Toad lives isn't it? It's not a real place.' I think it was because she wasn't a Londoner that she could constantly find the names so amusing, or maybe it simply

was because that's how she was, always taking a childlike fascination with the world. Maybe the truth of it was, that is why I loved her.

'Hurry… please,' said a voice. My consciousness snapped back. The shape wasn't a tarpaulin. Christ. It was a man collapsed on the track wearing a beige raincoat. He was about twenty feet away.

'Are you all right?' I managed to say, but I found it hard to move my legs.

'Please … Harry.'

'Look … are you all right?' I said again still finding a weird kind of inertia had the soles of my feet pinned to the spongy running track.

'Take this please, Harry,' said the man and he tried to lift an arm into the air. It reminded me from a scene in a film, or maybe it's a painting of a battlefield where a soldier holds up the colours of his regiment in a final defiant act.

Finally I managed to move closer.

'I'm not Harry,' I said. 'I'm Martin Evanson. I work for AF architects.' I have no idea why I said this, but probably I had shifted into automatic and I said it simply because I'd said it before.

'Oh,' he said. And then again, 'oh.' His face was clean-shaven and his hair gelled back. He had a familiar kind of face. The kind of face that's comforting in its simplicity and openness. But his skin was horribly pale. Even in the fading light I could see he was in a bad way.

'Are you all right?' I said. 'Shall I call for a –'

'No!' he swallowed. 'Please don't! You mustn't. Take this and go! Please take this. Will you take this for me?'

For the first time I realised he had something in his hand. An envelope.

'I'm not Harry,' I said. 'I'm Martin Evanson. I –'

'Work for an architect. I know. Please take it. I'm begging you. Please.' His eyes met mine and they were desperate. I reached out very slowly and grasped the envelope between my finger and thumb and lightly withdrew it from his grasp.

'Thank you,' he said. 'Now run Martin! Run! In God's name run or they'll come for you as well.' And his eyes closed and his head slipped onto the track. I felt my mouth fall open and then a moment later I was aware I was running. Obviously running was the wrong thing to do but I did it anyway and it felt like I was 10 again. It felt like I was going at a thousand miles an hour and the world was just a blur. My heart was virtually exploding and inexplicably I pictured myself talking to Joanne and saying, 'I could never move from London, the city is as much a part of me as my own heartbeat.'

I reached the edge of the woods gasping for air and began to take notice of what my legs were doing. I had a distant other-worldly memory of sprinting down the track faster than at any time in my life and then I must have lunged head long into the woods which is what sent the roosting birds into the air in a wild exhibition of flapping. Why the hell was I running? What the hell was I doing? I should call the police. I should do anything other than what I was doing at the moment. I tried to focus, but everything was turning slowly around me and my eyes felt like they were floating in my head. My feet locked to the ground and everything ground to a halt. I grasped at the idea that if I got back home everything would be all right again. I had to get back home. I had to just walk out of here the long way down through the park and get home. I lurched sideways and stumbled causing more rafts of birds to take off into the shifting haze of the ink-blue sky.

It was now 9.15pm I made a mental note not to look at my watch again because the time kept shifting in jumps. I had come back, ripped open the envelope, tried to make sense of the contents and then curled up on the sofa and felt like I was shaking. Not on the outside, but on the inside. As though my whole body was minutely vibrating. I didn't know whether to have tea, whiskey or cornflakes. In the end I had all three. It was a pretty strange meal but it worked to some extent because afterwards I felt strong enough to go upstairs to the top floor and have a long, hot shower. Finally I curled up in bed with the light on looking at the picture of Joanne on the bedside table and fell asleep. I woke once in the night. Turned off the light and then slept through.

2

The next day I called in sick. I had woken feeling empty inside and shuffled down the stairs to the kitchen to try and cook up a proper breakfast of eggs easy-over but I didn't get the timing of flipping the eggs quite right because my mind wasn't really on the job. Afterwards I sat on the sofa, turning the envelope over in my hands and seeing if there was anything I had missed the night before. On the address panel it said simply, '*your move*'. Inside was a single sheet of white writing paper and I studied it over again.

The top end of High Street in Harrow on the Hill is a sweeping parade of three storey Georgian and Victorian buildings that canter up the hill towards the church. I had decided to walk even though where I was going was a little way away. Part of the reason was that finding somewhere to park on Crown Street is virtually an occupation. Once you leave a space the chances are you will never find another. It's one of the few streets I know that still seems grouchy about the whole invention of the motorcar. It's simply way too narrow and hemmed in as it is, with short unforgiving pavements. There's only enough room to park a car outside your door as long as you have scoured the show rooms of the country for the thinnest model available. 'I like this car but do you have it in anything thinner?' is a phrase people living on Crown Street might have contemplated asking in car showrooms. So I was loathed to give up my car parking space and that was partly why I was walking and not taking my car.

But that was only part of the reason.

When I reached the school I took a little detour into the grounds so I could get a view of the running track down below. It was deserted. There was no police tent; no forensic scientists pouring over the ground dressed in their white baby grow overalls. I felt massively relieved, and headed back up the hill. In my inside jacket pocket was an envelope. And inside was a sheet of paper I had laboured over for around half an hour. I wondered why I was getting involved. Perhaps the desperate look on the man's face before he collapsed made me feel indebted to him, but what had happened after I left? The image of him lying on the running track came back in a white-hot charge. It was out of kilter with the day-to-day reality of everything around me, and I had to stop and clear my head near the church.

Joanne had attended the services at St Mary's on the hill. It wasn't that she was religious, even towards the end, but she loved the peacefulness. And perhaps St Mary's appealed to her particularly because it's a little fairy tale of a church nestling as it does among the trees with it's squat tower topped with an impossibly oversize spire. I had tried to explain to her once how London ran through my veins and that the buildings and the streets knew my secrets better than I did myself and that was enough religion for me. I was a Londoner and I was sure that meant something even if I didn't know what exactly.

My thoughts caught up with the present again and I found I had reached Kenton Road and the kettledrum noise of London traffic swamped me. I could have probably cut through the backstreets and trusted my sense of direction but I stuck to the main road anyway. When I turned a corner I saw a woman hauling a small dog along the pavement towards me. It was the same woman I had seen the previous evening.

'Mr Beagle only likes dog snacks in the shape of a bone,' she said as she passed by me, exactly as before as though this was in answer to a question I was about to ask. I nodded and then turned to watch her disappear before going on. Eventually I reached the Civic Centre and I just stood there like an idiot. There was still time not to do this. There was still time to walk away.

Maybe I stood there for five minutes. I simply stood letting my thoughts have free reign. Eventually I decided there didn't seem to be any good reason not to go in, so I walked up the steps. Inside there was a musty business-like atmosphere. People bustled backwards and forwards in the heavy gloom, many in suits, and others in casual clothes that seemed to come from another era. I ignored the reception desk and strode towards the far end where the lifts were arranged. I pressed the button on the nearest one and as I waited my mind re-wound to the envelope.

'Leave your next move for the white pieces in an envelope taped above the buttons in the lift number one in the Civic Centre, Station Road by 12pm tomorrow. The deal remains the same.'

That's what it had said on the piece of paper and below had been drawn a position in a chess game. I stepped in quickly when the lift arrived and before the doors closed I saw there was a new envelope taped above the buttons with the same familiar writing. I tore it down and opened it. There was a single sheet inside. *'Tape your move here,'* it said. *'My next move will be inside a copy of Remains of the Day by Kazuo Ishiguro, to be found in Pinner Library at 3pm.'*

Was this the beginning of something? Or the end of something? What was happening to me?

Back home I was hunched over a chessboard in the living room when the phone rang. I picked up after four rings. It was the office. I tried to sound downbeat and told them it was a stomach upset and I'd be in the next day. They wanted to know some detail about an extension for a house in Wealdstone and I explained it as best I could and then rang off. I had also bought a local paper and scanned it for any news about the guy on the running track but there was nothing. Maybe somebody collapsing wasn't news. Maybe that kind of thing happened every day.

I looked back at the board. Chess is a game I have only a slight knowledge of. I know the moves, and I had a little spell when I played quite a few games with a friend, sitting cross-legged on the floor with a whiskey in one hand and the room filled with his cigarette smoke and the music of Gil Scott Heron. But that had been years before and it had taken me a long while studying the position drawn on the paper before I could fathom out my next move.

2.15pm I took the Metropolitan Line northbound two stops to Pinner and then walked. The library was only a few streets away – a neat brick and glass affair with red railings. Inside the atmosphere was somewhere between a charity shop and a primary school. I tried to look slightly bored and wandered past some battered looking children's picture books and a large woman carrying a basket before I hunkered down behind a terminal. *Remains Of the Day* by Kazuo Ishiguro was on the shelves.

I pulled out the white spine and immediately saw there was an envelope jammed into the pages. I withdrew it, crumpled it into my pocket and walked to the exit trying not to move too fast but I was aware of the woman with the basket, staring.

On the tube home I watched the houses slip by, one after the other. Joanne had had all kind of plans. She wanted to move to Hatch End, not because she especially liked the area, in fact I'm not sure she had actually ever even been there, but simply because she liked the name. There were plenty of places she would have refused to live I'm sure. I remember her refusing to go through Ipswich one time, and we had to detour around because she thought the name sounded all wrong.

***

I sat on the sofa in the living room and turned the new envelope over in my hand. It had '*your move*' written on the front exactly as before. I compared it with the first envelope and the writing was identical. Inside was a sheet of paper with the chess game drawn out by hand, including the move I had left in the lift at the Civic Centre and a new one from my opponent. Underneath was written, '*Leave your next move for the white pieces in an envelope taped to a pillar of the temple in the grounds of Canons Park by 5pm The deal remains the same.*'

'*The deal remains the same.*' What deal was this? What was I involved with? I had no idea and looked at my watch. It was 3.30pm now. I had never been to Canons Park and got out the *A to Z*. It wasn't that far away but it was complicated by tube. It would take about twenty minutes in the car if there wasn't traffic but anything up to an hour if there was. I hadn't been on my bike for months and I went out through the kitchen to the small terrace where it sat leaning on the fence and gave it an inexpert shake. It seemed like it would work.

I set off with the deadline thirty-five minutes away. I partially memorised the route but trusted mostly to my sense of direction. If dolphins and sparrows can navigate between entire continents I reasoned, then surely I could get as far as Canons Park. Sadly my logic was flawed and I had to twice get out the *A to Z*. I guess sparrows don't have anything as complicated as the Honeypot Lane contra-flow system to worry about on their way to Africa or they'd be extinct. It was another warm evening and Canons Park looked beautiful. I left my bike against some railings and wandered through the grounds until I saw the crisp, white temple standing deserted in the languid evening light.

The envelope was taped high up on the back of one of the pillars. I had to jump up to pull it down and then I taped my own move slightly lower down. Afterwards I sat on the low step looking out over the grass and felt the sun on my arms. The pick up point for the next move was the following morning in a record shop in Pinner. The envelope would be tucked into a CD of Bruch's violin concerto. In the distance I could see someone walking a small dog.

On the journey home I passed a couple of bookshops on St. Anne's Road. At the second I stopped. I lent my bike against the glass and returned to it a little later having bought a copy of *Remains of the Day*. I hadn't read a novel in years.

3

I slept well and woke early. I went out and bought pain au chocolat, fresh fruit and yoghurt for breakfast and phoned the office bang on 8.30am to tell them I wouldn't be in that day and probably not the next. The idea of going to work seemed ludicrous and my act on the phone was less convincing than ever. Then I studied the chessboard. I was a knight up and couldn't see any imminent threats.

I cycled to Pinner. The envelope with the next move was tucked into the CD case, just as it should be, and on a whim I bought the Bruch album. The next deadline was tight. Headstone Manor in less than an hour, and I realised what I really needed was a pocket chess set, along with some envelopes and paper so I didn't have to go back home each time between moves. I got what I needed in Pinner and the rest of the morning I continued with the game. I found myself at the Roger Banister Stadium as well as the Harrow Arts Centre where I picked up an envelope with a key inside. It was for a locker in Hatch End swimming pool and the only way I could see to get access to the locker to retrieve the move was to actually go swimming. So I had to make a detour via home to pick up my swimming things. There was a message on the answer phone from the office. My hand hovered over the receiver but I decided not to call back. Then I headed off to the pool. I hadn't been swimming for years and the feeling of release when I got into the water was terrific.

6.00pm I was sitting on the sofa staring at a sheet of paper from the latest envelope feeling numb. I had played several more moves since the swim and the chess game was going well. It wasn't that that was causing me a problem. My opponent's position was hopeless. I was now two pieces up with a pawn threatening to queen. No it was something else. '*Your final move,*' it said on the paper. '*The running track Harrow School, 7pm sharp.*' For the first time I felt genuinely scared. Maybe I shouldn't go. Maybe I had taken this whole thing far enough. What did it all matter anyway?

I normally like this part of the walk. You finally leave the buildings behind and slip down the narrow lane through the trees. The sun was just setting and I stopped to look out over the deserted tennis courts and the running track. I could just make out a tiny figure standing on the far straight. I strained my eyes in the deepening dusk and it seemed they were wearing a long, light coloured raincoat.

'Come along Mr Beagle,' said a voice and I turned. It was the same woman I seen before hauling along her small brown and white dog. I opened my mouth but couldn't think of anything to say and she simply walked on not even making eye contact this time and I watched her yanking along her dog until she was out of sight.

I headed down the path, trying to make sense of it all. I turned right at the bottom and came out near the tennis courts. The figure was still there, standing alone on the running track. I followed the path around and then walked down the small flight of steps to the track. The man turned. 'You play a mean game of chess, Martin.' It was the same person I had met here two days before.

'You again? You're not – what is this? Was this all a trick?' I said.

'No, no of course not. Not a trick. Thank you for your participation. I'm from a company called *Perspective*. We're funded by a Government Arts Organisation.'

'A Government Arts Organisation? What do you mean?' I said.

'Our remit is to keep people feeling properly alive in areas serviced by the Metropolitan Line.'

'What *are* you talking about?'

'Relax, it's all right Martin, please. We have funding to improve the use of public and cultural services in this area. It's part of our remit to keep people feeling tip top. Otherwise living in London can get you down without you even noticing can't it?'

'Can it?' I said.

'Oh yes. So I need you to sign here to say you have significantly increased your use of public services in the last two days.' He waved a sheaf of papers and slipped a pen from his top pocket.

'Are you telling me this was all about improving my use of public services?'

'That's partly it of course, but it's also about making sure Londoners haven't lost that fighting spirit isn't it? To begin with we tried putting leaflets through people's doors but no one takes any notice of those these days do they? And I think on your file it said you had a friend pass away quite recently didn't you?'

'Yes,' I said.

'Yes, well there you go. Coh! Death eh? That can definitely be a downer. Anyway, sign here... please?' He pushed the papers toward me and pointed.

'You're serious?' I said.

'Oh yes. Sign here please to say you used the swimming pool and park and so on. And sign there to say how much more fully you now embody the spirit of London with particular regard to the area serviced by the Metropolitan Line.' I paused and then scribbled my name across the papers because it seemed as though he was actually telling the truth. 'Good,' he said. 'So, these are some complimentary egg cups and sports socks.'

'Right.' I took the gifts and clasped them awkwardly to my chest. 'So you're telling me this whole chess game was just something to make me feel more a part of London?'

'Exactly, exactly, very well put, I must remember that.'

'I can't quite believe it.'

'Well it's amazing what great work is done to keep traditions alive.'

'Is it?'

'Yes. By the way, I wanted to apologise that I'm so bad at chess. I did try to get them to change the game to Chinese Chequers but the creative department were very much against that.'

'Ah.'

'Yes. Well, I'm sorry about this, but I have another client now, so I'll have to ask you to run.'

'Run?' I said. 'Why?'

'Run. If you wouldn't mind? That way.' And suddenly blood came from his mouth.

I stepped back.

'Run. If you wouldn't mind?' he said collapsing onto the ground.

'Right,' I stared at his face, which had gone a horrible shade of white and then I turned and sprinted towards the cover of the trees just managing to cling onto my egg cups and socks. When I'd unhooked myself from the brambles I looked back through the heavy dusk. Another person was already on the running track walking tentatively toward the collapsed figure who held one hand in the air clasping something small and white in his fingers, and it looked to me very much like an envelope.

HAMMERSMITH & FULHAM
Brook Green

Brook Green

Daisy Goodwin

It must be the first day of term, thought Miss Frobisher. On summer mornings you could make out the birds in the plane trees, the thwack of tennis balls and the swish of a passing cyclist. But in the first week of September nothing could be heard above the grumble of car engines inching slowly around the Green. She usually arranged to be away this week, since she found the anxious voices of the mothers and the monosyllabic replies of their children too painfully reminiscent of the time when her job had been to say firmly, 'Goodbyes at the gate, please.' The girls had usually been relieved by her interventions, the mothers being the tearful ones. But this year the Lake Windermere hotel that ran fell-walking holidays for the visually impaired was full, and she was bound to stay in London.

She had hoped that by now, fifteen years after she had left the school, the rhythm of the terms would no longer disturb her. But she found it difficult to keep her white stick steady as she inched along the pavement to the newsagents.

So many schools, six of them crowded around the isosceles triangle of green between the Shepherd's Bush and Hammersmith Roads. In the old days she had made the year 8 girls do a project on local history. 'Brook Green,' she would tell them, 'was covered in market gardens, where vegetables were grown for the people living in the City of London. These days the nurseries of Brook Green produce a very different kind of cabbage.' She would pause, and then deliver the punch line: 'Or do you consider yourselves turnips?' Occasionally one of the kinder girls would laugh at this feeble joke, but generally the girls would stare back at her sullenly. At twelve their dignity was too fragile to brush off comparisons with brassicas. It had almost been a relief when she could no longer make out the exact contours of their doughy faces. In a year or two they would be all angles and shine, some of them beginning to get that big-eyed look that meant they had stopped eating properly. No, the gradual darkening of her vision had not been without its benefits.

She stepped carefully through a throng of voices speaking French. The Ecole Maternelle Française had the most fragrant parents. The scents, which Miss Frobisher had decided were worn by both sexes, were expensively dry and elusive. At the Catholic primary school across the road the perfumes were sweeter and more pungent. As she tapped her way towards her old workplace she began to make out the aroma of patchouli, vanilla and Clearasil that announced the proximity of teenage girls, and to hear the flap and slap of their sheepskin boots as they shuffled along the pavements and the tinny buzz of the headphones they wore in their ears. She would have liked to cross the road to avoid them, but she knew there was no pavement on the other side, so she put her head down and swung her cane wider than usual, hoping it would register in what she knew was the very narrow field of teenage vision.

As she approached the school gates she heard shouts of welcome peppered with acronyms and abbreviations. 'OMG, you didn't?' 'Eeeugh. TMI.' 'Laters.' 'Felix is over BTW.' Everything they said ended on a rising note, as if they were not stating but venturing. This change of cadence had only just started by the time she finished teaching, but now every young voice she heard on her daily outings around the Green uttered sentences that ended not with a full stop but with a question mark. They sounded more than ever like baby birds clamouring to be fed.

There was a tap on her shoulder. 'Miss Frobisher?' This voice was loud, clear and adult. 'It's Sophie Luxton, Ward-Bishop as was. I was in your history set. I'm here with my daughter Ruby, she's in the fourth form now. GCSEs next year, unbelievable how quickly they grow up. Say hello, Ruby.'

'Hello.' A small, sullen voice, quite unlike that of the mother. Miss Frobisher wondered why this woman was talking to her so loudly. Did she assume that because she was blind she must also be deaf? She turned her head towards the voice and said quietly, 'I'm sorry, I don't remember your name. But I usually remember faces. Why don't you describe yourself to me?' She had used this ploy before when accosted by former pupils. The girl, now woman, would always hesitate, unsure whether to describe herself in her current matronly incarnation or as the girl that had once gazed slack-mouthed at her as she explained the niceties of Stuart finance.

'Well, I had brown hair then, long and straight, and I still have blue eyes. I suppose the thing you might remember about me are my dimples. I used to get teased about them.'

Miss Frobisher heard the girl say, 'Muum, I've got to go.'

'All right, Ruby, you go on in. I'll see you tonight. Hang on, aren't you going to give me a kiss?' There was the sound of mouth brushing against reluctant cheek.

'Sorry about that, Miss Frobisher. She gets so impatient. But then so did I. People are always saying she is the spitting image of me at that age.' There was a little pause. Miss Frobisher had a policy of not reacting to these unwitting faux pas, like the visitors who would climb the seventy-three stairs to her flat on the other side of the Green and exclaim, 'Oh, how lucky you are to have such a wonderful view.' But Sophie Luxton, nee Ward-Bishop, was not easily abashed.

'I'm surprised you don't remember me, really. For all the wrong reasons. I'm afraid I made your life something of a misery. I feel embarrassed just thinking of how naughty I was.'

'Oh, I'm sure you weren't as bad as all that. And teachers are resilient souls.' She knew that all her former pupils were convinced they were unforgettable. But she could remember very few individuals now – only the shapes of girlhood from eager prepubescence through sullen plumpness to shiny-haired condescension. 'Goodbye, Miss Frobisher, I'll really miss you,' the shiny-haired ones would coo on the last day of term.

Suddenly, however, a memory returned, and she did remember Sophie Luxton, nee Ward-Bishop, after all.

When the macular degeneration had set in she had concealed its effects pretty well. After nearly twenty years at the school it was not so very hard to find her way around the corridors in the twilight of her deteriorating sight. She recognised her fellow teachers by their voices and by the sound of their walks. The head, who always wore heels, made a brisk tattoo on the marble floors that was quite unlike the tentative rubber-soled perambulations of the junior staff.

Of course homework had been a problem – she could no longer read the girls' essays. She had told them she couldn't be bothered to figure out their atrocious handwriting, and had ordered them to read their work aloud. This had been quite successful, as the prospect of being given a B or worse in public had made the girls work harder, and they could no longer copy each other's work. Indeed Miss Frobisher had dared to hope she might finish her twentieth year at the school with her finest set of results.

'Do you live near here, Miss Frobisher? It's funny, I can't stop myself calling you that. I suppose I should call you Celia now. It is Celia, isn't it?' Sophie Luxton, nee Ward-Bishop, leaned towards her, and Miss Frobisher smelled shampoo and expensive leather.

'Miss Frobisher is fine,' she said. 'I live across the Green, opposite the school, on the top floor.'

'Oh, how nice,' said Sophie. Miss Frobisher heard the jangle of keys. It seemed her ordeal was about to be over. 'Well, I'd best be off. Makes me feel seventeen again seeing you like this. How funny that I should be coming here with my daughter now. Goodbye, then.'

Miss Frobisher said nothing but waved her stick by way of farewell. She had always declined the offer of a guide dog, knowing that dogs drew people in while sticks kept them away.

She tapped on towards the newsagents, past the prep school where mothers stood in groups talking in anxious voices about entrance exams. 'I heard they only took four. The school really needs to prepare them better. I heard that the ones that got in were all *tutored*.'

She carried on past the tennis courts. The South African tennis coach shouted, 'Howzit, Miss Frobisher?' in between the thwack of tennis balls. He never forgot to say hello. She missed him in the winter months.

She wouldn't have been able to hide it forever, of course. The girls had guessed, and some of her colleagues had begun to suspect. But she might have scraped by until the end of the year if she hadn't given Sophie Ward-Bishop a B minus. It had been a terrible essay, a mess of cliches and generalisations not worth more than a B, but she had added the minus because of the creamy smugness of Sophie's delivery. The girl's indignant snort of dismay when she heard the mark had been really quite satisfying. But this was destined not to be the end of the matter.

The next day she had sensed the girls were excited about something. There were more giggles and squeaks than usual. She could feel barely suppressed hilarity every time she turned her head. There was a strange crackling sound as if some of the girls were wearing pvc macs, although given the summer weather that was unlikely. Whatever it was, she hoped that she would be able to ride it out until the end of the lesson, but then she heard the classroom door open and the Headmistress's smooth tones,

'And these are our Historians, we like to think of the sixth form as a smooth transition to …' the practised flow stopped and Miss Frobisher heard a gasp, followed by some snorts of laughter from the girls.

'Oh dear,' the Head was saying, to someone who accompanied her, parents probably, 'we seem to be interrupting something. Some kind of re-enactment perhaps. Shall we go straight on to the new Science block? We are so fortunate to have a really world class physics lab.'

As the door closed, the classroom exploded. Miss Frobisher heard a long hiss as if someone was deflating a lilo.

Later, in her study, the Head had spoken more in sorrow than in anger. 'I know, Celia, that sometimes the best thing to do is to ignore them, but was it wise to allow something quite so grotesque to remain in your classroom?'

Miss Frobisher said nothing, and the Head continued,

'It was so horribly lifelike. Do you think men actually use dolls like that for sex? I wonder where the culprit got it from? I hope it didn't come from home.' Miss Frobisher heard the Head sigh. 'What I don't understand is why any of our girls would do something like this. A sixth former too. Unless, of course, it was a message of some kind.' She paused for a moment. 'I just wish you'd told me, Celia. You didn't have to keep me in the dark like this.'

Miss Frobisher smiled ruefully, but the Headmistress didn't falter.

'An unfortunate choice of words, perhaps. But, honestly, Celia, we have worked alongside each other for so long. It's a question of trust. I could have helped you to … adjust.'

It had all been very swift. Compassionate leave. The promise of some coaching work, 'to tide you over'. One of the governors had put in a word with the Distressed Gentlefolks' Association and had found her the flat across the Green, 'so you won't be too cut off from your old life'.

Miss Frobisher allowed herself a little pause on the fifty-third stair, before climbing the last flight to her flat. Her visitors were always surprised that she could manage the stairs, as if her failing sight had impaired all her other faculties. She turned on the radio and heard Libby Purves announcing the line-up for Midweek. It included a man who had raised two million pounds for charity in sponsored sky dives despite losing both his legs in a waterskiing accident. She pressed the off button. Miss Frobisher did not want to hear about people who met adversity with courage, who used it as an 'opportunity'. She disliked the assumption that suffering made you a nobler person. One of the distressed gentlewomen who lived downstairs liked to tell her that when one door closes, another opens. In Miss Frobisher's experience the door had only ever been at best half open. And now it was quite shut.

She did not go out again the next morning, but waited till after lunch then the Archers repeat had finished. This was a good time, before the schools came out and the end of the working day, when the pavements were full of determined pedestrians talking on their phones and not looking out for old ladies with white sticks. As she pushed back the bolt of the front door she smelled the warm dusty scent of the plane trees. But there was something else as well – the aroma of cigarette smoke.

'Is somebody there?' she said. 'I don't want to trip over you coming down the steps.' She thought it must be a girl, since they quite often came to smoke here, the house being in a side street, and not in full view of the school.

'I'm sorry. I didn't know it was your house.'

Miss Frobisher had been right, it was a girl. She thought she recognised the voice. She never forgot a voice.

'I don't suppose you have a spare cigarette, do you?' she said. 'I used to smoke, but I had to stop when I went blind. Too dangerous, kept burning my fingers. But if you were to light a cigarette for me I would be very grateful. You never really stop wanting them, or at least I haven't.'

The girl said, 'Oh sure, no problem.' Miss Frobisher heard the sound of a match being struck, and then she felt a touch on her hand. She raised the cigarette to her lips and inhaled.

'Thank you. Now, did I meet you yesterday with your mother? What's your name? No, don't tell me, it's Ruby, isn't it?'

There was a moment's silence, and then the girl said, 'Yes. But how do you know? Can you still see things?'

'No, I'm totally blind. But I remember voices. So Ruby, how are you enjoying school?'

She could hear Ruby scuffing the step with her shoe.

'It's fine.'

Miss Frobisher knew all about 'fine'.

'Then why are you smoking on my front steps when you should be in your classroom learning something?'

'I don't know. I just needed to get out for a bit.' There were more sounds of shoe leather scuffing the steps.

'And what would your mother say if she knew what your were doing?'

'Oh, she'd be horrified. She loved being at school. Head Girl, Captain of everything. She's always telling me how great it was. But I'm not like her.'

Miss Frobisher waited for her to go on.

'I'm amazed I got in. All the other girls are really pretty and really clever. They make me feel fat and stupid. I'm the ugly duckling.'

Miss Frobisher felt the nicotine hit her, and then a flutter of pleasure. Was it the cigarette or the idea that Sophie Ward-Bishop's daughter was not turning out according to plan? She decided to nudge things a little further.

'It always was a competitive place. Sadly there's not much you can do about your looks or your brains. But you don't have to be fat.'

Miss Frobisher thought of the girls who had wasted away, their lemur-like eyes bulging, before they were whisked off to clinics by their desperate parents. Fifteen was the age when it started, usually. 'How old are you?' she asked.

'I'll be fifteen next month.'

'Quite old enough then to take control. You'll be a swan before you know it, Ruby. Give my regards to your mother. You can say you helped me across the road. Remember you can always be thin.'

Miss Frobisher set off towards the roar of traffic on the Shepherd's Bush Road. She decided she would buy some chocolate. There were some pleasures left in life after all.

EALING
Ealing Commondy

Ealing Commondy

Will Maxted

It was only light rain, so he took them the long way, through the park.

Jeremy had known what they wanted when they had first walked in. Thirty five years' experience that was. He was hearing out a phone-whinge about arrears on the office, and, on auto-pilot, guessed their tick boxes. First time. No chain. Unrealistic hopes. The bloke, Martin, seemed relaxed enough, as interested in looking around the office as at the particulars. But Chloe was an exclamation mark. Even though it had been a Saturday, she was in business dress, and sat bolt upright. Sure enough, while Martin smiled to himself, Chloe answered the questions. Jeremy typed them in carefully as if there were a point.

'Three bedrooms… Garden… One child…. Yes… Yes…' When they got to 'Catchment of Ealing Park Primary?' she just said 'yes', but briefly she was very still. Jeremy noticed such things. When he had first started in the office they had used index cards that had to be filled in by the client. Her tick in that box would have left a dent. He toyed with inventing others: 'Have You Suddenly Realised Your Application From For Primary School Has To Be In Shortly?' and, 'Are You Now Freaking Out?'

When he had got to the end of the questions, he hit the return key with a flourish. That showed he was now running an enormous computer programme, analysing vast databanks of potentially suitable properties. His nod at the screen's 'Nothing Suitable' suggested that this was only to be expected, that his properties were so desirable that, unless you paid cash as he was first mentioning them to you, they would be gone. Rather than the fact that all he had to sell at the moment was two bijou flats, in need of some reconstruction. Everyone seemed to want to go to the big boys these days, with their hungry young 'teams' and free coffee, and 360 degrees web video interactive … things. His confidence was a sham. Business was not booming.

But Chloe had worked him on the phone anyway. Trying to be charming, asking how he was, laughing but coming back to the point. Jeremy found it more impressive than flattering. The weeks passed and he felt the tone of her voice steadily going up.

And then … Someone handed him a briefcase full of banknotes saying, 'It's yours. Enjoy.'

Not literally, you understand. Literally what happened is that Mrs Isobel Turner, of Creighton Road, finally decided that her adult children were no longer going to visit her often enough to stop her moving to Devon. Not of the generation to shop around, she had just phoned up the agency she'd bought from thirty years earlier. Would he mind selling it again? Three bedrooms? South-facing garden? Jeremy almost had to wipe his chin before saying that wouldn't be a problem. He'd called Chloe for a 'heads up' before the particulars were prepared. That was this morning.

'This is Walpole Park,' he said, off-handedly, trying not to walk fast.

He talked about other things as they walked past Pitshanger Manor, and the SS Windrush memorial flowerbed. He led them past the teahut, and down the path alongside the water feature, and on past the bark-based play area. Now they were on the long tree-lined path, flanked by the open grassy spaces. He pointed out the back of Ealing Studios. He watched as Chloe's eyes flicked between the groups of people, usually including at least one mother and one small child. He thought of the Terminator scanning the biker bar.

It was Martin that eventually spoke up. 'Is this place sponsored by Maclaren Buggies?'

'Oh …' Jeremy smugged, '… yes, it's obviously a popular area for young families.'

Past the tennis courts opposite Lammas Park with a casual nod to that, round the corner, turning right when St Mary's came into view. Chloe scanned in the tiny front yards as well as the cosy front rooms, while Martin wandered along more vaguely. And then they were there. Jeremy paused on the front step.

'Obviously, South Ealing tube is just a couple of minutes walk that way,' he gestured. 'And as you probably know Ealing Park School is five minutes walk down there.' Chloe glanced, but returned her scan to the front door. Jeremy, briefly distracted by the fact that the front room's curtains were drawn at this time of the afternoon, felt that if he took too long with the keys, she might actually elbow him out of the way.

They waited as Jeremy fiddled, picking up some bits of post and putting them on the narrow shelf above the radiator. The floor tiles were the black and white tiles of an old cleaning advert. The wallpaper was muted, faded, stripes. A small faux chandelier lit photographs of people in haircuts and clothes no longer fashionable. Chloe had finished staring down the hall and was now bending sideways to glimpse the upstairs.

Jeremy opened his mouth to speak, but then a puzzle passed across his face. He closed his mouth, listening. They all heard it. He opened his mouth again, and looked at his watch. 'I thought she said she wouldn't be back until four.'

There was certainly a voice on the other side of the door to the front room. But, muffled though it was, Martin felt sure it was not the voice of an old lady. And it was strangely fluent, lively, if artificial. Martin realised what was strange: there was no interrupting second voice, and no changes in volume. Martin and Chloe looked at Jeremy. He looked at the door. 'Oops,' he said. 'I'd better just …' He stepped forward and knocked.

The voice kept going regardless.

Chloe brushed some imaginary dust of her skirt then put her shoulders back. Looking at Martin, she saucered her eyes at a point below his chin. Martin gazed back steadily, but he did straighten the tie she had made him wear. The voice paused, then kept coming again.

Jeremy knocked once more, and, coughing loudly, eased the door open slowly, leading into the gap with his head. He paused, said 'Ah,' and then pushed the door fully open. Opposite the doorway was a television, the sole source of light in the room. A confident voice was explaining how something, presumably the object on the screen that was being fondled by a stupid looking blonde woman with a mouth-only smile, also had modern and stylish looks. Jeremy moved on into the darkened room.

Martin followed Chloe after him. There was a smell that Martin couldn't place, but wasn't fresh bread or coffee. It was more like … oranges?

'Throw a little light onto the subject …' Jeremy had located a curtain rope and was tugging to pull the last few inches open as they came in. 'I think I'll turn that off for her', he said, now turning back from the window, 'if I can just find the … oh.'

They followed his gaze. The wallpaper here was light brown. Going round the room from the television opposite the door, there was a chimney breast with gas effect coal fire, then bookshelves bearing hardback books. Next to Jeremy and backed up against the window was the first of two sofas forming an L shape. The second one was against the wall next to the hall. That sofa was where the dead man was sitting.

Everything stopped. Maybe there was a joint intake of breath first, but for a moment there seemed to be just nothing apart from the body. It was the sort of pause you get when dragging a trolley suitcase along a bumpy pavement at speed, and it takes off. You know the noise is going to start again very soon, but for a beat the whole world seems weightless.

The dead guy's left hand lay on the cushion beside him, palm upwards.

The fingers curled lightly. It could have been the start of a conversational gesture, or he could have been ready to grip something. The way the possible movement was now made stone was the deadest thing Martin had ever seen.

The eyes were open, dry but unblinking in the new daylight. Unfocussed now, they were still pointed towards the television or, rather, Martin standing in front of it. Martin looked back at the man's wrinkled face. He tried to picture it moving to see what he had been like. There was nothing stern in the lines around the eyes. And the mouth, hanging open, was slight. Kindly, thought Martin. A kindly old man, sitting there in his striped pyjamas. Backless slippers. Their leather was cracked, but well loved, and with an oiled gleam.

The rest of the world was coming back into being. The voice on the television was saying that the object folded flat for ease of storage.

Martin glanced at Chloe, who was transfixed. Jeremy was now staring at the remote control in the body's right hand, resting on the arm of the sofa. Realising he was being assessed, Jeremy shuddered.

'Well … Ha. This is very …' He made a small gesture with his hands, unsure how best to recover the positive mood. 'I … Well. You do sometimes …'

Martin squatted down opposite the man, level with his face but still a respectful distance away. At least, thought Martin, this man looked relaxed now.

The voice on the television started listing prices.

The more Martin looked, the more he felt that the man would not have worn his age with bitterness. Perhaps it was just the relaxation of the muscles before rigor mortis set in, but Martin found it easy to imagine him content. He could picture him uncompetitively kicking a football around with grandchildren in the park before securing a break by offering to buy them ice-cream. Then, later, a well-earned pint with the son-in-law. Martin almost smiled. He felt it would have been nice to buy him one.

113

Jeremy spoke up again, 'I … er… was once going round a house and the dog was sick on the shoes of the woman I was showing round.'

Martin looked away from the old man's face for a moment. Then, slowly, he stood up and turned on Jeremy. He made a show of looking at Jeremy from head to toe in slow motion. He took in the sheen on the light grey suit, and worn silk tie, as if for the first time. He paused on the frayed shirt cuffs, and then went down the crease on the trousers that had largely disappeared. He looked back at the old guy to make his point.

'I expect,' he said coldly, 'that in your job, you've been in a lot of funny situations.' Jeremy started to say that well, no, it wasn't that, but Martin carried on. 'I think we should let you get hold of the owner and break the news to her before she arrives.' It's ok, he wanted to tell him.

Jeremy's fluster disappeared.

'I don't think that's a good idea,' he said.

'Oh, why not?' said Martin, not turning towards him.

Jeremy hesitated, then, pleased, said, 'Hang on. First, Chloe, are you ok?'

Martin snorted, but he did look back to Chloe. She nodded.

Clinging to this moral toehold, Jeremy mustered his best senior statesman delivery. These moments were won or lost as much by personality as rules. And by speaking slowly he gave himself a bit more time to think as he went.

'The elderly lady concerned does not have a mobile phone, but she is due here shortly. I don't think I should leave and let her discover this on her own, do you? Of course, I'd quite understand if you would want to leave her to it.'

Martin did now turn, and glared at Jeremy. In as even a tone as he could, he said, 'So what are you proposing? Are you going to doorstep her with the news?'

'No.' Jeremy's urge to disagree was accompanied by an acute

awareness he hadn't really thought this through. 'No... I thought I – we
– could, er, wait in the hall.'

'What?' Martin said, 'like a surprise party?'

'Well, I don't...'

'Martin...' Chloe's eyes bored into him.

'... I don't... On reflection, no, perhaps waiting in here would be
better.' Jeremy then felt a surge of relief in finding a good phrase. 'We would
be sitting with the body, as it were.'

Martin was now incredulous. 'I'm sure she'll love it if we're sitting
around watching telly with him. Shall I see if there're some beers in the
fridge?'

Chloe snapped: 'Martin!'

'Well, really,' he appealed. 'I'd be very happy to sit with him, but what's
an old lady going to think if we're all watching the shopping channel as if
we haven't noticed he's died? I think I preferred the idea of hiding behind
the front door so that we she opened it we could all shout, 'Sur-'

But Chloe held her right hand up, palm towards Martin. With her left
hand she made little fanning gestures to her face. 'I think ... I think this is
very upsetting and I need a tissue.' She looked to Jeremy. 'Could you tell me
where the bathroom is please?'

'Of course.' Jeremy tried a new tack, of speaking in tones that he
imagined a funeral director would use. Low, calm, understanding. As he
directed her to the downstairs toilet through the kitchen, he could feel
Martin bristling.

The three men waited in silence for Chloe to return, two of them conscious
that no decisions would be made without her, and with no goodwill left for
small talk. Martin looked at the old man again, and wondered about his life.
Had he done what he wanted to? Jeremy got his phone out and tapped on it
for a while. Something about the set of Martin's jaw made him stop.

Chloe returned. 'Thank you,' she said. 'They... she has a very nice
kitchen.'

'Yes,' Jeremy nodded morosely. Then he had a thought. As casually as he could, he added: 'She had it entirely refurbished last year.'

There was a deathly pause. The comment hung in the air like a smell.

With pointed slowness, Martin inched his head around from looking at the old man, to staring at Jeremy. But Jeremy was now studying his shoes. Chloe too declined to catch his eye. So Martin turned back to Jeremy, facing him square on, arms folded. He, at least, was going to stick up for the old guy.

But in the silence, an advertisement for a device that cut nose hair ran its course. A magazine rack with a pouch for jigsaws took its place.

So it was Chloe who spoke next. She too had had a thought.

'Really?' she said.

Jeremy nodded without looking up from his shoes.

'Well, I think Jeremy's right,' said Chloe. 'I think we should stay so we're ready to comfort the vendor.'

Martin said nothing, but he turned to face Chloe, still with his arms folded. Now she did look him in the eye. The poise that she had regained reminded him of their third date. During coffee, she had wound down her contributions, and just looked at him instead, those blue eyes … waiting. He had tried a few gambits, but got next to nothing back. 'No … yes … Since May…' But still she watched him. He was just about to ask her whether she thought the art of conversation was dying out, but almost for the hell of it first tossed out: 'Would you like to come back to my place?' She had smiled, and got up.

Right now, she was looking at him intently again. This time Martin simply stared back. She widened her eyes, and he said nothing. She smiled tightly and nodded in the direction of the open door. He was not, however, going to help. He looked between her and the old guy, and then made a point of sitting on the empty sofa.

'I'd be happy to sit with him for a bit.'

She stared at him some more, rolling her eyes to the door, but Martin's answer was just to turn to the dead guy and start contemplating him once more, leaving Chloe and Jeremy stranded.

An advert for an all-weather fondue set came and went. The flame was guaranteed to keep in light to moderate wind and drizzle. Chloe turned back to Jeremy, revealing a tissue in her hand.

'I wonder if there's somewhere I can dispose of this?'

'Of course,' Jeremy cooed, 'there's a fitted pull out bin in the kitchen alongside the built in appliances.' He smiled. 'But if you can't find that, try the dining room. It's off to the left from the kitchen, and leads on to the conservatory.'

Martin gritted his teeth.

She was gone for about five minutes, or at least long enough for a whole feature on the amazing range of uses for a curved knife.

'Thanks Jeremy,' she said on her return. Then, 'Martin, do you want to stretch your legs a little?'

'No thanks,' said Martin evenly. 'I think I forgot my tape measure. And actually I'm a bit busy showing some respect to this dead chap here, by staying with him for a while?'

Chloe shot him a look. There would be trouble, later, Martin knew. There would be tight lips, and frostiness. If he sought to break the ice by suggesting they were maybe both to blame for the atmosphere, he would get an articulate speech about exactly what he had done that was disappointing. He would almost certainly give way and accept it was all his fault, and, yes, she had done the right thing in difficult circumstances, not him, sorry.

And yet, and yet. This was typical. Martin would have been happy to stop in Acton. He'd always felt fine there. Or go to Chloe's homeground of Brentford. Sure, in neither place did you have the benefits of the militant middle class pushing their way into the classrooms, asking to see their children's colouring in books every other week, but neither did it feel like a theme park for young families fretting about centiles, with their tidy…

'Jeremy,' said Chloe, 'I wonder if it might be wise, before the vendor returns, to check that there's nothing too upsetting in the upstairs rooms?'

Jeremy looked up, surprised. 'Er…yes.' He caught up. 'Oh, yes… Allow me.'

Martin didn't look at them as they went out. He looked at the old guy. I bet you wouldn't be doing that, he thought. I bet when you bought your first house you were respectful, and polite, and … and overwhelmed with pride that you'd managed to save up enough money for your own place for you and your girl.

He tried to think of what Chloe would say when the old lady returned. It would probably be well judged, but clear. He realised he would feel no pride in her for that.

He could hear the tour going on upstairs, and saw the future. He'd be living in a house that would always be a monument to Chloe's focussed pushing. He wouldn't be able to tell himself that he had tried to stop her. It would be a permanent reminder of the unimportance of his belief that, so long as you treated people right, things would turn out ok.

And then he thought: this has to stop. He suddenly felt it with all his being.

He knew he was right. But he also knew that while the house was available, Chloe would not let it go. Even if he had the courage to keep up the resistance, to make the point, there would be prolonged unpleasantness. The arguments would not stop until he gave in, or the house was sold. He had to end this now.

He checked his watch. It was five to four. He stood up.

'Listen old chap,' he said, tucking some of the old guy's wilder hair behind an ear, before patting him on the shoulder, 'I'm just going to be a minute.'

Martin walked down the corridor towards the kitchen, heedless of the original features around him. He found the fridge: nothing. He went through cupboards until, with a smile, he found what he was after. He took two of them back down the corridor. As he turned back into the front room, he saw a shape coming up the path.

Jeremy and Chloe hurried down the stairs to greet the opening door. From where he was sitting, Martin could hear Jeremy breaking the news. Then it was the lady's voice. She was upset, but not hysterical. He could hear her talking about an 'old friend … just staying over … hadn't looked well …' He could make out that she said 'only staying over' several times. And then it was Chloe making a short and relieved speech about difficult times, and beautiful surroundings. There was her number if she wanted help, or just a chat. And whilst it was the wrong time now, if there was a desire to move on quickly, to put this behind her …

Soon, he heard his name being mentioned as her partner. Sitting with the body to keep him company, his respects, in all the circumstances. The talking stopped. There was a pause, and then the door opened slowly.

The old lady came in to find Martin sitting on the same sofa as the old guy. Both the men were perfectly still. The old guy was still sitting with his right arm resting on the arm of the sofa, the other by his side on a cushion. But now in that hand he held one of the cans of beer Martin had found in the cupboard. Martin sat in exact mirror image. He held the other can of beer in his right hand resting on the sofa cushion, next to the cold fingers of the older man. Martin's other arm again lay along the other sofa arm. A tableau of blokes watching TV, then.

Jeremy came in to see what the silence was about. He noticed first that the old lady opened her mouth, like, he now saw, the two men on the sofa. But no noise was coming out of any of them. Jeremy was torn between a sense that everything was going badly wrong, and a more minor but precise thought which it took him a moment to tie down. That was it: the two blokes, and now Mrs Turner too, looked like those living statues you see in Covent Garden who suddenly do things when you put a coin in their bowl. He found himself wondering what they might do, when

119

Chloe lost patience with tactfully waiting outside and came in to find the foursome with their mouths open. She, however, found words.

'MARTIN!' she screamed, 'WHAT THE HELL DO YOU THINK YOU'RE DOING?'

Martin spoke without moving, even his lips.

'Oh, you know. Just making myself at home.'

'You ... you ... *idiot*.'

Chloe turned. The others didn't move, but quickly heard the sound of the front door opening and closing in angry succession.

Martin stood up. He took the beer can from the old man's hand, and addressed the old lady directly.

'Madam, my apologies. I'm never going to be able to explain this to you, but I meant no disrespect to you or to this gentleman. I offer you my condolences, and wish you all the best.'

He too left the room. Jeremy and the old lady heard his footsteps go back to the kitchen cupboard, the sound of some placing. His footsteps came back down the corridor. Then there was the opening and closing of the door for a second time. There was a pause as Jeremy and Mrs Turner looked at the body, and then each other.

'How very strange,' said the old lady to Jeremy. 'Do you think they're interested?'

HILLINGDON

Holding Patterns

Holding Patterns

Rachael Dunlop

When you fly into Heathrow, you can see the whole of Britain. That's what Dawn's boss always said to new members of staff. His little joke, he said. Most of the workers in the coffee shop in Terminal Five had no idea what he was talking about.

'Don't believe me?' he'd say to their bewildered faces. 'Dawn knows what I'm talking about, don't you, Dawn?'

And Dawn would smile and nod and say nothing. Dawn was a local girl, unlike most of her co-workers, having lived in Hillingdon all her life. She knew he was talking about Little Britain Lake.

'Shaped just like Great Britain it is,' he'd continue, 'a mini sceptred isle.' (He fancied himself as a bit of a scholar as well as a joker.) 'Just north of the airport, pretty much all the planes circle over it at least once.'

Dawn remembered walking around Little Britain Lake when she was younger, holding her mum's hand, and looking up at the planes stacked up in the sky, a string of graduated pearls. She used to worry that the big planes and the little planes were going to crash into each other, until her mum explained that the planes were all the same size, but some were much higher up and further away, so looked smaller. And they were all going in circles anyway, so they couldn't crash into each other. Dawn wanted to ask her mum why they were going round in circles when they were supposed to be going places, but she didn't want to push her luck.

These days, as Dawn rode the bus to work at the airport, she would press her face to the window and watch the planes coming in to land. They dropped slowly out of the sky in lazy, loping descents, like they didn't really mean it, like they might at any moment change their minds and swoop back up. And why wouldn't they, Dawn wondered, when they saw where they were landing? When she thought of Heathrow, she thought *grey*: light grey concrete buildings, dark grey tarmac roads, planes and cars and buses coated in a grey fuel-infused dirt. And too much sky. Dawn didn't like all that sky over her head.

Inside the airport, too, things didn't have as much colour as they should. Dawn supposed it was something to do with the lighting – white fluorescent light bouncing off white tiled floors, bleaching everything in between.

It was different in the coffee shop – cosy, warm, all natural wood and plum-red walls. It smelled warm too. Dawn usually worked the first or last shifts, fitting them around her classes at sixth-form college. Early shifts were her favourite: she liked brewing up the first coffee of the day, before the machine started to overheat and scorch the coffee. She took her role as a barista very seriously and when there was time (which wasn't very often) she would linger over the ritual of brewing the espresso: waiting for the machine to heat up; drawing off a scant cup of hot water to prime the pump; carefully tamping the coffee into the holder so the water would flow through at just the right speed; steaming the milk until it was creamy and dense or frothy and filled with air, as required.

It was on one of the slow early morning shifts that Dawn first met Audrey. She was sitting at a small corner table, lingering over a rapidly cooling latte, a small black carry-on suitcase tucked behind her legs. She looked to be about the same age as Dawn's mum, which meant she was probably a good deal older. Dawn's mum looked every inch of her forty-four years, and then some. This woman took care of herself – she had the sort of skin where the edges of ageing had been blurred out by a lifetime of good habits. Her hair was neat and her clothes looked expensive, if a little out-of-date.

She'd been sitting at that table for a while, which wasn't so unusual. There were two types of customer in the coffee shop – those with time to kill and those with no time to spare. This woman wasn't checking her watch or leaning out to check the departures board outside the coffee shop. She was sitting quite still, elbows on the table, coffee cup cradled in mid-air, eyes gazing into the unseen distance. She looked, Dawn realised, relaxed. Like there was nowhere else she needed to be.

Dawn came out from behind the counter and started wiping down the tables, moving closer and closer to the woman in the corner. She took a quick glance over her shoulder to make sure the boss wasn't looking.

'I could heat that up for you.'

The woman looked surprised to be spoken to. 'Sorry?' she said.

'Your coffee. I can heat it up if you like. Not supposed to, really, but there's nothing worse than getting half way through a large latte and finding it's gone cold.'

The woman smiled. 'Nothing worse,' she agreed. 'Thank you.'

Dawn gave the cold coffee a shot of steam and returned it to the woman.

'Thank you ... Dawn,' she said, leaning in to read Dawn's name tag.

'No worries. It's quiet this morning. Where are you off to, then?'

'Where am I...?' For a moment the woman looked blank. 'Oh. I'm going to Kampala.' Now it was Dawn's turn to look blank. 'Uganda,' the woman explained.

'Oh, nice.' Dawn said, not knowing what else to say. Of all the places on the departure boards that she had dreamed of going to, Uganda wasn't one of them.

'My husband is working out there. Volunteering. He's a heart surgeon.'

Now Dawn was impressed. Not that the woman was married to a heart surgeon – that wasn't an achievement, just a fact. No, it was the idea that they had so much money he could afford to work for free, give his time for nothing. Dawn worked every free minute she had to justify the time she spent in college.

The woman finally checked her watch. 'I should make a move,' she said. 'Thanks for this.' She raised her now empty coffee cup in a half-salute and left.

The next evening, there was a thick stack of envelopes waiting for Dawn on the kitchen table, lying beside her dinner plate like a side order of paper and ink. It was late and her mum had eaten already. At least, Dawn hoped she had eaten. Sometimes she forgot and sometimes she just couldn't be bothered. Her mum was at the sink now, washing the pots. As Dawn sat down at the table, her mum pulled off her rubber gloves and lit a cigarette. She turned to face Dawn, leaning back against the sink and squinting at her daughter through the smoke.

'Mum, can't you wait 'til I've finished eating before you light up?' Dawn said.

Dawn's mum ignored her protests, taking a slow crackling drag on her cigarette and tipped the ash into the sink. 'Thought you weren't going to bother with applications,' she said finally, 'I thought we agreed.' Dawn dropped her eyes quickly from her mother's accusing gaze. She shuffled through the envelopes, checking off the names of the universities they were from.

'The careers advisor said I may as well,' Dawn replied. 'Keep my options open.'

'Did the careers advisor tell you where you're going to find the money from to go to university?'

'Everyone applies, it's no big deal,'

'Well, okay. So you applied. But why did you apply to all those places? I don't even know where half of them are, but I know they're far away. You'll have to move out, and then what am I going to do?'

'I had to apply where they offered the courses I might want, Mum.' Dawn said levelly. 'Just going through the motions.'

Dawn's mum stubbed out her cigarette and turned back to washing the dishes. 'Just going through the motions,' she mumbled into the grease-scummed water.

Dawn set the envelopes down, unopened, and started to eat. For as long as she could remember, life with her mum had been a delicate balancing act. She had explained it to the social worker like this: her mum was sitting at one end of a seesaw, with Depression sitting on the other end (she always thought of the illness like that, capitalised, personified). Dawn needed to run the length of the seesaw, end to end, like a gymnast on a beam, to keep things balanced. Only sometimes she didn't get it right, and her mum would crash to the ground, crushed by the weight she carried.

Things had been in pretty good balance for nearly a year now. Dawn's mum was holding down a job, and with Dawn's part-time work at the coffee shop, they were keeping their heads above water.

'I'll take a look at these later,' she said to her mum now, pushing the envelopes to the far side of the table. 'How was work today?'

About a month later, Audrey came into the coffee shop again. Just like the first time, she appeared early in the morning, when things were quiet. Dawn chatted to her while the boss was out the back arguing with a delivery guy over the wrong size of cup lids.

'So, your husband's still out in Africa then?'

'Yes, he'll be there another six months at least. He works at Harefield Hospital normally, but they've given him a year's sabbatical.'

'Hey,' said Dawn, 'my mum works at Harefield.'

'Really?' The woman took a small sip of her coffee, eyeing Dawn over the rim of her cup. 'Which department?'

'Oh, all of them, really. She's a cleaner.'

The woman smiled. 'Oh, well, she probably wouldn't know my husband, then. I'm Audrey by the way.'

'Audrey. Nice to meet you. Again.' Dawn took her hand. She was surprised to find the skin on Audrey's hand dry and chapped, and there was strong smell of something familiar, something clean yet not clean. It was the smell of industrial strength airport soap.

'So,' Dawn said, 'you're going out there quite often then? And that's okay with your work?'

'I don't work,' Audrey said. 'Haven't for a long time.' She said it quietly.

'Shit, sorry,' said Dawn. 'I mean sorry for being so nosey, not sorry you're not working, unless you want to work, then I'm sorry about that too. Sorry.'

Audrey laughed, and it was a surprising laugh, full and deep, although the tail end of it caught in a soft rasp at the back of her throat. She gave a little cough.

'Don't worry about it, Dawn. I don't mind. It's nice to have someone take an interest. I spend a lot of time on my own, now that my husband is... away.'

'So what do you do, if you don't work?' Dawn didn't imagine that Audrey spent her unemployed days like her mum did, under the duvet, or wandering around the flat like a whey-faced wraith, the depression draining her down to a deflated version of her better self.

'Well, I look after my husband when he's around. Run the house. His kids come to stay most weekends as well, so I have to deal with that.'

'*His* kids?' Dawn asked.

'He was married before. I stopped working when we got married. I didn't mind, because it was a job, you know, not a career. Just a job.'

Dawn thought about her university applications, and nodded. That's what she wanted: a career, not a job.

'But you know what, Dawn?' Audrey leaned forward, making sure Dawn could hear her over the increasing hubbub of the coffee shop, 'A job, a career, it doesn't matter, as long as you have something that's yours, all your own. If I wasn't Charles' wife, well, I'm not sure who I'd be. And that's no good, is it?'

Dawn shrugged, not knowing what to say. She looked over her shoulder and saw the queue building up at the counter and the boss looking daggers at her. She gave the table a quick wipe and lifted Audrey's empty cup.

'Gotta get back to work. No rest for the wicked,' she said. 'See you around.'

'Yes,' said Audrey, reaching around to pull her case from under the chair, 'see you around.'

Audrey leaves the coffee shop and strides purposefully across the concourse. She wants to make it look like she knows where she's going, but not too much. She stops every now and then to check the information boards, double-check a sign. She fishes into her handbag and pulls out a dog-eared boarding pass and looks from it to the departure boards and back down again.

Now, she thinks, where to go today? She decides to change terminals, she doesn't want to risk running into Dawn twice in one day.

Audrey heads down to the Tube. Thank god the transfers are free. Not much cash left in her pocket after she bought that coffee. She gets onto the train that will loop her round to the other terminals. Maybe she'll stay on for a while, circling. Her own personal holding pattern. It's quiet on the Tube so she takes a seat. She lifts her case up and holds it to her. It's a bit too big for her lap, but she doesn't want to risk losing it. She stares at her reflection in the window opposite, the glass transformed into a shaded mirror by the fast-moving blackness behind. She stares and she wonders how much of what she has told Dawn is a lie. Because sometimes none of it seems real, none of her life before.

'Isn't that your friend over there, Dawn?' the boss asked her. They were in Terminal One, where they'd borrowed some paper cups and filters from the other branch of the coffee shop. The boss liked to get out of Terminal Five every now and again. 'Time for a field trip!' he would declare.

Dawn looked to where he was pointing with his elbow, his arms full of slippery stacks of polythene-wrapped filter papers. The woman on the far side of the concourse looked like Audrey from behind, the same black coat (even though it was July) and carry-on case. Audrey had been in the coffee shop four, maybe five times in the past six months. She usually came in when it was quiet, and the boss had started turning a blind eye when Dawn stole ten minutes for a chat.

Dawn thought about calling out, but the woman was too far away. And there was something about the woman over there that didn't seem like Audrey, something about her body language that was off. Audrey always looked so relaxed, so poised. This woman looked a little hunched, furtive even.

As Dawn watched, the woman cast a quick glance over her shoulder then pushed herself into a lift just as the doors were closing. Two security guards cut across Dawn's line of sight and hurried over to the lifts, walkie-talkies barking in their hands.

'Nah, that wasn't her,' Dawn said. But in the split second when the woman had looked over her shoulder, Dawn had recognised her. It was Audrey. And now Dawn was lying, covering for her. Which didn't make any sense.

Dawn and her boss took the shuttle bus back to Terminal Five. They rode in silence, having exhausted the few possibilities for polite conversation on the way over. Dawn was happy to look out the window, watching the cars and buses and concrete go by. There wasn't a single person walking anywhere, as far as she could see. Everyone was in a vehicle of some sort. It was like some post-apocalyptic world where no one could survive on the outside. As the bus pulled into each terminal in turn, Dawn imagined she felt the tension relaxing on the bus, as safe harbour was reached. Watching people struggling off with their luggage, she speculated about their trips. She wondered, not where they were going, but why. Not the business travellers and the holidaymakers, but all those others. People who were running away from something, people who were running to something. Births, deaths, broken hearts. Dawn reckoned they were all good reasons for getting on a plane.

Audrey catches a glimpse of the security guards as the lift doors close. They didn't usually bother to move people on during the day, there must be some sort of security alert, she thinks. Or someone important coming through the airport. She sees Dawn, too, holding a pillar of stacked paper cups across herself like a ceremonial sword. Standing beside that boss of hers, the one who thinks quoting facts is the same as holding a conversation. She's a sweet girl, and has a lot on her plate for one so young. Audrey wonders what the date is. Dawn must be getting her A-level results soon. The girl has boxed herself into a corner, applying only to universities that will mean leaving home. As if she need something outside of herself to force her out the door. But Audrey understands why Dawn is afraid to go, afraid to leave her mum alone. Being alone is not good.

Audrey hopes Dawn hasn't seen her in the wrong terminal. Audrey likes the person she is when she's with Dawn. These days they talk more about Dawn and her life than about Audrey. Which is good, because Audrey sometimes has trouble remembering when she is. When and who.

There are plenty of people working in the airport who know Audrey, know what she is. You can't live at the airport twenty-four seven without people getting to know you, and she's not the only one. Last count, there were about a hundred of them. Audrey doesn't think of herself as homeless, though. She considers herself to be in transit. It's just that she doesn't know where she is going yet.

The day the A-level results came out, Dawn was working. She could have asked to swap shifts, when she saw the rota. She could have gone down to the college in the morning with her friends. But something stopped her, perhaps the wish to let fate take its course one last time. Soon enough she would have to make a decision, actually make a decision. All her life she had been fire-fighting, reacting to what life threw at her, rolling with the punches. The idea of taking control of her own life was more frightening than exhilarating.

She spent the morning making one coffee after another, filling cups, calling names, rarely looking up to check the faces that went with the outstretched hands. Every now and then she peered around to check who was sitting at the tables. She half-expected, half-hoped to see Audrey sitting at her usual table. Dawn hadn't reminded her mum of the date, there was no point in having them both on tenterhooks. But it would have been nice to have Audrey around. She told herself that Audrey would only be there if she had a flight that day, it wasn't as if she came to Heathrow just to have coffee in Dawn's shop. But ever since that day in Terminal One, Dawn had known, deep down, that Audrey's story didn't really add up. Which meant that she had been lying to Dawn for months. But it also meant that she came to see Dawn out of choice, which meant she could choose to be here today.

Dawn shook her head, shook herself out of this illogical train of thought. She checked her watch and ducked under the counter to grab her small backpack.

'Taking my break now,' she called out and elbowed her way out of the coffee shop without waiting for permission. She headed for the internet terminals in the middle of the concourse. They were arranged in a circle, their screens facing outwards and Dawn felt somehow exposed as she stood with her back to the crowds in the Departures hall. She swiped her cash card in the machine and logged herself on to the college website.

Her fingers prickled with nerves as she clicked the link to get her results. Scrolling, going too far, clicking back up the page, slowly, slowly. Her name. Another click. Words and letters on the screen, the keys to her future. Dawn let out the breath she had been holding. She pulled a scrap of paper out of her backpack and wrote down her results, even though there was no chance she would forget them. She stood up, put the piece of paper in her back pocket and logged out of the computer.

Audrey was waiting for her back at the coffee shop. She looked tired. She looked like she had been crying. She was tucked into the corner, her head down. Dawn almost didn't see her in the crowd.

'I lost my suitcase,' she said as soon as she saw Dawn, panic in her voice.

'You lost it? How?'

'Someone stole it while I was asleep.'

Dawn looked in Audrey's eyes and recognised what she saw there. She had seen the same look in her mum's eyes. Somehow, the loss of her bag was the last straw for Audrey, the thing that upset the precarious balance of whatever life she had. The world had become un-navigable to her and she was folding in on herself.

Dawn squeezed into the seat beside Audrey. Her break wasn't over yet, she still had five minutes. 'Tell me what happened,' she said.

Audrey sat up straighter in her seat, took a drink of her coffee and smoothed her hair behind her ears. It looked like she was literally pulling herself together, closing over the emotional rip at the seams she had just exposed. Dawn had never seen anything like it.

'It doesn't matter.' Audrey said firmly. 'Never mind that. Did you get your results yet?'

Dawn pulled the paper from her pocket and handed it over. Audrey unfolded it, smoothed it on the table and read it carefully. She looked back up at Dawn and smiled. 'Good girl,' she said quietly.

Dawn started to cry.

In her little black suitcase Audrey has a change of clothes, a few books and a photograph of her and Charles on their wedding day. She has some nice toiletries retrieved from the bins near the security gates, and she usually picks up a few bottles of water this way as well. She will be sad if they ever lift the limits on liquids in hand luggage. She gets a hot shower and washes her clothes once a fortnight at the Salvation Army centre. She picks up her dole cheque there too, it's her registered address for all her benefits. Otherwise she washes in the toilets at the airport. The soap dries out her skin horribly, but it's better than being dirty.

She takes out the photograph and looks at it every night before she goes to sleep. She looks so like a second wife in that picture. No white gown, no veil, just a nice dress, suitable for her age and a lunchtime registry office wedding. Charles wanted them to be married before he went to work in the hospital in Kampala. Two months later, Charles was dead, shot in the head execution-style. The Ugandan police said it was probably a case of mistaken identity, or a robbery gone wrong.

Charles hadn't written a will. Everything went to his teenaged children. The first wife swooped in and claimed the house for herself and the kids. Audrey wasn't going to argue with her. It was their home, they had just lost their dad, what was she supposed to do?

They sent Charles home in a box. She never saw his body. Sometimes Audrey can convince herself that he isn't really dead, that the police were the ones who had mistaken his identity, that he is still out there, in Uganda, and if she can only get to him, she can bring him home. Home.

On a warm evening in late September, Dawn and her mum took a walk around Little Britain Lake. The Canada geese honked and hooted as they came in to land on the water, sending the ducks and moorhens skittering and flapping away. Dawn and her mum took a seat by the water and started to lob pieces of stale bread out over the water, despite the sign telling them not to feed bread to the birds. Dawn had been feeding bread to the ducks all her life, and they seemed okay.

'Call me when you get there,' her mum said after a while, 'I mean, the minute you arrive, okay?'

Dawn laughed. 'Okay, mum.'

'How long does the coach take again?'

'To Edinburgh? Most of the day.'

'And everything is sorted with the halls of residence?'

'Mum, don't worry. I'm sorted.'

Dawn's mum took her hand, gave it a squeeze.

'I know you are, love. More sorted than I'll ever be.'

'Mum...'

'No, it's true,' her mum insisted, 'but at least I know it. And there's help there when I need it.'

Above their heads, the aeroplanes blinked and bobbed in the dusky sky. Some banked hard, their engines complaining, as they headed out to circle the city one more time. Others, the lucky ones, pulled out of their holding patterns and pointed their noses towards the Heathrow runway. Coming in to land.

HOUNSLOW
A Marriage Made in Hounslow

A Marriage Made in Hounslow

Rajinder Kaur

There had to be more than this. Fried chicken shops. Kiosks selling sim cards and phone chargers. The pound store. The 99p store. The 98p store. The gamblers. The old mothers clothed in black, baby in one arm, hand outstretched with the other. The clothes shops permanently on sale, the clothes shops permanently closing down. The derelict buildings. The cars with windows open and oversized speakers rumbling along the street. The school kids play fighting, one punch away from assaulting each other. A house that was not quite a home. And a man who was not quite a husband.

Kulvinder gathered her things and said goodbye to her colleagues. She worked part-time as a receptionist in the Civic Centre. Not the most challenging job for an IT graduate but it was better than no job at all. And it gave her some financial freedom from her husband, Arjun. Her husband. It still sounded strange despite the weddings and the protracted form filling, the waiting for her visa to be granted, and the new house on Gresham Road. The idea of having a husband was still alien to her. There were none of the sparks of having a lover, or the tingles of being someone's girlfriend. There was just him, and his job, and his Audi TT, which he could barely afford.

She decided to sit in Lampton Park for a while. It wasn't like her mother had said, as she prepped her for her first meeting with Arjun.

'You'll be going to London. There will be so much more to do. So much more to see. It'll be a big change anney.'

What her mother didn't say was that she was going to Hounslow. Kulvinder didn't expect to be picked up at Heathrow and then dropped off fifteen minutes later. It was a bit like living in an extension of the airport. Terminal Five and a bit. Arjun worked a short drive away in Acton, his parents lived barely one street away. Her world had actually grown smaller.

'It's an adjustment innit,' Arjun said once over dinner. 'It'll take some time.'

Time. It had nearly been a year. Kulvinder imagined her mother-in-law kept a calendar, where she marked off each day that her son remained childless. She had even mumbled something about her seeing a specialist. Kulvinder shrugged it off. What her mother-in-law didn't know was simply that she and Arjun rarely had sex. Some nights they even slept in different rooms. Her husband had tried to talk to her about it, but was too timid to make it an issue, and he certainly couldn't bring it up with his parents. He convinced himself it was all part of this mystery process they called a marriage. The weeks became months. And their lack of intimacy became normal.

It was some time after five, the sun a few hours from setting. Kulvinder started to walk towards home, changed her mind and headed to Hounslow Central station. She wanted to drift. She took the Tube heading east and got off at Hammersmith. She was in her work clothes, a strange mix of east and west: black trousers with a light orange kameez and chuni, and a denim jacket. Following a group of office workers she ended up outside a pub on Shepherd's Bush Road. She stood very still.

She had drunk alcohol before. Early on in the marriage Arjun made dinner one night, he opened a bottle of red wine. Kulvinder took a sip and nothing more, much to his chagrin. Another time she had drunk champagne with her colleagues at a Christmas dinner. Alcohol was a taboo, another barrier between herself and the life she had imagined when she was at university. Yet still she continued to hover by the entrance. A man coming out to smoke a cigarette held the door open for her.

'You coming in?' he asked.

She nodded and stepped just inside the building. If it was the Wild West, the bow tie wearing pianist might have stopped playing, or the needle would have skipped on the gramophone. The room hushed, the drinkers glanced at her, and then business resumed. Kulvinder walked gingerly to the bar. There was a bit of a wait and then a space opened up. She stood perfectly straight, paying close attention to what other people were ordering, not quite sure what words corresponded to which drinks.

The barman looked in her direction, and raised a finger to say 'shoot'.

'I'll have a pint of your best lager, please,' Kulvinder said mechanically.

The man raised an eyebrow.

'Are you sure?' he said. He had an Australian accent, which tallied with his blonde hair and broad shoulders.

Kulvinder paused, 'No. Is there a menu?'

He laughed. 'Why don't you have a glass of wine?'

Kulvinder shook her head.

'A Pimm's?'

'No. Just give me a lager, OK?'

The barman poured the pint, his hand lingering as he gave Kulvinder her change. There was a moment of eye contact, then he moved on to another customer, a knowing smile on his face. Kulvinder took her pint and sat at a small table near the entrance to the pub. She held the pint like it was milk of magnesia, blowing on the foam and taking the shortest of sips. It tasted terrible. She looked up and caught the barman watching her. She took a longer sip to show him she was in control. It was amazing – from sip to sip the taste of the lager changed. She stared into the half-empty pint glass and believed that it was half-full. She imagined that the barman was called Bruce or Greg and that he worked part-time and acted part-time. Or maybe he was a model. Whatever he was, he wasn't Arjun. He wasn't stocky, he didn't shave his head, and he was most certainly not an accountant.

143

Kulvinder finished the pint and stood up, feeling an unexpected giddy rush. She steadied herself and went to the ladies', splashing water on her face before striding past the bar on her way out, resolute that she would not look back at the barman. She went to the nearest shop and bought a packet of mints, ate five on the Tube journey home. The swaying of the train causing small waves of consternation in her stomach.

Arjun sat in the living room with the volume of the TV turned low. He held his mobile in his left hand, checking the screen every other minute. He hadn't eaten. He liked to have thought that he was waiting for Kulvinder to come home so they could eat together; what that really meant was that he was waiting for her to cook. His father's generation expected to be fed and looked after by their wives. In his generation it wasn't so clear. Even if he had gone to India to find a bride.

He looked at the framed photograph of them taken at their wedding in Jalandhar. Kulvinder looked beautiful in her red sari: slim, almond eyes, high cheekbones, fair skin. He looked dehydrated with dark patches around his eyes. He tried his best to quell the thought that he wasn't a good physical match for her, but every now and then it resurfaced like a whale gasping for air. His wife was over two hours late home. He looked at his mobile and wondered if calling her would show his concern, or his control. He heard the key in the lock and promptly turned the volume of the TV up.

Kulvinder took off her jacket and went upstairs. She changed into her house salwar kameez then went downstairs. Arjun was in the hall.

'I was worried,' he said, reaching out and touching her arm.

'I had to work late, then went for a walk, sorry,' she replied at first sounding harsh then softening. She touched his hand but didn't hold it. 'What shall we eat? There's some alloo gobi left over from last night.'

Arjun nodded then said, 'No wait, why don't we eat out tonight?'

They walked along the London Road and then settled on a chicken restaurant, which was a cut above the fast food places but not by much. Arjun ordered at the till and then they took their seats by the window. The pause before the food arrived was filled with casual talk about work. Kulvinder still felt a little tipsy. The food had helped steady her, what remained was a freer sense of what she could say. She got up and ordered two coffees, then sat back down next to her husband. She didn't want to be staring him in the face.

'Did you think it would be like this?' she asked.

'What, the chicken?'

'No. Marriage.'

Arjun put his coffee cup down and looked at his wife. She didn't look back. He realised that they were having a conversation that could shape the rest of the evening, perhaps even the rest of their lives.

'Honestly, I didn't think it'd be like this. I knew things would take time, but I don't feel like we've got to know each other, it's like we've got off on the wrong foot.'

Kulvinder didn't quite understand the simile but nodded. Her hand crept closer to his. Arjun expected her to talk; when she kept quiet, he continued.

'Sometimes I feel like you're not there. I mean you're there but your thoughts are somewhere else. Like you drift off.'

'Drift off?'

'I don't mean it exactly like that. I guess what it boils down to is that we don't know each other well enough. Maybe we don't know each other at all. What do you think?'

Kulvinder moved her hand back and drank some coffee.

'You know I had a very different life in India. My family and my friends. I thought coming to London would be a pacy lifestyle, but we don't seem to move. We go from day to day and nothing changes. There's no excitement.'

'No excitement? Well, what do you want to do?'

'I don't know.' Kulvinder drank some more coffee. She looked at him with a glint in her eye. 'Tell me one of your secrets.'

'One of my secrets?'

'Yes,' she touched his hand. 'Everyone married couple has secrets, isn't that what they say?'

Arjun made a non-committal sound then said the word 'secret' a few times, like he was looking up its meaning in a dictionary.

'OK, so here goes. But are you sure you want to hear this?'

Kulvinder nodded.

'Ok. So before I decided to follow the traditional Indian path to marriage, I went out with a girl for a couple of years.'

'A girl?' Kulvinder's nostrils flared, 'What girl?'

Arjun could feel a flop sweat coming in. 'It was nothing serious … Well, it was quite serious … But it ended. And it was good that it ended.'

'Who was she?'

'She was from my university.'

'What was her name?'

Arjun wished he had kept his mouth shut.

'Louise.'

Louise. Kulvinder could picture Louise and Arjun together, eating ice cream and strolling on a beach.

'You went out with a white girl,' she said more as a statement than a question. 'Well, I have a secret for you. Before I married you I went out with an Australian man.'

'An Australian man?'

'Yes, Bruce was his name.'

Kulvinder put her jacket on and got up to go. Arjun trailed behind her and kept a safe distance as they walked home. He caught up with her as she opened the front door.

'It was a long time ago,' he pleaded. 'You're acting like I cheated on you.'

'Have you cheated on me?'

'No!'

'Let's go to bed,' Kulvinder snapped.

'Bed?'

'Come on before I change my mind.'

Arjun followed her up the stairs, almost tripping as he tried to take two steps at once. Kulvinder held him on the landing and kissed him. It was an angry, territorial kiss. She thought of Louise as she undressed, while Arjun wondered how his wife had gone out with an Australian while she was living in India. There had to be more than this. But for one night, it was more than enough.

RICHMOND

I ♥ Richmond

I ♥ Richmond

Jonathan Green

Less than 1 minute ago via web...

RichmondGirl: I love you. Goodbye.

RichmondGirl: Hello?

RichmondGirl: Hello? Are you still there?

KewGuy: I love you. Goodbye.

RichmondGirl: So, this is it. This is really the end? But it can't be, not now. I love you!

KewGuy: Not like this. But look for me again in the spring, in the cherry blossom.

RichmondGirl: But I won't hear from you again? Not like this?

KewGuy: You know you can always talk to me if you need me, no matter where you are.

RichmondGirl: Making love, talking into the early hours, then making love again and falling asleep with the dawn.

RichmondGirl: Right now? Don't go yet. Talk to me some more. Talk to me right through the night, like we used to when we first met.

KewGuy: It's time for me to go.

RichmondGirl: So what happens now?

KewGuy: I'm glad.

RichmondGirl: I've taken the flat off the market.

KewGuy: Thank you.

RichmondGirl: In every plant, in every blossom, in every leaf. And I'll go there again and know that you're there too. Always.

RichmondGirl: I imagined you in every tree, ever flower, ever blade of grass. It's a place of life, not death, and there you'll live again.

RichmondGirl: But as I watched the last trickle of grey powder take flight on the breeze I felt warm like I used to feel when you held me after sex.

RichmondGirl: Anyway – I did it. I did want you asked – what you wanted – and I cried as I did it.

RichmondGirl: I ended up under a cherry tree. It was covered in blossom and it felt so peaceful there. Suddenly everything about it seemed right.

KewGuy: It sounds magical.

RichmondGirl: I can't believe we'd never been there before. It's beautiful, it really is. And it's so you. The Palm House is something else.

KewGuy: And do you know what the best part about it was? I shared it with you.

RichmondGirl: So I paid up and went in and you completed your journey at last.

RichmondGirl: But you never did. We went for coffee instead. Then supper. And we kissed outside the Tube and I knew then that this was something special.

RichmondGirl: And then I really realised for the first time where I was – outside Kew Gardens. The place you were going to when we first met.

RichmondGirl: I couldn't leave you there among the fag butts and the leaves and watch you join the stream of rubbish trickling down the drain.

RichmondGirl: It was the right time – I just knew it was. But I couldn't do it there, the rain pattering on the roof of the shelter.

RichmondGirl: And do you know what I did? I sat in the bus stop. I must have been there for over an hour. I watched four buses go past.

KewGuy: You were always better with anniversaries than me.

RichmondGirl: Do you know what today is? Today's the anniversary of our first meeting at the bus stop.

KewGuy: Tell me about it.

RichmondGirl: I did it. Today. I did what you asked me. Even though it broken my heart again for a moment, I did it.

.

.

.

RichmondGirl: I know. But let me enjoy it a while longer while I can. We ended up on Richmond Green, outside The Cricketer's, and watched the sun go down.

KewGuy: But you know this has to end sometime, don't you?

RichmondGirl: To be honest I take you most places with me now, hidden away inside my bag. Truth is I've got used to having you around again.

RichmondGirl: Do you know what we did today? This'll make you smile – wherever you are. We went shopping.

.

.

.

RichmondGirl: At least that was what I let you believe. My knight in shining armour.

KewGuy: As I remember, you got lost in the maze and I had to guide you out again.

RichmondGirl: But there's so much history tied up with the place already, I felt our history would be swamped. Besides, we only went there the once.

RichmondGirl: Don't get me wrong, it's a stunning setting – the red brick, the king's beasts, the lush green lawns and all...

RichmondGirl: I got as far as the gates of Hampton Court today. In fact I got as far as the ticket office and then I turned around and walked away.

.

.

.

KewGuy: And your love. That's what sustains me.

RichmondGirl: All?

KewGuy: Still is. Words are all I have now.

RichmondGirl: I waited for you outside on the grass and watched the joggers and dog walkers on the footpath. It was always words with you, wasn't it?

RichmondGirl: You always used to want to read everything, so I did what I did last time we went there together.

RichmondGirl: It was Marble Hill Park today. I went round the house, cursorily reading the information on display in the rooms, but I didn't stay long.

.

.

.

RichmondGirl: But that was never you. It seemed like a whole other life away.

RichmondGirl: I wandered down to St Mary's afterwards, just for a look at the old place again – must be something to do with this nostalgic kick

I'm on.

RichmondGirl: You weren't to know.

KewGuy: I'm sorry.

RichmondGirl: But we ran out of time, didn't we?

KewGuy: I know. That's something else I wish I'd been able to give you, so that you wouldn't be alone now.

RichmondGirl: And I couldn't help thinking that one of those children should have been ours.

RichmondGirl: I went home through Bushy Park and watched the deer, the ducks down at the fountain and the kids in the playground.

RichmondGirl: They wanted to know how I was and kept asking how I was coping. I couldn't stop smiling, knowing you were there too. It was our secret.

RichmondGirl: Chris and Julia invited me over for lunch yesterday, over at their new place in Teddington. You went too, but I didn't tell them that.

.

.

.

RichmondGirl: That's true.

KewGuy: No, it didn't. But then not much stops Tommy once he's put his mind to something.

RichmondGirl: Didn't stop Tommy though, did it?

KewGuy: It was a hot day, as I recall, but never so hot that you'd want to jump into the Thames surely, I thought.

KewGuy: I remember that time the Thames burst its banks and people were diving off the wall outside the White Cross into the river.

RichmondGirl: I sat there and watched the world and his wife go by. At least that was how it seemed to me.

155

RichmondGirl: By the time I reached Richmond itself again I was ready for a drink. So I got a pint and sat by the river.

RichmondGirl: Anyway, I cut through Kew and joined the Thames Path at Ferry Lane. I went right past Kew Gardens and the Old Deer Park, past Richmond Lock.

RichmondGirl: I want to remember you as you were, not as a box sliding between tatty red curtains as some old biddy plays the organ badly.

RichmondGirl: I walked past the crematorium but didn't go in. I've only been there the once, and once was enough.

RichmondGirl: I went for a walk along the river instead. I started at the White Hart in Mortlake, where we watched the Boat Race, and then headed west.

RichmondGirl: I thought about going to Ham House today. We used to talk about going there, but never did, so I didn't today. Couldn't see the point.

KewGuy: It's funny how a change in perspective changes so much more than just that.

KewGuy: I like hearing about all the old places, all the things we used to do together – evening shopping in Kingston.

RichmondGirl: Shopping in Kingston was never your favourite activity, was it? So I got a coffee to go and went home.

RichmondGirl: You were still with me, so I got on the 65 but took the bus to Kingston. I picked up some things in town but I felt like I'd lost my way.

RichmondGirl: I ate sandwiches by Peg's Pond, then followed the horse ride back past Pembroke Lodge, and back to Richmond Gate.

KewGuy: You used to love the seeing the rhododendrons in flower.

RichmondGirl: Then we cut through Duchess' Wood, past the Royal

Ballet School, past Pen Ponds and all the way down to the Isabella Plantation.

RichmondGirl: We visited Richmond Park together. I did a circuit of the place. We followed the horse ride from Richmond Gate to begin with.

RichmondGirl: So I decided to spend the day with you instead.

RichmondGirl: The sun was streaming in through the bedroom window and I turned to watch you sleeping – like I used to – but you weren't there.

RichmondGirl: I woke up this morning and, for the first time in three weeks, forgot that you'd gone.

.

.

.

KewGuy: It's the most real thing I've ever known.

RichmondGirl: I like the pain. Pain is real. It helps me to remember that – with you gone – that what we had was real.

KewGuy: It's only a poem. I know you won't forget really. I was only trying to make you feel better, to help ease your pain.

RichmondGirl: You're quoting bloody Christina Rossetti now? What if I don't want to forget?

KewGuy: And it will get easier, in time. It is better that you forget and are happy than you remember and are sad.

RichmondGirl: I know.

KewGuy: But you won't. I know you won't. If our experience taught us anything it's that life is precious and not to be wasted.

RichmondGirl: Sometimes I feel I could end it all, just like that.

KewGuy: And I meant it. But life is for the living and you're far from done living yours.

RichmondGirl: Forever, you said.

KewGuy: I know.

RichmondGirl: You were what was right for me.

KewGuy: That's alright. Don't worry. I understand. I probably would have done the same. Whatever's right for you. That's what's important now.

RichmondGirl: I suppose now's a good a time to tell you as any. I've put it on the market.

RichmondGirl: I don't know why I call it home anymore. It doesn't feel like home, not without you there. In fact...

KewGuy: How is the old place? The flat I mean?

RichmondGirl: That was like a mantra for us, wasn't it? So I turned around and headed home.

KewGuy: I remember. Never go anywhere on a match day, unless you're going to the match itself.

RichmondGirl: I ended up at Twickenham, at the stadium, but that felt wrong too. We hardly ever went and the traffic used to wind us up on match days.

RichmondGirl: So then I went past the golf course. But that was all you. It certainly isn't me so it could never be us, could it? It wasn't right.

RichmondGirl: Plenty of hopes and dreams there, that's for sure, but most of them end up in tatters and that wasn't what I wanted for you.

RichmondGirl: I started with Kempton Park but it didn't seem like the calmest place to spend eternity. And the atmosphere wasn't right.

RichmondGirl: I tried again today. Took you off the shelf and did a tour of some of your favourite sporting venues.

KewGuy: You will. One day.

RichmondGirl: You mean you're smiling now? I wish I could see your smile again.

KewGuy: Probably for the best. You always did know how to put a smile on my face.

RichmondGirl: I'm sorry, but I thought that if I told her it would only cause more problems than it was worth, so we went for coffee instead.

RichmondGirl: I was going to take you to the park, or down by the river, but I ran into Susan outside the bank and couldn't tell her what I was doing.

RichmondGirl: I made a start today. I put you in my bag – the one you bought me from Fat Face – and took you into town.

.

.

.

KewGuy: Like I said, there's no rush. It has to feel right.

RichmondGirl: I couldn't do it. I wasn't ready.

RichmondGirl: I took you down off the mantelpiece for the first time this morning. Gave the mantelpiece and you a good dust and then put you back again.

.

.

.

KewGuy: And when you're ready to say goodbye, scatter them there. Then move on.

KewGuy: That's for you to decide. Take your time, there's no hurry, but when you're ready and you think you've found the right spot.

RichmondGirl: But where?

KewGuy: I need you to take that urn from the mantelpiece and scatter the ashes inside somewhere that meant something to us both.

RichmondGirl: It feels like that was only a week ago, not five years. So what do you need me to do?

KewGuy: You've always loved me, just like I've always loved you, I think from the first moment we met at that bus stop outside Kew Gardens.

KewGuy: I know, but I know you will. You'll do it for me, because you love me.

RichmondGirl: What you're asking me to do feels like the hardest thing anybody's ever asked me to do, right now.

KewGuy: I know. Just like I could never forget you. But that's not what I'm asking you to do.

RichmondGirl: You have no idea how much I miss such simple intimacy. I don't want to forget you.

RichmondGirl: All I want is to and feel your hands on my body again. To feel you inside me. Just once more. To feel your fingers in my hair.

KewGuy: I want you to have time to heal. I want you to live a rewarding life. I want you to be happy, to fall in love again.

KewGuy: You have to. Not for me but for you, because it's not healthy. You can't stay like this for the rest of your life, weighed down by grief.

RichmondGirl: What if I don't want to?

KewGuy: Only you can do it, my darling.

KewGuy: You need to let me go. And only you can release me.

RichmondGirl: Sorry? No, it's me who should be sorry. It wasn't your fault was it?

KewGuy: I know. And I'm sorry.

RichmondGirl: The natural order of things? Neither is dying from cancer at 35!

KewGuy: But this isn't how it's meant to be. This isn't the natural order of things.

RichmondGirl: And I read them over and over and over again. We have a chance to say all those things that bastard illness prevented us from saying in time.

RichmondGirl: Is that such a bad thing? I mean, we can talk again. Well, not talk exactly, but when I read your posts, it's your voice I hear.

KewGuy: I'm trapped here.

RichmondGirl: Tell me.

KewGuy: I don't understand how I can be here either. But I think I understand why.

RichmondGirl: But how can we be talking like this, via Twitter?

KewGuy: It's me. And everything will be alright. You'll see. Trust me.

RichmondGirl: I so want it to be you. I so want you to be able to tell me everything will be alright again.

RichmondGirl: There's been a hole in my heart since you... since you died. It's like I'm just a shell, a shell hiding the great black gulf inside me.

KewGuy: I don't exactly understand it myself.

RichmondGirl: But why are you here? I mean I still can't quite believe it, but I want to. I want to believe it's you.

KewGuy: I don't know. I prefer not to ask in case it all comes to an end.

RichmondGirl: It really is you. But how can it be? How is that possible?

KewGuy: And the first thing you ever said to me was, 'Excuse me, does the 65 to Ealing go from here?'

KewGuy: Your first pet was a budgie called Sid. You love rum and raisin ice cream but you never ask for it because it makes you sound like your dad.

KewGuy: What else can I say to prove it to you? That your favourite biscuits are custard creams? You lost your virginity in 1992 on a camping trip?

RichmondGirl: It really is you?

KewGuy: I wanted to tell you that love like ours never dies, no matter what might happen to our bodies. The cancer couldn't take that away from us.

KewGuy: I know it sounds corny now, but what we shared was true love.

KewGuy: I wanted to tell you that I'll love you forever, that I've never felt about anyone the way I feel for you. That what we had was true.

KewGuy: But I wanted to say so much. I hadn't had a chance to say thank you for the last five years. For the best five years of my life.

KewGuy: I didn't say anything – I couldn't. But I squeezed your hand as tight as I could as I slipped away, until I couldn't even feel anything.

RichmondGirl: And what did you say?

KewGuy: You said to me, 'Those geraniums could do with some more water.'

KewGuy: You held my hand in yours and having told me that you'd love me forever, after you'd kissed my eyes, my lips, my cheeks...

KewGuy: As I was lying there in that hospital bed, the cancer eating me up from the inside, unable to even open my eyes...

RichmondGirl: What was the last thing I said to you?

KewGuy: Anything. Go on. Ask me.

KewGuy: As me something. Ask me anything. Something only you and I could possibly know.

RichmondGirl: In fact I can't believe I'm even carrying on with this charade, playing your pathetic little games. Is this what you get off on you sicko?

RichmondGirl: I watched your coffin slide beyond those disgusting, tatty red curtains while some old biddy played some ruddy dirge on the organ.

RichmondGirl: It can't be you! How could you be watching me?

KewGuy: The sight of you, looking so upset, yours eyes puffy and red with tears, tore me apart.

RichmondGirl: Don't say that!

KewGuy: I know. I was there too, watching you.

RichmondGirl: Never mind lost – you're dead! I sat there by your beside watching you die.

KewGuy: I understand how you must be feeling right now. I can hardly believe it myself. But you must believe, otherwise I'm lost.

RichmondGirl: Go away! Leave me alone! I'll have you reported for this.

KewGuy: Because I know you want it to be true with all your heart.

KewGuy: Because I know you. Because right now, no matter how impossible this may seem I know that you want it to be true.

RichmondGirl: How do you know what I do or do not want? Who are you to make that call?

KewGuy: You don't mean that. You don't want that, not really.

RichmondGirl: FUCK OFF! There, is that better?

KewGuy: You never did like swearing online, did you?

RichmondGirl: F*** off! and leave me alone!

KewGuy: This isn't a joke. It's really me.

RichmondGirl: Who is this? What kind of sick joke do you think you're playing?

KewGuy: I know you're there and I know how strange, how unreal this must seem, but please respond.

KewGuy: Are you there, my darling?

KewGuy: Hello?

KewGuy: Hello? Is there anybody there?

33 days ago via web...

WANDSWORTH
Chicken Run

Chicken Run

Melanie McGee

How many fish slices does one woman need? This is a question many an enquiring mind has asked. In Shirley's case, 'about 73' would appear to be the correct answer. Or at least that's the conclusion Shirley herself comes to as she stands on the street in her finest 'moving house outfit' (brown slacks that cling in such a way as to display one hell of a camel-toe, and a maroon fleece), and attempts to jam another bin liner full of pointless kitchen implements into the boot of her lilac Fiat thingameejig.

She doesn't even like cooking. Were you to offer up your dough balls, with the express intent of having Shirley tease them into something delicious upon which to nibble, the result would be some sub-standard fumbling and a quick resolution by way of calling in the professionals – i.e. she'd dump them in the trash, buzz up the those trusty chaps at Pizza GoGo (opposite the funeral parlour on West Hill – no connection inferred) and demand two of their finest 'Beefy Ones' with extra garlic slices and a bottle of pop to boot. So how, in the name of Rod, Jane and Freddy, she has ended up with three bin liners full of cooking utensils is a mystery only Jessica Fletcher can solve.

She shoves one last box of possessions into the footwell and goes back to waggle her key in the lock of the front door for the last time. As she posts the key back through the letterbox with the penchant for human finger-flavoured snacks, she recalls the day she'd first bowled through the door as a grumpy 23 year old. The rental agency had sent a right haughty sort to show her in. This posh (but bonkers) woman spent a good 40 minutes explaining how to sit on a sofa correctly so as not to damage it, and precisely which ecologically sound cleaning products should be used on different surfaces. She had to admit that even now, at a slightly more grown-up 33 years old, she still put malt vinegar on her chips more regularly than on the tap fittings.

Despite the strange estate agent she had been excited to move into her first home. Ok it was rented and ok it was small but it was only four minutes from Wandsworth Town station and the newsagent across the road stayed open 24 hours – a vital tool in feeding her obsessive Monster Munch habit. All in all, a score, so today she isn't exactly brimming with glee.

The realization that she would need to pack away her fish slices and ship out thundered into her life as she splayed out on the sofa the Friday before last. She was keenly eyeing up *Cash in the Attic* while slowly pushing a corned beef sandwich into her face when she detected the sound of her telephone bell. Placing the receiver to her ear, the drum within picked up the unmistakable sound of her mother's voice. This in itself was not unusual, Doreen called Shirley every second week without fail, but it was the urgency with which Doreen jabbered that caused Shirley to peel her peepers away from the box and fire up the ears for some serious listening time.

'It's my chickens,' yelped Doreen, 'they've run amok!' (Doreen had kept chickens in the back garden of her semi-detached, three-bed, post-war, red-brick, with-views-over-the-sea property, since 1964).

'What, mother, precisely do you mean when you say *amok*?' was the sensible question with which Shirley replied.

'Amok, you silly girl, AMOK! Did I spend all that money on an education for you not to understand the word 'amok' when I use it? Good Lord child, put a dictionary on your Christmas list and after Santa has delivered it, study it with earnest.'

'I went to state school mother, you didn't pay a bean, and I am in clear possession of the dictionary definition, I simply wish for you to clarify it in relation to Biffy, Jean and Poirot.' Poor old Shirley did well to keep her lip buttoned down, many other girls would have bitten back at such verbal abuse, but Shirley knew it was the panic talking. Since Doreen's beloved Jim had dropped stone dead from a heart attack in the yogurt aisle of a Tesco Metro some three years past, she'd noticed her mother becoming kerfuffled on a distinctly more frequent basis, so she played it calm and waited for the facts to come forth.

'They've snuck into the house Shirley! How, I simply don't know! I was in the kitchen nook, fingering through an old copy of Fanny Craddock's 'Bon Viveur Recipes' with a view to whipping up a boiled beef platter, when I heard the unmistakable sound of claw upon lino, I looked down and there, Shirley, was Biffy, tap-dancing across the floor. Before I knew it Jean and Poirot had joined him and now they've formed some sort of be-feathered conga-line and are making their way towards the downstairs loo. Oh Shirley, your Father's ashes are in there, what if they've got a mind to knock him clean out of his urn. They know he never had love for them. Perhaps they are out for revenge.'

'Mother. Calm down, please. It's Biffy, Jean and Poirot, not a herd of rabid elephants. They've crept into the house plenty of times before and they've never had a mind for revenge, so just take a big deep breath. You know perfectly well how to round them up and flush them out. You've done it a million times. Just get something to flap about and wave it at them until they head back out of the door.'

Shirley spoke with level authority and after repeating these instructions a few times Doreen gathered herself together, replaced the telephone back in it's cradle, grabbed the tea-towel with the stain where Princess Diana's nose should be, and ushered those naughty wee beaks back outside.

***

Most of this is, of course, by the by. Doreen's chickens were back in the garden and Shirley caught the last 10 minutes of *Cash in the Attic* so, in theory, all was once again right with the world. But the confusion in her mother's voice sat queerly in Shirley's belly for the rest of the day. The following day it was that same queer feeling that prompted her to rap on the door of her boss's office, look him squarely in the eye and hand him the resignation lemon. She then called her estate agent and gave her the very same treatment. She had made the momentous decision to leave Wandsworth Town and go home to look after her mother. This is why, on this cold Saturday afternoon, we find her ramming all her worldly goods into her daft little car, ready to set off for the grey and dismal coastal town of her birth.

Pinging up the old engine she looks back at her flat in Shoreham Close for the last time and with a sharp pang of sadness prodding at her slightly pudgy tummy she pulls out onto Barchard Street ready to turn right onto Wandsworth Town's notorious gyratory system one final time.

Within moments said pang of sadness is replaced by a yowl of frustration. The queue on Fairfield Street to join the traffic on the main high street is long enough to make Shirley squint. Not that this should surprise her, and nor does it. The appalling traffic situation on this one-way system is so well known it has dropped its last name. It's just that on this, her parting trip from a decade spent in the most wonderful city the Baby Jesus (and/or any other deity that may/may not exist) ever did create; she wants it to feel a little bit dramatic. She even had a finger on the volume button ready to crank up the stereo so she can whizz away whilst singing along to that … erhem … iconic end of an era tune 'Don't you, forget about me'. True, she was no Molly Ringwald and in Wandsworth Town she had never found her Judd Nelson, but it was the end of something special all the same and she does not want her final departure to consist of three hours sat behind a rusty Renault Cleo with an unsmiling child staring coldly into her eyes from his back seat as if Lucifer himself has inhabited his body and is trying to kidnap her soul so he can drag it back to Hell – or perhaps the boy is just in a bad mood. Either way, it is not the finale she has imagined. She removes her finger from the volume button. The desire to sing, all but disappeared.

As she slowly inches towards the traffic lights at the end of Fairfield Street she concentrates hard on avoiding the stare of the maniac child in the Renault Cleo in front and gazes about the place willy-nilly in (she believes) an effort to save her soul from Hell.

Studying the town hall that sits alongside the driver's side seems like a useful distraction. A funny old place, half traditional and beautiful and the other half modern and downright ugly, she's never had cause to venture inside, but the constant stream of wedding guests that gather outside the Civic Suite has always made her smile … except for the time she'd been wandering by and a lady in the most beautiful sari she'd ever set eyes upon asked her to take a picture of her family. Slightly overwhelmed by the glamour of the occasion Shirley had gone all out to take the best photo she could, ushering the family further and further to the left in order to get the fancy-pants part of the building in the background. Sadly, whilst she was 'art directing' children, aunties and elderly relatives like she was the next David Bailey, she was unaware that she was guiding them into a pile of disgusting dog-bottom deposits. An elderly grandfather in his best brogues was the first to notice – by way of his slipping base-over-apex. Eek! The lady with the beautiful sari was the second. As she helped 'Pops' up from the floor she smeared the horrible stuff all along the hem edge of her outfit. Crikey it chiffed too. All Shirley could do was blush, apologise and try to wipe it off with a snotty old tissue.

It didn't work. This lovely looking woman and the sore-bottomed old boy had to go to the wedding smelling like, well, there's no other word for it – POO!

Shirley turns her head back to the evil child; even he is preferable to that embarrassing memory! But the thought soon leaves her brain as the light turns green and she zips onto Wandsworth High Street, out of the eye-line of the devil-child and the dastardly town hall.

However it seems a kernel of melancholic reminiscence has penetrated her noggin and it isn't prepared to slip on its coat and leave any time soon. As she inches slowly down the High Street past Wandsworth College, with it's wonderful 'middle earth' style turrets, more thoughts from the past tiptoe into her conscious.

Back in 2005 Shirley had undertaken a Legal Secretarial course. It was an attempt to haul herself out of the admin team at the distinctly murky solicitors firm at which she worked. However, her attempts at advancing her career, like her attempts at cookery, were decidedly unpalatable. When faced with the inevitable final examinations that one must undertake when attempting something that ends in a certificate, she did precisely zero revision. Not a pip.

Her lack of revision was not down to laziness, oh no, somewhat queerly, the responsibility lay firmly at the feet of a family of mice. Yes, mice.

Every third evening Shirley would traipse up the winding wooden staircase with the ornate banister carvings (it always made her feel like she was in a Harry Potter movie) and into the college library. She'd flip open the books with study in mind. However, within minutes she would spot one of these little mice. Sometimes it would be the mother, herding her young sprouts along the side of the bookcase and back to their hole. Other times it'd be the father, briefcase in his tiny paw, bowler hat perched atop his furry head, off for a hard day in the office …

Ok ok, so perhaps he wasn't *actually* wearing a bowler hat or carrying a brief case. And perhaps he was just performing run-of-the-mill scurrying activity rather than making his commute to work – but it was precisely these sorts of contemplations that occupied Shirley's mind. A mind that should have been focused upon probate documents and particles of claim but instead it played out a little vermin based soap opera for it's own amusement, and before she knew it, the library would have closed and all she'd have done was sketch a few mousey pictures in her pad.

For weeks this continued. She trotted off to study with the best of intentions – and achieved nowt. It's sad to think that the provision of one or two mousetraps would have seen Shirley take an altogether more professional path. Mind you, a girl who can be distracted by the smallest of mammals and their imaginary lives is perhaps one not best suited to the cut and thrust of the legal business.

It's true, the failure of her career did nibble away at her happy bone (in a manner not dissimilar to those naughty little mice nibbling away at a delicious cheese supper) but Shirley, ever of the philosophical view (and easily distracted bonce) shrugs the memory off with ease as she puts the car into 2nd gear and moves steadily forward, crossing the Garrett Lane junction, before once more coming to a halt. This time next to that legendary Wandsworth Town eatery, the Diana Fish Bar. Ho, what a place! She's seen a few things in there … or at least she thinks she has. Shirley has never actually set foot in the place without having first downed a significant skinful, so it's fair to say that the sights and sounds of which she believes to have experienced may have been nothing more than 'gin on the wind'. Not that it is a place only suitable for drunken fools, yee gods no. The fish/chicken/burger/kebab selection is of the widest and finest quality a human being in possession of a mouth and a tummy can wish for. It just so happens that she has only ever frequented the premises late-night and drunken – more often than not with Becky – a fellow Wandsonite with a straw-like barnet but a cracking pair of norks.

The waft of vinegar and kebab meat drifts through the car window and plays around the inner edges of Shirley's nostrils, firing off neurons in the brain that tickle the memory bank in such a way that Becky's 30th birthday comes flooding to the fore …

'Sausages,' blathered Shirley as the clock tinkled 2am and they weaved their merry way across the bridge towards Diana's after several hours spent throwing alcohol at their faces. 'Large and battered,' Becky confirmed.

These plonkers arrived on wobbly pins at Wandsworth's battered sausage Mecca, gazed through crossed-eyes at those significantly more sober purveyors of fine meat goods and ordered no less than 16 battered sausages. Yep. That's right. Ten. Plus. Six.

Six.

Teen.

The reasoning? They had never eaten 16 battered sausages before, and all women of 30 full years should have their '16 battered sausages' badge. Apparently.

'Not good reasoning,' Shirley acknowledges, these two years on, but reasoning all the same.

They paid for the requested goods and began to weave their way home along Wandsworth Plain, passing the small sack of steaming pork delights betwixt them and guessing at what went on in the big buildings housed behind the iron railings that lined the road.

Neither saw the small hound that had snuck up on tippy-toes behind them. A furry chap, with the traditional wet snout and wagging tail combination, he'd not had a sniff of food since breakfast and sausages just happened to be his most loved of all the world's foods. The scent had passed across his little snoz a good way back and he'd been creeping up on the sozzled idiots for some 30 yards.

His pounce at the grease stained bag was an inevitable maneuver. The girls, however, did not consider it inevitable, nor even a possibility, given they hadn't caught wind of the be-pawed fellow at all. And so, when he leapt from behind, his jaws drooling with sausagey desire, Becky made her own leap, three feet into the upwards and flung the bag out of reach, up into the air... only to watch it land on the other side of some iron railings. Zoiks.

The dog saw that there was no way he'd get his chops around those meaty little treats now and began to howl.

Becky and Shirley joined in. However, never one to sit about howling for long Becky decided action must be taken. 'Rub the rest of that sausage on my arm Shirl, I'll have our battered friends back here soon enough.' Shirley had a mere two inches remaining of the one she'd been noshing at the time of the incident, and she obliged Becky without question, smearing the fatty beast up and down the fleshy forearm of poor inebriated Becky until the grease glistened proudly in the moonlight. With angry determination Becky shoved her arm through the irons bars right up to the tonsils and made swift purchase upon the bag they so desired. Shirley let out a 'whoop!'

Of course it was only when Becky tried to pull back her arm that they registered the real situation. She was stuck and stuck fast.

Shirley grabbed hold of Becky's trunk and gave it a tug, but predictably the alcohol prevented any significant success, and so after 20 minutes of pulling Shirley had to leave Becky sitting on the path, all alone save for the damned dog, one arm lodged between the bars and the rest of her glutinous body spread out on concrete, while she pegged it to the fire station on West Hill and roused those handsome chaps with the enviably large hoses to ask for their help.

Oh the shame – not merely of having to explain the situation to the sober and decidedly stern firemen, but of coming back to find Becky slumped against the railings, fast asleep, with her face pressed into the bag of cold sausages. Shame, shame, shame.

The memory made blood flow generously to her cheeks and the heat brought her sharply back to the present – and not a moment too soon. Her onion being occupied with thoughts of the past almost leads to a shunt up the rear in the here and now, when she fails to notice the traffic shift forward. Yikes! Some idiot in a silver BMW gifts her a right good blast on his horn for not moving quickly enough and as she whacks her foot to the pedal and hares forward he zooms past her and she clocks that it is Michael.

Ahhh Michael. What a knob. He is pushing pension age, easily, with all the beer-bellied, hairy-eared attributes that so often accompany it, yet he mysteriously has the arrogance of 20-year-old packing a serious trouser-snake. SuperTed alone knows why, but Shirley had made it quite clear she never wanted to discover the answer.

Michael is one of the 'gentlemen' she encountered when fighting against the proposition to build two gynormous tower blocks on the recently flogged off Ram Brewery site. Shirley stuck her oar right into the proceedings when she discovered that this wonderful old patch of Wandsworth, many parts of which were built back when dinosaurs still roamed the earth (well ok, the 1830s) were under threat from bad-guy movie-type villains. These fellows, with scars on their faces and long, black, twiddleable moustaches, planned to redevelop most of the site in a way wonderfully sympathetic to the finest aspects of Wandsworth Town. However, for reasons known only to Mystic Meg herself, they fancied blasting their lovely plans all to cock by plonking down two tower block erections at one end of the site. The disproportionate size of which (at least in Shirley's mind) were completely bonkers. Good old Wandsworth Town, a place filled with cute terraced streets, independent shops, and an untouched character, needed help. But it needed more than one knight in shining amour, it needed an army of them, and so although Shirley was more accustomed to pink frocks and kitten heels, she'd readily poured herself into said armour and joined the fight.

Michael had been one of the villains in favour of the dastardly plan. He'd sat in all the public meetings silent and cold, only ever speaking to make comment on the perceived advantage of the bloomin' things. Never smiling, never laughing. Shirley was consistently distracted by his straight-backed pose and his thin little lips – she could happily imagine a white cat nestling in his lap, pushing it's furry head up to meet Michael's boney-fingered strokes. Sometimes he caught her staring. She had to look away quickly. He gave her the heebie-jeebies. Urgh.

Stony cold and icy as he was, Shirley was fully prepared to respect the opinions of her opponents, after all he lived in Wandsworth Town too. She was not, however, prepared to respect the sort of man who would happily sidle up to her after one particular public meeting and whisper in her shell, 'I saw you staring at me. I know you want me and I am fully prepared to take you for dinner…as long as you wear something a little lower cut around your knockers. That blouse comes up too high around your neck.'

An interesting approach, yes, but successful it was not. Unless receiving an elbow to the throat is considered a success … Still, it had put all thoughts of his being scary out of her brain. A sleazy old idiot? Yes. But scary? Pah!

As he zooms past her in his great big motor vehicle tooting his darned horn she realizes that leaving Wandsworth Town right now may not be the worst thing to happen. If the proposed planning is to go through she's fairly certain she'd be hotfooting it elsewhere anyway. She isn't sure where she'd skedaddle to, anywhere that has managed to keep the concrete and glass monstrosities at bay she guesses. It is important to her, to live in a place with character and charm. She doesn't believe that being in a major city means function has to preside over form. Shirley chose to live in Wandsworth Town for a reason – and it wasn't just the 24hr access to Monster Munch. She thought it a homely little place, full of community, tradition and beauty. The sort of place families from across the world can come to and feel a part of. A place where women can walk in safety after dark. A place where kids have a good chance of achieving a half decent education – as long as they ignore the mice, that is. So although many other locals may disagree, hoofing great tower blocks just don't fit into her particular view of Wandsworth Town.

And *that* Wandsworth Town, as it stands now, is, she realises, what she wants to remember. The good times, the funny memories, the happy places. She is certain that sticking around to watch it try to accommodate such disproportionate development will make her chin tremble and her balls leak. So maybe, she reasons, leaving now, on a high, is what it's all about? Wandsworth Town would become her personal Jim Morrison (always remembered at it's best that is, not dead in a bath).

The last set of lights flash amber and she can see the A3 turn-off winking at her. She smiles, the pang of sadness now all but behind her, and so, finally, is the dastardly one-way system. It's time to move on. Zipping away she whacks her little beast into forth, cranks the volume, and fires up the vocal cords. 'Hey hey hey hey... ooohhhh ... don't you, forget about me ...'

LAMBETH
The Hunt

The Hunt

Tom Bromley

The first time I hear the scream, I'm convinced someone is being murdered. High, piercing, inhuman, eerie, its scores the south London night like a scalpel. I wake with a start, and in the silent echo that follows, wonder if I was dreaming. Then the scream is there again – an anxious, anguished, tortured howl. In the second silent echo, my mind starts to race. Someone is being assaulted, mugged, killed. I sit up in bed.

'What?' Abi's head hasn't moved from her pillow, her waterfall of auburn hair cascading down towards the duvet.

'Can't you hear it?'

'Hear what?' she murmurs. The screaming, of course, has stopped. There is nothing more than the pulse of night whispering through the window. I looked at the clock radio. Three seventeen.

'There was a scream,' I say. 'A nasty one. I think something is going down.'

'Are you sure?' Abi's head of hair doesn't move.

'I'm not making it up, Abs.'

The silence continues. We sit there listening, like a still life painting. No movement, no sound, nothing. Then, just when I think I might have been hearing things after all, I hear the scream again.

'There,' I whisper. 'I told – ' Abi's hand reaches across to touch me on my side, to tell me to shush. It stays there, holding me, and I can feel the tautness of her arm, the tightness as she is straining to hear, to listen, to identify.

'It's alright,' she says, her hand relaxing. 'It's just a fox.'

'A fox?' I feel relieved, surprised, confused. 'Is it ok?'

'Very ok,' Abi reassures, with that elegant air of female authority. Her hand is directing me now, gently tugging at my T-shirt to guide me back down into the bed. 'That's what the French would call *la petite mort*.'

I spoon in behind her, feel the warm 'S' of her body against mine. 'Bloody foxes,' I say, my initial concern now turning to annoyance. 'They should go back to the country they came from.'

'Hey,' Abi chides gently. 'They've got just as much right to be here as you have.'

'I guess,' I say, a little defensively. 'Well. If they're going to move in, they should still be a bit more respectful of the rest of us. We don't keep *them* awake when we're, you know…'

'We *could*,' Abi suggests, taking my hand and guiding it down.

* * *

The following morning, under the four-sided clock at Waterloo Station, the horses, hounds and huntsmen are beginning to gather. As the morning trains arrive from Windsor and Winchester, Guildford and Goldalming, so the disparate members of the Lambeth Hunt are starting to congregate: the bloodhounds scuttling under the automatic ticket barriers, the huntsmen on horseback vaulting over the top.

As the dogs scuffle around at the horses' hooves, panting away like the lapping of waves, the huntsmen, in their central line red jackets and northern line black riding hats, sip from stirrup cups and chat away.

'Is this your first time on an urban hunt? Oh it's *such* fun.'

'The rural hunts are so complicated these days, what with having to keep an eye on the regulations. I mean, you can still hunt, but you have to be so careful not to get caught.'

'And then that chappie realised that London was exempt under some ancient bylaw or other. Bloody genius he was.'

'Much more fun in the city. And so many urban foxes waiting to be bagged.'

'I don't suppose you know the rule about pigeons, do you?'

'Afraid not. Have you tried the port? 1983 I think, absolutely marvellous.'

In the centre of the circle line of riders, sitting astride a handsome, hardy looking off-white horse, is the Master of the Hunt: a man of ruddy complexion, generous in girth and filthy rich in the thigh department.

'Gentlemen,' he calls crisply, bringing the twitter of conversations to a halt. 'I think we're going to have to make a start, even though not everyone is present – thanks to the trains for being as punctual as ever. I hope that, like Clarence here,' he patted his horse firmly, 'you managed to show your appreciation in the appropriate manner.'

Calming the snorts and sniggers with a raised hand, the Master continued. 'May I start by welcoming you all to today's meet. Marvellous to see so many familiar faces, and some new friends among us as well. For those who haven't been on an urban hunt before, I'll just familiarise you with the rules.' With a theatrical flourish, the Master pulled out of his pocket a blank sheet of paper, which to cheers from the assembled huntsmen he waved around, before to even greater cheers, he ripped into shreds. 'There *are* no rules, as long as we inform the mayor of our intentions. You'll be pleased to know that not only does the mayor have no objections,' he paused to let the cheers ring round the station concourse, 'but he might even join us later today on his bicycle!'

As the applause died down, the Master began his summing up. 'So the vermin fox thought he'd got clever by coming and living in the city, did he? Well, he reasoned without the Lambeth Hunt. He might think he can come and go as he pleases, ripping up the residential flowerbeds,

rummaging through rubbish bins, killing and eating the Queen's swans …'
the Master was less certainly about the last one, but it always got a rise from
his men, '… but we're here to show him otherwise – to run the rotten so-
and-so out of town and send him back into the countryside where we can
kill him properly!'

At which point, the Master noticed one of the whippers-in waving at
him and holding a phone up.

'Is that our first sighting?'

'We've found one, sir! One of the outriders has just called. He's at a
block of flats in Tulse Hill.'

The Master signalled for his stirrup cup. 'To Tulse Hill then! And the
fox's Waterloo!' he acclaimed, the silver glinting in the station lights.

'Fox's Waterloo!' the hunt roared back. After a swift pause for the
downing of drinks, a lone bugle sounded. To the bark of the bloodhounds
and the clatter of hooves, the hunt was on its way.

As the red sea of jackets raced down Kennington Road, past the Oval and
on towards Camberwell and Denmark Hill, through Ruskin Park and on
towards Herne Hill and Brockwell Park, up ahead in a residential street, all
was quiet. A black-jacketed huntsman (he was not yet qualified to wear the
red) was crouched behind a blue Ford Fiesta, keeping his eyes on the block
of flats that his bloodhound had led him to. That their quarry was in there
was without question: the young huntsmen had learnt over the years that
his bloodhound's nose was better than anything in finding a fox. All he had
to do was make the call, and wait.

It was a warm and sunny summer's morning in south London, and the
young huntsman paused to take off his riding helmet, and for a few seconds
allow the cool breeze to ripple through his hair. The huntsman wondered,
not for the first time, when he would be awarded his red coat, and allowed
to ride with the main pack. He knew, too, that this was initiation, that it was

part of him earning his place among the other riders. If he made sure that this hunt was successful, there wouldn't be too many more rides, he felt sure, before his promotion.

As he stayed crouched behind the car, his horse happily chomping away on the front lawn of a nearby garden, the huntsman felt a sharp and insistent feeling in his bladder. He knew that he shouldn't have had that second cup of coffee. Actually, his real mistake was too many pints the night before, which was why he was having to drink the coffee in the first place. One bucket sized Americano after another was not his smartest move. It was no good, the huntsman thought: I am going to have to have a piss. He glanced up at the block of flats. No movement. It'll be fine, he told himself: thirty seconds isn't going to make much difference. Stroking his bloodhound and telling him to 'stay' and to 'watch', the huntsman slipped down the side of a neighbouring house, and began to piss prime Italian coffee up against the wall.

Barely, though, had the huntsman got past his first Americano, before the Bloodhound started barking.

'Fuck,' thought the huntsman, craning to see what the Bloodhound was barking at. Then, with a clip clop of horror, he heard the one thing worse than the four horsemen: the rest of the hunt arriving. Zipping up hurriedly, the huntsman sprang back out to his viewing point to the sinking feeling that not only had he lost his prey, but also his chances of promotion. 'Well … ?' asked the Master, pulling up on his white horse, his face moist from the exertion of the ride.

'Oh yes,' said the huntsman. 'That's him alright. You're just in time.' He shook his head. 'Vicious looking thing. Big bushy coat and everything. Could be hiding anything under there.'

'So which way did he go?' the Master asked.

'Right,' the huntsmen looked despairingly at his hound for help. 'That way,' he pointed, as he saw a flash of bloodhound movement disappear round the corner. 'Maybe he is heading for the bus stop.'

The hunt arrived at the main road to see a red double decker number two pulling away. But further on, in the same direction, there was a 201 and a 432. Coming up was a 435. And heading the other direction was a 639.

'Crap,' said the young huntsman.

'It's like the Italian Job,' said a whipper-in. 'Which one do we follow?'

'All of them,' said the Master, through gritted teeth. 'He's a clever one. But he's not going to outfox me.' Splitting the hunt up into smaller groups, he pointed to the young huntsman. 'You,' he said, 'don't let the number two out of your sight. And keep in touch with me.'

By the time I wake up, Abi has gone, the indentations of where she'd been in the bed nothing but a fading memory. I lie there for a moment, my mind remembering the night before, then roll over and look at the clock. Ten thirty-five. After everything that happened, I'm glad to be on the late shift today.

I get up, put on a dressing gown and slouch through to the kitchen to put the kettle on. The morning sunlight is streaming into the kitchen, making me blink a little. As the kettle hums, I see the note that Abi has left for me on the kitchen table: *Good Evening! Hope I didn't wake you when I left – chicken defrosting on the side for supper tonight. See you then, Foxy Lady x*

I yawn a smile, and as the kettle boils, I pour the water into a mug, leaving it for a moment to allow the teabag to infuse. As I wait, I look out across the garden – the criss-cross of potted plants on the patio, the stretch of lawn that Abi is nagging me to mow, and next door's tree that is hanging over at the back, speckling the far corner with a canopy of shade.

It's as I'm looking out that in the dark far corner I see something reflect and sparkle. I look again, and realise that what I can see in the shadows is a pair of bright green animal eyes looking at me. As my eyes adjust and focus, I can just about make out the creature's ears, the sharpness of its nose, the shape of its silhouette. For a second I think, so *you're* the one who woke me up. Then I remember, well it wasn't *all* bad you waking me up, and find myself softening a little.

The fox though, just keeps staring at me. As I take the tea bag out, find some milk, give the tea a stir, I keep glancing back to the corner of the garden, keep seeing the twin sparkle of green looking back at me. It's like a natural version of CCTV, locked in and recording every my every moment. I stand there, in the morning sun, the steam from my mug of tea spiralling towards the ceiling – watching the fox, watching the fox watching me.

As the number two weaved its way towards Brixton, one of the outriders managed to catch up with the bus, and trot alongside peering in.

'Nothing here,' he said, dropping back. 'If he's on this bus, he's sat on the top deck.'

'Do you think he's going to go to catch the tube at Brixton?' the whipper-in asked, as the bus continued towards the underground station. 'What do we do then?'

'You don't let him,' the Master's voiced cracked over the radio. 'Whatever you do, don't let him go to ground.'

'I've heard that some of these urban foxes are a bit street,' said the whipper-in. 'Didn't you say he had a big thick coat this one? He could be concealing *anything* under that.'

Brixton High Street, as usual, was a bunfight. The huntsmen were glad they were on horseback, able to see out above the jostle and the bustle, the hangers out and the hangers on. In the middle of the road, a duvet-wearing homeless man was doing battle with a preacher over ownership of a traffic island.

'It's closed,' the whipper-in said, pointing at the fluorescent-jacketed heavies at the entrance to the tube station. Look, the tube station is shut.'

As the number two bus pulled up to its stop, and the passenger door opened, word quickly spread back that the station was closed.

'Where is he?' crackled the Master's voice. 'Can you see him?'

'Everyone's getting back on,' said the young huntsman. 'If he's on this bus, he's decided not to get off.'

'Keep watching,' said the Master. 'Where does the bus go next?'

'Up South Lambeth Road,' the huntsman said, looking at a map. 'Then Vauxhall, Pimlico, Victoria, Hyde Park Corner, Marble Arch and Marylebone.'

'He won't be going that far,' the Master's voice crackled. 'I still think he'll go to ground at the first opportunity. Which by my reckoning is the next tube station you'll meet.'

It's the fox that blinks first in our staring match. Its ears give the faintest of twists, like tiny radars, detecting something I cannot see or hear. I strain to work out what she has sensed, but whatever it is, is beyond my wavelengths. I think I see her nose twitching too, now. And the faintest of glances to her right.

Then, to my surprise, the fox emerges from the shadows. One part nonchalantly to two parts purposefully, she pads across the garden towards me. As sun catches the colours in its coat – the richness of the orange red, the paintbrush dip of white on the tail – one can't help but think, what a beautiful creature. This fox is no shrinking violet: a few soft silent steps later, and she is stood by the back door, her features distorted by the corrugated glass. With a paw raised up, there's a scratch scratch scratch. My god, I think. She wants to come in.

At first I stand there, not quite sure what to do. Then I see the fox's ear flick again, distorted through the frosted door, and this time I can hear what she is hearing. There's a low but definite rumble down the street, a little like thunder but more alive, a rumble that's getting louder all the time. I hear a horn and a crash, and even though I'm stood in my kitchen in south London, I find myself thinking of Jericho, the trumpets, and the walls coming down.

The fox scratches on the door again. It lets out a little scream: quiet but loud, like when you shout in a whisper. And this time, having listened to her cries carefully in the night, I know instantly that her shout is different. This scream isn't one of desire, this is desperation. I'm not really sure what is coming our way, but like Abi in the middle of the night, I'll trust her female intuition. I open the door and the fox scuttles in. She's looking and listening and sniffing around – checking her surroundings for an escape route, a sign of a trap. But however nervous she is of me, it's obviously nothing to the rumble that is getting louder and louder. As I push the back door to, she cowers under the table, makes herself small and out of sight.

Now the rumble is tuning into focus. From a fuzzy mess I can now make out an ever-clearer chorus of dogs, horses and shouting. It's the dogs I see first, leaping over from next door's garden, zigzagging across the lawn like metal detectors after gold. Can they smell the fox's scent? One hound can certainly sense something, because he's following the fox's footprints across the lawn, looking across at me with menace. His blood is up, I think, as I do my best to block his view. He knows.

Then, with an almighty crash, the first of the huntsmen leaps over the fence, bringing half of it down with him, like a bad show jumper. He lands on the lawn and with another leap is off and out the other side. It so quick, and I'm so surprised, that I don't have time to say or shout anything. But I recover myself as the fellow huntsmen gallop through and like an irate farmer I'm shouting, 'Get Off my Land!' The bloodhound, I'm sure, still thinks that he has his prey, but as the rest of the hounds follow the horses, he issues me with a final, curdling snarl, before chasing after his pack.

As the rumble subsides, and the city hum slowly returns, I look back across at where the fox is sitting. She is curled up now in a semi-circle, her head down and resting, like any other domestic animal. It is only later, after I have gone out into the garden to inspect the damage from the hunt, that I discover that not only has the fox disappeared without so much as

191

a goodbye or a thank you, but the chicken breasts that were defrosting on the side for supper have vanished too.

'Target is off the bus. Repeat, target is off the bus.'

'Where are you huntsman?'

'By that big Irish pub at the top of Stockwell Road. Target is crossing Clapham Road and heading for the tube station.'

'I *knew* he'd go to ground.'

'What's the procedure, sir? Am I authorised to go down there?'

'This is a Code Red situation, huntsman. Whatever you do, don't let him get on that train.'

'Absolutely, sir.' The huntsman looked across as the whipper-in. 'Release the dogs.'

With a whistle and a cry, the whipper-in gave the instruction, and the hounds streaked across Clapham Road, howling and barking and jumping on and over cars, screeching to a halt. And as the harshness of their barks disappeared down the long escalator to the platforms, so the sound of screams – high, piercing, inhuman, eerie – travelled back up to the surface.

'What?' crackled the master's voice. 'What is going on there?'

The young huntsman, struggling to keep up with the pace of the pack, leapt over the ticket barrier and raced down the escalator, three steps at a time, in their wake. He almost tumbled over in his haste, almost knocked over by the bodies that rushed out in the opposite direction. Down he descended onto the platforms, to the northbound train now going nowhere. As soon as he stepped through the open doors into the carriage, he knew something had gone horribly wrong. He reached for his radio, but even if he could speak, the crackle of the line is cut off underground. There's nothing down here but silence, and the body of a man, in jeans and a light denim jacket, in a pool of blood on the floor.

MERTON
White Wedding

White Wedding

Jessica Ruston

Hamilton House, Southside Common, Wimbledon. 8am

Tara White woke up on the morning of her wedding day, and blinked, feeling the unfamiliar bed beneath her, before remembering that she was not at home, in the Balham flat she shared with Tom. She was at 'home', in the attic room of her parents' house in Wimbledon village. She stretched, and her feet hit the end of the carved wooden sleigh bed that had been hers since childhood and which she had insisted on sleeping in last night, the Last Night of her single years, putting Lucy, her oldest friend and bridesmaid in the bigger double room next door. Her back ached because of the old mattress, and she was regretting her sentimental symbolism a little.

She could hear the high-pitched whirr of the coffee grinder as her father began his morning routine. He put a lot of store by routine, did David White, JP. She knew that he would be walking slowly around the kitchen, whistling to himself, filling in the *Times* Sudoku (fiendish), and laying the table for breakfast. Soon she would smell the fresh coffee as he carried a cup up to her mother in bed. Tara smiled. She couldn't wait for him to see her in her dress.

Her dress. She gave a little shiver of excitement as she let her eyes rest on it, hanging on its satin padded hanger on the back of the bedroom door. It was a slim column of white lace, its train falling softly into a pool at the back, the front corseted and strapless with a lace jacket that she would wear in the church and that had scalloped edges to highlight her collarbones. A pair of ivory Louboutins would provide a flash of red as she walked up the aisle towards Tom.

There was a knock at her door. The luxury of being at home and being brought coffee in bed. She'd drink it, chatting to her father, and then she was going to have to get a move on. The cars were coming at 11.45. And, though the bride was traditionally late, Tara had no intention of keeping Tom waiting a single minute. She was desperate to be married to him, to be his wife. Mrs Tom Beaton. No, Tara White was not going to be late.

Tibbett's Corner Roundabout. 8am

Tom Beaton opened his eyes, very slowly, and then shut them again very quickly as they were filled with a rush of agonising, bright yellow light. It felt as though someone was burning the back of his brain with a laser beam. As though he was in an operating theatre and had woken up halfway through some kind of procedure. Oh God. He felt as though he were dead. Though as soon as that thought had appeared, it was replaced by the decision that death would probably be preferable to how he felt. His stomach lurched. He was hot. Very hot, and yet, he could feel a strange breeze over his body. As though he were outside, wearing no clothes. He shook his head – he must be half-dreaming still – and groaned out loud at the pain of it. Jesus.

'Arrgukkugh'. The sound that came out of his mouth was only half-human, and as it emitted forth from his throat, he became suddenly aware of a strange taste in his mouth, sticky and herbal and unmistakably alcoholic. He swallowed hard to stop himself throwing up. Slowly, the situation was becoming clear to him. He was not dead, not had he been abducted by aliens; he was simply terribly, horribly hungover. That was alright. He had been hungover before. He took a deep breath. Why had Tara left the window open all night? No. Not Tara. She was at her parents. Benjy must have opened it to stop him feeling sick in the night. Good old Benjy. But oh God, he would be in trouble if he didn't sort this hangover out before he got to the church. Coffee. He needed coffee, and mouthwash, and fast.

His hot flush of a few moments ago had passed, and now he was freezing. Ok. Come on, Beaton. Stir yourself. You didn't go through Sandhurst for nothing.

He opened his eyes for the second time. And this time, though he would have liked to have shut them once more, he was unable to, because they were wide with shock.

In front of him, a bright red 93 bus was passing just a few feet from his naked, hairy body. As it sailed down the road towards Wimbledon Village, he saw teenagers sniggering in the back window, and the outraged face of a middle-aged woman with her mouth open. Trust me, I'm more surprised than all of you, he thought to himself, as he scrambled to cover himself with his hands, and looked around desperately for his clothes. Fucking hell. Fuck! Not far away, Tom could hear a police siren. He looked around, and, covering himself with his cupped hands, legged it over the round and into the undergrowth on the edge of the Common.

Hamilton House. 8.15 am

'Come in,' she called, and shifted over to make space for him to sit on the edge of her bed.

But the head that appeared in her doorway wasn't the bushy-eyebrowed one of her father, but the pale and worried face of her mother, pale pink velvet dressing gown clutched around her thin body.

'What's the matter, Mum?'

'He's gone,' Carrie White replied, looking bemused.

Tara pushed herself up on one elbow. What was her mother talking about? Oh God. Had Tom changed his mind? Tara went hot and her mouth went dry. Being jilted at the altar was her most dreaded fear. Ever since … She shut her eyes. Not again. Please, please, not again.

But her mother was shaking her head. This wasn't to do with Tom.

'Dad,' her mother was saying. 'He got up half an hour ago as usual, made the coffee, and then came upstairs, got dressed and walked out of the door. Wearing his cords. He didn't even bring me a cup of coffee. Wearing his cords.'

'Mum. Calm down,' Carrie was on the verge of tears. 'He's probably just gone for a walk. To get the papers.' But the papers were delivered and David never went for a walk before breakfast. Her mother was shaking her head. 'Mum, spit it out, what now?'

She looked at Tara with teary eyes.

'He said – he said he was leaving. He said he couldn't believe what I'd done, and he was leaving.' And Carrie burst into tears.

Cannizaro House Hotel, Wimbledon Common. 9am

'They're meant to be getting here at what time?' Mr Proudfoot, the maitre d' of Cannizaro House's restaurant asked Jane, the hotel's wedding planner, though he knew the answer perfectly well. He just needed to hear it one more time.

'Twelve o'clock.'

Mr Proudfoot nodded slowly. 'Twelve o'clock,' he repeated. And they both stood and stared at the large room before them, which, just a couple of hours previously had been in perfect condition, the twelve round tables in their positions, each with their ten chairs covered in white slip covers adorned white bows, the cutlery gleaming, ready and waiting for the fresh flower arrangements to be placed in their centres and the final touches to be completed. Now, though, the tables were invisible under a thick layer of damp, sooty, plaster dust.

Beyond, the smaller room where the ceremony itself was to have taken place, and where the fire had started, was even worse. The once pale green and cream curtains were now just a few frazzled strips of frayed fabric. In the bar, the bottles of champagne that had been chilling in ice buckets had popped and exploded in the heat, and shards of green glass covered the floor.

'I suppose we should be thankful for small mercies,' Jane said.

'Which would be?' Mr Proudfoot asked.

'Well.' She crossed her arms, searching her mind for an upside to the situation. Jane liked to think of herself as a positive, glass half-full kind of a person. She thought it was important to count one's blessings. But even she was struggling, now.

'At least it happened sooner, rather than later. Imagine if the fire had started during the wedding. You've got to admit, that would have been worse.'

Mr Proudfoot gave a tiny nod. He did indeed have to admit that yes, that would have been worse.

'And,' she continued, having got into her stride, 'maybe it's good luck. Like rain.'

'Like rain.' That was pushing it, for Mr Proudfoot, and Jane began to lead him away. They didn't have much time to decide what on earth they were going to do.

'Come on. We'll go to my office and make a plan. At least nothing else is going to go wrong, now.'

Mr Proudfoot's brow knitted together, and he frowned. 'You're probably right.'

At that moment, his mobile phone buzzed in his jacket pocket, and he answered it. As he listened, Jane could see his Adam's apple sink down in his throat, and then bob back up again, and he began to sweat a little, on his forehead. That was not a good sign. Mr Proudfoot did not believe in displays of emotion in front of members of staff.

'That was the florist,' he said, slowly. 'She was phoning from a hospital trolley in St Mary's. She's gone into labour six weeks early.'

He swallowed, his Adam's apple bobbing again. 'She's very sorry, but she's been unable to finish the table decorations and flowers, and she can't deliver them. For obvious reasons.'

He and Jane surveyed the devastation in front of them once more. Jane sighed.

'To be honest, Mr Proudfoot, I think that's the least of our worries,' she said.

Jane was nothing if not pragmatic.

Outside in the garden of the hotel, as he and Jane rushed past, Mr Proudfoot noticed that a tall man with unusually bushy eyebrows was sitting on one of the benches, leaning forward with his elbows on his knees, and smoking a pipe. Strange. But he didn't have time to worry about it. He had a wedding reception to try and salvage. Mr Proudfoot had never let a bride down, not in all the thirty-nine years of his career in hospitality, and he wasn't going to start now.

Hamilton House. 9.45am

The White family's kitchen was not, as it should have been less than two hours before Tara's wedding, full of the bustle and activity of the last minute preparations, neighbours dropping in to wish her well and the bouquets that she had so carefully chosen, tight little puffs of freesias and lily of the valley and roses bound with white ribbons resting in long, shallow boxes on the scrubbed pine table. The flowers weren't there at all. But, just like Mr Proudfoot at the hotel, the flowers were the least of the White family's worries.

'But Mum, *why*? I don't understand.'

Lucy, Tara's oldest friend was standing by the hob, making coffee, her face made up and her hair in rollers, wearing an oversized men's shirt and boxer shorts. The phone rang and she leant over to answer it. 'That's probably him now,' she said.

'Do you think it's some sort of mid-life crisis?' Tara asked. Carrie's face crumpled.

'No,' she sobbed. 'It's all my fault. I've been a stupid, stupid woman, and I've ruined everything. The whole wedding's spoilt and it's all because of me.'

Tara's face began to show her frustration. 'Mum, you have to *tell me* what's happened, or I can't …'

'Um,' said Lucy. 'I'm afraid I've got bad news.'

Carrie and Tara's heads jerked up in unison. 'Tom?'

'No. The … .Well, it doesn't look as though today's going to be going ahead exactly as planned. But Carrie, I can tell you that this, at least, isn't your fault.'

Tara, Carrie and Lucy stood, pale-faced among the wreckage of the hotel function room. Despite the hurried clearing up Mr Proudfoot and Jane had done, there was no disguising the fact that no wedding reception was going to take place in the hotel that day.

'Bloody hell,' said Lucy.

From behind them came the familiar sound of Benjy sucking air through his teeth, a habit he'd picked up at school and which Carrie was always berating him for. Now, though, she just turned around in relief.

'Benjy!'

'Man. This is really fucked up.'

'Well. Yes. That would seem to sum up the situation,' said Carrie.

'I went to the house and Mrs Watson said you were all here.'

'Why were you coming to the house, Benjy? You're meant to be with Tom,' Tara snapped.

'Yeah,' Benjy said, rubbing his neck. 'About that …'

Tara took one look at the guilty expression on her brother's face, and at the room around her, and burst into tears.

Just then, Benjy lifted his head and looked out of the tall window that stretched from floor to ceiling, behind where his sister was standing, sobbing.

And he saw something that made his bushy eyebrows shoot up in surprise, and relief.

'Don't cry Tara – hey, don't cry! You'll make your face all puffy. And ugly,' he said seriously. Despite herself, she laughed.

'He's had a bit of a shaving disaster, that's all. Cut his ear because he was all shaky.'

'Oh God,' Tara's lip trembled.

'He might be half an hour late, he's got to have a few stitches, but he's going to be fine. It's all going to be fine.'

Benjy pulled his sister to him and patted her shoulder as she sobbed. He nudged his mother, and pointed to the lawn beyond the window.

Sitting on a bench, smoking a pipe, was David White. Carrie raised her eyebrows in surprise. Because, beyond the forlorn figure of her husband, was the other missing player in the days planned events – her not-quite son-in-law, flanked by what looked like two policemen, gesticulating wildly at Benjy from behind a small shrub. And, if Carrie White wasn't mistaken, it looked very much as though the shrub was the only thing he was wearing.

Carrie White took a deep breath. It was time to pull herself together. She gently stroked her daughter's cheek.

'Benjy's right, Tara. Stop crying. It's all going to be ok.'

Tara sniffed. 'But how?' she wailed.

'Don't you worry about that. You go home with Lucy. Wash your face, do your make-up, get dressed. Have a stiff drink. I'm certainly going to.'

Tara looked at her mother in surprise. Carrie continued.

'That's right. A double gin and tonic. And then, Mr Proudfoot here and I, and Jane ...' she looked to the pair for support. Mr Proudfoot stood tall and gave a little bow.

'Have got work to do.'

Cannizaro Gardens. 12.30pm

Tara stood, legs trembling slightly, holding on to her father's arm, around the corner of the hotel, waiting for the string quartet to start playing her entrance music.

'Good job it's a nice day,' David White said. 'One stroke of luck, at least.'

Tara smiled. They were silent for a moment.

'Why did you leave, this morning, Daddy?' she asked, quietly. David gave a deep sigh.

'Because I'm an old fool,' he said. 'Because I found out your mother had been keeping something from me – for my own good - and I threw my toys out of the pram. I should have thanked her. Instead I behaved like a spoilt child.'

'But what? She wouldn't tell me anything.'

David looked at his daughter in her lace wedding dress, her face glowing and excited, showing no sign of her earlier tears. And he leant down and kissed her forehead.

'Just a silly thing. Storm in an old fool's teacup. I'm sorry I let you down. I saw red. I would never have missed the wedding, you know. I wouldn't do that to you.'

She nodded. 'I know, Daddy.' She smiled at him. He wasn't telling her the whole truth. But she wasn't going to push him on it, not now.

The music changed. Tara took a deep breath. And slowly, she and her father, walked around the corner of the building, into the sunshine.

The sloping gardens that sat at the back of the building had been hurriedly transformed by a team of helpers, gathered and headed by Mr Proudfoot. Hotel staff, guests who had arrived early, even a couple of students who had been studying (sunbathing) on towels in the garden, had all been pressed into service. Chairs had been carried out from the function room on the backs of the volunteers, like ants carrying crumbs. Dust from the collapsed ceiling was wiped off where possible, and where not sheets that trailed onto the grass looked almost like the smart chair covers that had been planned.

Tara was carrying a hastily put together bouquet of roses that Jane had run to the florist in the village for, tied with the only ribbon she had been able to find at the last minute. It came from the party shop, and had pink kittens on it, but they were only small, and from a distance it just looked like a random pattern. She hoped. There were no table centres – there were no tables. And instead of the ornate floral columns that were to have provided the decoration for the ceremony, the gardens provided the backdrop.

As Tara and Tom walked back down the makeshift aisle, the string quartet playing 'I do, I do, I do', a great cheer went up from the crowd that had assembled to watch the wedding.

'Bigger congregation than we'd bargained for,' Tom said, grinning, and waving at his cricket team, in their whites, who had turned up when they had heard what had happened. As had Carrie's book club, all of the White's neighbours from the street, Tara's hairdresser, the guys from the wine shop in town … Carrie had spent half an hour on the phone, rallying the troops. 'If Tara can't have the wedding she planned, I'm going to make sure she gets the wedding she deserves,' she had said.

They reached the end of the aisle, and a swarm of small children who had been on a nature day in the park rushed up to them, showering them with handfuls of daisies (the petals that were to be used as confetti were still in the back of the florist's car, in St George's car park).

A stream of waiters emerged from inside the hotel, bearing trays of canapés. The hotel kitchen had been undamaged, and as soon as he had been given the all clear by the fire brigade, the chef had raced back inside to get the job done. One of the ushers had been dispatched to Majestic wine for new glasses and bags of ice, and cases of champagne had been quickly chilled in the kitchen sinks.

Tara turned to Tom. 'Did you really cut yourself shaving? I can't see anything wrong with your ear.' She stood on tiptoe to look, and kissed it.

Tom took a deep breath. Behind his new wife, he could see his father-in-law take Carrie in his arms, and begin to slowly dance around the lawn. There would be time. There would be time for Tom to tell Tara where he had woken up that morning, and why his feet were covered in little scratches. And why a couple of local PCSOs were among the people watching them get married, having almost arrested Tom as he made his way across Wimbledon Common for indecent exposure, until he had explained his predicament. There would be time for David White to explain to Tara just why he had walked out of the house that morning. To explain about the letter that Carrie had kept hidden from him, with the results of the tests that he had had done some months ago at Parkside. There would be time for all of that and more. But for now, Tom just kissed his wife.

'No, he said,' I didn't cut myself shaving.

'Thought not. Benjy always was a bad liar. Tell me on the plane?'

Tom nodded. He watched David and Carrie waltzing slowly around the gardens, her cheek on his shoulder.

'Yes. I'll tell you on the plane. Oh, and I've got a surprise for you.'

'I'm not sure how many more surprises I can take today, to be honest.'

'You'll like this one. I promise. It turns out that the chauffeur who was going to drive us away started the fire. Because he'd been fired for being drunk.'

Tara closed her eyes. 'Tom. Seriously…'

'Wait, wait, wait … I've organised something else. Something better. I promise.'

She opened them again. 'You promise?'

'I do. I do, I do, I do….'

When Tara and Tom reached the hotel driveway, she burst out laughing. The fire engine had been festooned with ribbons and balloons begged and borrowed from every shop in the area while they had been enjoying their improvised reception. The firemen in their blue overalls were lined up in the driveway, making an aisle for Tom and Tara to walk through, and, as they reached the end, two of them swept Tara up and deposited her gently on the side of the vehicle, then gave Tom a leg up to join her.

'As good as the back of a Merc?' Tom asked.

'Better,' she said.

'I'm sorry today hasn't gone how we planned. I'm sorry about your big white wedding, babe.'

Tara grinned, and kissed him. 'But I did. Look. Look at all the people who helped, who made it happen, despite everything. How could it be any bigger, or whiter, or more weddingy?'

They looked down from the engine, at hundreds of people in the driveway of the hotel, cheering and blowing kisses, handkerchiefs waving in the air. And she threw her bouquet into the crowd, as the fire engine pulled away, its horn beeping, and it floated down towards the ground and into the arms of Jane, who caught it, and gave out a little 'ooh' of pleasure, and determinedly did not look at Mr Proudfoot, who stood, stiff and still perfectly groomed beside her. And blushed, as he reached down and took her hand in his.

KINGSTON UPON THAMES
Streetlights

Streetlights

Patrick Binding

For just a moment, everything is light; blinding shimmering golden light dancing on the surface of the water. For just a moment, the seams that bind the vast depths of the sky with the surface of the water are consumed; everything is consumed by the blinding shimmering golden light and he has to look away. Compelled by the river beneath, he looks back, captivated by the infinitely fracturing and rejoining golden light.

He shares the walk down towards the water's edge with an older man with an open, sincere face who looks about the same age as his father. Although the older man's walk is laboured, he notices a purpose in his stride. The older man, seemingly lost to his thoughts, beams a smile with a short nod and says something about it being a lovely day for it and he beams a smile with a short nod back and overtakes the older man and continues along the path.

There are lovers sitting beside the river, students reading, friends running, Police community support officers patrolling, young families cycling, older families sailing, schoolboys rowing and a small girl who looks about the same age as his niece taking a tiny handful of breadcrumbs from a plastic bag held open by her attentive mother. The small girl carries the breadcrumbs with great care the short distance to the river bank and throws them at a pair of expectant swans and then turns gleefully and toddles back to her mother and takes another tiny handful of breadcrumbs and carefully carries them to the river bank and throws them and then turns even more deliriously to take another tiny handful: and he continues along the path.

For just a moment, his attention is drawn to the vast verdant parkland to his right. During the war, this was where the Supreme Headquarters of the Allied Expeditionary Force (SHAEF) readied itself for D-Day. Eisenhower found nearby Coombe Hill the perfect antidote to the pressure-cooker intensity of Whitehall and was chauffeured down to Bushy Park by his alleged mistress, Kay Summersby, to oversee every last detail of the plans for the mother-of-all beach landings. There used to be American servicemen all over this part of south-west London. He wonders what those real-life Supermen from sprawling stateside metropolises: Austin, Texas; Denver, Colorado; Indianapolis, Indiana; Milwaukee, Wisconsin; Portland, Oregon; Buffalo, New York, must have made of the quaint 1940s Royal Borough of Kingston upon Thames. But the bombs fell here too, in retaliation for SHAEF's subsequent successes, most terrifying of all, the Doodlebug, sent over by the Nazis from the Pas-de-Calais.

Half a dozen brilliant green parakeets swoop over the parkland and settle in the branches of a nearby tree. Neither the lovers nor the students nor the friends nor the Police community support officers nor the young families nor the older families nor the schoolboys give any indication whatsoever that they are aware of their presence and he finds this more incredible than the fact that there are half a dozen brilliant green parakeets perched in the branches of a nearby tree in Kingston. There are flocks of brilliant green parakeets all over this part of south-west London. Legend has it that the original birds either escaped from aviaries during the storms of 1987, were accidentally released from a film set at nearby Pinewood, Shepperton or Teddington studios, or were owned by Jimi Hendrix. Like the American servicemen, he wonders what these most exotic of creatures must make of their surroundings. How do they reconcile the immense blinding cold winters of suburban Surrey with the dense Amazonian heat or choking Indian throb of their native habitats, where admittedly they are more likely to be trapped, plucked and put in a curry? Conversely, if they are second or even third generation immigrants then they are practically as British as he.

Somebody is aware of the brilliant green parakeets perched in the branches of a nearby tree and that is a homeless man who has rolled up his dirty cargo pants to reveal pale grimy legs and looks about the same age as his sister. The homeless man is leaning against a fence next to a boatyard deep in conversation with a little Jack Russell with only one ear. Every so often, the homeless man gestures towards the brilliant green parakeets and each time the Jack Russell's scruffy little head obediently follows the direction of his master's outstretched arms. As he watches, the scruffy little Jack Russell does an amusing double-take, and the homeless man erupts first with mirth then sorrow. In turn, he is sure that the brilliant green parakeets are aware of the attentions of the homeless man and the scruffy little Jack Russell as they shift listlessly in the branches of the nearby tree, glancing in their direction and then they flutter and rise, taking-off in a vibrant commotion towards Richmond Park.

At the half-way point of his walk, close to the imposing outer walls of Hampton Court, he takes a seat on a bench next to a girl with dark brown hair who looks about his age. She wears a denim jacket tied around the waist of a black summer dress and is purposefully lost in a book of short stories about vampires. He has a swig of water from a half-empty bottle in his green satchel, then, after a brief pause, takes out exactly the same book. 'Of all the books in published history' he says in an unconvincing Bogart-esque tone. 'This could be the start of a beautiful reading group?' she replies with a sideways frown and a much more passable accent. He laughs, noticing that she wears her hair up to expose a tribal necklace and that her eyes are copper-coloured, framed by freckles and accentuated with black eyeliner which comes to a point just past the corners of her eyes. 'So, what's the verdict?' he asks, motioning to her book. 'My jury's out. I'm sucking it and seeing. But from what I've read so far, so good. You?' She raises her eyebrows. 'I've read better. I've read worse. But it sure is original!' They laugh together and, almost imperceptibly, she shifts her body to face him and asks 'Say, has anyone ever told you you look like …' 'Colin Farrell?' he responds without hesitation. She shakes her head and squirms indignantly. 'No, Fred from Breakfast at Tiffany's?' For a moment he is speechless, having long felt an affinity with that very character. 'So, that would make you Holly Golightly, right?' 'Well, I do have a no-name cat and a Japanese landlord upstairs.' She smirks. 'By the way, I'm Emilia. 'Oscar.'

Emilia explains how she'd adopted Cat from Hounslow Animal Welfare Society. He'd been rescued from a French magician who'd used him as a prop the same way most others use rabbits and doves. So, she said, this meant every so often Cat performed tricks out of the blue. He could stick his tongue out, fake sneezes, walk backwards on his front paws and even meow 'La Marseillaise', although Emilia had only witnessed Cat's piece de resistance twice and both times she'd been stoned. 'And what about your Japanese landlord?' She shakes her head. 'Never heard him meow La Marseillaise, stoned or otherwise, but you should try his homemade Sake!' 'I should …' he smiles, noticing how the golden light is dancing in her eyes. The hint at potential familiarity makes them both look away and a comfortable silence settles between them. He asks if she is from London and she points over the river towards Thames Ditton. As he looks across, a gleaming pleasure cruiser ambles past and for just a moment he is captivated by their reflection replicated over and over in sequence across its slender windows. 'I grew up in the north west,' he tells her, 'but moved to London. New Malden,' he motions back towards Kingston, 'about ten years ago, to follow a girl.' She shakes her head. 'Will you boys never learn?' She asks whether he had noticed anywhere on his walk where she could buy ice-cream and when he responds in the negative, suggests they head back towards Kingston before it's too late in the day.

Soon enough, they come across an ice-cream van parked by the side of the river and he asks Emilia what she would like, saying that this is his treat. When she protests, he tells her that she is hurting an old man's feelings. She asks for a 99 Flake. 'With bits and juice?' he asks. She gives him a puzzled look. 'Hundreds and thousands and strawberry sauce,' he explains. 'Just juice.' She smiles with a disarming shrug. He walks over to the ice-cream van and places their order. The heat of the day is now beginning to wane and she unbuttons her denim jacket, and places it over her shoulders as he pays for and passes her the ice-cream. She immediately takes a giant lick and motions for them to continue their stroll beside the river.

Other than the ambling pleasure cruiser, the river is still. The schoolboys have completed their herculean practice-laps, returned to their rowing clubs, heaved-out, washed-down and stowed their boats, showered and emerged, exhausted but energised, to amuse themselves in the town centre until the imposition of their curfews. The older families have moored and secured their launches and now find themselves engrossed in preparations for intimate evening meals with their neighbours during which too much valuable wine will be consumed and their companionship reaffirmed through the retelling of favourite memories. The young families will be serving small warm portions of grown-up food and then, as brightly-patterned pyjamas are climbed into and milk teeth scrubbed, a chorus of pleas for just one more story before lights out will sound all over Kingston. He thinks back to the little girl with the tiny fistful of breadcrumbs and reflects that his niece will be pleading louder than most. The friends have long-finished their runs and gone their separate ways, either farewelling until the next weekend or to reconvene later in the evening. The Police community support officers have filled-out their reports for what was an unusually quiet day, changed out of their stifling

217

uniforms and blended back into the civilian population. The students will be snatching convenient, cheap and unnutritious suppers before rendezvouing to jest and flirt in front of heaving bars or make hard-earned spending money behind them. But where do the brilliant green parakeets nest and what of the homeless man and the scruffy little Jack Russell with only one ear? And as for the lovers …

As they finish-off their cones, she asks him to tell her a joke. 'What, like a made-up story about a performing cat?' She punches him playfully on the arm and reaches into her purse, producing a badly-focused picture of a cat walking backwards on his front paws. He scratches his head, purses his lips and says 'Okay. You ready? Here's one of my best. A man walks into the Doctor's dressed only in Clingfilm. The Doctor says "Well I can clearly see you're nuts"'. Emilia walks around and away from him protesting 'That's awful!' 'Let's see you do better then.' She thinks for just a moment, then says 'I'll tell you something funny that happened to me recently instead.' She explains that she had just returned from a ten-day yoga retreat on the west coast of India where she had been awoken by a bell at 4.30 every morning and, for the following twelve hours, put through a gruelling round of yoga routines of ever-increasing intensity, interspersed with guided meditation, a minimum quantity of food and all this conducted in absolute silence. As a special treat on the afternoon of the last day, her cohort of international delegates were lead by their Swami to an idyllic beach and invited to recite a traditional song from their culture. Emilia thought that the idea was that everyone would join in, so chose "If you're happy and you know it". As she clapped, nodded and stomped along, she was aware that no-one was joining in, but put that down to the fact that she was first up and, after ten days of silence, it would inevitably take time for the ice to melt. She soon realised the error of her ways when the second delegate from Sweden sang an ancient Norse sea shanty, the third from Sri Lanka a mystical chant translated from Sanskrit, the fourth from New Zealand a sacred Maori funereal blessing and so on. 'How embarrassing' he whispers. 'Good job you don't blush'. 'Yeah, now I know how Raymond Stantz felt when he thought of the Stay Puft Marshmallow Man!'

The golden light is starting to fade now and he asks if she has any plans to watch the World Cup final later. She shakes her head slowly, smiling and he asks if she likes football. Again she shakes her head slowly, widening her smile. Undaunted, he says that they should head back towards Kingston together for a drink. Under the streetlights, Kingston is amber. The whole of Kingston, its roads and its pavements, its walls and its buildings, its grass and its trees, its men and women, their clothes and their dogs and their shiny cars, her hand he is holding and even the few clouds above. If there was never any sunlight again, the whole of Kingston would be amber for ever. On the bridge, they pause and he leans forward, closing his eyes and slowly kisses her lips. Lost to the moment, he feels an energy all around them which almost lifts him off the ground. Emilia opens her eyes and looks up at him mischievously. 'Hmm, what would Holly do?' 'Probably jump off the bridge!' Her face suddenly becomes serious and she leans over the edge of the bridge seemingly gauging the drop to the water below. 'You can swim can't you?' she says, poking him in the stomach. He nods his head slowly, frowning, at which point she takes a short running jump and pushes herself up and over the ledge. For just a moment he pauses, shaking his head in disbelief, then rushes to the ledge. Looking down into the void, he is just able to make out where she has broken the surface of the water below. As she surfaces, Emilia shouts up gleefully 'And what would Fred do?'

He falls and everything is darkness; immense blinding cold darkness enshrouding under the surface of the water. For just a moment, the seams that bind the vast depths of the water with the surface of the water are consumed, everything is consumed by immense blinding cold darkness. As he nears Emilia, he feels the energy pulling him towards her outstretched arms and the amber of Kingston's streetlights fading behind them. 'I think we're going to miss kick-off. I'm sorry,' she gasps as he reaches and pulls her towards him. 'And I think we're going to struggle to match this first meeting of our beautiful reading group.'

SUTTON

Belmont Nights

Belmont Nights

Nicola Monaghan

1. Night Bus

The night bus trundled along, onward, endlessly, past all the battered shop fronts on its way to the very edge of London. Charlie was getting used to this journey now, beginning to know its sway and flow across the streets, to recognise the places where the signs were so out of date they still read 01 for the dial code.

London no longer looked strange or exotic to her. Bizarre to think now how south London had when she'd first moved there, in a knock off, run down, shabby kind of way. It had looked like a place other families lived, other types of people who weren't like Charlie's folks back home. Now, though, it just looked like Clapham or Balham or Tooting or Sutton. It was just places on the way home to Belmont, about as exotic as a cup of tea. Charlie had wanted to move to London, wished for it with every birthday candle until she expected it to happen and, inevitably, it had come as a bit of an anticlimax.

For starters, she wasn't sure she lived in London at all. Belmont was officially London. It was the very edge of the London borough of Sutton and, some of it at least, was even in the *A to Z*, which had to mean something. She had walked to the very edge of London one day, followed the map like Alice down the rabbit hole. She wasn't sure what she thought might happen. It hadn't been far from her dingy little studio flat that she'd stood, one foot in London and one in Surrey. An old gent walking past had given her a funny look. She didn't know exactly what she had expected it to feel like, but it wasn't like this.

The bus shuddered as it pulled out from a stop and Charlie's stomach flipped. She thought about that night's gig. It had gone okay but she hadn't been on top form. She wasn't sure about the band she was working with. They were called *Something for the Weekend* and she'd kind of liked the name, which was why she'd auditioned. Of course, they'd loved her. A young, punkish, pretty girl with long blonde hair and a nose stud who could really play the drums; she never exactly had problems getting bands to take her on. This one, though, wasn't working out as well as she would have liked. She hated to admit it, but they were a bit of an old man band. The singer must have been late forties if he was a day. Tonight, she'd been put off by his sex face when he was singing. She'd noticed some male singers did this, holding the microphone like it was a lover, face up and close and eyes pulled tight, and she was just certain it was the same face they'd pull when they came. The thing that had disturbed Charlie tonight is that she'd been kind of fascinated by Zed's version of this face. She'd hardly been able to look away but it hadn't been like rubbernecking; she'd been kind of attracted. She shuddered, thinking about it. He was way too old!

The bass player, Adam, he was younger, but he wasn't exactly a dude or anything. He was already balding, and wore the rest of his hair long and lank, as if that might make up for it. He was incredibly talented, and could play anything but he worked as a music teacher. She couldn't imagine him making it in the real world. By rights, based on talent, Adam should have been really famous but he didn't have the X-factor – there was no other way to describe it. She hated that show, with a passion, it was the one thing in the business she had sworn she'd never have any part of. But there was something to it, to the idea of what it took to make it as a musician or band. It wasn't about looks, not really. It was something much less definable than that. Charisma or a presence maybe. The thing that was missing in Adam almost defined what it took, when Charlie really thought about it and, despite his age, Zed had it in spades.

Weekend, as they were known to fans, got plenty of gigs. Zed lived in Tooting and so a lot of their performances were in pubs around there but they were offered stuff in town regularly too. They were entertaining and they didn't play their own stuff so the punters could sing along. That was what it boiled down to, Charlie thought. They would never make it big, though, get to recording their own songs or even writing them. Zed talked about it sometimes, his eyes far away with hope and his face red with the force of his ideas, but he never got round to putting pen to paper. Charlie was a realist; as much as she liked them, these guys were a stepping stone, a chance to be seen out and about and picked up by someone better. People who were going somewhere.

Meanwhile, she was going somewhere. Home, eventually. It would be a while, yet, though. The bus banked a corner viciously and sent her flying to the window. She'd been miles away. She was still miles away, not even in Sutton yet. It had started raining, making wet tracks down the massive windscreen in front of her. She watched through the glass as the borough she lived in came into view. She felt cold, and pulled her coat around her. Perhaps she would look for somewhere more central to live soon. Zed had mentioned a mate who was looking for lodger. She wasn't sure she'd be able to afford it but maybe she'd be better going without food than living such a trek out of the way. She would like to be able to tell people that she lived in London without feeling like she was lying to them.

2. Last Train

Charlie had run so fast for the train and got so out of breath she still felt kind of shaky the other side of Clapham Junction. It had been an early doors gig but it had still been a hair's breadth thing whether she made the train on time. In the week, the last train to Belmont left at ten to eleven. Even on the weekend it was only half past. And it had become a point of principle that she should catch the train wherever possible no matter what it took.

The thing was, the alternative was the night bus. There was something totally depressing about the mix of people you got on these particular vehicles. Like it was the folks who'd missed out on getting somewhere with their lives. You could see it in their faces, half drunk maybe, or stoned or high, but whatever else they were disappointed to find themselves where they were. It was like a microcosm or whatever the shit they call it; where you were in terms of transport home of a night was where you were in life. Only people with no choices rode the night bus. Charlie didn't fit with them. She had no money and so no choices by default, but that was only a time of life thing. It would change, once she'd made it, even once she started getting regular session work that would change. But the scary thing about being on the bus was that it might not. Charlie always sat at the front, on the top deck, so that she could avoid the other people, but she couldn't help catching their reflections in the massive windscreen. She would look at the older women reproduced there, examine their faces, the way they slouched as they sat and she could see the disappointment, and wonder what it was they'd wanted and missed out on. She'd began to do anything she could to avoid ending up on that bus at the end of the night.

And so her life had become a succession of rushed packing at the end of the gig and trying to chivvy up the blokes to load the van as quickly as possible so that she could dash for the train. Her main image of herself these days involved running from the party with her shoes coming off; Cinderella plays the drums and legs it so that she doesn't have to sit with the pumpkins on the bus. She usually made it. There was something comforting about travelling on the train, maybe to do with the steady rhythm of its motion. Despite the fact it was still public transport, and that there was still the odd dodgy drunk travelling with her, the train was more like being in London. Perhaps this was because she'd always taken the bus back when she lived in Birmingham and dreamed of a life in the capital city. It hadn't panned out exactly the way she'd thought it would, but she'd not been a silly naïve girl and had known her dreams of trendy flats with minimalist furnishings were years away so that didn't bother her. It was other things, really, that did, long journeys home after gigs and the way people's faces twisted as they said 'Belmont? Isn't that in Surrey somewhere?'

Sex face Zed had mentioned that mate of his again tonight, the one who was looking for a lodger. The money was quite a bit more than she was paying at the moment for the flat to herself in Belmont. Her studio was only two rooms, one for living and eating and a tiny bathroom, but it was all hers. She wasn't at all sure she'd like sharing with a mate of Zed's. He would be quite a lot older than her, she was guessing. The idea of living with someone Zed's age was not attractive. It was a bit like the sex face. There was something about the extra experience these men had that appealed to her and that, in itself, was frightening.

At last, tonight, the puzzle of Zed's nickname worked itself out. Charlie had been wondering for ages, but she'd been too shy to ask. Some woman he'd dated years ago came to say hello, and she'd called him Pete, much to Adam bass player's amusement. Zed explained that the nickname came from playing darts down the pub. He said there were a million blokes with the first initial P in his generation, lots of Peters and Pauls and Patricks. He'd got fed up of having to put down two initials and it getting confusing anyway and so one day he'd just walked up and written Z on the board and it had stuck. Charlie was kind of relieved to hear his story. There was an explanation that made sense and the name wasn't just some posey contrivance.

The whole event made her think differently about Zed, though. It was as if knowing his real name gave her extra information about who he was as a person. She tried to fit the word to him; Pete. It didn't suit and so she understood why the nickname had taken over. She wondered if she'd feel differently had she known him as Pete first, but somehow doubted it. It seemed that he well and truly was Zed, was destined to have that name, and that he'd have been a different person if he'd not walked up to that chalkboard one day and wrote a new self upon it. She sat on the train thinking about Zed and a shiver went through her; she was getting a crush on him, despite the age difference and even despite the sex face or, more shockingly, a little because of it. She pushed all that to the back of her mind and thought about how it had felt tonight, the way everything came together after near disaster on the second track.

She had played really well, even she knew it. Sometimes it was hard to tell how you'd done but tonight it had been really obvious. Being a drummer, especially a female drummer, was full of contradictions. Charlie always got noticed: an attractive girl on drums has novelty value, but that didn't mean her contribution to the music was always understood. Only other drummers ever seemed to get it. The best kind of drummers were the ones so good you didn't see their tracks. And yet these drummers were the people who held it all together, when it came down to it. In fact, they were more than that, a strong heartbeat that made the sound whole and healthy. They'd all played well, though. Even Adam had looked pumped at the end of their second set. They'd sat having drinks afterwards and his eyes had shone as he went on about how they were 'gelling' at last.

The train pulled into Sutton station and was held there for a moment. A drunk on the platform was talking on his mobile phone, then said 'shit' quite loudly as the announcement went off and he scrambled to cut off the line. Charlie watched, wondering who he'd been talking to and why he'd been lying. She studied the man as he sat there and stared at the floor, no doubt concocting excuses for when he got home, get-out clauses. She looked at his face and clothes, the way he sat, searching for things about him that would give someone a clue he was untrustworthy. There was nothing. He looked frighteningly normal. Pissed, but ordinary.

The activities of the evening had taken their toll on Charlie and she wanted to close her eyes and sleep but didn't. She was too worried about not waking up and missing her stop. Belmont was the end of the line and she didn't know where the trains went when they left but she certainly didn't want to end up any further out of town, or miles from her flat with no way of getting back. She felt lost enough already, without a midnight trip to the middle of nowhere. So she kept her eyes open and stared out of the window. It had begun to rain and she watched the snail trails of water as they made patterns on the outside of the glass.

A moment's panic made her sit up and start out of her daze as she thought about her savings. It was an issue she was trying not to think about and she found, the more she did this, the more it snuck up and jumped out on her at quiet moments. The money was running out. She would need a job soon, the kind you go to every day and where you answer to the boss, even to pay the rent on her hovel in the middle of nowhere. She didn't want to work in a supermarket or office but knew she had limited options. She needed something that she could fit in around her gigs. She wondered if she could just about get away with working in a pub, if they were flexible with rotas and she was organised. It seemed a better option that the others that came to mind.

The train was approaching Belmont now. She pulled on her coat and steeled herself for the walk. She shivered; more in response to the thoughts she'd been having about getting a job than to do with the cold. In fact, despite the rain, it was quite a mild night. She hugged herself, though, as she stepped onto the dark platform. She put thoughts about work and running out of money to the back of her mind. She would think about all of that tomorrow. She would think about Zed tomorrow too, she knew, but that was a different matter and it made her cold all over for other reasons.

3. Taxi

Charlie's crush on Zed had built over the next couple of weeks and so, when he invited her round to his place, she'd agreed. She'd thought it was what she wanted.

Tooting was still lively when she got off the Tube. Young girls walked in groups, tottering on heels to the local bars and restaurants. The air smelled of curry and made Charlie feel hungry. She hoped that Zed had plans for food, even if it was just takeaway pizza or something. It struck her for a second that he could have at least offered to meet her from the station. She consulted her *A to Z* as subtly as she could. Someone had warned her once that you should be careful. If people thought you were a tourist they might try to mug you or rip you off. She pulled the book to the top of her bag and tried to open it and read it while still keeping it the other side of the zip. It was no good; she couldn't see a thing and, anyway, she guessed she looked even more clueless trying to read something inside her bag. She moved to the tube station wall and leaned against it as she pulled out the *A to Z* and worked out her route. It wasn't far but he could have met her.

Despite this oversight of his, as she walked down Tooting High Street towards the right road, Charlie let herself drift into a daydream. She imagined Zed as the big romantic, sweeping her away, lifting her and carrying her to his room where they'd make love for days, finally emerging only so that they could fetch her things from the flat in Belmont. Then she would live in Tooting, which was definitely London, no mistaking that.

The road Zed on lived was five minutes' walk from the Tube station.

She checked her *A to Z* again as she saw the sign, and turned right. And then she was there; outside Zed's door. She took a deep breath. Was this really what she wanted? As she rapped the door knocker she realised she was still holding her breath. Moments later the door was open and he was stood in front of her. As soon as she saw him she thought about the sex face, and wondered if she did really have a crush on him or if it was all some weird fascination with the way he sang.

Any part that was left of the fantasy she'd had about living with Zed was blown clean away as she walked into his house. It was a two up two down terrace place, so it wasn't like there wasn't the room, except there was something about the place that said there wasn't the room in Zed for a partner. It took one look round for her to see it clearly. Zed was a bachelor. Everything about his house was set that way; the leather chairs and the furry rug with the lamp that pulled down over it, the bar in the basement and all that shit. Zed lived alone and he liked it that way. There was a moment of disappointment, followed quickly by relief, followed by Charlie remembering that she was only young and didn't want that serious shit anyway. A fling with an older, more experienced man could be just the ticket.

Zed offered Charlie a drink as soon as she walked in but it didn't materialise quickly. She sat and watched as he fiddled with his stereo, a real boy's toys job with an amp and serious speakers, and she chewed at her nails and thought how she could really do with a drink. Ten minutes later she gave up on waiting and asked if she could help herself. He looked up through his fringe, seeming helpless. He stood up straight. 'Shit, sorry,' he said. 'Being a bit crap.' He poured her a glass of the same wine he was drinking without asking what she wanted.

After that, though, Charlie was never without a drink. Three glasses on and she was waiting for Zed's move, fascinated with how it might pan out. She figured whatever else, he'd be smooth and that his moves might leave her breathless, awed in the sense of how sophisticated he was compared to the boys she'd dated before. But the night went on and no moves materialised. He poured her drink after drink, cracking open more wine bottles until she wondered if that was his move, getting her ratted. Certainly boys in sixth form had tried that one before and she was not exactly impressed.

The drink ran out and there was an awkward silence. Then Zed bent towards Charlie, fluttering his lashes and saying 'There's something in my eye.' It was like a spell was broken. Her crush was built on that layer of sophistication she'd thought she'd seen but this one little mistake scraped that away completely. Now all she could see was how yellow his teeth were from smoking and his tummy, the way it bulged above his jeans and, worst of all, the sex face he always pulled when he was singing and, it would seem, when there was something in his eye.

Charlie put down her glass and left the house without saying anything. Zed did not call after her. She phoned for a minicab on her mobile and waited outside. She couldn't really afford a taxi but she didn't have much choice; it was too late for the Tube and she was too freaked out to deal with the night bus on top of all the rest. It was lonely around Zed's street, so she waited right next to the door, figuring she could easily run straight back in if the outside of his place became scarier than the inside. It didn't.

Sitting in the soft leather seats of the taxi, Charlie decided she could never see Zed again. It was too excruciating. She would resign from the band and look for that job, and find new people to play with, closer to her age and maybe girls too, if such a band existed in south London. She would avoid Tooting altogether. She couldn't bump into him, she really couldn't deal with that. It was a relief now to be based all the way out in Belmont and know how unlikely it was that she'd see Zed or any of his mates there. Maybe Belmont was Surrey and not London but it didn't matter. Zed's parents had called him Peter but that wasn't what he was meant to be and this could be the same kind of deal. She liked to think that life made some decisions for you; it just made sense.

The taxi whizzed through the quiet night-time streets and before she knew it she was crossing the border from the borough of Merton and into Sutton. She tried to imagine floating above the city, high enough that it looked like a map. She looked down on herself, gliding towards the edge of London. Something about this picture made her think of the past, where people thought you could sail off the edge of the world.

It was only as the taxi rounded the bend and headed across the railway bridge near Belmont station that a thought struck Charlie; maybe Zed actually had had something in his eye.

4. Vauxhall Corsa

It had been a busy night at *The Belmont* and Charlie's legs hurt as she walked. There was something pleasant about feeling so tired, though, like you'd worked hard and now you deserved the rest you were about to get. The sense of a job well done. After all her worrying, Charlie found working for a living quite satisfying. The landlord of the pub had been great too, and given her all the lunchtime shifts, agreeing that evenings could be negotiable. Not that she was gigging that much, anyway. Her new band, *The Buzbies*, were much closer to where she saw herself belonging but they didn't have the rep to get loads of engagements yet. They played their own stuff, which was that much harder to sell to local pubs than if you were prepared to do covers. They were the real thing, though, she was sure of that. All three of her new band mates were blokes but they were at least a similar age to her. In fact, the lead singer was a year or two younger.

As Charlie walked, her heels clicked along the pavement. She noticed the sound, the way it echoed, and she played with it, faster, slower, 4-4 time, then 3-4 like a waltz, drumming her own way home. She hadn't spoken to any of the other members of *Weekend* since that night at Zed's. She'd sent Zed an email the next day resigning from the band and he'd been good enough not to reply or try to ring her. She'd been relieved and, at the same time, disappointed. The ambitious young drummer inside her thought he could have at least tried a little harder to keep her. Perhaps he'd just got something in his eye again.

All of the lads in the new band lived in Belmont or Sutton. They stayed at home with their parents, *indoors*, as they called it. She'd seen their houses, picking up and dropping off equipment with them in the bass player's van. They were detached jobbies on what estate agents would call 'well appointed' streets. They reminded her of home, Sutton Coldfield, and her parents' house, which made her feel a little sick for those people and places. She started ringing her mum more often.

The converted house that contained Charlie's studio flat came into view. She was happy to see it. It might have been pokey and basic but it was all hers. She still wasn't sure if she lived in London or Surrey. It didn't matter. Outside, Oliver's car was waiting for her. Oliver also pulled a sex face when he was singing but, on one so young, it didn't look so seedy. They'd been dating a few weeks now, approximately half the time she'd been in the band, not that she was counting or anything. She entertained the odd fantasy about where their life might go in the long run, but none of these daydreams revolved around real estate or lettings.

The door opened beside her and she ducked inside, smiling. 'Hey,' she said, climbing into the passenger seat and removing her shoes. She rubbed her feet. She was sore from standing up for so long but it wasn't that bad of a feeling. 'What you been doing?'

Oliver smiled a grin that lit up his whole face. 'I been writing a song, baby.'

She fell back into the seat of his car feeling totally content. He indicated, then pulled out into the road. Charlie wasn't convinced she was in exactly the right place yet but she knew she was moving in the right direction.

CROYDON

How Lucky You Are

How Lucky You Are

Debi Alper

If it wasn't for the photo on his mobile, Max would have no proof that he'd met Ishraqi in real life. It would be easy to believe that she was just a dream. A figment of his twisted imagination.

Max's mum was always telling him his imagination was twisted. His teachers said that was a good thing. Max was creative, they said. The Brit School in Croydon was the ideal setting to nurture his strengths and guide him onto constructive paths. Or some such crap.

Max didn't buy it. Okay, the Brit was a vast improvement on his old school and it was great not to have to wear uniform. But along with the music and performing arts you still had to do the same old boring stuff like Maths and English.

This time last year, he'd been full of enthusiasm for his new school. Until the day he came home to find a bulging rucksack sitting in the hallway. His dad had sat him down, explained how he felt stifled and needed to get away. He was going off travelling, to 'find himself', he said. Max was old enough to understand.

'Look after your mum for me,' his dad had said. 'She'll be fine – probably better off without me.'

Yeah right, Dad. That's why I heard her crying every night for weeks after you left. Fuck off then and if you do manage to find yourself in Thailand or wherever you are, give yourself a kick in the bollocks from me.

Burrowing deeper under his duvet, Max squinted at the grainy image on his mobile screen. Two teenagers, sitting side by side on a concrete wall on the concourse outside the UK Borders Agency building in Croydon Town Centre.

Their arms were linked. Ishraqi was wearing the beanie he'd nicked for her and they were both grinning into the camera.

You would think they'd known each other for ages.

You would think they had a future ahead of them.

You wouldn't think that a moment after the photo was taken, Ishraqi would walk away and Max would never see her again.

Closing his eyes, Max drifted back.

Dan stood at the door of the bus, glaring at Max.

'You can't bunk off,' he objected. 'We've got a Maths assessment today.'

Max shrugged.

'Which, you twat, is the exact reason why I'm bunking off.'

Dan shook his head in disgust.

'You're mad, y'know? You're lucky to have a place at the Brit – and you're just wasting it.'

He jumped off the bus and walked away up the road.

Max sat back in his seat and planned his day. IKEA or one of those big warehouse places out of town? Nah. Boring even if he did have money to spend, which of course he didn't. He could always hang out at the recreation ground at Duppas Hill... Maybe hook up with some other cool kids, kick a ball about, smoke and chill. He might even strike lucky and get to share a spliff.

Peering through the grime on the bus window, Max checked the sky. Uniformly grey with some darker clouds that looked to be heading their way. Were they rain clouds? If he'd concentrated harder in geography lessons, he'd probably know that. Ah well. Best not to risk it.

He decided to stay in the town centre where he could always duck into the Whitgift Centre if it did rain. Jumping off the bus, he pulled his hood down low over his eyes. Just a week ago he'd been bunking and bumped into a teacher who had scooped him up and insisted he return to school.

No sign of the rain, so he headed over to the flat expanse of concrete near the bus stop to have a fag. There was the usual bunch of people milling round outside the vast concrete and glass block looming up into the sky. The sign said the building was the UK Borders Agency and there was a Union Jack fluttering above it, but Max had no idea what went on in there. There was always a diverse group of people hanging out on the concourse, but that didn't mean anything. London's a diverse city. Croydon's a diverse borough.

Besides, Max was sixteen and was focused inwards, unaware of anyone else unless they made a direct impact on him.

Extracting a crumpled packet containing tobacco and Rizlas from the pocket of his skinny jeans, he sat down on a low wall and began the ritual of rolling the thinnest possible fag. The task was engrossing so he was only subliminally aware of the two women hovering in front of him, the older one talking on her mobile.

It was at that moment The Wanker came onto the scene. Everyone knows the type. Shaved head, tattoos, vicious dog, hatred of anyone they think is different . . . The dog was on a long lead and his leering bullet-headed owner was letting it run among the crowd, snarling and snapping at legs. Animal and man shared a physical resemblance that obviously extended to a mutual sense of what constitutes fun.

While Max was hunched oblivious, licking the adhesive strip on his rollup, the dog ran straight for the two women in front of him, circling the older woman's leg. As she struggled to keep balance, she grabbed hold of her companion who in turn staggered, tottered and fell.

Onto Max's lap.

'Oi! Watch it!' Max yelped, holding his fag up out of harm's way.

'Sorry. Sorry,' the girl gasped.

It was obvious she was embarrassed as she scrambled to extricate herself. Dog and owner moved on in search of new victims. The older woman was still on the phone and the girl had gone redder than Max thought possible. He peered up at her and decided she was fit in a shy sort of way. Not the usual goth type he went for – her black hair looked natural for a start - but she had really nice dark eyes.

''S'all right,' Max said with what he hoped was a winning smile.

He wriggled along the wall to make some space. The girl had allowed curtains of dark curly hair to fall forward to cover her blushes. After a moment's hesitation, she perched on the edge of the wall next to him.

'You bunking?' Max asked, patting his pockets for his lighter.

The girl looked shocked.

'No,' she replied. 'I am here for an appointment. To this place.'

She indicated the concrete hulk behind them. Her English was good – better than many of Max's London-born friends – and she had an accent he thought only added to her cuteness factor.

'So what happens in this place?' he asked, not because he was particularly interested in the building, but it was as good a conversation opener as anything else he could think of.

He'd tracked down his lighter but it was thwarting his efforts to look cool by refusing to spark. At that point, the other woman ended her call, leaned over and lit his rollup for him.

'It's part of the Home Office,' she said, sheltering the flame with a cupped hand. 'It's where they deal with immigration – refugees and asylum seekers.'

It wasn't long before the three had exchanged stories. Max thought his was really boring compared to both of theirs. The older woman was called Alexsa and she had a job in a refugee centre as a support worker. She'd originally come to England from Kosovo, as a refugee herself. The blushing girl was Ishraqi. She had left Iran a year and a half ago, after both her parents were arrested at an anti-government demonstration.

'You came here alone?' Max asked trying to wrap his head round what it must feel like to be a kid and leave everything that's familiar and everyone you know to go to a strange country where you don't even understand the language.

'I came here as an un-accom-panied minor,' Ishraqi said, pronouncing the words with care and checking with Alexsa that she'd got it right. 'But Alexsa found me a place to live with an Iranian family and a school too. I learn English and next week I take my GCSEs.'

Max could see she was trying to look modest but was proud of her achievements. To be honest, he was pretty impressed himself and, somewhat to his own surprise, felt no desire to tease her for being a neek.

'So where are your parents now?' he asked.

Ishraqi shuffled her feet and it was Alexsa who replied, though not to the question he had asked.

'Look, guys,' she said. 'I've just been told Ishraqi won't be seen for another few hours.' She turned to the girl. 'We can wait inside. I've got case notes to work on. Have you got a book to read? Or some revision to do?' She gave an apologetic grimace. 'I'm sorry. It's going to be boring but there's nothing we can do about it. We need to stay close in case they call us.'

Seeing his potential diversion about to disappear inside the concrete block, Max felt a lurch of disappointment swiftly followed by a spark of creative genius.

'Hey! I've got an idea,' he said. 'How about Ishraqi and I hang out together?'

He looked into the girl's eyes. They were very brown and very deep.

'I can show you round Croydon,' he added, hoping that sounded a more attractive prospect than he knew it to be.

Alexsa looked dubious.

'I don't think ...' she began.

To Max's delight, Ishraqi cut in.

'Oh, please, Alexsa. We would be careful. What could go wrong? If I stay here with you I will just be bored and worry about the appointment …'

Alexsa gave the pair a long hard look, scrutinising Max through narrowed eyes.

'You don't have a mobile, Ishraqi. I wouldn't be able to contact you …'

'No worries,' Max said. 'You can take my number.'

They both made puppy dog eyes at Alexsa and watched her resolve crumble.

'Okay,' she said, though she still sounded doubtful. 'But you stay in public where you can be seen at all times, you understand? As soon as I hear her appointment's coming up, I'll give you a ring.'

Max quite liked the idea of acting as a tour guide. An empty day filled with something unexpected and different. Why not? It helped that the person he would be guiding was fit. Ishraqi was suitably grateful and he gave Alexsa his mobile number. Alexsa gave Ishraqi a fiver and told her to get a sandwich or something for lunch before walking into the building and leaving them to face the day together.

They stood in the middle of the pavement while Max tried to decide their first destination. Ishraqi gazed round. Blocks of shops, offices and multi-storey car parks towered over them and traffic whooshed past on the dual carriageway. Buses, trucks and cars jostled for space while in the middle of the road trams trundled on humming wires and rails on their own designated track.

'I think we'll start with an overview,' Max said to show how seriously he was taking his role.

He looked at Ishraqi but she appeared frozen. Time for him to take charge.

'C'mon,' he said grabbing her hand.

She allowed him to tow her in his wake as they ran to the tram stop and leapt on board. Finding two seats at the back, they settled in to watch south London roll past their window.

'We'll just take the loop round the town centre,' Max reassured her when she reminded him they mustn't go too far.

'It's so … grey,' she murmured peering out the window. 'No trees and not even much sky with all these buildings.'

'Oi! You dissing my country?' Max teased.

To his dismay, Ishraqi turned round, her eyes wide with horror.

'Oh no!' she protested. 'That would be rude. I would never …'

'Hey, lighten up,' he said nudging her in the ribs. 'I was only joking.'

Seeing she still looked agitated he decided to change the subject.

'So what's your country like then?'

Ishraqi turned back to the window with a sigh.

'There is no future for me in my country,' she said, her voice so quiet he had to lean over to hear her. 'I do not even know where my parents are or if they are still alive.'

Max felt his stomach turn. Just that morning he'd had a huge row with his mum. She drove him crazy with her nagging about homework and taking responsibility and all that crap. But what if she disappeared and he didn't know if he would ever see her again? The thought was too awful to contemplate. Time for another change of subject.

'So what GCSEs are you taking?'

Blimey. Was that ever a wrong move … ? Or maybe a right one because at least it got Ishraqi animated and talking. She listed twelve subjects and then asked what he was taking.

'As few as I can get away with,' he confessed. 'I love music though.'

He told her about his new guitar and amp and an idea occurred to him.

'I've got a gig next weekend,' he said. 'Performing with my band at a club in Purley. Why don't you come? Bring a friend if you like. Or I could meet you and take you there if you're nervous about going on your own.'

'You are in a band?' Ishraqi said, clearly impressed.

'Yep. Death Rat Millennium.'

Ishraqi looked blank.

'The band's name,' he explained. 'You know – rats?'

He stuck his teeth over his lower lip and wiggled his fingers like ears. Ishraqi hesitated for a moment and then began to giggle. At first, Max wasn't sure whether or not to be offended, but her giggles were infectious and before they knew it they were both holding each other up, helpless with laughter, while all around them pensioners and harassed mums with buggies gave secret smiles, remembering how it felt to be young.

'I'm sorry,' Ishraqi gasped when she'd managed to regain control. 'I would love to come. But my GCSEs …'

'Oh, come on,' he replied. 'You've got to have a break from revision every now and then. You can meet the other members of the band. They're cool.'

He was already imagining introducing Ishraqi to his friends.

'Yes,' he would say. 'She's an Iranian asylum seeker,' her exotic status upping his street cred no end.

'But they might think that I am a gropie …' she said.

'A *what*?'

'A gropie. Is that not the right word for a girl who follows a band around?'

'Oh!' Max exclaimed as the penny dropped. 'You mean a groupie!'

And then there they were, collapsing in giggles all over again until Max noticed they had completed the loop of the town centre. He grabbed her hand and they jumped off the tram and headed for the underpass into the Whitgift Centre. As they walked into the temple of the gods of retail, Ishraqi said she had never been in such a large shopping centre before. She stood on the chequered floor in the middle of the towering structure and circled slowly, staring up at the soaring white columns, the ranks of escalators, layer upon layer of shops …

They had lunch in Subway, using Alexsa's fiver and then Max told her he'd show her where to find the coolest gear. Ishraqi was wearing jeans and a sweatshirt which were okay but nothing special.

'You're gonna need something for the gig,' he told her.

When she said she didn't have any money, he flashed her a knowing smile but didn't reply.

Max had thought showing Ishraqi round for the day would be no more than an interesting diversion, but as the time passed he found he was having more fun then he'd anticipated. Once her initial shyness had worn off, she was good company, laughing at his jokes and not moaning when he spent ages admiring the latest mobiles. Other girls would have flounced off ages ago. Ishraqi said she had never owned a mobile and laughed at Max's horrified expression when he said he didn't think he could live without his.

They wandered in and out of stores until they found themselves in H&M, where he persuaded her to try on hats.

'A hat can make all the difference,' he said, feeling like a TV style guru.

After several attempts, he declared a red and black beanie suited her best. Her dark hair tumbled from beneath the wool, framing her face and emphasising her delicate features. With a wistful smile, Ishraqi replaced the hat on the display and turned away. She didn't think anything of it when Max grabbed her hand a moment later and hauled her from the shop.

'Time to go,' he muttered, his eyes darting left and right.

They emerged into the open air and Max stopped to roll a fag. Ishraqi watched as he licked the gum and sparked the lighter, which worked this time.

'Could I have a try, please?' she asked.

Max raised his eyebrows, surprised.

'I feel like I want to try new things today,' she said, looking at him sideways through her lashes. 'Things I've never done before.'

Max passed her the rollup. She sucked and sputtered, handing it back with an expression of disgust.

'We'll just have to come up with something else new for you to try,' he said with a suggestive smirk she couldn't fail to interpret.

Ishraqi blushed but met his gaze full on. They wandered off into the subway, holding hands. In the middle of the underpass, Max stopped, turned Ishraqi towards him and told her to close her eyes. She did as she was told and felt him doing something to the top of her head.

'Open your eyes,' he said.

Obeying instructions, she reached up to feel her head. She lowered her hands and looked at what she held.

'Max! You stole this?' She looked like she was wrestling with her emotions. 'You did this for me?' she whispered.

He nodded, swallowing. Was she going to have a go at him for shoplifting? Maybe even insist he take the hat back? If she did, that would be the end of it. He'd take her back to that Borders Agency place and leave her there. He'd achieved what he wanted and got through most of the day anyway. He looked at her, bracing himself for rejection.

'Max,' she said, her eyes swimming with tears. 'That's so kind. You took a big risk for me. Thank you.'

Max resisted the urge to pump the air in triumph and instead pulled her towards him.

'So why are you crying then?' he asked.

Ishraqi looked away for a moment, her face screwed up like a much younger kid. Yet, at the same time, Max had the weird thought that she looked older and wiser than he would ever be.

'When I first come here to this country,' she said, 'it felt so strange to be able to wear whatever I like. I could choose if I wear a hat or not. Or jeans. Or a short skirt.'

Max looked blank so Ishraqi explained that in Iran she could never leave her home without being covered up from head to foot.

'My mother used to say a day would come when women would be more free,' she said, her eyes were bright with longing. 'We used to dress up together and sometimes she would let me use her makeup. But if we went outside our home we had to be sure no one could see us. Until I came here, no one outside my family and closest girlfriends had even seen my hair.'

It was way beyond Max's comprehension. He searched for something sensitive and intelligent to say and reckoned he did pretty well under the circumstances.

'Your hair is beautiful. And anyway, this is your home now,' he said pulling her closer.

To his delight, she didn't duck away. It wasn't a full on snog, but the kiss was sweet all the same. They drew back and he bit through the label on the hat and rearranged it on her head.

'Next stop, Fairfield Halls,' he announced. 'They have some pretty naff stuff on there but sometimes there's good bands too. I've spotted some really famous people coming in for rehearsals and that.'

As if in confirmation, no sooner had they arrived in front of the imposing theatre than Max saw a familiar figure heading towards them from a cab.

'Shit! That's Jools Holland! Quick.'

Once again, Ishraqi found herself running to keep up with him as he headed straight for the man striding across the pavement to the theatre. Five minutes later, they were both clutching the napkins they'd taken from Subway, now emblazoned with her first ever celebrity autograph.

Just as Max was trying to decide how he could possibly top that, his mobile rang. He squinted at the screen and didn't recognise the number.

'Is it Alexsa?' Ishraqi asked the disappointment evident in her voice.

It was. Apparently Ishraqi would be seen shortly. They had ten minutes to get back to the Borders Agency.

Alexsa watched the young couple walking towards her, arm in arm. Their heads were close together and they were laughing. Ishraqi was wearing a new hat, which really suited her. Max must have bought it for her. It had been a risk but she was glad she had gone with her instincts and decided to trust them both. They seemed to have bonded and had a good time. Alexsa knew the girl was blocking on the possibilities of what might happen at her appointment and she wanted her to have a day she could remember. Just in case …

She had tried many times to explain to her young client about the problems that stemmed from when she had first entered the country. Ishraqi's uncle had pulled some strings and paid for forged papers that said she had a place at a college and was eligible for a student visa. There was no such place of course, but the family had been desperate. Her uncle told Ishraqi that once she was safely in the UK, she should contact a refugee centre he had heard about.

That was how the two women had first met, Ishraqi having used a public phone to call the number she'd been given. By a lucky coincidence, Alexsa had been at the airport that day on another case. The switchboard operator called her and she had met up with the young refugee. Back at the office with a Farsi interpreter, she remembered how her heart had sunk as Ishraqi explained how she'd entered the country.

Alexsa had tried then to explain the implications. If only Ishraqi had declared she was seeking asylum as soon as she'd arrived, things would have been so much easier. They managed to find the girl a place to live and get her enrolled in a school but her status was in jeopardy. As far as the government was concerned, Ishraqi had committed a criminal offence by entering the country under false pretences. Her application for asylum had been turned down, as had her appeal. Alexsa was attempting to make a special appeal on humanitarian grounds that the girl's life could be at risk if she was forcibly returned to Iran.

The timing was bad though. With an election coming up, the government were desperate to demonstrate how hard they were on failed asylum seekers, which is how Ishraqi was currently classified. After several years' experience, Alexsa knew things could go badly wrong at this appointment and her chest tightened as she watched the laughing couple walk towards her.

'C'mon,' she said, masking her anxiety with a tight smile. 'You will be called in a few minutes. We need to go inside.'

Max said he'd wait for them but just as they were about to go, he called them back on impulse and asked Alexsa to take a photo on his mobile. He snuggled up to Ishraqi on the same low wall where they had first met a few hours earlier.

Alexsa clicked the shutter. Max turned to Ishraqi and kissed her for the second time. This time the kiss lasted a little longer and he pulled back with a reluctant pout.

'We have to go now,' Alexsa insisted, twitching from foot to foot.

Max waved goodbye and then hunched over his mobile to text all his friends to tell them that, while they'd spent the day sweating over Maths assessments, he'd had a really cool time with a new girlfriend. Feeling smug, he pressed 'send' and then settled back for a smoke while he waited for the others to return.

Nearly two hours later, the lights in offices, shops and on the streets were winking on. The buses and trams were filling with rush hour commuters. Max's stomach growled and he wondered what his mum would be cooking for tea. His tutor would probably have phoned her to say he hadn't been in, so he'd have to negotiate his way through that. He thought about Ishraqi not knowing if her parents were alive or dead and resolved not to argue with his mum for once. It must be hard for her since his dad buggered off, coping with her own feelings as well as his. She only wanted what was best for him and he knew he wasn't exactly easy either.

Half an hour later, he texted his mum and said he would be home a bit late but would be starving when he got there.

Half an hour after that, he was getting cold. He jumped up from the wall and paced round in circles, blowing on his fingers, and wishing his jeans weren't too tight for him to put his hands in his pockets to keep warm.

Ten minutes later, he tried phoning Alexsa, but the call went straight to voicemail.

Fifteen minutes after that, he saw Alexsa walking out of the glass doors. She was alone, her eyes red, her feet dragging as if she was reluctant to leave. Max ran over, his heart pounding.

'Where … ?'

Alexsa shook her head.

'I'm sorry, Max,' she said, resting her hand on his shoulder. 'They're deporting her. They took her out the back entrance. She's already on her way to Tinsley House.'

'Where … ?' Max said again, as though that was the only word he had access to.

'It's an Immigration Removal Centre near Gatwick,' she said. 'I'm so sorry, Max. I didn't expect this myself. I thought we might still have a chance …'

'But … but … she's got GCSEs next week ...'

Even as he said the words, he realised how stupid they made him sound. But he didn't care. It was wrong. It was just wrong.

'Where will they send her?' he asked, struggling to keep his voice even.

'Back to Iran.'

She squeezed his shoulder, pulled out a pack of cigarettes, took one for herself and gave one to him. Barely aware of what he was doing, he leaned forward for the light and took a deep drag.

'Iran?' he breathed. 'Alexsa – her life could be at risk there. Surely if they knew that they wouldn't …'

He broke off at the pain in the woman's eyes.

'I'm so sorry, Max.'

'There has to be something we can do! She's still in the country. I'll organise a protest on Facebook. I'll get people involved. I know! We could contact Jools Holland. I bet he'd help. We can stop this, Alexsa, we can … We must!'

Alexsa put her arms round Max's thin shoulders and hugged him. He didn't care that he was crying or that people might be watching. He didn't care …

'Go home, Max,' Alexsa told him. 'Go home to your mother. Work hard. Take your exams. And know always how lucky you are.'

When Max arrived home late, his mother took one look at his face and bit off the angry lecture she had been preparing. Instead, she folded her son in her arms and waited for the time he would be ready to talk to her.

Index of Contributors

CATHERINE HETHERINGTON

Catherine Hetherington a psychologist by background has previously written for academic journals and is now working for an energy company. This is her first foray into creative writing.

DAISY GOODWIN

Daisy Goodwin is a TV producer and writer. She writes regularly for the *Sunday Times* and her first novel *My Last Duchess* will be published in August by Headline Review.

daisygoodwin.co.uk

DEBI ALPER

Debi Alper is the author of the Nirvana series of thrillers set in SE London. The first two, *Nirvana Bites* and *Trading Tatiana*, have been published by Orion. She also works as a freelance editor and mentor and hosts creative writing classes.

debialper.co.uk

JEMMA WAYNE

An author, playwright and journalist. After graduating from Cambridge University in 2002, she began her career as a reporter before seeing the publication of her first non-fiction book, *Bare Necessities*, in 2005. While continuing to work as a freelance journalist, in 2009 her first stage play, *Negative Space*, opened to critical acclaim.

jemmawayne.com

JESSICA RUSTON

Jessica Ruston was born in 1977. She is the author of *Luxury*, published by Headline Review, and two non fiction books. She came to Wimbledon to attend the School of Art at the age of 19, and ended up staying.

jessicaruston.com

JONATHAN GREEN

Jonathan Green has written for such diverse properties as *Fighting Fantasy*, *Games Workshop*, *Sonic the Hedgehog*, *Doctor Who*, *Star Wars* and *Teenage Mutant Ninja Turtles*. He is also the creator of the popular steampunk *Pax Britannia* line, published by *Abaddon Books*.

jonathangreenauthor.blogspot.com

MELANIE MCGEE

Mel McGee writes stuff and things. She is 5' 3" tall. She has lived in Wandsworth Town for the past 10 years and she has no intention of leaving. Mainly because she is in love with her hairdresser, Leanne (not in a sexy sexy way).

NEIL RAMSORRUN

Neil Ramsorrun was born in 1979, and after 5 years or so of writer's block, began his literary career with a gold star from Miss Green for the short story 'When I grow up, I want to be a vet'. Neil now runs a social enterprise in Camden working with young people and creative technology. He is allergic to most animals.

neilramsorrun.com

NICOLA MONAGHAN

Nicola Monaghan's debut novel *The Killing Jar* was published in 2006 to critical acclaim and went on to win a Betty Trask, the Authors' Club First Novel Award and the Waverton Good Read. She has since published a second book *Starfishing* and *The Okinawa Dragon*, a novella, as well as a number of stories and articles in anthologies and magazines.

nicolamonaghan.co.uk

NIKESH SHUKLA

Nikesh Shukla is a London-based author and poet who has played in America, India, Kenya and nationwide across the UK. He is resident poet for the BBC Asian Network.

nikeshshukla.wordpress.com

PATRICK BINDING

Patrick Binding. Birmingham born. Manchester schooled. Lost in Asia. Found in Melbourne. Earning his keep as an Educational Consultant and keeping his nose outta trouble learning about the world and running marathons.

RACHAEL DUNLOP

Rachael Dunlop is a writer of short stories and the blog *Butterflies*. She was the winner of the NYC Midnight Creative Writing Championships in 2009 and is herself a fierce champion of all short fiction forms.

rachaeldunlop.blogspot.com

RAJINDER KAUR

Rajinder Kaur loves to write comedy stories about Punjabi life. She is also partial to chocolate and cats.

TENA ŠTIVIČIĆ

Tena Štivičić was born in Zagreb, Croatia. Her award winning plays *Can't escape Sundays*; *Perceval*; *Pssst*; *Two of Us*; *Goldoni Terminus*; *Fragile*; *Fireflies*; *Seven Days in Zagreb* have been performed and produced across Europe and translated to more than ten languages. Her book of columns *The Countdown* has made the top of non-fiction charts in Croatia. Tena lives in London and writes in English and Croatian.

TIM SCOTT

Tim Scott appeared on Radio 4 in the comedy series *And Now In Colour*, and *The Skivers*. He directed and stared in the surreal ITV comedy series *Dare to Believe* and has written a number of children's books as well as two science fiction novels. In 2003 he won a BAFTA for writing and directing the ITV children's programme *Ripley and Scuff*.

TOM BROMLEY

Tom Bromley is an editor and author of nine previous books. His latest book, *All in the Best Possible Taste*, is published by Simon and Schuster in Autumn 2010.

WILL MAXTED

Will Maxted came to London, and his Notting Hill bedsit, amid a riot which was not his fault. He has since met and married the love of his life, and has two lovely children and some rabbits which make a mess. Most recently burgled in Paddington.

About Glasshouse Books

Glasshouse books has a simple mission statement:

To publish books for people who don't read.

Certainly this is open to interpretation. To clarify it means we're trying to reach people who can read, but choose not to read books, be it because they don't have the time, or they don't know what to read, or we're simply not publishing books to cater to their tastes.

Each of our titles focusses on a different area of the market, from helping young people make their first steps into professional life, to celebrating the richness and diversity of london. Uniquely we commission every title we publish.

As part of our remit to reach more readers, we make versions of our titles available to read exclusively on our website:

glasshousebooks.co.uk

In 2010 we will be publishing 5 titles, each one beautifully designed, printed to respect the environment and featuring many exciting debuts.

Books for *me, you, everyone.*

Our titles: *100, Boys & Girls, Bloody Vampires, 33 East* and *33 West*

GLASSHOUSE
B O O K S

LONDON
metropolitan
university

BOYS & GIRLS

Edited by Paul Burston

GLASSHOUSE
B O O K S

A Glasshouse Books Collaboration

Design by Eren Butler

Edited by Bobby Nayyar and Charlotte Judet

Assisted by Kate Du Vivier

Typeset in Arno Pro & Champagne & Limousines

First published 14. 07. 2010

ISBN 978-1-907536-35-9

Glasshouse Books
58 Glasshouse Fields
Flat 30, London
E1W 3AB

glasshousebooks.co.uk

facebook.com/GlasshouseBooks

Printed and bound in Great Britain by TJ International Ltd, Padstow, Cornwall

How to order

Please email sales@glasshousebooks.co.uk or call 020 7001 1177. Alternatively, you can buy online at glasshousebooks.co.uk.

For trade enquiries please contact Turnaround on 020 8829 3000 or email orders@turnaround-uk.com

100
£10
9781907536007

Bloody Vampires
£10
9781907536663

33
£15
IN 2 VOLUMES

BOYS & GIRLS
£10
9781907536090

Me. You. Everyone.

glasshousebooks.co.uk

Bernhard Schlink was born in Germany in 1944. A professor of law at the University of Berlin and a practising judge, he is the author of the major international bestselling novel *The Reader, Flights of Love* and several prize-winning crime novels. He lives in Bonn and Berlin.

Walter Popp was born in Nuremberg in 1948. He studied law at the University of Erlangen and spent postgraduate and research time at Cambridge University and in the USA, where he worked alongside Bernhard Schlink. In 1978, he started a law practice in Mannheim before moving to France in 1983. He now lives in a Provençal village with his teenage daughter and works as a translator.

Self's Punishment

BERNHARD SCHLINK & WALTER POPP
Translated from the German by Rebecca Morrison

PHOENIX

A PHOENIX PAPERBACK

First published in Great Britain in 2004
by Weidenfeld & Nicolson
This paperback edition published in 2005
by Phoenix,
an imprint of Orion Books Ltd,
Orion House, 5 Upper St Martin's Lane,
London WC2H 9EA

A CIP catalogue record for this book
is available from the British Library

ISBN 0 75381 821 3

Typeset by Deltatype Ltd, Birkenhead, Merseyside

Printed and bound in Great Britain by
Clays Ltd, St Ives plc

www.orionbooks.co.uk

Contents

Part Three

Part One

I

Korten summons me

At the beginning I envied him. That was at high school. The Friedrich Wilhelm in Berlin. I was getting the last bit of wear out of my father's old suits, had no friends, and couldn't pull myself up on the horizontal bar. He was top of the class, in PE too, was invited to every birthday party, and when the teachers called him Mr Korten in class, they meant it. Sometimes his father's chauffeur collected him in the Mercedes. My father worked for the state railway and in 1934 had just been transferred from Karlsruhe to Berlin.

Korten can't stand inefficiency. In gym, he taught me how to do the upward circle forwards and the full-turn circle. I admired him. He also showed me what makes girls tick. I trotted along dumbly at the side of the little girl who lived on the floor below and attended the Luisen, just opposite the Friedrich Wilhelm, and gazed adoringly at her. Korten kissed her in the cinema.

We became friends – studied together, national economy for him, law for me – and I was in and out of the villa at Wannsee. When his sister Klara and I got married, he was our witness, and presented me with the desk that is still in my office today, heavy oak, with carved detail and brass knobs.

I hardly work there these days. My profession keeps me on the move, and when I drop in to the office briefly in the evenings, my desk isn't piled high with files. Only the answering machine awaits, its small window letting me know how many messages I have. Then I sit in front of the empty surface and, fiddling with a pencil, listen to what I should take on and what I should avoid, what I should sink my teeth into and what I shouldn't lay a finger on. I don't like getting my fingers burnt. But they can just as easily get jammed in the drawer of a desk you haven't looked in for a long time.

The war was over in five weeks for me. A wound that got me home. Three months later they'd patched me together again, and I completed my legal clerkship. In 1942, when Korten started at the Rhineland Chemical Works in Ludwigshafen and I began at the public prosecutor's office in Heidelberg, we shared a hotel room for a few weeks before we found our own apartments. The year 1945 saw the end of my career as a prosecutor in Heidelberg, and he was the one who got me the first cases in the financial world. Then he began his rise, and he didn't have much time, and Klara's death heralded an end to the Christmas and birthday visits. We move in different circles and I read about him more often than I see him. Sometimes we bump into each other at a concert or a play and we get on. Well, we're old friends.

Then . . . I remember the morning clearly. The world was at my feet. My rheumatism was at bay, I had a clear head, and I looked young in my new blue suit – I thought so anyway. The wind wasn't carrying the familiar chemical odour in the direction of Mannheim, but towards the Pfalz. The baker at the corner had chocolate croissants and I was having breakfast on the pavement in the sun. A young woman was walking along Mollstrasse, drew closer and grew prettier, and I put my disposable container on the window sill and followed her. A few steps later, I was in front of my office in the Augusta-Anlage.

I am proud of my office. I've had smoked glass put in

4

the door and windows of this former tobacco shop, and on the door in elegant golden letters:

'*Gerhard Self – Private Investigations*'.

There were two messages on the machine. The company chairman of Goedecke needed a report. I'd proved his brand manager guilty of fraud, but the manager had contested his dismissal before the labour court. The other message was Frau Schlemihl from the Rhineland Chemical Works requesting her call be returned.

'Good morning, Frau Schlemihl. Self here. You wanted to talk to me?'

'Hello, Doctor Self. General Director Korten would like to see you.' No one apart from Frau Schlemihl addresses me as 'Doctor'. Since I stopped being a public prosecutor, I've not used my title. A private detective with a Ph.D. is ridiculous. But being the good personal assistant Frau Schlemihl is, she's never forgotten Korten's introduction when we first met at the beginning of the 1950s.

'What about?'

'He would like to tell you over lunch at the executive restaurant. Is twelve-thirty convenient?'

2

In the Blue Salon

In Mannheim and Ludwigshafen we live beneath the gaze of the Rhineland Chemical Works. It was founded in 1872, seven years after the Baden Aniline and Soda Factory, by Professor Demel and Entzen, His Excellency, both chemists. The Works have grown since then, and grown and grown. Today they encompass a third of the developed land of Ludwigshafen and boast around a hundred thousand employees. In collaboration with the wind, the rhythm of RCW production determines whether the region, and which part, will reek of chlorine, sulphur, or ammonia.

The executive restaurant is situated outside the grounds of the plant and enjoys its own fine reputation. Besides the large restaurant for middle management, there is a separate area for directors with several salons still decorated in the colours that Demel and Entzen synthesized in their early successes. And a bar.

I was still standing there at one. I'd been informed at reception that the general director would unfortunately be somewhat delayed. I ordered my second Aviateur.

'Campari, grapefruit juice, champagne, a third of each.' The red-haired, freckled girl helping out behind the bar today was happy to learn something new.

'You're doing a great job,' I said.

She looked at me sympathetically. 'The general director's keeping you waiting?'

6

I'd waited in worse places, in cars, doorways, corridors, hotel lobbies, and railway stations. Here I stood beneath gilded stucco and a gallery of oil portraits where Korten's face would hang one day.

'My dear Self,' he said, approaching. Small and wiry, with alert blue eyes, grey crew-cut, and the leathery brown skin you get from too much sport in the sun. In a band with Richard von Weizsäcker, Yul Brynner, and Herbert von Karajan he could take the Badenweiler, Hitler's favourite march, play it in swing, and he'd have a worldwide hit.

'Sorry to be so late. You're still at it, the smoking and the drinking?' He frowned at my pack of Sweet Aftons. 'Bring me an Apollinaris! How are you?'

'Fine. I'm taking it a little slower these days, not surprising at sixty-eight. I don't take every job any more and in a couple of weeks I'll be sailing the Aegean. And you're not relinquishing the helm yet?'

'I'd like to. But it'll take another year or two before anyone can replace me. We're going through a sticky patch.'

'Should I sell?' I was thinking of my ten RCW shares deposited at the Baden Civil Servants' Bank.

'No, my dear Self,' he laughed. 'In the end these difficult phases always turn out to be a blessing for us. But still there are things that worry us, long term and short term. It's a short-term problem I wanted to see you about today and then put you together with Firner. You remember him?'

I remembered him well. A couple of years ago Firner had been made director, but for me he'd always remain Korten's bright-eyed assistant. 'Is he still wearing Harvard Business School ties?'

Korten didn't respond. He looked reflective, as though

7

considering whether to introduce a company tie. He took my arm. 'Let's go to the Blue Salon. It's ready.'

The Blue Salon is the best the RCW has to offer its guests. An art-deco room, with table and chairs by van de Velde, a Mackintosh lamp, and on the wall an industrial landscape by Kokoschka. Two places were set. When we were seated a waiter brought a fresh salad.

'I'll stick to my Apollinaris. I've ordered a Château de Sannes for you. You like that, don't you? And after the salad a *Tafelspitz*?'

My favourite dish. How nice of Korten to think of it. The meat was tender, the horseradish sauce without a heavy roux, but rich with cream. Korten's lunch ended with the crunchy salad. While I was eating, he got down to business.

'I'm not going to get well acquainted with computers at this point. When I see the young people sent to us from university these days, who take no responsibility and are incapable of making decisions without consulting the oracle I think of the poem about the sorcerer's apprentice. I was almost glad to hear the system was acting up. We have one of the best management and business information systems in the world. I've no idea who'd want to know, but you could find out on the terminal that we're having *Tafelspitz* and salad in the Blue Salon today, which employees are currently training on the tennis court, which marriages among the staff are intact and which are floundering, and at what intervals which flowers are planted in the flowerbeds in front of the restaurant. And of course the computer has a record of everything that was previously housed in the files of payroll, personnel, and so on.'

'And how can I help you with this?'

'Patience, my dear Self. We were promised one of the safest possible systems. That means passwords, entry

8

codes, data locks, Doomsday effects, and what have you. All of this is supposed to ensure no one can tamper with our system. But what's happened is just that.'

'My dear Korten . . .' Addressing each other by our surname, a habit from schooldays, is something we'd held on to, even as best friends. But 'my dear Self' annoys me, and he knows it. 'My dear Korten, as a boy even the abacus overwhelmed me. And now I'm supposed to tinker about with passwords, entry codes, and data what-do-you-call-them?'

'No. All the computer business is sorted out. If I understand Firner correctly, there's a list of people who could have created the mess in our system. Our sole concern is finding the right one. That's exactly where you come into it. Investigate, observe, shadow, ask pertinent questions – the usual.'

I wanted to know more, but he fended me off.

'I'm none the wiser myself. Firner will go into it with you. Let's not spend all of lunch talking about this miserable situation – there's been so little opportunity to meet since Klara's death.'

So we talked about the old days: 'Do you remember?' I don't like the old times, I've packed them away and put a lid on them. I should have sat up and paid attention when Korten was talking about the sacrifices we'd had to make and ask for. But it didn't occur to me until much later.

So far as the current day went we had little to say to each other. I wasn't surprised his son had become a member of parliament – he had always seemed precocious. Korten seemed to hold him in contempt but was all the prouder of his grandchildren. Marion had been accepted into the Student Foundation of the German People, Ulrich had won a 'Young Research' prize with an essay about the twinning of prime numbers. I could have told him about my tomcat, Turbo, but let it go.

9

I drained my mocha, and Korten officially ended the meal. The restaurant supervisor bid us farewell. We set off for the Works.

3
Like getting a medal

It was only a few steps away. The restaurant is opposite
Gate 1, in the shadow of the main administrative building,
a twenty-floor banality that doesn't even dominate the
skyline.

The directors' elevator only has push-buttons for floors
fifteen to twenty. The general director's office is on the
twentieth floor, and my ears popped on the way up. In the
outer office Korten entrusted me to Frau Schlemihl, who
announced my arrival to Firner. A handshake, my hand
clasped in both of his, an 'old friend' instead of 'my dear
Self' – then he was gone. Frau Schlemihl, Korten's
secretary since the fifties, has paid for his success with an
unlived life, has faded elegantly, eats cakes, wears a pair of
unused spectacles round her neck on a thin gold chain.
She was busy. I stood at the window and looked out over
the jumble of towers, sheds and pipes to the trading port
and to a hazy Mannheim. I like industrial landscapes and
would be hard pressed to choose between the romance of
industry and the forest idyll.

Frau Schlemihl interrupted my idle musings. 'Doctor
Self, may I introduce you to our Frau Buchendorff? She
runs Director Firner's office.'

I turned around. There stood a tall, slim woman of
about thirty. She wore her dark-blonde hair up, which lent
her youthful face with its rounded cheeks and full lips an
air of experienced competence. Her silk blouse was

11

missing the top button, and the one below was open. Frau Schlemihl looked on disapprovingly.

'Hello, Doctor.' Frau Buchendorff reached out her hand and looked at me squarely with her green eyes.

I liked her gaze. Women only become beautiful when they look me in the eye. There's promise in such looks, even if it's a promise not kept, nor even proffered.

'May I take you through to Director Firner?' She preceded me through the door, with a pretty swing to her hips and bottom. Delightful that tight skirts are back in fashion.

Firner's office was on the nineteenth floor. At the elevator I said to her, 'Let's take the stairs.'

'You don't look like my idea of a private detective.'

I'd heard this often enough. In the meantime I know how people imagine private detectives. Not only younger. 'You should see me in my trench coat.'

'I meant it in a positive way. The guy in the trench coat would have his work cut out for him with the dossier Firner's going to give you.'

Firner, she'd said. Was she involved with him?

'You know what it's all about, then?'

'I'm one of the suspects even. In the last quarter the computer paid five hundred marks too much into my account each month. And via my terminal I do have access to the system.'

'Have you had to pay the money back?'

'I'm not the only one. Fifty-seven colleagues are affected and the firm is considering whether to ask for it back.'

In her office she pressed the intercom. 'Director, Herr Self is here.'

Firner had put on weight. The tie was now from Yves Saint-Laurent. His walk and movements were still nimble, and his handshake hadn't grown any firmer. On his desk lay a bulging folder.

'Greetings, Herr Self. It's good that you're taking this on. We thought it best to prepare a dossier with the details. By now we're certain we're dealing with targeted acts of sabotage. We have managed to limit the material damage thus far. But we have to reckon with new surprises at any time and can't rely on any information.'

I looked at him enquiringly.

'Let's start with the rhesus monkeys. Our long-distance correspondence, unless it's urgent, is saved in the word-processing system and the fax is sent out when the cheaper night rate applies. That's how we deal with our Indian orders, for example, and every half-year our research department requires around one hundred rhesus monkeys with an export licence from the Indian Ministry for Trade. Two weeks ago, instead of a hundred, an order went out for a hundred thousand monkeys. Luckily the Indians thought this odd and double-checked with us.'

I imagined 100,000 rhesus monkeys at large in the plant, and grinned.

Firner gave a pained smile. 'Yes, well, the whole thing does have its comic aspects. The mix-up with the tennis court bookings caused a lot of amusement too. Now we have to check every fax one last time before it's sent out.'

'How do you know it wasn't just a typo?'

'The secretary who wrote the message gave a printout of it as usual to the responsible party to have it proofed and initialled. The printout contains the correct number. So the fax was tampered with while it was in the queue on the hard-drive waiting to be sent. We've also examined the other cases in the dossier and can discount errors of programming or data gathering.'

'Good, I can read about that in the file. Tell me something about the circle of suspects.'

'We approached that in a conventional way. Among the employees who have right of access or access possibilities we eliminated those who've proven their worth here for more than five years. As the first incident occurred seven months ago, we can also discount all those who were only employed after that time. In some cases we could reconstruct what happened the day the system was meddled with; for example, the day of the fax message. Those absent that day are scored off. Then we examined virtually all input on a selection of terminals over a specific period of time and dug up nothing. And finally,' he smiled smarmily, 'we can rule out the directors.'

'How many does that leave?' I asked.

'A good hundred.'

'Then I've got years of work. And what about outsider hackers? You read about stuff like that.'

'We were able to eliminate that with the help of the telecom office. You speak of years – we can see it's not an easy case. And yet time is pressing. The whole thing isn't just a nuisance: with all the business and production secrets we have in the computer, it's dangerous. It's as though, in the midst of battle—' Firner is a reserve officer.

'Forget the battles,' I interrupted. 'When would you like the first report?'

'I'd like you to keep me constantly up to date. You can avail yourself of the men from security, from the computer centre and the personnel department, call on their time as you like. I needn't tell you that we ask for utmost discretion. Frau Buchendorff, is Herr Self's ID ready?' he asked over the intercom.

She entered the room and handed Firner a piece of plastic the size of a credit card.

Firner came round the desk. 'We took a colour photo of you as you entered the administration building and scanned it in straight away,' he said proudly. 'With this ID you can come and go in the complex as you please.'

He attached the card with its plastic clip to my lapel.

It was just like getting a medal. I almost felt obliged to click my heels.

4

Turbo catches a mouse

I spent the evening hunched over the dossier. A tough nut to crack. I tried to recognize a structure in the cases, a pattern to the incursions into the system. The culprit, or culprits, had managed to worm their way into payroll. For months they'd transferred 500 marks too much to the executive assistants, among them Frau Buchendorff, had doubled the vacation benefits of the low-wage groups, and deleted all salary account numbers beginning with a 13. They had meddled with intra-company communication, channelled confidential messages at the directors' level to the press department, and suppressed the automatic reminders of employees' anniversaries of service that were distributed to department heads at the beginning of the month. The programme for tennis court allocation and reservation confirmed all requests for the Friday most in demand so that one Friday in May, 108 players assembled on the sixteen courts. On top of that there was the rhesus monkey story. I could understand Firner's pained smile. The damages, around five million, could be handled by an enterprise as large as the RCW. But whoever had done it was able to saunter through the company's management and business information system at will.

It was getting dark. I turned on the light, switched it off and on a couple of times, but, although it was binary, no deeper revelation about electronic data processing came to me. I pondered whether any of my friends understood computers, and noticed how old I was. There was an ornithologist, a surgeon, a chess grandmaster, the odd legal eagle or two, all gentlemen of advanced years to whom the computer was, as for me, a terra incognita. I reflected on what sort of person it is who can work with, and likes, computers, and about the perpetrator of my case – that it was a single perpetrator was becoming pretty clear.

Belated schoolboy's tricks? A gambler, a puzzle-lover, a joker, pulling the leg of the RCW in grand style? Or a blackmailer, a cool-headed type, effortlessly showing that he was capable of bigger coups? Or a political action? The public would react sensitively if this measure of chaos came to light with a business that handled highly toxic material. But no. The political activist would have thought out different incidents. And the blackmailer could long since have struck.

I shut the window. The wind had changed.

The next day I wanted first to talk to Danckelmann, the head of Works security. Then on to the files of the hundred suspects in the personnel office. Although I was hardly hopeful that the trickster I had in mind would be recognizable by his personnel files. The thought of having to examine one hundred suspects by the book filled me with utter horror. I hoped that word of my hiring would get around and provoke some incidents through which the circle of suspects could be narrowed.

It wasn't a great case. It only struck me now that Korten hadn't even asked whether I wanted to take it on. And that I hadn't told him I'd think it over first.

The cat was scratching at the balcony door. I opened up and Turbo laid a mouse at my feet. I thanked him, and went to bed.

5
With Aristotle, Schwarz,
Mendeleyev, and Kekulé

With my special ID I easily found a parking place for my old Opel at the Works. A young security guard took me to his boss.

It was written all over Danckelmann's face that he was unhappy about not being a real policeman, let alone a proper secret serviceman. It's the same with all Works security people. Before I could even start asking my questions he told me that the reason he'd left the army was because it was too wishy-washy for him.

'I was impressed by your report,' I said. 'You imply there could be hassle from communists and ecologists?'

'It's hard to get your hands on the guys. But if you put two and two together, you know which way the wind is blowing. I have to tell you that I don't quite understand why they brought you in from outside. We'd have managed to sort it out ourselves.'

His assistant entered the room. Thomas, when he was introduced to me, seemed competent, intelligent, and efficient. I understood why Danckelmann could hold sway as head of security. 'Have you anything to add to the report, Herr Thomas?'

'You should know that we're not simply going to leave the field open for you. No one is better suited than us to catch the perpetrator.'

'And how do you intend to do that?'

'I don't have the least intention of telling you that, Herr Self.'

'Yes, you do. Don't force me to point out the details of my assignment and the powers conferred on me.' You have to get formal with people like that.

Thomas would have remained resolute. But Danckelmann interrupted. 'It's okay, Heinz. Firner called this morning and told us to offer unconditional cooperation.'

Thomas made an effort. 'We've been thinking about setting a trap with the help of the computer centre. We'll inform all system users about the provision of a new, strictly confidential and, this is the decisive point, absolutely secure data file. This file for saving specially classified data is empty, however, it doesn't exist, to be precise, because no data will be entered. I'd be surprised if the announcement of this absolute security doesn't challenge the perpetrator to prove his ability by infiltrating the data file. As soon as it's entered, the central computer will show the coordinates of the user and our case is over.'

That sounded easy. 'So why are you doing it only now?'

'The whole story didn't interest a soul until one or two weeks ago. And besides,' his brow furrowed, 'we here at security aren't the first to be informed. You know, security is still regarded as a collection of retired, or even worse, fired policemen who might be capable of setting an Alsatian on someone climbing over the fence, but who have nothing in their heads. Yet these days we're pros in all questions of company security, from the protection of objects to the protection of people, and data. We're currently setting up a course at the technical college in Mannheim which will offer certification in security studies. In this, as ever, the Americans are—'

'Ahead,' I finished. 'When will the trap be ready?'

'This is Thursday. The head of the computer centre

wants to see to it himself over the weekend, and on Monday morning the users are to be informed.'

The prospect of wrapping the case up on Monday was enticing, even if the success wouldn't be mine. But in a world of certified security guards guys like me don't have much of a place anyway.

I didn't want to give up immediately, however, and asked, 'In the dossier I found a list with around a hundred suspects. Does security have any further information on one or another of them, something that's not in the report?'

'It's good that you mention that, Herr Self,' said Danckelmann. He heaved himself up from his office chair and as he came over to me I noticed he walked with a limp. He followed my gaze. 'Vorkuta. In nineteen forty-five, age eighteen, I was taken to a Russian prisoner-of-war camp. Came back in fifty-three. Without old Adenauer I'd still be there. But to return to your question. We are in fact privy to some information about the suspects that we didn't want to include in the report. There are a couple of political cases that the Secret Service keeps us up to date on. And a few with problems in their private life – wives, debt, and so on.'

He rolled off eleven names. As we worked through them I quickly gathered that the so-called political ones concerned only the usual trifles: signed the wrong leaflet as a student, stood as candidate for the wrong group, marched at the wrong demonstration. I found it interesting that Frau Buchendorff was among them. Along with other women she had handcuffed herself to the railings in front of the house of the Minister for Family Affairs.

'Why were they doing it?' I asked Danckelmann.

'That's something the Secret Service didn't tell us. After divorcing her husband, who apparently coerced her into such things, she stopped attracting attention. But I

20

always say, whoever was political once can't shake it off from one day to the next.'

The most interesting person was on the list of 'Losers', as Danckelmann called them. A chemist, Frank Schneider, mid-forties, divorced several times. A passionate gambler. He'd grown conspicuous when he started going to the wages office too often to ask for advances.

'How did you latch on to him?' I asked.

'It's standard procedure. As soon as someone asks for an advance a third time, we take a look at him.'

'And what does that mean exactly?'

'It can, as in this case, involve going so far as shadowing a person. If you want to know, you can talk to Herr Schmalz, who did it at the time.'

I had a message sent to Schmalz that I'd expect him for lunch at twelve noon at the restaurant. I was about to add that I'd be waiting for him by the maple at the entrance, but Danckelmann brushed me aside. 'Leave it. Schmalz is one of our best. He'll find you all right.'

'Here's to teamwork,' said Thomas. 'You won't hold it against me that I'm a bit sensitive when our responsibility for security is removed. And you are from the outside. But I have enjoyed our pleasant chat, and' – he laughed disarmingly – 'our information on you is excellent.'

On leaving the redbrick building where security was housed, I lost all sense of direction. Maybe I used the wrong stairs. I was standing in a yard along the lengths of which the company security vehicles were parked, painted blue with the company logo on the doors, the silver benzene ring and in it the letters RCW. The entrance at the gable end was fashioned as a portal with two sandstone pillars and four sandstone medallions from which, blackened and mournful, Aristotle, Schwarz, Mendeleyev, and Kekulé regarded me. Apparently I was standing in front of the former chief administration building. I left the yard, and came to another, its façades completely covered with Virginia creeper. It was oddly quiet; my footsteps resounded exaggeratedly on the cobblestones. The buildings appeared to be disused. When something struck my back I whirled around in fright. In front of me a garishly bright ball gave a few more bounces and a young boy came racing after it. I retrieved the ball and approached the boy. Now I could make out the windows with net curtains in the corner of the yard, behind a rosebush, next to the open door. The boy took the ball from my hands, said 'thank you', and ran into the house. On the nameplate by the door I recognized the name Schmalz. An elderly woman was looking at me suspiciously, and shut the door. Again it was absolutely quiet.

6

A veal ragout on a bed of mixed greens

When I entered the restaurant, a small, thin, pale, black-haired man addressed me. 'Herr Self?' he lisped. 'Schmalz here.'

My offer of an aperitif was declined. 'No thank you, I don't drink alcohol.'

'And what about a fruit juice?' I didn't want to forgo my Aviateur.

'I have to be back at work at one. Happy if we could directly . . . Little to report anyway.'

The answer was elliptical, but without sibilants. Had he learned to eradicate all 's' and 'z' words from his working vocabulary?

The lady at the reception area rang the bell for service, and the girl I'd seen serving at the directors' bar took us up to the large dining hall on the first floor to a window table.

'You know how I love to begin a meal?'

'I'll see to it straight away,' she smiled.

To the headwaiter Schmalz gave an order for 'A veal ragout on a bed of mixed greens, if you would.' I was in the mood for sweet and sour pork Szechuan. Schmalz eyed me enviously. We both passed on the soup, for different reasons.

Over my Aviateur I asked about the results of the investigation of Schneider. Schmalz reported extremely precisely, avoiding all sibilants. A lamentable man, that

Schneider. After a row over his demand for an advance, Schmalz had tailed him for several days. Schneider gambled not only in Bad Dürkheim but also in private backrooms and was accordingly entangled. When his creditors had him beaten up, Schmalz intervened and brought Schneider home, not seriously injured, but quite distraught. The time had come for a chat between Schneider and his superior. An arrangement was entered into: Schneider, indispensable as a pharmaceutical researcher, was removed from work for three months and sent to a clinic, and the relevant circles were informed that they were not to allow Schneider to gamble any more. The security unit of the RCW used its influence around Mannheim and Ludwigshafen.

'A good three-year gap while the guy lay low. But in my opinion he remained a ticking bomb, even ticking today.'

The food was excellent. Schmalz ate his at a rush. He didn't leave a single grain of rice on his plate – pedantry of the food neurotic. I asked what, in his opinion, should be done with whoever was behind the computer shambles.

'Above all, interrogate him thoroughly. And then make him get in line. He can't be a threat to the plant any more. Bright guy. He could . . .'

He flailed around for a non-sibilant synonym for *certainly* or *surely*. I offered him a Sweet Afton.

'Prefer my own,' he said, and took a brown plastic box from his pocket containing homemade filter cigarettes. 'Made by my wife, no more than eight a day.'

If there's one thing I hate, it's homemade cigarettes. They are way up there with crocheted modesty covers for toilet paper. The mention of his wife reminded me of the janitor's apartment with the nameplate 'Schmalz'.

'You have a young son?'

He looked at me guardedly and deflected the question with a 'Meaning what?'

I told him about how I'd lost my way in the old factory, of the enchanted atmosphere of the overgrown yard and the encounter with the little boy with the brightly coloured ball. Schmalz relaxed and confirmed that his father lived in the janitor's flat.

'Member of our unit, too. The general and he knew one another well from the war. Now he . . . keeping an eye on the old plant . . . In the morning we take the boy to him, my wife being an employee here in the company, too.'

I learned that lots of the security people had lived in the compound and Schmalz had more or less grown up there. He'd been through the rebuilding of the Works after the war and knew its every corner. I found the idea of a life spent between refineries, reactors, distilleries, turbines, silos, and tank wagons, for all its industrial romance, oppressive.

'Didn't you ever want to look for a job beyond the RCW?'

'Couldn't do that to my father. His motto: we belong here. Did the general throw in the towel? No, nor do we.' He looked at his watch and leapt up. 'Too bad, can't linger. Am on personal security' – words he spoke almost error free – 'duty at one o'clock. Kind of you to invite . . .'

My afternoon in the personnel office was unproductive. At four o'clock I conceded I could quit studying the personnel files once and for all. I stopped by to see Frau Buchendorff, whose first name I now knew to be Judith, also that she was thirty-three, had a degree in German and English, and hadn't found a job as a teacher. She'd been at the RCW for four years, first in the archives, then in the PR department where she'd come to Firner's attention. She lived in Rathenaustrasse.

'Please don't get up,' I said. She stopped feeling for her shoes with her feet under the table, and offered me a coffee. 'I'd love one. Then we can drink to being

25

neighbours. I've read your personnel file and know almost everything about you, apart from how many silk blouses you own.' She was wearing another one, this time buttoned up to the top.

'If you're coming to the reception on Saturday, you'll see the third one. Have you received your invitation already?' She slid a cup over to me and lit a cigarette.

'What reception?' I peered at her legs.

'We've had a delegation from China here since Monday, and as a finale we want to show them that not only our plants, but also our buffets are better than the French. Firner thought it would be a chance for you to get to know a couple of interesting people for your case, informally.'

'Shall I also have the chance to get to know you informally?'

She laughed. 'I'm there for the Chinese. But there is one Chinese woman, I haven't figured out what she's in charge of. Perhaps she's a security expert, who wouldn't be introduced as such, so a kind of colleague of yours. A pretty woman.'

'You're trying to fob me off, Frau Buchendorff! I shall have to lodge a complaint with Firner.' Scarcely had the words left my lips than I regretted them. An old man's hackneyed charm.

7

A little glitch

The next day the air lay thick over Mannheim and Ludwigshafen. It was so muggy that, even without moving, my clothes stuck to my body. Driving was staccato and hectic, I could have used three feet to work the clutch, the brake, and the gas pedal. Everything was clogged on the Konrad Adenauer Bridge. There'd been a collision, and immediately after it another one. I was stuck in a traffic jam for twenty minutes. I watched the oncoming traffic and the trains, and smoked to avoid suffocating.

The appointment with Schneider was at half past nine. The doorman at Gate 1 told me the way. 'It's not even five minutes. Go straight on, and when you come to the Rhine it's another hundred metres to your left. The laboratories are in the light-coloured building with the large windows.'

I set off. Down at the Rhine I saw the small boy I'd met yesterday. He'd tied a piece of string to his little bucket and was ladling water out of the Rhine with it. He emptied the water down the drain.

'I'm emptying the Rhine,' he called, when he saw and recognized me.

'I hope it works.'

'What are you doing here?'

'I'm going to the laboratories over there.'

'Can I come with you?'

He shook out his little bucket and came. Children often

27

attach themselves to me, I don't know why. I don't have any, and most of them get on my nerves.

'Come on then,' I said, and we made our way together to the building with the large windows.

We were about fifty metres away when several people in white coats came rushing out of the entrance. They raced along the banks of the Rhine. Then there were more, not only in white coats, but also in blue overalls, and secretaries in skirts and blouses. It was an odd spectacle, and I didn't see how anyone could run in this heat.

'Look, he's waving at us,' the little boy said, and indeed one of the white-coats was flailing his arms and shouting something at us I couldn't understand. But I didn't have to understand; it was obviously about getting away as quickly as possible.

The first explosion sent a cascade of glass shards raining down the road. I grabbed the little boy's hand, but he tore loose. For a moment it was as though I were paralysed: I didn't feel any injury, heard a deep silence in spite of the continuing rattle of glass, saw the boy running, skidding on the glass shards, regaining his balance then finally falling two steps later and somersaulting forward from the impetus of movement.

Then came the second explosion, the scream of the little boy, the pain in my right arm. The bang was followed by a violent, dangerous, evil-sounding hissing. A noise that struck panic into me.

It was the sirens in the distance that made me act. They awakened reflexes inculcated in the war to flee, to help, to seek cover, and give protection. I ran to the boy, tugged him to his feet with my left hand, and dragged him in the direction we'd just come from. His little legs couldn't keep up, but he pedalled his feet in the air and didn't let go. 'Come on, little one, run, we've got to get out of here, don't slow down.' Before we turned the corner I looked back. Where we'd been standing a green cloud was rising into the leaden sky.

In vain I waved at the ambulance tearing past. At Gate 1 the guard took care of us. He knew the little boy, who was clinging tightly to my hand, pale, scratched, and frightened.

'Richard, in the name of God what happened? I'll call your grandfather right away.' He went over to the phone. 'And I'll call the medics for you. That doesn't look good.'

A splinter of glass had torn open my arm and the blood was staining red the sleeve of my light-coloured jacket. I felt dizzy. 'Do you have a schnapps?'

I only faintly recall the next half-hour. Richard was collected. His grandfather, a large, broad, heavy-set man with a bald head, shaved clean at the back and sides, and a bushy, white moustache, gathered up his grandson effortlessly into his arms. The police tried to get into the Works to investigate the accident, but were turned away. The doorman gave me a second and a third schnapps. When the ambulance men came they took me with them to the Works doctor, who put stitches in my arm and wrapped it in a sling.

'You should lie down for a while next door,' said the doctor. 'You can't leave now.'

'Why can't I leave?'

'We have a smog alarm, and all traffic has been stopped.'

'What's that supposed to mean? There's a smog alarm, and no one can leave the centre of the smog?'

'Your understanding of it is completely wrong. Smog is a meteorological overall occurrence and has no centre or periphery.'

This I considered complete nonsense. Whatever other sort of smog there might be, I'd seen a green cloud growing larger. It grew larger right here over the compound. And I was supposed to stay here? I wanted to talk to Firner.

In his office a crisis headquarters had been set up. Through the door I could see policemen in green, firemen in blue, chemists in white, and some grey gentlemen from the management.

'What actually happened?' I asked Frau Buchendorff.

'We had a little glitch on site, nothing serious. But the authorities foolishly turned on the smog alarm, and that caused some excitement.'

'I got myself some little scratches at your little glitch.'

'What were you up . . . ah, you were on your way to Schneider. He's not here today, by the way.'

'Am I the only injured person? Were there any deaths?'

'What are you thinking of, Herr Self? A few first-aid cases, that's all. Is there anything else we can do for you?'

'You can get me out of here.' I had no desire to battle my way through to Firner and be saluted with a 'Greetings, Herr Self.'

A policeman sporting several badges of rank emerged from the office.

'You're driving back to Mannheim, aren't you, Herr Herzog? Would you mind taking Herr Self with you? He got a few scratches and we don't want to keep him waiting here any longer.'

Herzog, a vigorous type, took me with him. Gathered in front of the gates to the Works were some police vans and reporters.

'Do avoid having your photograph taken with that bandage, please.'

I had absolutely no desire to be photographed. As we drove past the reporters I bent down to reach for the cigarette lighter, which was low on the dashboard.

'Why did the smog alarm go off so rapidly?' I asked on our drive through deserted Ludwigshafen.

Herzog proved to be well informed. 'After the spate of smog alarms in the autumn of nineteen eighty-four we in Baden-Württemberg and the Rhineland–Palatinate started an experiment with new technology on a new legal basis, with overriding authority over both states. The idea is to record the emissions directly, to correlate with the weather report, rather than just setting off the smog alarm when it's already too late. Today the model had its baptism of fire. Until now we've only had dry runs.'

'And how is cooperation with the Works? I gathered that the police were being turned away at the gate.'

'That's a sore point. The chemical industry is fighting the new law tooth and nail. At the moment there's a complaint about infringement of the constitution before the Federal Constitutional Court. Legally we could have entered the plant, but we don't want to rock the boat at this stage.'

The smoke of my cigaret̶ ̶ ̶ ̶ting Herzog, and he rolled down the windo̶ ̶ ̶ ̶ ̶ ̶aid, rolling it up straight away, 'co̶ ̶ ̶ ̶ ̶ ̶ut your cigarette.' A pungent̶ ̶ ̶ ̶ ̶ ̶r, my eyes began to strea̶ ̶ ̶ ̶ ̶d we both had a co̶

'It's just as̶ ̶ ̶ breathing ap̶ ̶ ̶ Adenauer ̶ ̶ officers s̶ ̶ edge of̶ ̶ The ̶ ̶ wit̶ h̶ afternoon, to be able to get out the workers and the RCW employees. That would considerably relieve the problem of rush-hour traffic. Some may have to spend the night at their workplace. We'd inform them of this via radio and loudspeaker vans. I was surprised before how quickly we cleared the streets.'

'Are you considering evacuation?'

'If the chlorine gas concentration doesn't decrease by half in the next twelve hours we'll have to clear east of Leuschnerstrasse and maybe also Neckarstadt and Jung-busch as well. But the meteorologists are giving us grounds for hope. Where should I let you off?'

'If the carbon monoxide concentration in the air permits it, I'd be delighted if you'd drive me to Richard–Wagner-Strasse and let me off at my front door.'

'The carbon monoxide concentration alone wouldn't have been enough for us to set off any smog alarm. It's the chlorine that's bad. With that I prefer to know people are safely at home or in their office, not, at any rate, out on the street.'

He drew up in front of my building. 'Herr Self,' he added, 'aren't you a private detective? I think my predecessor had something to do with you – do you remember the case with the senior civil servant and the sailboat?'

'I hope we're not sharing a case again now,' I said. 'Do you know anything yet about the origins of the explosion?'

'Do you have a suspicion, Herr Self? You certainly happened to be at the site of the occurrence. Had you an eye on the RCW?'

'Forget about it. My job is innocuous by comparison. A different direction.'

'If you come down to headquarters . . .' He looked skywards.

Herzog proved to be well informed. 'After the spate of smog alarms in the autumn of nineteen eighty-four we in Baden-Württemberg and the Rhineland-Palatinate started an experiment with new technology on a new legal basis, with overriding authority over both states. The idea is to record the emissions directly, to correlate with the weather report, rather than just setting off the smog alarm when it's already too late. Today the model had its baptism of fire. Until now we've only had dry runs.'

'And how is cooperation with the Works? I gathered that the police were being turned away at the gate.'

'That's a sore point. The chemical industry is fighting the new law tooth and nail. At the moment there's a complaint about infringement of the constitution before the Federal Constitutional Court. Legally we could have entered the plant, but we don't want to rock the boat at this stage.'

The smoke of my cigarette was irritating Herzog, and he rolled down the window. 'Oh Lord,' he said, rolling it up straight away, 'could you please stub out your cigarette.' A pungent odour had penetrated the car, my eyes began to stream, on my tongue was a sharp taste, and we both had a coughing fit.

'It's just as well my colleagues outside have their breathing apparatus on.' At the exit to the Konrad Adenauer Bridge we passed a roadblock. Both police officers stopping traffic were wearing gas masks. At the edge of the approach were fifteen or twenty vehicles. The driver of the first one was in the midst of talking with the police officers. With a colourful cloth pressed to his face, he looked funny.

'What's going to happen with the rush-hour traffic this evening?'

Herzog shrugged. 'We'll have to wait and see how the chlorine gas develops. We hope, in the course of the afternoon, to be able to get out the workers and the RCW employees. That would considerably relieve the problem of rush-hour traffic. Some may have to spend the night at their workplace. We'd inform them of this via radio and loudspeaker vans. I was surprised before how quickly we cleared the streets.'

'Are you considering evacuation?'

'If the chlorine gas concentration doesn't decrease by half in the next twelve hours we'll have to clear east of Leuschnerstrasse and maybe also Neckarstadt and Jungbusch as well. But the meteorologists are giving us grounds for hope. Where should I let you off?'

'If the carbon monoxide concentration in the air permits it, I'd be delighted if you'd drive me to Richard-Wagner-Strasse and let me off at my front door.'

'The carbon monoxide concentration alone wouldn't have been enough for us to set off any smog alarm. It's the chlorine that's bad. With that I prefer to know people are safely at home or in their office, not, at any rate, out on the street.'

He drew up in front of my building. 'Herr Self,' he added, 'aren't you a private detective? I think my predecessor had something to do with you – do you remember the case with the senior civil servant and the sailboat?'

'I hope we're not sharing a case again now,' I said. 'Do you know anything yet about the origins of the explosion?'

'Do you have a suspicion, Herr Self? You certainly didn't just happen to be at the site of the occurrence. Had attacks been anticipated on the RCW?'

'I don't know anything about it. My job is innocuous by comparison and takes a quite different direction.'

'We'll see. I might have to call you down to headquarters to ask you a few more questions.' He looked skywards. 'And now pray for a gusty wind, Herr Self.'

I walked up the four flights of stairs to my apartment. My arm had started to bleed again. But something else was worrying me. Was my job really going in a quite different direction? Was it coincidence that Schneider hadn't come to work today? Had I cast off the idea of blackmail too quickly? Had Firner not told me everything after all?

8

Yes, well then

I washed down the chlorine taste with a glass of milk and tried to change the bandage. The telephone interrupted me.

'Herr Self, was that you leaving the RCW with Herzog? Have the Works called you in for the investigation?'

Tietzke, one of the last honest journalists. When the *Heidelberger Tageblatt* folded, he'd got a job with the *Rhine Neckar Chronicle* by the skin of his teeth, but his status there was tricky.

'What investigation? Don't get any wrong ideas, Tietzke. I had other business at the RCW and I'd be grateful for you not to have seen me there.'

'You've got to tell me a little bit more if I'm not supposed simply to write what I saw.'

'With the best will in the world I can't talk about the job. But I can try to get you an exclusive interview with Firner. I'll be calling him this afternoon.'

It took half the afternoon before I caught Firner between two conferences. He could neither confirm sabotage nor rule it out. Schneider, according to his wife, was in bed with an ear infection. So Firner, too, had been interested in why Schneider hadn't come to work. He reluctantly agreed to receive Tietzke the next morning. Frau Buchendorff would get in touch with him.

Afterwards I tried calling Schneider. No one picked up, which could mean anything or nothing. I lay down on my bed. In spite of the pain in my arm I managed to fall asleep and woke up again in time for the news. It was reported that the chlorine gas cloud was rising in an easterly direction and that any danger, which had never really existed anyway, would be over in the course of the evening. The curfew, which had never really existed either, would be lifted at ten o'clock that night. I found a piece of gorgonzola in the fridge and used it to make a sauce for the tagliatelle I'd brought back from Rome two years ago. It was fun. It took a curfew to make me cook again.

I didn't need a watch to know when ten o'clock came around. Out on the streets a din broke out as if a Mannheim football team had won the German championship. I put on my straw hat and walked to the Rose Garden. A band calling itself Just For Fun was playing golden oldies. The basins of the terraced fountains were empty, and the young folk were dancing in them. I foxtrotted a few steps – gravel and joints crunched.

The next morning in my letterbox I found a postal door-to-door delivery from the Rhineland Chemical Works that contained a perfectly worded statement on the incident. 'RCW protects life,' I discovered, also that a current focus of research was the conservation of the German woodlands. Yes, well then. The delivery included a small plastic cube with a healthy fir-seed suspended in it. How cute. I showed the object to my tomcat and put it on the mantelpiece above the fireplace.

Out on my stroll around the neighbourhood I picked up my week's provision of Sweet Aftons, bought a warm meatloaf sandwich, with mustard, from the butcher on the marketplace, visited my Turk with the good olives, watched the Green Party members at their info-stand on Parade-Platz fruitlessly trying to disturb the harmony between the RCW and the population of Mannheim and

Ludwigshafen. Among the bystanders I noticed Herzog being supplied with fliers.

In the afternoon I sat in Luisenpark. It costs something, just like Tivoli. So at the beginning of the year, for the first time, I'd acquired a year's pass. I wanted to get my money's worth out of it. When I wasn't watching pensioners feeding the ducks I read Keller's *Green Henry*. Frau Buchendorff's first name had led me to the Judith in the book.

At five o'clock I went home. Sewing a button onto my dinner jacket took me a good half-hour with my dodgy arm. I took a taxi from the Wasserturm to the RCW restaurant. There was a banner stretched over the entrance with Chinese characters on it. On three masts flew the flags of the People's Republic of China, the Federal Republic of Germany, and the RCW, flapping in the wind. To the right and left of the entrance were two Rhineland maidens in folk costume, looking about as authentic as Barbie dolls dressed as Munich beer-maids. The procession of cars was in full swing. It all looked so upright and dignified.

9

Groping the décolleté of the economy

Schmalz was standing in the foyer.

'How's your little son doing?'

'Good, thank you. I would like to talk and thank you later. I'm tied up now.'

I went up the stairs and through the open double-doors into the large function suite. People were clustered in small groups, the waitresses and waiters were serving champagne, orange juice, champagne with orange juice, Campari with orange juice, and Campari with soda. I ambled around a bit. It was like any other reception before the speeches were given and the buffet is opened. I sought familiar faces and found the red-haired girl with the freckles. We smiled at each other. Firner drew me into a circle and introduced me to three Chinese men whose names were made up of various combinations of San, Yin, and Kim, as well as Herr Oelmüller, head of the computer centre. Oelmüller was trying to explain computerized data protection in Germany to the Chinese. I don't know what they found so funny about that but in any event they laughed like the Hollywood Chinese in a Pearl S. Buck adaptation.

Then came the speeches. Korten was brilliant. He covered everything from Confucius to Goethe, left out the Boxer Uprising and the Cultural Revolution, and touched on the former RCW branch in Tsingtao solely to weave in the compliment to the Chinese that the last head of branch there had learned a new process for the production of ultramarine from the Chinese.

The Chinese delegation leader replied no less elegantly. He recounted his university years in Karlsruhe, took his hat off to German culture and the economy, from Böll to Schleyer, spoke technical jargon I didn't understand, and closed with Goethe's 'The Orient and Occident can no longer be divided'.

After the president of the Rhineland-Palatinate's speech even a less superb buffet would have seemed exciting. For my first helping I chose the saffron oysters in a champagne sauce. Good thing that there were tables. I hate the stand-up receptions where you have to juggle cigarette, glass, and plate – really you should be fed at them. I spotted Frau Buchendorff at a table with a free chair. She was looking charming in her raw-silk, indigo-coloured suit. The buttons of her blouse were there in their entirety.

'May I join you?'

'You can get another chair, unless you plan on perching the Chinese security expert on your lap straight away?'

'Tell me, did the Chinese pick up on the explosion?'

'What explosion? No, seriously, they were up at Castle Eltz first thing yesterday, and then they tried out the new Mercedes on the Nürburg Ring. When they got back, everything was over. Today the press has really been going at it, mainly from the meteorological angle. How's your arm? You're something of a hero – that couldn't get into the papers, of course, though it would have made a lovely story.'

The Chinese lady appeared. She had everything that German men who dream of Asian women could dream of. Whether she was in fact a security expert I wasn't able to establish either. I asked whether there were private detectives in China.

'No plivate plopethy, no plivate detectives,' she

38

answered, and asked whether there were also female private detectives in the Federal Republic of Germany. This led on to observations about the waning women's movement. 'I've lead almost evelything published in Gehmany in the way of women's books. Why is it that men in Gehmany ahrite women's books? A Chinese man would lose face.'

Fohtunate China.

A waiter brought me the invitation to Oelmüller's table. On the way I selected a second course of sole roulades, Bremen-style.

Oelmüller introduced me to the gentleman at his table, who impressed me with his pedantic skill in arranging his sparse hair over his head: Professor Ostenteich, head of the law department and honorary professor at Heidelberg University. No coincidence that these gentlemen were dining together. Well, back to work. Since my talk with Herzog, a question had been bothering me.

'Could the gentlemen explain the new smog model to me? Herr Herzog of the police talked about it, said it is not entirely uncontroversial. What, for example, am I to understand by the direct recording of emissions?'

Ostenteich felt called upon to lead the discussion. 'That is *un peu délicat*, as the French would say. You should read the expert opinion by Professor Wenzel that most meticulously lays out the relevant distribution of powers, and unmasks the legislative hubris of Baden-Württemberg and the Rhineland–Palatinate. *Le pouvoir arrête le pouvoir* – the Federal law on Emissions Protection blocks any special paths the states might choose. Added to that is freedom of property, protection of entrepreneurial activity, and a company's privacy. The legislator hoped to disregard that with a single stroke of the pen. But *la vérité est en marche*, the Federal Constitutional Court in Karlsruhe still exists, *heureusement*.'

'And how does this new smog alarm model work?' I looked at Oelmüller invitingly.

Ostenteich didn't relinquish his lead quite so easily. 'It's good that you enquire about the technical side of things, too, Herr Self. Herr Oelmüller can explain all that to you in a minute. The crux, *l'essence*, of our problem is: the state and the economy only have a beneficial juxtaposition and cooperation if a certain distance prevails between the two. And, please allow me this rather bold picture: here the state has overstepped itself and groped the décolleté of the economy.' He roared with laughter, and Oelmüller dutifully joined in.

When quiet had again descended, or, as the French would say, *silence*, Oelmüller said, 'Technically the whole thing isn't a problem at all. The basic process of environmental protection is the examination of the vehicles of emissions – water, or air – to check the concentration of harmful substances. If an emission exceeds the accepted levels, one attempts to trace its source and shut it off. So, smog may be created if some factory or other emits more than their allowance. On the other hand, smog may also be created if the level of the emissions at the individual factories remains within the stated limits, but the weather cannot cope.'

'How does whoever's in charge of the smog alarm know what sort of smog he's dealing with? He surely has to react quite differently to each.' The business was beginning to enthrall me. I postponed my next trip to the buffet, and shuffled a cigarette out of the yellow packet.

'Correct, Herr Self, indeed both sorts require a different reaction, but they're difficult to tell apart using conventional methods. It's possible, for example, that traffic has to be stopped and factories have to grind to a halt because a single coal power station that drastically oversteps its accepted emission level can't be identified and stopped in time. What makes the new model irresistible is that, theoretically at least, problems like the one you raised can be avoided. Via sensors, emissions are measured where they originate and transmitted to the Regional Computing Centre that consequently always knows where which emissions are occurring. Not only that, the RCC feeds the emissions data into a simulation of the local weather expected in the next twenty-four hours – we call it a meteorograph – and the smog can be to a certain extent anticipated. An early-warning system that doesn't look as good in practice as it sounds in theory because, quite simply, meteorology is still in its infancy.'

'How do you view yesterday's incident in this respect? Did the model prove its worth?'

'The model worked all right yesterday.' Oelmüller tugged the end of his beard, contemplatively.

'No, no, Herr Self, here I must expand upon the technicians' perspective to present the broader picture. In the old days, quite simply, absolutely nothing would have happened. Yesterday instead we had chaos with all the loudspeaker announcements, police controls, curfews. And to what purpose? The cloud dispersed, without any assistance from environmentalists. Yesterday's event just fanned the flames of fear and destroyed trust and damaged the image of the RCW – *tant de bruit pour une omelette*. I think this is the very case to make clear to the Federal Constitutional Court how disproportionate the new law is.'

'Our chemists are checking whether yesterday's counts really justified the smog alarm,' Oelmüller inserted. 'They immediately began to evaluate the emissions data, which we also record in our MBI, management and business information, system.'

'At least they deigned to grant the industry online

access to the state emissions analysis,' Ostenteich interjected.

'Do you consider it possible, Herr Oelmüller, that the accident and the incidents in the computer system are in some way connected?'

'I've thought about it. Here practically all production processes are controlled electronically, and there are multiple links between the process computers and the MBI system. Manipulations via the MBI system – I can't completely discount it, in spite of all the built-in security measures. Regarding yesterday's accident, however, I don't know enough to say whether a suspicion in that direction makes sense. If so, I would hate to think what could be in store for us.'

Ostenteich's interpretation of yesterday's accident had almost made me forget my arm was still in a sling. I raised my glass to the gentlemen and made my way over to the buffet. With a loin of lamb in its herb crust on my prewarmed plate, I was steering my way to Firner's table when Schmalz came up to me.

'May my wife and I invite the doctor to coffee?' Schmalz had evidently dug out my title and gladly adopted it to neutralize another sibilant.

'That's extremely kind of you, Herr Schmalz,' I thanked him. 'But I'll hope you'll understand that until the end of this case, my time is not my own.'

'Oh, well, another time, maybe.' Schmalz looked downcast, but understood the Works came first.

I looked around for Firner and found him on his way to his table with a plate from the buffet.

He stood still for a moment. 'Greetings, have you found out anything?' He held his plate awkwardly at chest level to hide a red-wine stain on his dinner shirt.

'Yes,' I said simply. 'And you?'

'What's that supposed to mean, Herr Self?'

'Let's imagine there's a blackmailer who wants to demonstrate his superiority, first of all by manipulating the MBI system and then by creating a gas explosion. Then he demands ten million from the RCW. Who in the company would be the first person to get that demand on his desk?'

'Korten. Because he's the only one who could decide about sums of that size.' He frowned and glanced instinctively at the slightly raised table where Korten was sitting with the head of the Chinese delegation, the president, and other heavyweights. I waited in vain for an appeasing remark like 'But Herr Self, whatever are you thinking?' He lowered his plate. The red-wine stain did its bit to reveal a tense and uncertain Firner beneath the veneer of relaxed serenity. As though I were no longer there, he took a few steps towards the open window, lost in thought. Then he pulled himself together, rearranged the plate in front of his chest, nodded curtly at me, and moved in a determined fashion to his table. I went to the toilet.

'Well, my dear Self, making progress?' Korten arrived at the next stall and fumbled with his fly.

'Do you mean with the case or the prostate?'

He peed and laughed. Laughed louder and louder and had to put a hand out on the tiles to support himself, and then it came back to me, too. We'd stood next to each other like this before, in the urinals at the Friedrich Wilhelm. It had been planned as a preparatory measure for playing hookey, and then, when the teacher noticed we were missing, Bechtel was to stand up and say, 'Korten and Self were feeling sick and went to the lavatory – I can go in quickly and check how they are.' But the teacher checked on us himself, found us there having a great time, and, as a punishment, left us standing there for the rest of the lesson, supervised by the janitor.

43

'Professor Barfeld with the monocle will be here any minute,' snorted Korten. 'Barfing Barfer, here comes Barfing Barfeld.'

I remembered the nickname, and we stood there, trousers open, clapping each other on the shoulder. Tears sprang to my eyes and my belly hurt from all the laughing.

Back then things almost took a nasty turn. Barfeld reported us to the headmaster and I had already envisaged my father raging and my mother weeping and the scholarship evaporating into thin air. But Korten took it all on his shoulders: he had been the instigator and I'd just joined in. So he got the letter home, and his father only laughed.

'I've got to go.' Korten buttoned up his fly.

'What, again?' I was still laughing. But the fun was over and the Chinese were waiting.

IO

Memories of the blue Adriatic

When I returned to the hall it was all drawing to a close. Passing, Frau Buchendorff asked how I was getting home, I couldn't be driving with my arm.

'I took a taxi before.'

'I'd be glad to give you a lift, since we're neighbours. Quarter of an hour by the exit?'

The tables were deserted. Small knots of people formed and dispersed. The red-haired girl was still standing with a bottle at the ready, but everyone had had plenty to drink.

'Hello,' I said to her.

'Did you enjoy the reception?'

'The buffet was good. I'm amazed there's anything left over. But seeing there is – could you pack a little something for a picnic tomorrow?'

'How many in your party?' She bobbed an ironic curtsy.

'For two, if you have time.'

'Oh, can't do that. But I'll have something packed for two nonetheless. Just a moment.'

She disappeared through the swing-doors. When she returned she had with her a largish box. 'You should have seen the face of our chef. I had to tell him that you're peculiar but important.' She giggled. 'Because you've dined with the general director he took it on himself to add a bottle of Forster Bischofsgarten Spätlese.'

45

When Frau Buchendorff saw me with the carton she raised an eyebrow.

'I've packed the Chinese security expert. Didn't you notice how petite and dainty she is? The delegation leader shouldn't have let her go with me.' In her presence all I could think of were stupid jokes. If this had happened to me thirty years ago I'd have been forced to admit I was in love. But what was I to make of it at an age where falling in love no longer happens?

Frau Buchendorff drove an Alfa Romeo Spider, an old one without the ugly rear spoiler.

'Should I put the roof up?'

'I usually ride my motorbike in swimming trunks, even in winter.' It was getting worse and worse. And on top of it, a misunderstanding – she was putting up the roof. All because I hadn't dared say that I could think of nothing finer than to be on the road on a mellow summer night with a beautiful woman at the wheel of a cabriolet. 'No, leave it, Frau Buchendorff, I like driving in a sports car with the top down on a mellow summer night.'

We drove over the suspension bridge, below us the Rhine and the harbour. I looked up at the sky and the cables. It was a bright and starry-clear night. When we turned off the bridge and before we were submerged in the streets, Mannheim with its towers, churches, and high-rises lay before us for a moment. We had to wait at traffic lights and a heavy motorbike drew up alongside. 'Come on, let's drive out to the Adriatic,' shouted the girl on the back of the bike to her boyfriend, through his helmet against the noise of the engine. In the hot summer of 1946 I'd often been out at the gravel pit, its name imbued with Mannheimers' and Ludwighafeners' yearning for the South. Back then my wife and I were still happy and I enjoyed our companionship, the peace, and the first cigarettes. So, people still went out there, more

46

rapidly and easier these days, a quick dip in the water after the movies.

We hadn't spoken throughout the journey. Frau Buchendorff had driven fast, and with focus. Now she lit a cigarette.

'The blue Adriatic – when I was small we sometimes drove out in our Opel Olympia. There was coffee substitute in the thermos flask, cold cutlets, and vanilla pudding in the preserving jar. My big brother was streetwise, a rocker, as they called it; on his moped he soon went his own way. Back then the notion of going for a quick dip in the night was just getting fashionable. It all seems so idyllic now, looking back – as a child I always suffered those outings.'

We'd reached my house but I wanted to savour a little longer the nostalgia that had engulfed us both.

'In what way suffered?'

'My father wanted to teach me how to swim but had no patience. My God, the amount of water I swallowed.'

I thanked her for the ride home. 'It was a beautiful drive.'

'Goodnight, Herr Self.'

I I

Terrible thing to happen

A glorious Sunday saw the last of the good weather. At our picnic by the Feudenheim Locks my friend Eberhard and I ate and drank much too much. He had brought a miniature wooden crate with three bottles of a very decent Bordeaux, and then we made the mistake of downing the RCW Spätlese, as well.

On Monday I woke up with a blazing headache. On top of that the rain had coaxed out the rheumatism in my back and hips. Perhaps that's why I dealt with Schneider all wrong. He had reappeared, not flushed out by the Works security service, just like that. I was to meet him in a colleague's laboratory; his own had been burnt to a shell in the accident.

When I entered the room he straightened up from the fridge. He was tall and lanky. He invited me with an indeterminate flick of the hand to take a seat on one of the lab stools and remained standing himself, shoulders stooped, in front of the refrigerator. His face was ashen, the fingers of his left hand yellow from nicotine. The immaculate white coat was supposed to hide the decay of the person inside. But the man was a wreck. If he was a gambler then he was the sort who had lost and had no shred of hope left. The sort who fills out a lottery ticket on a Friday, but doesn't bother to look on the Saturday to see if he's won.

'I know why you want to talk to me, Herr Self, but I've nothing to tell you.'

'Where were you on the day of the accident? You'll know that surely. And where did you disappear to?'

'I unfortunately do not enjoy great health and was indisposed in recent days. The accident in my laboratory was a real blow, important records of research were destroyed.'

'That's hardly an answer to my question.'

'What do you really want? Just leave me alone.'

Indeed, what did I really want from him? I was finding it more and more difficult to picture him as the brilliant blackmailer. Broken as he was, I couldn't even imagine him the tool of some outsider. But my imagination had duped me in the past and there was something not right about Schneider. I didn't have that many leads. His, and my own, misfortune that he'd found his way into the security files. And there was my hangover and my rheumatism and Schneider's sulky, whiny manner that was getting on my nerves. If I couldn't intimidate him then I might as well kiss my job goodbye. I gathered myself for a fresh attack.

'Herr Schneider, we are investigating sabotage resulting in damages reaching into the millions and we're acting to prevent further threats. I've encountered nothing but cooperation during my investigation. Your unwillingness to lend your support makes you, I'll be perfectly honest, a suspect. All the more so as your biography contains phases of criminal entanglement.'

'But I put a halt to the gambling years ago.' He lit a cigarette. His hand was trembling. He took some hasty drags. 'But, okay, I was at home in bed and we often unplug the telephone at the weekend.'

'But Herr Schneider. Security was round at your house. There was nobody home.'

'So you don't believe me anyway. Then I won't say another word.'

I'd heard that often enough. Sometimes it helped to convince the other person I believed whatever he said. Sometimes I'd understood how to address the deep-seated trouble at the source of this childish reaction so that everything came gushing out. Today I was capable of neither one nor the other. I'd had it.

'Right, then we'll have to continue our discussion in the presence of Security and your superiors. I'd have liked to spare you that. But if I don't hear from you by this evening . . . Here's my business card.'

I didn't wait for his reaction, and left. I stood under the awning, looked into the rain and lit a cigarette. Was it also raining on the banks of the Sweet Afton? I didn't know what to do. Then I recalled that the boys from Security would have set their trap and I went over to the computer centre to take a look. Oelmüller wasn't there. One of his co-workers whose badge revealed him to be a Herr Tausendmilch showed me on screen the message sent to users about the false data file.

'Should I print it out for you? It's no problem at all.'

I took the printout and went over to Firner's office. Neither Firner nor Frau Buchendorff were there. A typist regaled me on the subject of cacti. I'd had enough for one day and left the Works.

If I'd been younger I'd have driven out to the Adriatic regardless of the rain to swim off my hangover. If I could just have got into my car I'd maybe have done it anyway, regardless of age. But with my injured arm I still couldn't drive. The guard, the same one as on the day of the accident, called a taxi for me.

'Ah, you're the fellow who brought in Schmalz's son on Friday. You're Self? Then I have something for you. He scrabbled beneath the control and alarm desk and came back up with a package that he handed over with ceremony.

'There is a cake inside as a surprise for you. Frau Schmalz baked it.'

I had the taxi take me to the Herschel baths. It was women's only day in the sauna. I had it take me to the Kleiner Rosengarten, my local, and ate a saltimbocca romana. Then I went to the movies.

The first movie showing in the early afternoon has its charm, regardless of what's playing. The audience consists of tramps, thirteen-year-olds, and frustrated intellectuals. When there were still students who lived out of town, they went to the early showing. Pupils who matured earlier used to go to the early showing to make out. But Babs, a friend who's headmistress of a high school, assures me that pupils now make out at school and are all made out by one o'clock.

I'd ended up in the wrong theatre – the cinema had seven of the things – and had to watch *On Golden Pond*. I liked all the actors but when it was over I was glad I no longer had a wife, a daughter, or some little bastard of a grandson.

On the way home I looked in at the office. I picked up a message that Schneider had hanged himself. Frau Buchendorff had spoken with extreme matter-of-factness on the answering machine and asked to be called back immediately.

I poured myself a sambuca.

'Did Schneider leave a note?'

'Yes. We have it here. We think your case is over now. Firner would like to see you to talk about it.'

I told Frau Buchendorff I'd be there straight away, and called a taxi.

Firner was light of heart. 'Greetings, Herr Self. Terrible thing to happen. He hanged himself in the laboratory with an electric cable. A poor trainee found him. We tried everything to revive him of course. No use. Read the suicide note, we have our man.'

He handed me the photocopy of a hastily scrawled sheet of paper, apparently meant for his wife.

My Dorle – forgive me. Do not think you didn't love me enough – without your love I'd have done this a long time ago. I can't go on now. They know everything and leave me no option. I wanted to make you happy and give you everything – may God grant you an easier life than in these past dreadful years. You deserve it so much. I embrace you. Unto death – your Franz.

'You have your man? This leaves everything open. I spoke with Schneider this morning. It's gambling that had him in its clutches and drove him to death.'

'You're a defeatist.' Firner bellowed with laughter in my face, his mouth wide open.

'If Korten thinks the case has been solved, he can of course relinquish my services at any time. I believe, though, that you're jumping to conclusions. And you yourself don't take them that seriously. Or have you already deactivated the computer trap?'

Firner wasn't impressed. 'Routine, Herr Self, routine. Naturally the trap is still in place. But for the time being the matter is over. We just have a few details to clear up. How, above all, Schneider managed to manipulate the system.'

'I'm quite certain you'll be on the phone to me soon.'

'Let's see, Herr Self.' Firner, honest to God, stuck his thumbs into the waistcoat of his three-piece suit and played 'Yankee Doodle' with his remaining fingers.

On the way home in the taxi I thought about Schneider. Was I responsible for his death? Or was Eberhard responsible for bringing so much Bordeaux that I had been hungover today and too gruff with Schneider? Or was it the senior chef, with his Forster Bischofsgarten Spätlese that finished us off? Or the rain and the rheumatism? The chains of cause and guilt went on and on into infinity.

Schneider in his white lab coat was often in my thoughts in the days that followed. I didn't have much to do. Goedecke wanted a further, more detailed report on the disloyal branch manager, and another client came to me not realizing he could have got the same information from the town clerk's office.

On Wednesday my arm was on the mend and I could finally collect my car from the RCW parking lot. The chlorine had eaten into the paint. I'd add that to the bill. The guard greeted me and asked whether the cake had been good. I had left it in the taxi on Monday.

12

Among screech owls

While playing Doppelkopf with my friends, I presented them with the problem of chains of cause and guilt. A couple of times a year we meet on a Wednesday in the Badische Weinstuben, to play cards: Eberhard, the chess grandmaster; Willy, the ornithologist and an emeritus of the University of Heidelberg; Philipp, surgeon at the city hospital; and myself.

At fifty-seven Philipp is our Benjamin, and Eberhard our Nestor at seventy-two. Willy is half a year younger than me. We never get particularly far with our Doppelkopf, we like talking too much.

I told them about Schneider's background, his passion for gambling, and how I'd cast suspicion on him that I didn't really believe in myself but nonetheless had used to take him harshly to task.

'Two hours later the man hangs himself. Not, I think, because of my suspicion, but because he could foresee the uncovering of his continued gambling addition. Am I to blame for his death?'

'You're the lawyer,' said Philipp. 'Don't you have any criteria for this sort of thing?'

'Legally I'm not guilty. But it's the human aspect that interests me.'

The three of them looked at a complete loss. Eberhard ruminated. 'Then I wouldn't be allowed to win at chess any more because my opponent might be sensitive and might take a defeat so to heart that he kills himself over it.'

'So, if you know that defeat is the drop that will make the glass of depression overflow, leave him alone and look for another opponent,' Philipp suggested.

Eberhard wasn't satisfied with Philipp's hypothesis. 'What do I do at a tournament where I can't select my opponent?'

'Well, among screech owls . . .' Willy began. 'It gets clearer by the day why I love screech owls so much. They catch their mice and sparrows, take care of their young, live in their tree-hollows and cavities in the earth, don't need any company, nor a state, are courageous and sharp, true to their family. There's real wisdom in their eyes, and I've never heard any such snivelling outpourings about guilt and expiation from them. Besides, if it's not the legal but the human side that interests you, all people are guilty of all things.'

'Put yourself under my knife. If it slips from my grasp because a nurse is turning me on, is everyone here guilty?' Philipp made a sweeping hand gesture. The waiter understood it as the ordering of another round and brought a pils, a Laufen Gutedel, an Ihring Vulkanfelsen, and a grog for Willy, who was suffering from a cold.

'Well, you'll have us to deal with if you hack up Willy.' I raised my glass to Willy. He couldn't drink back to me, his grog was still too hot.

'Don't worry, I'm not stupid. If I do something to Willy, we won't be able to play Doppelkopf any more.'

'Exactly, let's play another round,' said Eberhard. But before we could start he folded his cards together pensively and laid the little pile on the table. 'Although, seriously, I'm the eldest so it's easiest for me to broach the subject, what's to become of us if one of us . . . if . . . you know what I mean.'

'If there are only three of us left?' Philipp said with a grin. 'Then we'll play Skat.'

'Don't we know another fourth player, someone we could bring in now as a fifth?'

'A priest would be no bad thing at our age.'

'We don't have to play every time, we don't anyway. We could just go out for a meal, or do something with women. I'll bring a nurse for each of you, if you like.'

'Women,' said Eberhard mistrustfully, and took up his hand of cards again.

'The idea of a meal isn't a bad one.' Willy asked for the menu. We all ordered. The food was good and we forgot about guilt and death.

On the way home I noticed that I'd managed to distance myself from Schneider's suicide now. I was just curious as to when I'd next hear from Firner.

13

Are you interested in the details?

It's not often I stay home in the mornings. Not only because I'm out and about a lot, but because I can barely keep away from the office even if there's nothing for me to do there. It's a relic from my time as an attorney. Perhaps it also stems from the fact that as a child I don't remember my father ever spending a workday at home, and back then you worked six days a week.

On Thursday I was the leopard that changed its spots. The previous day my video recorder had come back from the repair shop. I'd rented a couple of Westerns. Even though they are scarcely shown any more I've remained true to them.

It was ten o'clock. I'd put on *Heaven's Gate*: I'd missed it at the cinema and it was unlikely to be shown there again, and I was watching Harvard graduates at the graduation party in their tails. Kris Kristofferson stood a decent chance. Then the telephone rang.

'I'm glad to reach you, Herr Self.'

'Did you think I would be at the blue Adriatic in this weather, Frau Buchendorff?' Outside the rain was pouring down.

'Ever the old charmer. I'll put you through to Herr Firner.'

'Greetings, Herr Self. We believed the case was over, but now Herr Oelmüller tells me that something has happened in the system again. I'd be happy if you could come over, today if possible. What's your schedule like?'

We agreed on 4 p.m. *Heaven's Gate* was about four hours long, and you shouldn't sell yourself too cheaply.

On the drive to the Works I pondered why Kris Kristofferson had cried at the end. Because early wounds never heal? Or because they heal and, one day, are nothing more than a bleached-out memory?

The gateman at the main gates greeted me like an old friend, hand on the brim of his cap. Oelmüller was distanced. The other member of the party was Thomas.

'Remember I told you about the trap that we'd planned and instigated?' said Thomas. 'Well, today it snapped shut . . .'

'But the mouse ran away with the cheese?'

'That's one way of putting it,' Oelmüller said sourly. 'Here is exactly what occurred: yesterday morning the central computer reported that our bait data file had been opened via terminal PKR 137 by a user with the number 23045 ZBH. The user, Herr Knoblauch, is employed in the main accounting department. He was, however, at the time the file was accessed, in a meeting with three gentlemen from the tax authority. And the said terminal is at the other end of the Works at the purification plant and was being serviced by our own technician off-line.'

'Herr Oelmüller means to say that the machine wasn't workable during its inspection,' added Thomas.

'Which means that another user and another terminal are hidden behind Herr Knoblauch and his number. Didn't you figure the culprit would disguise himself?'

Oelmüller took up my question eagerly. 'Oh yes, Herr Self. I've spent the whole of last weekend thinking through how we can catch the culprit regardless. Are you interested in the details?'

'Try me. If it gets too difficult I'll let you know.'

'Good, I'll attempt to keep it comprehensible. We've seen to it that when a special control command is issued by the system, the terminals that are logged on will set a special switch in their working memory. It's not noticeable to the user. The safety precaution was sent to the terminals at the moment the bait data file was accessed. Our intention was that all terminals in dialogue with the system at that second could later be identified by the state of the switch, and this even independent of the terminal number the culprit could have used to disguise himself.'

'Could I imagine it being like a stolen car being identified not by its false licence plate, but by the engine number?'

'Well, yes, somewhat along those lines.' Oelmüller nodded at me encouragingly.

'And how do you explain that, in spite of all this, there was no mouse in the trap?'

Thomas responded. 'At the moment we have no explanation. Something you may be considering – outside intervention – we still discount. The wiring the telecom people installed to trace things is still in place and signalled nothing.'

No explanation. And that from the specialists. My dependence on their expertise bothered me. I could follow what Oelmüller had described. But I couldn't check his premises. Possibly the pair of them weren't particularly bright and it wasn't a big deal to outwit their trap. But what was I supposed to do? Immerse myself in computers? Follow up the other leads? What other leads were there? I was at a loss.

'The whole thing is very embarrassing for Herr Oelmüller and myself,' said Thomas. 'We were sure we'd trap the culprit and stupidly we said so. Time is ticking by and nonetheless the only possibility I see is to go through all our assumptions and conclusions with a fine-toothed comb. Perhaps we should also speak to the man who set up the system, don't you think, Herr Oelmüller? Can you tell us, Herr Self, how you are going to proceed?'

'I've got to sift through everything in my head first.'

'I'd like us to stay in touch. Shall we get together again on Monday morning?'

We were standing and had said our goodbyes, when my thoughts returned to the accident. 'What, incidentally, came out of the investigation of the causes of the explosion? And did the smog alarm function properly?'

'According to the RCC it was right that the smog alarm went off. So far as the cause of the accident is concerned, we have at least arrived at the point where we know it had nothing to do with our computer. I don't have to tell you how relieved I was. A broken valve – the engineers will have to answer for that.'

14

Lousy reception

With good music playing I can always think well. I'd
switched the stereo on but hadn't started playing *The
Well-Tempered Clavier* as I wanted to fetch a beer from the
kitchen first. When I returned, the neighbour on the floor
below had turned her radio up loud, making me listen to
her current favourite: 'We are living in a material world
and I am a material girl . . .'

I trampled on the floor, to no avail. So it was off with
the dressing gown, on with the shoes and jacket, and down
the stairs I went to ring the doorbell. I intended to ask the
'material girl' if there was no consideration left in her
'material world'. No one answered, nor was any music
coming from the flat. Obviously no one was home. The
other neighbours were away on holiday and there's
nothing but the attic above my flat.

Then I realized that the music was coming from my
own loudspeaker. I don't have a radio attached to the
system. I fiddled with the amplifier and couldn't get rid of
the music. I put on the record. Bach in the *forti* sections
easily managed to drown out the sinister other channel,
but the *piani* he had to share with the newscaster of
South-West Radio. My stereo was apparently screwed up.

Perhaps it was due to the lack of good music that I
didn't get much more thinking done that evening. I played
through a scenario in which Oelmüller was the culprit.
Apart from the psychology it all fitted. He certainly wasn't

61

the rascal or prankster – could he be the blackmailer? According to everything I'd ever gathered about computer criminality, people who worked with a computer would make different use of it for criminal purposes. They would use the system but not make a mockery of it.

The next morning I went to a radio repair shop before breakfast. I'd tried out the stereo again and the interference had gone. That really did annoy me. I can't abide unpredictable machinery. A car may be roadworthy and a washing machine still wash, but if the last, most insignificant indicator light doesn't work with Prussian precision, my mind will know no rest.

I got a competent young man. He had compassion for my lack of technical know-how, almost called me 'Grandpa' in friendly condescension. Of course, I know that radio waves aren't brought to life by the radio – they're always there. The radio merely makes them audible, and the young man explained to me that practically the same circuit that achieves this in the receiver is also present in the amplifier and that, under certain atmospheric conditions, the amplifier may act as a receiver. There was nothing you could do about it, just had to accept it.

On the way from Seckenheimer Strasse to my café in the arcades by the Wasserturm I bought a newspaper. At my kiosk, lying next to *Süddeutsche* is always the *Rhine Neckar Chronicle* and for some reason the abbreviation RNC stuck fast in my head.

When I was sitting in Café Gmeiner, coffee in front of me, awaiting my ham and eggs, I got that feeling of wanting to say something to someone but not remembering what. Was it related to the RNC? It struck me that I hadn't read Tietzke's interview with Firner yet. But that wasn't what I was looking for. Hadn't someone spoken to me yesterday about the RNC? No, Oelmüller had said the

RCC had had reason to trigger the smoke alarm. That was apparently the office responsible for the smog alarm and analysis of emission data. But there was something else I wasn't getting. It had something to do with the amplifier functioning as a receiver.

When the ham and eggs arrived I ordered another coffee. The waitress didn't bring it until I'd asked for a third time. 'Sorry, Herr Self, I've got lousy reception today. I'm miles away. I was taking care of my daughter's boy last night because the young folk have a subscription for the opera and got back late yesterday. Wagner's *Götterdämmerung* went on and on.'

Lousy reception, miles away, long-distance. Of course, that was it, the long-distance reception at the RCC. Herzog had told me about the direct emission model. The same emission data are also recorded in the RCW system, Oelmüller had said. And Ostenteich had spoken of the online connection with the state monitoring system. Somehow the computer centre of the RCW and the RCC had to be connected. Was it possible to penetrate the MBI system via the RCC? And was it possible that the people at RCW had simply forgotten this? I cast my thoughts back and remembered clearly that there had been talk of the terminals in the plant and of telephone lines to the outside when we'd been discussing possible breaches in the system. A cable running between RCC and RCW, as I was now picturing it, had never been mentioned. It belonged neither to the telephone lines nor to the terminal connections. It differed from those by not being a mode of direct communication. Rather a silent flow of data migrated from the various sensors onto tape. Data that interested no one at the plant and could be immediately forgotten unless there happened to be an alarm or an accident. I understood why the musical confusion on my stereo had preoccupied me for so long: the interference came from inside.

I played around with my ham and eggs and the multitude of questions going through my mind. Above all I needed additional information. I didn't want to speak with Thomas, Ostenteich, or Oelmüller now. If they had forgotten an RCW–RCC connection, that would ultimately cause them more concern than the connection itself. I needed to take a look at the RCC and find someone there who could explain system connections to me.

From the phone booth next to the restroom I gave Tietzke a call. The RCC, it transpired, was the Regional Computer Centre in Heidelberg. 'To a certain degree even trans-regional,' said Tietzke, 'as Baden-Württemberg and the Rhineland–Palatinate are hooked up to it. What do you have in mind, Herr Self?'

'Do you ever let up, Herr Tietzke?' I retorted, and promised him the rights to my memoirs.

15

Bam bam, ba bam bam

I drove straight to Heidelberg. In front of the law school I found a parking space. I walked the few steps to Ebert-Platz, the former Wrede-Platz, and found the Regional Computer Centre in the old building with the two entrance pillars where the Deutsche Bank used to be. The doorman sat in the former banking hall.

'Selk from Springer Publishing,' I introduced myself. 'I'd like to talk to one of the gentlemen from emission supervision, the publishing house called ahead.'

He picked up the telephone. 'Herr Mischkey, there's someone here from Springer Publishing, he says he wants to talk to you and has an appointment. Should I send him up?'

I interjected. 'Can I talk to Herr Mischkey myself?' And as the doorman was sitting at a table not screened by glass and since I was already reaching for it, he handed the receiver to me, nonplussed.

'Hello, Herr Mischkey, Selk from Springer Publishing here, you know? We'd like to include a report on the direct emission model in our computer journal, and after talking with the industry I'd like to hear the other side. Will you see me?'

He didn't have much time but invited me up. His room was on the second floor, the door was open, the view opened onto the square. Mischkey was sitting with his back to the door at a computer that had his full concentration and on which he was typing with two fingers at great speed. He called over his shoulder, 'Come on in, I'll be finished in a second.'

I looked around. The table and chairs were awash with computer printouts and magazines from *Computer Weekly* to the American edition of *Penthouse*. On the wall was a blackboard with 'Happy Birthday, Peter' scrawled on it in smudged chalk. Next to that Einstein was sticking his tongue out at me. On the other wall were film posters and a still that I couldn't assign to a particular film. 'Madonna,' he said without looking up.

'Madonna?'

Now he did look up. A distinctive, bony face with deep furrows in the brow, a small moustache, an obstinate chin, all topped with a wild mop of greying hair. His eyes twinkled at me in delight through a pair of intentionally ugly spectacles. Were the national health glasses of the fifties back in fashion? He was wearing jeans and a dark-blue sweater, no shirt. 'I'll call her up on screen for you from my film file.' He beckoned me over, typed in a couple of commands, and the screen filled in a flash. 'You know how it is when you're fishing for a tune that you can't quite remember? Problem of all music and movie buffs? I've solved that with my file, too. Do you want to hear music from your favourite film?'

'*Barry Lyndon*,' I said, and in the space of seconds came the squeaky but unmistakable start of the Sarabande by Handel, bam bam, ba bam bam. 'That's fantastic,' I said.

'What brings you here, Herr Selk? As you can see, I'm very busy at the moment and haven't much time to spare. It's to do with emissions?'

'Exactly, or rather, with a report on them for our computer journal.'

A colleague entered the room. 'Are you messing around with your files again? Do you expect me to deal with the registration data for the church? I must say I find you extremely uncooperative.'

'May I introduce my colleague Grimm? That's really his name, but with two "m's" – Jörg, this is Herr Selk from the computer journal. He wants to write about the office culture in RCC. Keep going, you're being most authentic.'

'Oh, Peter, really . . .' Grimm puffed out his cheeks. I placed them both in their mid-thirties, but one came across like a mature 25-year-old and the other like a man in his fifties who's aged badly. Grimm's grimness was only accentuated by his safari suit and his long, thinning hair. I kept what was left of my hair trimmed short. I wondered whether my hair situation might still get worse at my age, or whether the balding was over, just as getting pregnant is over for post-menopausal women.

'You could have called up the church report on your computer ages ago, by the way. I'm in the middle of the traffic census. It has to go out today. Yes, Herr Selk, it doesn't look good for the two of us. Unless you want to buy me lunch? At McDonald's?'

We arranged to meet at twelve-thirty.

I strolled up the main street, impressive evidence of the city council's will towards destruction in the seventies. It wasn't drizzling at the moment. Yet the weather couldn't make up its mind what to offer for the weekend. I decided to ask Mischkey about the meteorograph. In the Darmstadt shopping centre I came across a record shop. Sometimes I like to sample the zeitgeist, buy the representative record or the representative book, go to see *Rambo II* or watch an election debate between the chancellor and his challenger. There was a special offer on for Madonna. The girl at the till took a look at me and asked if she should gift-wrap it. 'No. Is that the impression I give?'

I walked out of the Darmstadt shopping centre and saw Bismarck-Platz ahead of me. I'd have liked to visit the old man on his pedestal. But the traffic didn't allow it. On the corner I bought a packet of Sweet Aftons, and then time was up.

16

Like an arms race

It was rush hour at McDonald's. Mischkey pushed us skilfully to the front. Following his recommendation, I chose a Fish Mac with mayonnaise, a small portion of fries with ketchup, and a coffee.

Mischkey, tall and lanky, ordered a quarter-pounder with cheese, a large portion of fries, three portions of ketchup, another small hamburger to 'fill the little gap afterwards', an apple pie, two milkshakes, and a coffee.

The full tray cost me almost 25 marks.

'Not expensive, is it? For lunch for two. Thanks for inviting me.'

First of all we couldn't find two seats together. I wanted to move a chair to a free space, but the chair was attached to the floor. I was bemused; neither as an attorney, nor as a private detective, had I ever come across the offence of theft of restaurant chairs. Eventually we installed ourselves at a table with two high school students who eyed Mischkey's assortment enviously.

'Herr Mischkey, the direct emission model file led to the first lawsuit dealing with computers since the national census, the first, also, to reach the Federal Constitutional Court. The computer journal wants a legal report from me since legal journalism is my field. But I've realized I need to figure out more of the technical side, and that's where I'd appreciate some information.'

'Mmm.' He chomped contentedly on his quarter-pounder.

'What sort of data-sharing is there between yourselves and the industrial firms you supervise the emissions for?'

Mischkey swallowed. 'I can tell you a thousand things about that, the transmission technology, the hardware, the software, you name it. What do you want to know?'

'Perhaps as a lawyer I can't formulate the questions precisely enough. I'd like to know, for example, how a smog alarm is triggered.'

Mischkey was in the process of unwrapping the hamburger for that little gap afterwards and drenching it in ketchup. 'That's actually quite banal. Sensors are attached at the points where the harmful substances escape from the plant, and we receive round-the-clock reports on the fallout. We record the levels and simultaneously they go into our meteorograph. The meteorograph is the result of the weather data we get from the German weather service. If emissions are too high or the weather can't cope with them, an alarm sounds in the RCC and the smog alarm machinery chugs into motion – as it did most excellently last week.'

'I've been told the factories receive the same emissions data as you. How does that work technically? Are they also linked to the sensors, like two lamps on a two-way adaptor?'

Mischkey laughed. 'Something like that. Technically it's a bit different. Since there's not one, but lots of sensors in the factories, the individual lines are already brought together within any one factory. From that collection point, if you like, the data come to us via fixed cable. And the factory in question draws its data from the collection point like we do.'

'How secure is that? I was thinking the industry might have an interest in falsifying the data.'

That got Mischkey's attention and he let his apple pie sink down without taking a bite. 'For a non-technician you ask some pretty good questions. And I have things I'd like to say about that. But I think that is for after this apple pie.' He gazed tenderly at the sickly pastry, which was giving off a synthetic cinnamon smell. 'We shouldn't stay here, we should finish our lunch in the café in Akademie-strasse instead.' I groped for a cigarette and couldn't find my lighter. Mischkey, being a non-smoker, couldn't help me.

The way to the café took us through the Horten department store; Mischkey bought the new *Penthouse*. We lost each other briefly in the crowds but found each other again at the exit.

In the café Mischkey ordered a piece of Black Forest gateau, a mixed-fruit tart, and a pastry to accompany his pot of coffee. With cream. Obviously he was a good burner of food. Thin people who can shovel so much down make me envious.

'And what about a good response to my good question?' I asked, picking up the thread.

'Theoretically there are two exposed flanks. First of all you could play around with the sensors, but they're so well sealed that it wouldn't go unnoticed. The other possible breach is the connection between the collection point and the factory's cable. There the politicians agreed to a compromise I consider rotten through and through. For at the end of the day you can't discount the possibility that, from this connection, emissions data may be falsified or, even worse, the programme of the smog alarm systems tampered with. Naturally we've built in security measures that we're constantly fine-tuning, but you can view this as being like an arms race. Every defence system can be out-tricked by a new attack system and vice versa. A never-ending, and never-endingly expensive, spiral.'

I had a cigarette in my mouth and was going through all my pockets looking for the lighter. In vain again, naturally. Then Mischkey, from the right breast pocket of his fine nappa leather jacket, took out two disposable lighters packed in plastic and cardboard, one pink, the other black. He tore open the packet.

'Is pink all right, Herr Selk? Compliments of the department store.' He winked at me, pushed the pink one over the table, and offered me a light from the black one.

'Former public prosecutor deals in stolen lighters.' I could just picture the headlines, and fiddled a bit with the lighter before pocketing it and thanking Mischkey.

'But what about the opposite direction? Would it be possible for someone to penetrate the factory's computer from the RCC?'

'If the factory's cable leads to the computer and not to an isolated data station . . . But actually you should be able to work that out yourself after all I've said.'

'So you really face off like the two superpowers, with offensive and defensive weapons.'

Mischkey tugged at his earlobe. 'Be careful with your comparisons, Herr Selk. If we follow your analogy, capitalist industry can only be the Americans. That leaves us employees of the state in the role of the Russians. As a public servant,' he straightened up, pulled back his shoulders, and made a suitably stately face, 'I must renounce this impertinent insinuation most strongly.' He laughed, slouched down, and gobbled his pastry.

'Something else,' he said. 'Sometimes I'm amused by the thought that the industry that fought for this damaging compromise has damaged itself. One competitor could naturally take advantage of our network to tamper with the system of another. Isn't that sweet, the RCC as the turntable of industrial spying?' He spun his pastry fork on his plate. When it stopped, the prongs were pointing at me.

I suppressed a sigh. Mischkey's amusing, playful reflections suggested an explosion in the circle of suspects. 'An interesting variant. Herr Mischkey, you've been a great help. In case I think of anything else may I give you a call? Here's my card.' I felt around in my wallet for the business card with my private address and telephone number on which I pose as freelance journalist Gerhard Selk.

We shared the route back to Ebert-Platz.

'What does your meteorograph say about the coming weekend?'

'It'll be fine, no smog, not even rain. It looks like a weekend at the pool.'

We said goodbye. I took the Römer roundabout to Bergheimer Strasse to get petrol. Listening to it running through the hose I couldn't help thinking of the cables between the RCW and the RCC and now God knows which factories. If my case was one of industrial espionage, I thought on the motorway, then there was something missing. The incidents in the RCW system, so far as I could recall, didn't add up to a case of espionage. Unless the spy had used them to cover his tracks. In which case, wouldn't his only reason have been that he feared someone was on his trail? And why should he fear that? Did one of the first incidents perhaps risk undoing him? I needed to take another look at the reports. And I needed to call Firner and get hold of a list of the firms connected to the smog alarm system.

I reached Mannheim. It was three o'clock, the blinds of Mannheim Insurance had already closed for the evening. Only the windows that showed an illuminated M at night were still on duty. M as in Mischkey, I thought.

I liked the man. I also liked him as a suspect. Here was

the joker, the puzzle-lover, the gambler I'd been looking for from the beginning. He possessed the necessary imagination, the requisite talent, and was sitting in the right place. But it was no more than a hunch. And if I wanted to nail him with that he'd serenely send me packing.

I'd tail him over the weekend. Right now I had nothing but a feeling and I didn't see how else I could follow the lead. Maybe he'd make a move that would bring me new ideas. Had it been winter I'd have stocked up at the bookshop for the weekend on computer crime. Shadowing someone is a cold and hard business in winter. But in summer it's fine. Mischkey was going to the pool.

17

Shame on you!

Mischkey currently lived in Heidelberg at number 9, Burgweg, drove a Citroën DS cabriolet with the licence plate HD-CZ 985, was unmarried and childless, earned 55,000 marks as a senior civil servant, and had a personal loan from the Co-operative Savings Bank for 30,000 marks, which he was paying back in an orderly fashion: all this I'd been told on Friday by my colleague Hemmelskopf at the credit bureau. On Saturday at 7 a.m. I was at Burgweg.

It is a small stretch of street, closed to traffic, and the upper part of it becomes a footpath leading to the castle. The residents of the five or so houses in the lower part are allowed to park their cars there and have a key for the gate that divides Burgweg from Unteren Faulen Pelz. I was glad to see Mischkey's car. It was a beauty, bottle-green with gleaming chrome and a cream-coloured hood. That's where the loan money had gone. My own car I parked in the hairpin bend of Neue Schlossstrasse from which steep, straight stairs lead to Burgweg. Mischkey's car was facing uphill; if he were to drive off I ought to have time enough to be in Unteren Faulen Pelz when he arrived. I positioned myself in such a way that I could watch the entrance without being visible from the house.

At half past eight a window opened at eye-level in the house I had taken to be the neighbour's and a naked Mischkey stretched out into the already mild morning air.

I just had time to slip behind the advertising column. I peered out. He was yawning, doing some forward bends, and hadn't seen me.

At nine o'clock he left the house, walked to the market by Heiliggeist Kirche, ate two salmon rolls there, drank a coffee in the drugstore in the Kettengasse, flirted with the exotic beauty behind the bar, made a phone call, read the *Frankfurter Rundschau*, had a quick game of power chess, bought some more stuff, went home to drop off the shopping, and came out again with a big bag and got into his car. Now it was time to go swimming, he was wearing a T-shirt with 'Grateful Dead' printed on it, cut-off jeans, Jesus sandals, and had thin, pale legs.

Mischkey had to turn his car but the gate below was open so I had real trouble getting my Opel behind him in time, one car between us. I could hear the music blasting from his stereo at full volume. 'He's a pretender,' sang Madonna.

He took the motorway to Mannheim. There he drove at eighty past the ADAC pavilion and the Administrative Court, along Oberen Luisenpark. Suddenly he braked sharply and took a left. When the oncoming traffic allowed me to turn I could no longer see Mischkey's car. I drove on slowly, and kept an eye out for the green cabriolet. On the corner of Rathenaustrasse I heard loud music die out all of a sudden. I nudged forward. Mischkey was getting out of his car and going into the corner house.

I don't know what struck me, or what I noticed first, the address or Frau Buchendorff's silver car gleaming in front of Christuskirche. I rolled down the right-hand window and leaned over to take a look at the building. Through a cast-iron fence and an overgrown garden I looked up at the first-floor balcony. Frau Buchendorff and Mischkey were kissing.

Of all people, the two of them had to be involved! I

didn't like it at all. Tailing someone you know is bad enough, but if you're discovered you can always pretend it's a coincidental meeting and extract yourself reasonably well. Theoretically that could also be the case for two people, but not here. Would Frau Buchendorff introduce me as private detective Self, or Mischkey as freelance journalist Selk? If things progressed to swimming I'd be staying outside. Too bad, I'd been looking forward to it and had packed my Bermudas especially. They were kissing fervently. Was that something else I didn't like?

I assumed they would set off in Mischkey's car. It was waiting with the top down. I drove a little further into Rathenaustrasse and parked so that the garden gate and Citroën were reflected in my back mirror. Half an hour later they drove past me, and I hid behind my newspaper. Then I followed them through what we call the Suez Canal to Stollenwörth-Weiher.

It's in the south of town and has two club swimming pools. Frau Buchendorff and Mischkey went to the Post Office Pool. I stopped my car outside the entrance. How long do young people in love go swimming these days? In my day at Müggel Lake it could go on for hours, probably that hadn't changed much. I had dismissed the idea of swimming but the prospect of sitting in the car, or leaning propped against it for three hours made me cast about for a different solution. Was this pool within sight of the other one? It was worth a shot.

I drove round to the swimming pool opposite and packed my Zeiss binoculars in my swimming bag. I'd inherited them from my father, a regular officer who lost the First World War with them. I bought an entrance ticket, pulled the Bermudas on and my stomach in, and stepped into the sunshine.

I found a space from which I could view the other pool.

The lawn was full of families, groups, couples, and singles, and some of the moms too had dared to bare their breasts.

When I extracted my binoculars from my bag I encountered the first, reproachful eyes. I pointed them at the trees, at the few seagulls there were, and at a plastic duck on the lake. If only I'd taken my ornithology guide, I thought, I could use it to inspire their confidence. Briefly I got the other pool in my sights; so far as distance was concerned I could have easily tailed the two of them. But I wasn't allowed to.

'Shame on you!' said a family father whose paunch hung over his bathing trunks, and his breasts over his paunch. He and his wife were the last thing I'd want to look at, with or without binoculars. 'Stop it right now, you peeping Tom, you, or I'll smash them.'

It was absurd. The men around me didn't know which way to look, whether to see everything or nothing, and I don't think it's too old-fashioned to believe the women knew exactly what they were doing. And there I was, not interested in the whole business at all – not that it couldn't have interested me, but at the moment it really didn't, now I only had my job on my mind. And now of all times I was suspected of lecherousness, accused, convicted, and pronounced guilty.

Such people can only be dealt with using their own weapons. 'Shame on you,' I said. 'With your figure you really ought to wear a top,' and tucked my binoculars into the bag. I also stood up and topped him by a full head. He contented himself by twitching his mouth disapprovingly.

I jumped into the water and swam over to the other pool. I didn't even have to get out; Frau Buchendorff and Mischkey had lain down near the water in the baking sun. Mischkey was just cracking open a bottle of red wine so I figured I had at least an hour. I swam back. My adversary had pulled on a Hawaiian shirt, was solving crosswords with his wife, and left me in peace. I fetched a bockwurst with fries and lots of mustard and read my newspaper.

An hour later I was waiting back at the car in front of the other pool. But it wasn't until six p.m. that the pair of them came through the turn-stile. Mischkey's thin legs were red, Frau Buchendorff had her shoulder-length hair loose and her tan was emphasized by her blue silk dress. Then they drove back to her place in Rathenaustrasse. When they came out again, she had on a boldly checked pair of Capri pants and a knitted leather sweater, and he was in a pale linen suit. They walked the few steps to the Steigenberger Hotel in the Augusta-Anlage. I skulked around in the hotel lobby until I saw them leave the bar with their glasses and make their way to the restaurant. Now I headed for the bar and ordered an Aviateur. The barman looked puzzled, I explained the mixture to him, and he nodded approvingly. We got talking.

'We're pretty damn lucky,' he said. 'There was a couple in here just now, wanted to eat in the restaurant. A card slipped out of the man's wallet and landed on the bar. He tucked it away again immediately but I'd seen what was on it: *Inspecteur de bonne table* with that little Michelin man. He was one of those people, you know, who do those guides. Our restaurant is good, but still, I alerted the maître d' right away, and now the two of them will get service and a meal they'll never forget.'

'And you'll get your star at last, or at least three sets of crossed knives and forks.'

'Let's hope so.'

Inspecteur de bonne table – well, damn. I don't think there are identity cards of that sort. I was simultaneously fascinated by Mischkey's imagination, and uncomfortable with this little con game. Also the state of German gastronomy gave me reason for concern. Did you have to resort to such means to get decent service?

I knew I could call it a day so far as tailing them was concerned. The two of them, after a last calvados, would return either to Frau Buchendorff's or to Mischkey's in Heidelberg. I would take a Sunday morning walk to Christuskirche and quickly ascertain whether both cars, no cars, or only Frau Buchendorff's were in front of the house in Rathenaustrasse.

I went home, gave the cat a can of cat food, and myself a can of ravioli, and went to bed. I read a bit more of *Green Henry* and wistfully pictured myself at Lake Zurich before falling asleep.

18

The impurity of the world

On Sunday morning I took tea and butter cookies back to bed and mulled things over. I was certain: I had my man. Mischkey corresponded in every way to the image I'd formed of the culprit. He was a puzzle-lover, a joker, and a gambler, and his con-man's impulses rounded off his profile. As an employee of the RCC he had the opportunity to penetrate the systems of the interconnected firms, and as Frau Buchendorff's boyfriend he had the motive to select RCW. The raising of the executive assistant salaries was an anonymous friendly gesture to his girlfriend. This circumstantial evidence alone wouldn't stand up in court if everything there was handled by the book. Yet it was convincing enough for me to think less about whether he was the one than about how to convict him.

To confront him in front of witnesses so that he'd fold under the weight of his guilt – ridiculous. To set him a trap, along with Oelmüller and Thomas, this time targeted and better prepared – on the one hand I wasn't sure of success, and on the other I wanted to have this duel with Mischkey myself with my own weapons. No doubt about it, this was one of those cases that packed a personal punch. Perhaps it even offered too personal a challenge. I felt an unhealthy mixture of professional ambition, respect for my opponent, burgeoning jealousy, the classical rivalry of the hunter and the hunted, and even envy for Mischkey's youth. I know much of this is simply the impurity of the world: only fanatics believe they can escape it and only saints do. Yet, it bothers me sometimes. Because so few people admit to it I tend to think I'm the only one who suffers from it. When I was a student at university in Berlin my professor, Carl Schmitt, presented us with a theory that neatly differentiated the political from the personal enemy, and everyone felt justified in their anti-Semitism. Even then I was preoccupied by the question of whether the others couldn't stand their own impurity and had to cover it up, or whether my ability to erect a barrier between the personal and the objective was under-developed.

I made some more tea. Could I get a conviction via Frau Buchendorff? Could I get Mischkey, through her, to tamper once more, this time identifiably, with the RCW system? Or could I make use of Grimm and his obvious desire to put one over on Mischkey? Nothing convincing came to mind. I'd have to rely on my talent for improvisation.

I could spare myself any further tailing, but on my way to the Kleiner Rosengarten, where I sometimes meet friends for lunch on a Sunday, I didn't take my usual route past the Wasserturm and the Ring, but instead walked past the Christuskirche. Mischkey's Citroën was gone and Frau Buchendorff was working in the garden. I crossed to the other side of the street so I wouldn't have to say hello to her.

19

Anyone for tennis?

'Good morning, Frau Buchendorff. How was your week-end?' At half past eight she was still sitting over her newspaper, opened to the sports page, and was reading the latest on our newest tennis marvel. She had the list of roughly sixty businesses linked to the smog alarm system laid out for me in a green plastic folder. I asked her to cancel my appointment with Oelmüller and Thomas. I only wanted to see them after the case was solved, and even then preferably not.

'So you're crazy about our tennis wunderkind, too, Frau Buchendorff?'

'What do you mean, "too"? Like yourself, or like millions of other German women?'

'I do find him fascinating.'

'Do you play?'

'You'll laugh, but I have difficulty finding opponents with whom I don't wipe the floor. In singles, younger players can sometimes beat me just because they're fitter, but in doubles I'm almost invincible with a reasonable partner. Do you play?'

'To brag like you, Herr Self, I play so well that it gives men complexes.' She stood up. 'Allow me to introduce myself. South-west German Junior Champion nineteen sixty-eight.'

'A bottle of champagne against an inferiority complex,' I offered.

'What's that supposed to mean?'

'It means that I'll beat you, but, as a consolation, I'll bring a bottle of champagne. However, as mentioned, preferably in mixed doubles. Do you have a partner?'

'Yes, I have someone,' she said pugnaciously. 'When should we do it?'

'I'd opt for this afternoon at five, after work. Then it won't be hanging over us. But won't it be difficult to get a court?'

'My boyfriend will manage it. He seems to know someone at the court reservation office.'

'Where will we play?'

'At the RCW sports field. It's over in Oggersheim, I can give you a map.'

I hurried to get into the computer centre and had Herr Tausendmilch, 'but this remains between the two of us,' print me out the current status of the tennis court reservations. 'Are you still here at five o'clock?' I asked him. He finished at four-thirty but was young and declared himself willing to make me another printout at five on the dot. 'I'll be glad to tell Firner how efficient you are.' He beamed.

When I got to the main gate I bumped into Schmalz. 'The cake proved palatable?' he enquired. I hoped the taxi driver had eaten it.

'Please pass on my warm thanks to your wife. It tasted quite excellent. How is little Richard?'

'Thank you. Well enough.'

Don't worry, poor Richard. Your father wants you to be extremely well. He just can't risk the sibilant.

In the car I took a look at the printout of the tennis court reservations, although it was already clear to me that I wouldn't find a reservation for Mischkey or Buchendorff. Then I sat in the car for a while, smoking. We actually didn't have to play tennis; if Mischkey turned up

84

at five and a court was reserved for us, I had him. Nonetheless I drove to Herzogenried School to inform Babs, who owed me a favour, that she was duty-bound to play doubles. It was the morning break and Babs was right: kids were carrying on with one another in every corner. Lots of students had their Walkmans on, whether standing alone or in groups, playing, or smooching. Wasn't the outside world enough, or was it so unbearable for them?

I found Babs in the staffroom talking to two student teachers.

'Anyone for tennis?' I interrupted, and took Babs to one side. 'Really, you must play tennis with me this afternoon. I need you urgently.'

She kissed me, reservedly, as is appropriate for a staffroom. 'What an opportunity! Didn't you promise me a springtime excursion to Dilsberg? You only let me clap eyes on you when you want something. Nice to see you, but I'm annoyed.'

That's how she was looking at me, both delighted and pouting. Babs is a lively and generous woman, small and compact, and agile. I don't know many women of fifty who can dress and act so lightly without trying to play young. She has a flat-ish face, a deep furrow above the bridge of her nose, a full, determined, and at times severe mouth, brown eyes beneath hooded lids, and closely cropped grey hair. She lives with her two grown-up children, Röschen and Georg, who are far too comfortable at home to make the leap to independence.

'And you really forgot we went to Edenkoben for Father's Day? If you did, then I'm the one to be annoyed.'

'Oh dear – when and where do I have to play tennis? And do I get to find out why?'

'I'll collect you from home at quarter past four, all right?'

'And you'll take me at seven to choir; we're rehearsing.'

'Gladly. We're playing from five till six at the RCW tennis courts in Oggersheim, mixed doubles with an executive assistant and her boyfriend, the chief suspect in my current case.'

'How thrilling,' said Babs. Sometimes I have the impression she doesn't take my profession seriously.

'If you'd like to know more I can fill you in on the way. And if not, that's all right too, you just have to behave naturally.'

The bell rang. It sounded the way it did in my day. Babs and I went out into the corridor, and I watched the students streaming into the classrooms. They didn't just have different clothes and hairstyles, their faces were different from the faces back then. They struck me as more conflicted and more knowing. But the knowledge didn't make them happy. The children had a challenging, violent, and yet uncertain way of moving. The air vibrated from their shouts and noise. It almost felt threatening and I was cowed.

'How do you survive this, Babs?'

She didn't understand me. Perhaps because of the noise. She looked at me questioningly.

'Okay then, see you this afternoon.' I gave her a kiss. A few students wolf-whistled.

I appreciated the peace of my car, drove to the Horten parking lot, bought champagne, tennis socks, and a hundred sheets of paper for the report I'd have to write that evening.

20

A lovely couple

Babs and I were at the grounds shortly before five. Neither the green nor the silver cabriolet was parked there. It was fine with me to be first. I'd changed into my tennis things at home. I asked them to put the champagne on ice. Then Babs and I perched ourselves on the uppermost step of the flight of stairs leading from the restaurant terrace of the clubhouse to the courts. The parking lot was in view.

'Are you nervous?' she asked. During the drive she hadn't wanted to know more. Now she was just asking out of concern for me.

'Yes. Perhaps I should stop this work. I'm getting more involved in the cases than I used to. This time it's difficult because I find the main suspect very likeable. You'll get to know him in a moment. I think you'll warm to Mischkey.'

'And the executive assistant?'

Could she sense that, in my mind, Frau Buchendorff was more than just a supporting actress?

'I like her, too.'

We had chosen an awkward place on the steps. The people who had played until five went trooping up to the terrace, and the next lot came out of the changing rooms and bustled down the stairs.

'Does your suspect drive a green cabriolet?'

When my view was clear too I saw that Mischkey and Frau Buchendorff had just pulled up. He sprang out of the car, ran round and flung open her door with a deep bow.

She got out, laughing, and gave him a kiss. A lovely, vibrant, happy couple.

Frau Buchendorff spotted us when they reached the foot of the stairs. She waved with her right hand and gave Peter an encouraging nudge with the left. He, too, raised an arm in greeting – then he recognized me, and his gesture froze, and his face turned to stone. For a moment the world stopped turning, and the tennis balls were suspended in the air, and it was absolutely still.

Then the film moved on, and the two of them were standing next to us, and we were shaking hands, and I heard Frau Buchendorff say, 'My boyfriend, Peter Mischkey, and this is the Herr Self I was telling you about.' I went through the necessary introduction rituals.

Mischkey greeted me as though we were seeing each other for the first time. He played his part composedly and skilfully, with the appropriate gestures and the correct sort of smile. But it was the wrong role, and I was almost sorry that he played it with such bravado, and would have wished instead for the proper 'Herr Self? Herr Selk? A man of many guises?'

We went over to the groundsman. Court eight was reserved under Frau Buchendorff's name; the groundsman pointed it out to us curtly and ungraciously, involved as he was in an argument with an older married couple who insisted they had booked a court.

'Take a look yourselves, if you please, all the courts are taken and your name isn't on the list.' He tilted the screen so that they could see it.

'I can't allow this,' said the man. 'I booked the court a week in advance.'

His wife had already given up. 'Oh, leave it, Kurt. Maybe you mixed things up again.'

Mischkey and I exchanged a quick glance. He wore a

disinterested expression but his eyes told me his game was up.

The match we launched into is one I'll never forget. It was as though Mischkey and I wanted to compensate for what had been lacking in open combat before. I played beyond my capabilities, but Babs and I were properly thrashed.

Frau Buchendorff was in high spirits. 'I have a consolation prize for you, Herr Self. How about a bottle of champagne on the terrace?'

She was the only one to have enjoyed the game uninhibitedly and didn't mask her admiration for her partner and her opponents. 'I hardly recognized you, Peter. You're enjoying yourself today, aren't you?'

Mischkey tried to beam. He and I didn't say much as we drank the champagne. The two women kept the conversation going.

Babs said, 'Actually, that wasn't really a game of doubles. If I weren't so old, I'd hope you two men were battling for me. But as it is, you must be the one they're wooing, Frau Buchendorff.'

And then the two women were on to age and youth, men and lovers, and whenever Frau Buchendorff made some frivolous remark, she gave the silent Mischkey a kiss.

In the changing rooms I was alone with Mischkey.

'How does it go from here?' he asked.

'I'll hand in my report to the RCW. What they'll do with it, I don't know.'

'Can you leave Judith out of it?'

'That's not so easy. She was the bait to a certain extent. How else could I explain how I got on to you?'

'Do you have to say how you got on to me? Isn't it enough if I simply confess that I cracked the MBI system?'

I thought it over. I didn't believe he wanted to make

trouble for me, nor could I see how that would be possible. 'I'll try. But don't pull any fast ones. Otherwise I'll have to submit that other report.'

Back at the car park we joined the two ladies. Was I seeing Frau Buchendorff for the last time? I didn't like the thought.

'See you soon?' was her goodbye. 'How's the case coming along by the way?'

21

You're such a sweetheart

My report for Korten turned out to be short. Nonetheless, it took me five hours and a bottle of Cabernet Sauvignon before my draft was finished at midnight. The whole case replayed in front of me, and it wasn't easy to keep Frau Buchendorff out of it.

I saw the RCW–RCC link as the exposed flank of the MBI system that allowed not only people from the RCC but also other businesses connected to the RCC to access the RCW. I borrowed Mischkey's characterization of the RCC as the turntable of industry espionage. I recommended disconnecting the emission data recording system from the central system.

Then I described, in a sanitized way, the course my investigation had taken, from my discussions and research in the Works to a fictive confrontation with Mischkey at which he had declared himself willing to repeat a confession and to reveal the technical details to the RCW.

With an empty, heavy head I went to bed. I dreamt of a tennis match in a railway carriage. The ticket inspector, in a gas mask and thick rubber gloves, kept trying to pull out the carpet I was playing on. When he succeeded we continued to play on the glass floor, while beneath us the sleepers raced by. My partner was a faceless woman with heavy, hanging breasts. Her movements were so powerful, I was constantly afraid she'd crash through the glass. As she did I woke up in horror and relief.

In the morning I went to the offices of two young lawyers in Tattersallstrasse whose under-burdened secretary sometimes typed for me. The lawyers were playing Amigo on their computers. The secretary promised me the report for eleven o'clock. Then, back in my office, I looked through the mail, mostly brochures for alarm and security systems, and called Frau Schlemihl.

She hemmed and hawed a great deal, but eventually I got my lunchtime meeting with Korten in the canteen. Before I collected the report, I booked a flight on the spot at the travel agent's for that evening to Athens. Anna Bredakis, a friend from university days, had asked that I give her plenty of prior warning. She had to get the yacht she'd inherited from her parents sail-worthy and assemble a crew from amongst her nieces and nephews. But I'd prefer to be in Piraeus, haunting the harbour bars, rather than reading about Mischkey's arrest in the *Mannheimer Morgen* and having Frau Buchendorff connect me to Firner, who'd congratulate me with his silver tongue.

I arrived half an hour late for lunch with Korten, but I couldn't use that to make a point. 'Are you Herr Self?' asked a grey mouse at reception who'd caked on too much rouge. 'Then I'll call the general director straight away. If you'd be so kind as to wait.'

I waited in the reception hall. Korten came and greeted me rather curtly. 'Things not advancing, my dear Self? You need my help?'

It was the tone of a rich uncle greeting his tiresome, debt-producing, and money-begging nephew. I looked at him in bewilderment. He might have a lot of work and be stressed and hassled, but I was hassled, too.

'All I need is for you to pay the bill in this envelope. You could also listen to how I solved your case, but then again you could also let it be.'

'Not so touchy, my dear friend, not so touchy. Why

didn't you tell Frau Schlemihl right away what this is about?' He took my arm and led me into the Blue Salon once again. My eyes searched in vain for the redhead with the freckles.

'So, you've solved the case?'

I briefly summarized my report. When, over the soup, I came onto the slip-ups of his team, he nodded earnestly. 'Now you see why I can't hand over the reins yet. Nothing but mediocrity.' I didn't comment. 'And what sort of man is this Mischkey?'

'How do you imagine someone who orders a hundred thousand rhesus monkeys for your plant and deletes all account numbers that begin with thirteen?'

Korten grinned.

'Exactly,' I said. 'A colourful character, and a brilliant computer expert to boot. If you'd had him in your computer centre, these mess-ups wouldn't have happened.'

'And how did you get on to this brilliant chap?'

'What I choose to say on that is contained in the report. I don't have any wish to expand greatly on that now. Somehow I find Mischkey likeable and I don't find it easy to turn him in. I'd appreciate it if you weren't too severe, not too hard – you know what I mean, don't you?'

'Self, you're such a sweetheart!' Korten laughed. 'You've never learned to do things thoroughly or not at all.' And then, more reflectively, 'But perhaps that's your strength – your sensitivity lets you get inside things and people; it lets you cultivate your scruples, and at the end of the day you do actually function.'

He rendered me speechless. Why so aggressive and cynical? Korten's observation had got me where it hurt, and he knew it and blinked with pleasure.

'Don't worry, my dear Self, we won't cause any

unnecessary trouble. And about what I said – I admire it in you very much, don't get me wrong.'

He was making it even worse and looked me mildly in the face. Even if there was some truth in his words – doesn't friendship mean treading carefully when it comes to the lies the other person builds into his life? But there wasn't any truth in it. I felt a surge of fury.

I didn't want dessert any more. And preferred to have my coffee in the Café Gmeiner. And Korten had a meeting at two.

At eight I drove to Frankfurt and flew to Athens.

Part Two

I

Luckily Turbo likes caviar

In August I was back in Mannheim.

I always enjoy going on vacation and the weeks in the Aegean were spent in a glow of brilliant blue. But now I'm older I enjoy coming home more, as well. After Klara's death I redecorated the apartment. During our marriage I hadn't managed to assert myself against her taste and so, at fifty-six, I caught up on the pleasures of decorating that other people delight in when they're young. I do like my two chunky leather sofas that cost a fortune and also hold their own with the tomcat, the old apothecary shelves where I keep my books and records, and the bunk-bed in my study I had built into the niche. Coming home I also always look forward to Turbo, whom I know is looked after well by the next-door neighbour but who does, in his quiet manner, suffer in my absence.

I'd put down my suitcases and opened the door when, with Turbo clinging to my trouser leg, I beheld a colossal gift hamper that had been placed on the floor of the hallway.

The door to the next-door apartment opened and Frau Weiland greeted me. 'How nice that you're back, Herr Self. My, you're tanned. Your cat has missed you very much, haven't you, puss wuss wuss wuss? Have you seen the hamper yet? It came three weeks ago with a chauffeur from the RCW. Shame about the beautiful flowers. I did consider putting them in a vase, but they'd be dead now anyway. The mail is on your desk as always.'

I thanked her and sought refuge behind the apartment door from her torrent of words.

From *pâté de foie gras* to Malossol caviar it contained every delicacy I like and dislike. Luckily Turbo likes caviar. The attached card, with an artistic rendition of the firm logo, was signed by Firner. The RCW thanked me for my invaluable service.

They'd paid, too. In the mail were account statements, postcards from Eberhard and Willy, and the inevitable bills. I'd forgotten to cancel my subscription to the *Mannheimer Morgen*; Frau Weiland had stacked the papers neatly on the kitchen table. I leafed through them before putting them in a bin bag, and sampled the musty taste of old political excitement.

I unpacked and threw a load in the washing machine. Then I did my shopping, had the baker's wife, the head butcher, and the people in the grocer's shop comment admiringly on my rested appearance, and enquired after news as though all sorts must have happened in my absence.

It was the summer holidays. The shops and the streets were emptier, my driver's eyes picked out parking spaces in the most unlikely of places, and a stillness infused the town. I'd returned from my break with that lightness of spirit that allows you to experience familiar surroundings as new and different. It all gave me a floating sensation that I wanted to savour. I put off my trip to the office until the afternoon. Fearfully, I made my way to the Kleiner Rosengarten: would it have shut down for the holiday? But from a distance I could see Giovanni standing in the garden gate, napkin over his arm.

'You come-a back from the Greek? Greek not good. Come on-a, I make you the gorgonzola spaghetti.'

98

'*Si*, old Roman, great.' We played our German-converses-with-guest-worker game.

Giovanni brought me the Frascati and told me about a new film. 'That would be a role for you, a killer who could just as easily be a private detective.'

After the spaghetti gorgonzola, coffee, and sambuca, after an hour with the *Süddeutsche* by the Wasserturm, after an ice-cream and another coffee at Gmeiner I gave myself up to the office. It wasn't as bad as all that. My answering machine had announced my absence until today and not recorded any messages. In amongst the newsletters from the Federal Association of German Detectives, a tax notice, advertisements, and an invitation to subscribe to the *Evangelical State Encyclopedia* I found two letters. Thomas was offering me a teaching appointment on the security studies course at the technical college of Mannheim. And Heidelberg Union Insurance asked me to get in touch as soon as I returned from my holiday.

I dusted a little, flicked through the newspapers, got out the bottle of sambuca, the jar with the coffee beans, and poured myself a measure. While I reject the cliché of whisky in the desk of a private detective, there's got to be some sort of bottle. Then I recorded my new message, made an appointment with Heidelberg Union Insurance, put off replying to Thomas's offer, and went home. The afternoon and evening were spent on the balcony, seeing to this and that. The account statements got me calculating and I realized that with the jobs so far I'd almost fulfilled my annual target. And coming after the holiday, too. Most reassuring.

I managed to hold on to my sense of floating into the following week. The insurance fraud case I'd taken on I worked through without getting involved. Sergej Mencke, a mediocre ballet dancer at Mannheim National Theatre, had taken out a high insurance policy on his legs and promptly suffered a complicated break. He'd never dance again. A million was the sum in question and the insurance company wanted to be sure all was above board. The notion that a person could break their own leg repelled me. When I was a small boy, as an example of male willpower, my mother told me how Ignatius of Loyola re-broke his leg himself with a hammer when it healed crookedly. I've always abhorred self-mutilators, the young Spartan who let his belly be mauled by a fox, Mucius Scaevola, and Ignatius of Loyola. But so far as I was concerned, they could all have had a million if it meant them disappearing from the pages of our schoolbooks. My ballet dancer claimed the break occurred when shutting the heavy door of his Volvo; on the evening in question he was running a high fever, had to get through a performance nonetheless, and afterwards wasn't himself. That's why he'd slammed the door although his leg was still hanging out. I sat in my car for a long time trying to imagine whether such a thing was possible. There wasn't much more I could do with the summer break that had scattered his theatre colleagues and friends in every direction.

Sometimes I thought about Frau Buchendorff and about Mischkey. I hadn't found anything about his case in the papers. Once I happened to walk along Rathenaustrasse and the second-floor shutters were closed.

2

Everything was fine with the car

It was pure coincidence that I got her message in time one afternoon in September. Normally I don't listen to any of the calls that come in the afternoon until the evening, or the next morning. Frau Buchendorff had called in the afternoon and asked if she could talk to me after work. I'd forgotten my umbrella so had to go back to the office, saw the signal on the answering machine, and called back. We agreed to meet at five o'clock. Her voice was subdued.

Shortly before five I was in my office. I made coffee, rinsed the cups, tidied the papers on my desk, loosened my tie, undid my top button, pushed my tie up again, and moved the chairs in front of my desk back and forth. Finally they stood where they always stand. Frau Buchendorff was punctual.

'I really don't know if I should have come. Maybe I'm only imagining things.'

She stood, out of breath, next to the potted palm. She smiled uncertainly, was pale, and had shadows beneath her eyes. As I helped her out of her coat her movements were nervous.

'Take a seat. Would you like a coffee?'

'For days I've done nothing but drink coffee. But, yes, please do give me a cup.'

'Milk and sugar?'

Her thoughts were elsewhere and she didn't reply.

Then she fixed me with a look of determination that forced down her scruples and insecurities.

'Do you know anything about murder?'

Carefully I put the cups down and sat myself behind the desk.

'I've worked on murder cases. Why do you ask?'

'Peter is dead, Peter Mischkey. It was an accident, they say, but I simply can't believe it.'

'Oh, my God!' I got up, paced back and forth behind my desk. I felt queasy. In the summer on the tennis court I'd destroyed a part of Mischkey's vitality, and now he was dead.

Hadn't I ruined something for her, too, then? Why had she come to me anyway?

'You met him just that one time playing tennis, and he did play pretty wildly, and it's true, he was also a wild driver, but he never had an accident and drove so confidently with such concentration – what happened doesn't fit.'

So she knew nothing about my meeting with Mischkey in Heidelberg. Nor would she refer to the tennis match that way if she knew I'd turned Mischkey in. It seemed he'd told her nothing, nor had she, in her role as Firner's personal assistant, discovered anything. I didn't know what to make of that.

'I liked Mischkey and I'm terribly sorry, Frau Buchendorff, to learn of his death. But we both know that not even the best of drivers is immune to road accidents. Why don't you believe it was an accident?'

'You know the railway bridge between Eppelheim and Wieblingen? That's where it happened, two weeks ago. According to the police report, Peter skidded out of control on the bridge, broke through the railings, and crashed down onto the tracks. He had his seatbelt on, but the car buried him beneath it. His cervical vertebra was broken and he was killed on the spot.' She sobbed convulsively, brought out a handkerchief, and blew her nose. 'Sorry. He drove that route every Thursday; after his sauna at the Eppelheim baths he rehearsed with his band in Wieblingen. He was musical, you know, played the piano really well. The section over the bridge is straight as an arrow, the roads were dry, and visibility was good. Sometimes it's foggy but not that evening.'

'Are there any witnesses?'

'The police didn't trace any. And it was late, around eleven p.m.'

'Did they check the car?'

'The police say everything was fine with the car.'

I didn't have to enquire about Mischkey. He'd have been taken to the forensic medicine department, and if any alcohol or heart failure or any other failure had been ascertained the police would have told Frau Buchendorff. For a moment a vision of Mischkey on the stone dissection table came to me. As a young attorney I often had to be present at autopsies. I had a sudden image of his abdominal cavity being stuffed with wood shavings and sewn up with large stitches at the end.

'The funeral was the day before yesterday.'

I considered. 'Tell me, Frau Buchendorff, apart from the details of the event, do you have any reason to doubt that it was an accident?'

'In recent weeks I often barely recognized him. He was morose, dismissive, turned in on himself, sat at home a lot, hardly wanted to join me on anything at all. Once he even threw me out, just like that. And he evaded all my questions. Sometimes I thought he had someone else, but then again he'd cling to me with a kind of intensity he hadn't shown before. I was at a complete loss. Once, when I was especially jealous . . . You'll think, perhaps, I'm not coping with my grief and am being hysterical. But what happened that afternoon . . .'

I topped up her cup and looked at her encouragingly.

'It was on a Wednesday that we'd both taken off to spend more time together. The day started badly and it wasn't the case that we wanted to spend more time with one another; actually I wanted him to have more time for me. After lunch he suddenly said that he had to go to the Regional Computing Centre for a couple of hours. I knew very well that wasn't the truth and was disappointed and furious and could feel his frostiness and imagined him with someone else and did something that I think is actually pretty lousy.' She bit her lip. 'I followed him. He didn't drive to the RCC, but into Rohrbacher Strasse and up the hill on Steigerweg. It was easy to follow him. He drove to the War Cemetery. I'd been careful to keep an appropriate distance. When I reached the cemetery he'd parked his car and was striding up the broad path in the middle. You know the War Cemetery, don't you, with that path that seems to lead straight to heaven? At the end of it there's a man-size, chiselled block of sandstone that looks like a sarcophagus. He went up to it. None of this made any sense to me and I hid in the trees. When he'd almost reached the block two men stepped out from behind it, suddenly and quietly, as if they'd come out of nothingness. Peter looked from one to the other; he seemed to want to turn to one of them, but didn't know which.

'Then everything went like lightning. Peter turned to his right, the man to his left took two steps, grabbed him from behind, and held him tightly. The guy on the right punched him in the stomach, over and over. It was quite unreal. The men seemed detached somehow, and Peter made no attempt to defend himself. Perhaps he was just as paralysed as I was. And it was over in a flash. As I started to run, the one who'd punched Peter took his glasses from his nose with an almost careful gesture, dropped them, and crunched them beneath his heel. Then just as silently and suddenly, they left Peter and disappeared again behind the sandstone block. I heard them running away through the woods.

'When I reached Peter he had collapsed and was lying awkwardly on his side. I . . . but that doesn't matter. He never told me why he had gone to the cemetery and been beaten up. Nor did he ever ask me why I'd followed him.'

We were both silent. What she'd recounted sounded like the work of professionals and I could understand why she doubted Peter's death was an accident.

'No, I don't think you're being hysterical. Is there anything else that seemed odd to you?'

'Little things. For example, he started smoking again. And let his flowers die. He was apparently strange with his friend Pablo as well. I met him once during that time because I didn't know what else I could do and he was worried, too. I'm glad you believe me. When I tried to tell the police about the thing in the War Cemetery they weren't in the least bit interested.'

'And that's what you want me to do, to carry out the investigations the police neglected?'

'Yes. I can imagine you're not cheap. I can give you ten thousand marks and in exchange I'd like clarity about Peter's death. Do you need an advance?'

'No, Frau Buchendorff. I don't need any advance, nor can I tell you now whether I'll be taking on the case. What I can do is conduct a kind of pre-investigation: I have to ask the obvious questions, check the evidence, and only then will I decide whether to take the case. Do you agree?'

'Good, let's do it that way, Herr Self.'

I noted down some names, addresses, and dates, and promised to keep her informed. I took her to the door. Outside the rain was still falling.

3

A silver St Christopher

My old friend in the Heidelberg police force is Chief Detective Nägelsbach. He's just waiting for retirement; since starting as a messenger at the age of fifteen at the public prosecutor's office in Heidelberg he may have constructed Cologne Cathedral, the Eiffel Tower, the Empire State Building, Lomonossov University, and Neuschwanstein Castle from matches, but the reconstruction of the Vatican, his real dream, is simply too much alongside his police work, and has been postponed for his retirement. I'm curious. I've followed my friend's artistic development with interest. In his earlier works the matches are somewhat shorter. Back then his wife and he removed the sulphur heads with a razor blade; he hadn't known that match factories also distribute headless matches. With the longer matches the later models took on a gothic, towering quality. Since his wife no longer needed to help with the matches she began reading to him as he worked. She started with the first book of Moses and is currently on Karl Kraus's *The Torch*. Chief Detective Nägelsbach is an erudite man.

I'd called him in the morning and when I was with him at ten o'clock in police headquarters he made me a photocopy of the police report.

'Ever since data protection came on the scene no one here knows what he's allowed to give out. I've decided not to know what I'm not allowed to give out,' he said, handing me the report. It was only a few pages long.

'Do you know who oversaw the accident protocol?'

'It was Hesseler. I thought you'd want to talk with him. You're in luck, he's here until noon and I've let him know you'll be coming by.'

Hesseler was sitting at a typewriter, pecking away laboriously. I'll never understand why policemen are not taught to type properly. Unless it's supposed to be a form of torture for the suspects and witnesses to watch a typing policeman. It is torture; the policeman brushes away at the typewriter helplessly and aggressively, looking unhappy and extremely determined – an explosive and fearful mixture. And if you're not induced to make a statement then at least you're deterred from altering the statement once it has been written and completed by the policeman, regardless of how unfamiliar he's rendered it.

'Someone who'd driven over the bridge after the accident called us. His name's in the report. When we arrived the doctor had just turned up and clambered down to the accident vehicle. He saw immediately that nothing could be done. We closed the road and secured the evidence. There wasn't much to secure. There was the skid mark showing that the driver simultaneously braked and swung the steering wheel to the left. As to why he did that there's no indication. Nothing points to the fact that another vehicle was involved, no shattered glass, no trace of body paint, no further skid mark, nothing. A strange accident all right but the driver lost control of his vehicle, that's all.'

'Where is the vehicle?'

'At Beisel's scrapyard, behind the Zweifarbenhaus, the brothel behind the railway station. The professionals examined it. I think Beisel will scrap it soon. The storage fees are already higher than the scrap price.'

I thanked him. I looked in on Nägelsbach to say goodbye.

'Do you know *Hedda Gabler*?' he asked me.

'Why?'

'It cropped up yesterday in Karl Kraus and I didn't understand whether she drowned or shot herself or neither of the above, and whether she did it in the sea or in a vine arbour. Karl Kraus is pretty complicated at times.'

'All I know is that she's one of Ibsen's heroines. Why not read the play next? Karl Kraus can easily be interrupted.'

'I'll have to talk to my wife. It would be the first time we interrupted something.'

Then I drove to Beisel. He wasn't there. One of his workers showed me the shell.

'Do you know what's going to happen with the car? Are you family?'

'I think it'll get scrapped.'

Looking at it from the rear right you'd have thought it was almost unscathed. The top had been down when the accident occurred and closed by the towing company, or by the expert, due to the rain; it was in one piece. On the left-hand side the car was completely crushed at the front and gashed open at the side. The axle and the engine block were twisted to the right, the hood was folded into a V, the windshield and the headrests lay on the back seat.

'Ah, scrapped. You can see, yourself, that there's not much to the car now.' So saying, he peered at the stereo with such obvious furtiveness that it caught my attention. It was completely intact.

'I won't take the stereo from you. But could I look at the car now, alone?' I slipped him a ten-mark note and he left me in peace.

I walked round the car once more. Strange, on the right headlight Mischkey had stuck black sticky tape in the shape of a cross. Again I was fascinated that the right side seemed almost intact. When I took a close look I discovered the blotches. They weren't easily visible against the bottle-green paintwork, nor were there many. But they looked like blood and I wondered how it had got there. Had Mischkey been pulled out of the car on his side? Had Mischkey bled at all? Had someone hurt themselves during the recovery? Perhaps it was unimportant but whether it was blood or not now interested me so much that I scraped off some shavings of paintwork where the stains were into an empty film canister with my Swiss penknife. Philipp would get the sample tested.

I pushed back the top and looked inside. I saw no blood on the driver's seat. The side pockets of the doors were empty. A silver St Christopher was attached to the dashboard. I picked it up; maybe Frau Buchendorff would like to have it even though it had let Mischkey down. The radio and cassette player reminded me of the Saturday I'd followed Mischkey from Heidelberg to Mannheim. There was still a cassette inside that I took out and pocketed.

I don't have much of a clue about the inner workings of cars. So I refrained from staring blankly at the motor or crawling under the wreck. What I'd seen was plenty to give me a picture of the car's collision with the railings and the descent onto the tracks. I retrieved my small automatic camera from my coat pocket and took a couple of pictures. Along with the report Nägelsbach had given me were some photos but they were scarcely recognizable on the Xerox.

4

I sweated alone

Back in Mannheim, the first thing I did was drive to the city hospital. I located Philipp's room, knocked, and went in. He was in the process of hiding his ashtray, complete with smouldering cigarette, in the drawer of his desk. 'Ah, it's you.' He was relieved. 'I promised the senior nurse I'd stop smoking. What brings you round my way?'

'I've a favour to ask you.'

'Ask me over a coffee, let's go to the canteen.' As he strode ahead, white coat billowing, a cheeky one-liner for every pretty nurse, he looked like a lecherous Marcus Welby, MD. In the canteen he whispered something at me about the blonde nurse three tables away. She shot him a look, the look of a blue-eyed barracuda. I'm fond of Philipp but if he's gobbled up one day by a barracuda like that he'll deserve it.

I fetched the film canister from my pocket and placed it in front of him.

'Sure, I can get your film developed in the X-ray lab. But now you're shooting pictures you're not comfortable taking to the photo shop? Well, Gerd, that's a shocker.'

Philipp really did have one thing on the brain. Was it the same with me when I was in my late fifties? I thought back. Following the stale years of marriage to Klara I'd experienced those first years as a widower like a second springtime. But a second spring full of romance – Philipp's pose as the gay Lothario was alien to me.

'Wrong, Philipp. There are some grains of paint in the film canister with something on them and I need to know whether it's blood, if possible which blood group. And it doesn't come from a deflowering on the hood of my car, as you're doubtless thinking, but from a case I'm working on.'

'The one doesn't necessarily contradict the other. But, whatever, I'll see to it. Is it urgent? Do you want to wait?'

'No, I'll give you a call tomorrow. How are things, by the way? Shall we drink a glass of wine sometime?'

We decided to meet on Sunday evening in the Badische Weinstuben. As we were leaving the canteen together he suddenly shot off. An Asian nurse's aid was stepping into the elevator. He made it just before the doors closed.

Back in the office I did what I should have done a long time ago. I called Firner's office, exchanged a few words with Frau Buchendorff, and was put through to Firner.

'Greetings, Herr Self. What's up?'

'I'd like to thank you very much for the hamper that was waiting for me when I got back from holiday.'

'Ah. You were on holiday. Where did it take you?'

I told him about the Aegean, about the yacht, and that I'd seen a ship full of RCW containers in Piraeus. He'd gone walking in the Peloponnese as a student and now had business every so often in Greece. 'We're protecting the Acropolis from erosion, a Unesco project.'

'Tell me, Herr Firner, how did my case proceed?'

'We took your advice and severed our system from the emission data site. We did so immediately after your report and since then haven't had any further annoyances.'

'And what did you do with Mischkey?'

'A few weeks ago we had him here with us for a full day and he had a great deal to say about the system connections, points of entry, and possible security measurements. A capable man.'

'You didn't get the police involved?'

'That didn't strike us as particularly opportune. From the police it gets into the press – we don't like that sort of publicity.'

'And the damages?'

'We considered that, too. If it interests you: some of our people found it unbearable simply to let Mischkey go after calculating the damage he caused at five million. But at the end of the day, fortunately, economic sense triumphed over the legal aspect. Also over the legal reflections of Oelmüller and Ostenteich, who wanted Mischkey's case to be brought before the Federal Court. It wasn't a bad idea: before the Federal Court the Mischkey case would have demonstrated the dangers to which businesses are prey under the new emissions law. But it would have brought undesirable publicity. Besides, we're hearing, via the Economics Ministry, about rumblings from Karlsruhe that would make any further arguments on our part unnecessary.'

'So, all's well that ends well.'

'That would have a somewhat cynical ring to it, I think, in the knowledge that Mischkey went on to die in a car crash. But you're right, for the Works the matter had a happy ending, all things considered. Will we be seeing you here again? I had no idea that the general and yourself were such old friends. He told me about it when my wife and I spent an evening at his home recently. You know his house in Ludolf-Krehl-Strasse?'

I knew Korten's house in Heidelberg, one of the first to be built in the late fifties from the perspective of personal security. I can still remember Korten one evening proudly demonstrating the cable car to me that connects the house, situated high up on the steep cliff above the street, with the entrance gate. 'If there's a power cut, it runs on my emergency power supply.'

Firner and I said our goodbyes with a few niceties. It was four o'clock, too late to make up for the missed lunch, too early to eat dinner. I went to the Herschel baths.

The sauna was empty. I sweated alone, swam alone beneath the high cupola with its Byzantine mosaics, found myself alone in the Irish-Roman steam bath and on the roof terrace. Shrouded in a large, white sheet, I dozed off on my deck chair in the rest room. Philipp was roller-skating through the hospital corridors. The columns he passed were shapely female legs. Sometimes they moved. Philipp avoided them, laughing. I laughed back at him. Then I suddenly saw that it was a scream that gashed his face. I woke up and thought of Mischkey.

5

Hmm, well, what do you mean by good?

The proprietor of Café O had expressed his personality in an interior design that summarized everything that was fashionable at the end of the seventies, from the imitation fin-de-siècle lamps and the hand-operated orange juice squeezer to the little bistro tables with the marble tops. I wouldn't want to know him.

Frau Mügler, the dancer, I recognized by the severe black hair pulled back into a little ponytail, her angular femininity, and her look of sincere engagement. She'd gone as far as she could to look like Pina Bausch. She was sitting at the window, drinking a glass of freshly squeezed orange juice.

'Self. We spoke on the phone yesterday.' She looked at me with raised eyebrows and nodded almost imperceptibly. I joined her. 'Nice of you to take the time. My insurance firm still has some questions regarding Herr Mencke's accident that his colleague may be able to answer.'

'How did you hit on me in particular? I don't know Sergej especially well, haven't been here in Mannheim for long.'

'You're simply the first one back from vacation. Tell me, did Herr Mencke strike you as particularly exhausted and nervous in the last few weeks before the accident? We're looking for an explanation for its strange nature.' I ordered a coffee; she took another orange juice.

'Like I said, I don't know him well.'

'Did anything attract your attention?'

'He seemed very quiet, oppressed at times, but what do you mean by "attract attention"? Perhaps he's always like that, I've only been here six months.'

'Who from the Mannheim National Theatre knows him particularly well?'

'Hanne was closer to him at some point, so far as I know. And he hangs out with Joschka a lot, I think. Maybe they can help you.'

'Was Herr Mencke a good dancer?'

'Hmm, well, what do you mean by good? Wasn't exactly Nureyev, but then I'm no Bausch. Are you good?'

I'm no Pinkerton, I could have replied, but that wouldn't have been appropriate for my role.

'You won't find another insurance investigator like me. Could you give me the last names of Hanne and Joschka?'

I could have saved my breath. She hadn't been there long; don't forget, 'and in the theatre we're all on a first-name-terms basis. What's your first name?'

'Hieronymus. My friends call me Ronnie.'

'I didn't want to know what your friends call you. I think first names have something to do with one's personality.'

I'd love to have run out screaming. Instead I thanked her, paid at the counter, and left quietly.

6

Aesthetics and morality

The next morning I called Frau Buchendorff. 'I'd like to take a look at Mischkey's apartment and things. Could you arrange for me to get in?'

'Let's drive over together after office hours. Shall I pick you up at three-thirty?'

Frau Buchendorff and I took the back roads to Heidelberg. It was Friday, people were home early from work and getting their homes, yards, gardens, cars, and even the pavements ready for the weekend ahead. Autumn was in the air. I could feel my rheumatism coming on and would have preferred to have the top up, but I didn't want to appear old and kept quiet. In Wieblingen I thought about the railway bridge on the way to Eppelheim. I'd go there in the next few days. Now, with Frau Buchendorff, the detour hardly seemed appropriate.

'That's the way to Eppelheim,' she said, pointing past the small church to the right. 'I have the feeling I should take a look at the spot, but I can't do it yet.'

She left the car in the parking lot at Kornmarkt. 'I called ahead. Peter shared the apartment with a friend who works at Darmstadt Technical University. I do have a key but didn't want just to turn up.'

She didn't notice I knew the way to Mischkey's apartment. I didn't try to play dumb. No one answered our ring and Frau Buchendorff opened the front door. The lobby contained cool air from the cellar: 'The cellar goes down two levels into the hillside.' The floor was made of heavy slabs of sandstone. Bicycles were propped against the wall decorated with Delft tiles. The letterboxes had all been broken into at some point. Only a faint light trickled through the stained-glass windows onto the worn stairtreads.

'How old is the house?' I asked as we climbed to the third floor.

'A couple of hundred years. Peter loved it. He had lived here since he was a student.'

Mischkey's part of the apartment consisted of two large interlinking rooms. 'You needn't stay here, Frau Buchendorff, while I'm looking around. We can meet afterwards in a café.'

'Thanks, but I'll manage. Do you know what you're looking for?'

'Hmm.' I was getting my bearings. The front room was the study with a large table at the window, a piano and shelves against the remaining walls. In the shelves files and stacks of computer printouts. Through the window I could see the rooftops of the old town and Heiligenberg. In the second room was a bed with a patchwork quilt, three armchairs from the era of the kidney-shaped table, one of the aforementioned tables, a wardrobe, television, and a stereo system. From the window I looked left up to the castle and right to the advertising column I'd stood behind weeks ago.

'He didn't have a computer?' I asked in astonishment.

'No. He had all sorts of private stuff on the RCC system.'

I turned to the shelves. The books were about mathematics, computing, electronics, and artificial intelligence, films and music. Next to them an absolutely beautiful edition of *Green Henry* and stacks of science fiction. The spines of the files indicated bills and taxes, guarantee certificates and instruction manuals, references and documents, travel, the public census, and computer stuff I barely understood. I reached for the folder of bills and leafed through it. In the references file I discovered that Mischkey had won a prize in his third year of high school. On his desk was a pile of papers that I looked through. Along with private mail, unpaid bills, programming notes, and sheet music, I came across a newspaper cutting.

RCW honoured the oldest fisherman on the Rhine. While he was out fishing yesterday on the river, Rudi Basler, who had turned ninety-five years old, was surprised by a delegation from the RCW headed by General Director Dr H. C. Korten: 'I didn't want to pass up the opportunity of congratulating the grand old man of Rhine-fishing personally. Ninety-five years old and still as fresh as a fish in the Rhine.' Our photo captures the moment in which General Director H. C. Korten shares the happiness of the celebrated man and presents him with a gift hamper . . .

The picture had a clear shot of the gift hamper in the foreground; it was the same one I'd received. Then I found a copy of a short newspaper article from May 1970.

Scientists as forced labourers in the RCW? The Institute for Contemporary History has picked up a hot potato. The most recent monograph from the *Quarterly of Contemporary History* deals with the forced labour of Jewish scientists in German industry from 1940 to 1945. According to this, renowned Jewish chemists among others worked in degrading conditions on the development of chemical war materials. The press officer of the RCW pointed to a planned commemorative publication for their 1972 centenary in which one contribution will deal with the firm's history under National Socialism, including the 'tragic incidents'.

Why had this been of interest to Mischkey?

'Could you come here for a moment?' I asked Frau Buchendorff, who was sitting in the armchair in the other room, staring out of the window. I showed her the newspaper article and asked her what she made of it.

'Yes, recently Peter had started asking for information on this or that about the RCW. He never had before. Regarding the matter of the Jewish scientists I even had to copy the article from our commemorative publication.'

'And where this interest stemmed from he didn't say?'

'No, nor did I push him to tell me anything because talking was often so difficult towards the end.'

I found the copy of the commemorative publication in the file entitled 'Reference Chart Webs'. It was next to the computer printouts. The R, the C, and the W had caught my eye as I was casting a resigned farewell glance at the shelves. The file was full of newspaper and other articles, some correspondence, a few brochures and computer printouts. So far as I could see, all the material was linked to the RCW. 'I can take the file with me, can't I?'

Frau Buchendorff nodded. We left the apartment.

On the homeward journey on the motorway the roof was closed. I sat with the file on my knees and felt like a schoolboy.

Suddenly Frau Buchendorff asked me, 'You were a public prosecutor, Herr Self, weren't you? Why did you actually stop?'

I took a cigarette from the packet and lit it. When the pause grew too long I said, 'I'll answer your question, I just need a moment.' We overtook a truck with a yellow tarpaulin, 'Fairwell' on it in red letters. A great name for a removal firm. A motorbike droned past us.

'At the end of the war I was no longer wanted. I'd been a convinced National Socialist, an active party member, and a tough prosecutor who'd also argued for, and won, the death penalty. There were some spectacular trials. I had faith in the cause and saw myself as a soldier on the legal front. I could no longer be utilized on the other front following my wound at the start of the war.' The worst was over. Why hadn't I simply told Frau Buchendorff the sanitized version? 'After nineteen forty-five I first worked on my in-laws' farm, then in a coal merchant's, and then slowly started doing private investigations. For me, my work as a public prosecutor didn't have a future. I could only see myself as the National Socialist I'd been, and certainly couldn't be again. I'd lost my faith. You probably can't imagine how anyone could believe at all in National Socialism. But you've grown up with knowledge that we, after nineteen forty-five, only got piece by piece. It was bad with my wife, who was a beautiful blonde Nazi and stayed that way till she became a nice, round Economic Miracle German.' I didn't want to say any more about my marriage. 'Around the time of the Monetary Reform they started to draft incriminated colleagues back in. I could have returned to the judiciary then, too. But I saw what the efforts to get reinstated, and the reinstatement itself, did to my colleagues. Instead of feeling guilt they only had a sense that they'd been done an injustice when they were expelled and that this reinstatement was a kind of reparation. That disgusted me.'

'That sounds closer to aesthetics than morality.'

'It's hard to tell the difference any more.'

'Can't you imagine anything beautiful that's immoral?'

'I see what you mean, Riefenstahl, *Triumph of the Will* and so on. But since I've grown older I just don't find the choreography of the masses, the bombastic architecture of Speer and his epigones, and the atomic blast brighter than a thousand suns beautiful any more.'

We had stopped by my door and it was approaching seven. I'd have liked to invite Frau Buchendorff to the Kleiner Rosengarten. But I didn't dare.

'Frau Buchendorff, would you care to dine with me in the Kleiner Rosengarten?'

'That's nice of you, many thanks, but I won't.'

7

A raven mother

Quite against my principles I'd taken the file with me to dinner.

'Working and eating izza no good. The stomach is ruined.'

Giovanni pretended to seize the file. I clung to it tightly. 'We always work, we Germans. Not the dolce vita.'

I ordered calamari with rice. I abstained from spaghetti because I didn't want to get any sauce stains on Mischkey's file. Instead I spilled some Barbera on Mischkey's letter to the *Mannheimer Morgen* with which he'd enclosed an advertisement.

> Historian at the University of Hamburg looking for oral evidence from workers and employees of the RCW from the years before 1948 for a study of social and economic history. Discretion and reimbursement of expenses. Replies to box number 379628.

I found eleven responses, some in spidery handwriting, some laboriously typed, that answered the ad with not much more than name, address, and phone number. One response came from San Francisco.

Whether anything had come of the contacts wasn't revealed by the file. It contained no notes by Mischkey at all, no clue as to why he'd put this collection together, and what his intentions were. I found the contribution to the commemorative publication photocopied by Frau Buchendorff, and further on the small brochure of an anti-chemical-industry action group – '100 Years RCW – 100 Years Are Enough' – with essays on work accidents, suppression of strikes, the entanglement of capital and politics, forced labour, union persecution, and party contributions. There was even an essay about the RCW and the church with a picture of the Reich Bishop Müller in front of a large Erlenmeyer retort. It struck me that during my Berlin student days I'd got to know a Fräulein Erlenmeyer. She was very rich and Korten said she came from the family of the aforementioned retort. I'd believed him, the similarity was undeniable. What had become of Reich Bishop Müller? I wondered.

The newspaper articles in the file dated back to 1947. They all bore reference to the RCW but otherwise appeared to be ordered randomly. The pictures, sometimes blurred in the copies, showed Korten first as a simple director, then as general director, showed his forerunner General Director Weismüller, who had retired shortly after 1945, and General Director Tyberg whom Korten had replaced in 1967. The photograph of the hundred-year anniversary had captured Korten receiving Chancellor Kohl's congratulations and next to him he seemed small, delicate, and distinguished. The articles were full of news about finance, careers, and production, and now and again about accidents and slip-ups.

Giovanni cleared my plate away and placed a sambuca in front of me without a word. I ordered a coffee to go with it. At the neighbouring table a woman of around forty was sitting, reading *Brigitte*. From the cover I saw its lead article was 'STERILIZED – AND NOW WHAT?' I gathered my courage.

'Yes, indeed, now what?'

'I'm sorry?' She looked at me in confusion and ordered an amaretto. I asked her if she came here often.

'Yes,' she said. 'After work I always come here to eat.'

'Are you sterilized?'

'Believe it or not, I am sterilized. And after my sterilization I had a child, the sweetest little boy.' She laid down *Brigitte*.

'Incredible,' I said. 'And does *Brigitte* approve of that?'

'The case doesn't crop up. It's more about unhappy women and men who realize they want children after they've been sterilized.' She nipped at her amaretto.

I crunched a coffee bean. 'Doesn't your son like Italian food? What does he do in the evenings?'

'Would you mind if I joined you rather than screeching the answer through the entire restaurant?'

I stood up, pulled back a chair invitingly, and said I'd be delighted if she – well, the usual things you say. She brought a glass with her and lit a cigarette. I looked at her more closely, the somewhat tired eyes, the stubborn mouth, and the tiny wrinkles, the lacklustre ash-blonde hair, the ring in one ear and the Band-Aid on the other. If I didn't watch out I'd be in bed with this woman within three hours. Did I want to watch out?

'To come back to your question – my son is in Rio with his father.'

'What's he doing there?'

'Manuel is eight years old now and goes to school in Rio. His father studied in Mannheim. I almost married him, because of the residence permit. When the child arrived he had to return to Brazil and we agreed he'd take him with him.' I frowned at her. 'Now you consider me a raven mother. But I didn't get sterilized for the fun of it.'

A raven mother, indeed. Or at least an irritating one. According to German fairy tales, raven mothers and fathers push their fledglings from the nest. I never found out whether this does justice to real ravens, but it seemed to apply to her and I didn't have any particular desire to keep flirting. When I remained silent, she asked, 'Why the interest in the sterilization thing anyway?'

'First something clicked in my mind, because of the cover of *Brigitte*. Then you interested me, how composed you were as you dealt with the question. Now it feels too composed, the way you talk about your son. Perhaps I'm too old-fashioned for this kind of composure.'

'Composure can't be imparted. A shame that prejudices are always confirmed.' She took her glass and wanted to leave.

'Could you just say first what RCW brings to mind?' She gave me a frosty look. 'I know, it's a stupid-sounding question. But the RCW has been in my mind all day and I can't see the wood for the trees.'

She responded earnestly. 'A whole lot comes to mind. And I'll tell you, because there's something about you that I like. RCW to me stands for the Rhine Chemical Works, contraception pills, poisoned air and poisoned water, power, Korten—'

'Why Korten?'

'I massaged him. I give massages as it happens.'

'So you are a masseuse?'

'Masseuses are our impure sisters. Korten came for six months with back problems and he spoke a bit about himself and his work during the sessions. Sometimes we got into proper discussions. One time he said, "It's not reprehensible to use people, it's just tactless to let them notice." That stayed in my mind for a long time.'

'Korten was my friend.'

'Why "was"? He's still alive.'

Yes, why 'was'? Had our friendship been buried in the meantime? 'Self, you sweetheart' – again and again the words had gone through my head in the Aegean and sent a shudder down my spine. Submerged memories had resurfaced, blended with fantasy, and forced their way into my sleep. With a cry, I'd awoken from the dream bathed in sweat: Korten and I hiking through the Black Forest – I knew very well that it was the Black Forest in spite of the high cliffs and deep gullies. There were three of us, a classmate was with us, Kimski or Podel. The sky was deep blue, the air heavy and yet surreally clear. Suddenly stones crumbled and bounced away silently down the slope, and we were hanging from a rope that was fraying. Above us was Korten and he looked at me and I knew what he expected of me. Still more of the cliff tumbled silently into the valley; I tried to claw my way up, to secure the rope and pull up the third man. I couldn't do it and tears of helplessness and despair came to my eyes. I got out my penknife and started to cut through the rope beneath me. I have to do it, I have to, I thought, and cut. Kimski or Podel fell into the ravine. I could see it all at once, flailing arms, getting smaller and smaller in the distance, gentle mockery in Korten's eyes, as though it were all a game. Now he could pull me up and when he almost had me at the top, sobbing and bleeding, 'Self, you sweetheart' came once again, and the rope broke . . .

'What's wrong? What's your name, by the way? I'm Brigitte Lauterbach.'

'Gerhard Self. If you didn't come in your own car – may I after this bumpy evening offer you a lift home in my jolting Opel?'

'Yes, please. I'd have taken a taxi otherwise.'

Brigitte lived in Max-Joseph-Strasse. The goodbye peck on the cheek turned into a long embrace.

'Would you like to come up, stupid? With a sterilized and raven mother?'

8

An everyday sort of blood

While she fetched wine from the fridge I stood there in her living room with all the awkwardness of the first time. You're still wary about what might not grate: a canary in a cage, a Peanuts poster on the wall, Yevtushenko in the bookshelves, Barry Manilow on the turntable. Brigitte was guilty of none of the above. Yet the wariness was there – perhaps it's always in one's self?

'Can I make a phone call?' I called through to the kitchen.

'Go right ahead. The phone's in the top drawer of the bureau.'

I opened the drawer and dialled Philipp's number. It rang eight times before he picked up.

'Hello?' His voice sounded oily.

'Philipp, Gerd here. I hope I'm disturbing you.'

'You bet, you crazy dick. Yes, it was blood, blood type O, rhesus negative. An everyday sort of blood, so to speak, age of the sample between two and three weeks. Anything else? Sorry, but I'm tied up here. You saw her yesterday, remember, the little Indonesian in the elevator. She brought her friend along. It's all action.'

Brigitte had come into the room with a bottle and two glasses, poured it, and brought a glass over to me. I'd handed her the extension, and Brigitte looked at me in amusement at Philipp's last sentences.

'Do you know anyone at forensics in Heidelberg, Philipp?'

'No, she doesn't work at forensics. At McDonald's at the Planken, that's where she works. Why?'

'It's not Big Mac's blood type I'm after, but Peter Mischkey's – he was examined by forensics at Heidelberg. And I'd like to know if you can find out. That's why.'

'But it doesn't have to be right now. Come round instead, let's talk about it over breakfast. Bring someone with you though. I'm not slogging my guts out so you can come along and lick the cream.'

'Does she have to be Asian?'

Brigitte laughed. I put my arm round her and she snuggled into me demurely.

'No, my home is like a Mombasa brothel, all races, all classes, all colours, all lines of business. And if you're really coming, bring a bottle.'

He hung up. I put my other arm around Brigitte too. She leant back into my arms and looked at me. 'And now?'

'Now we take the bottle and the glasses and the cigarettes and the music over to the bedroom and lie down in bed.'

She gave me a little kiss-and-send in a bashful voice: 'You go ahead, I'll be right there.'

She went into the bathroom. Amongst her records I found one by George Winston, put it on, left the bedroom door open, switched on the bedside lamp, undressed, and got into her bed. I felt a little embarrassed. The bed was wide and smelled fresh. If we didn't sleep well tonight, the fault would be all ours.

Brigitte came into the bedroom, naked, with only the earring in her right ear and the plaster on her left earlobe. She whistled along to the George Winston. She was heavy round the hips, had breasts which were large and couldn't help but sag a little, broad shoulders, and a protruding collarbone which gave her an air of vulnerability. She slipped beneath the covers and into the crook of my arm.

'What happened to your ear?' I asked.

'Oh,' she laughed in embarrassment, 'combing my hair, I kind of combed the ring out of my ear. It didn't hurt, I just bled like a pig. The day after tomorrow I have an appointment with a surgeon. He'll make a clean wound of the tear and patch it together again.'

'Would you mind me removing your other earring? Otherwise I'll be afraid of tearing it out, too.'

'You're such a passionate guy?' She took it out herself. 'Come on, Gerhard, let me take off your watch.' It was nice to have her bending over me like that, fumbling with my arm. I pulled her down to me. Her skin was smooth and fragrant. 'I'm tired,' she said in a sleepy voice. 'Will you tell me a bedtime story?'

I felt relaxed. 'Once upon a time there was a little raven. Like all ravens he had a mother.' She pinched my side. 'The mother was black and beautiful. She was so black that all the other ravens appeared grey next to her, and she was so beautiful that all the other ravens appeared ugly next to her. She herself didn't realize it. Her son, the little raven, could see and knew it very well. He knew much more besides: that black and beautiful is better than grey and ugly, that raven fathers are as good and as bad as raven mothers, that you can be wrong in the right place and right in the wrong place. One day after school the little raven flew away and got lost. He told himself that nothing could happen to him: in one direction he'd be sure to encounter his father, and in the other his mother. Nonetheless he was afraid. Beneath him he could see a land stretching far and wide with small villages and large, gleaming lakes. It was pretty to look at, but frighteningly unfamiliar to him. He flew and flew and flew . . .' Brigitte's breathing had grown regular. She snuggled comfortably into my arms again and started to snore softly, her mouth slightly open. I carefully withdrew my arm from under her head and put out the light. She turned onto her side. So did I and we lay there like spoons in the cutlery case.

When I woke up it was just after seven and she was still asleep. I crept out of the bedroom, shut the door behind me, looked for and found the coffee machine, got it going, pulled on my shirt and trousers, took Brigitte's set of keys from the bureau, and bought croissants in Lange Rötterstrasse. I was back at her bedside with the tray and coffee and croissants before she woke up.

It was a lovely breakfast. And lovely afterwards together again beneath the covers. Then she had to leave to take care of her Saturday morning patients. I wanted to drop her off at her massage practice in the Collini Centre, but she preferred to walk. We didn't arrange another meeting. But when we embraced at her front door we could hardly pull ourselves apart.

9

Clueless for hours

It was a long time since I'd spent a night with a woman. Afterwards, returning home is like coming back to your own town after a holiday. A short period of limbo before normality kicks in again.

I prepared a special rheumatism tea, purely prophylactic, and lost myself in Mischkey's file once again. On the top was the photocopied newspaper article that had been lying on Mischkey's desk and that I'd shoved in the file. I read the connected commemorative piece entitled 'Twelve Dark Yards'. It touched only briefly on the forced labour of Jewish chemists. Yes, these had existed, but the RCW had also suffered with the Jewish chemists in this oppressive situation. In contrast with other big German businesses, RCW had generously compensated forced labourers immediately after the war. Using South Africa as an example, the author portrayed how alien any kind of mandatory employment situation was to the character of the modern industrial enterprise. Moreover, employment in the plant had lowered the rate of suffering in the concentration camps; the survival rate of the RCW forced labourers was proven to be higher than that of the average concentration camp population. The author dealt extensively with the RCW's participation in the resistance, remembered the condemned communist workers, and depicted in detail the trial of the general director-to-be Tyberg, and his erstwhile colleague Dohmke.

Memories of the trial came back to me. I'd led the inquiry then, while my boss, Södelknecht, the senior public prosecutor, had led the prosecution. The two RCW chemists were sentenced to death for sabotage and for some violation of the Race Laws, which I didn't recall. Tyberg managed to escape; Dohmke was hanged. The whole affair must have been at the end of 1943, beginning of 1944. At the start of the fifties Tyberg returned from the USA after succeeding very quickly there with a chemical company of his own, came back to RCW, and soon thereafter was made general director.

A large part of the newspaper article was devoted to the fire of March 1978. The press had estimated the damages at 40 million marks, no deaths or injuries were reported, and statements from the RCW were printed, according to which the poison released from the burnt pesticides posed absolutely no danger to the human body. I'm fascinated by such findings of the chemical industry: the same poison that annihilates the cockroach, which is supposed to be able to survive a nuclear holocaust, is no more harmful to humans than a barbecue on a charcoal grill. In the *Stadtstreicher* magazine I found documentation by the group The Chlorine Greens that the Seveso poisons TCDD, hexachloroethane, and trichloroethylene had been released by the fire. Numerous injured employees were swept off in hush-hush fashion to the company's own treatment clinic in the South of France. Then there was a collection of copies and cuttings about the capital stakes of the RCW and about an inquiry by the Federal Antitrust Office, which dealt with the role of the plant within the pharmaceutical market and which went nowhere.

I sat for hours in front of the computer printouts, clueless. I found data, names, figures, curves, and incomprehensible acronyms such as BAS, BOE, and HST. Were these printouts of the files Mischkey had managed privately at RCC? I needed to talk to Grimm.

At eleven I started to call the numbers on the responses to Mischkey's ad. I was Professor Selk of Hamburg University, wanting to pick up the contacts initiated by his colleague for the social and economic history research project. The people on the other end were dumbfounded; my colleague had told them that their oral testimony wasn't of any use to the research project. I was puzzled; one phone call after the other with the same empty result. From some of them I gathered at least that Mischkey hadn't attached any value to their statements because they'd only started work at the RCW after 1945. They were annoyed because if my colleague had put out an ad that referred to the end of the war they could have saved themselves the trouble of responding. 'Reimbursements of expenses, it said, are we going to get our money from you now?'

I'd just put down the receiver when the phone rang.

'It's impossible to get through to you. What woman have you been talking to all this time?' Babs wanted to make sure I hadn't forgotten we were going to a concert that evening. 'I'm bringing Röschen and Georg. They enjoyed *Diva* so much they don't want to miss Wilhelmenia Fernandez.'

Of course I had forgotten. And while I'd been perusing the file, some little coil in my brain had disconnected so that it could play with the possibility of an evening arrangement incorporating Brigitte. Were there any tickets left?

'Quarter to eight at the Kleiner Rosengarten? I might be bringing someone with me.'

'So it was a lady on the phone. Is she pretty?'

'I like her.'

It was only to be thorough that I wrote to Vera Müller

133

in San Francisco. There was nothing specific I could ask her. Perhaps Mischkey had asked her specific questions, my letter attempted to find out just that. I picked it up and walked to the main post office on Parade-Platz. On the way home I bought five dozen snails for after the concert. I also got fresh liver for Turbo; I felt guilty about leaving him alone the night before.

Back home I was about to make a sandwich with sardines, onions, and olives. Frau Buchendorff prevented me. She'd had to type something for Firner that morning at the plant, was on her way home through Zollhofstrasse passing the Traber-Pilsstuben, and was quite certain she recognized one of the men from the War Cemetery.

'I'm in a phone-box. He hasn't emerged, I don't think. Could you come over straight away? If he drives off, I'll follow him. Head back home if I'm not here and I'll call you later, when I can.' Her voice cracked.

'My God, girl, don't do anything stupid. It's enough to jot down his registration number. I'm on my way.'

I O

It's Fred's birthday

In the stairwell I almost flattened Frau Weiland. Driving off, I nearly took Herr Weiland with me. I drove via the railway station and the Konrad Adenauer Bridge, past blanching pedestrians and reddening traffic lights. When I drew up five minutes later in front of the Traber-Pilsstuben, Frau Buchendorff's car was still facing it in the No Stopping zone. No sign of her, though. I got out and went into the pub. One bar, two or three tables, a jukebox and pinball, maybe ten guests and the proprietress. Frau Buchendorff had a glass of Pils in one hand and a meat patty in the other. I placed myself next to her at the bar. 'Hello there, Judith. You're back in the neighbourhood, are you?'

'Hello, Gerhard. Join us for a beer?'

I ordered two meat patties to go with the beer.

The guy on her other side said in a thick Austrian accent, 'It's the boss's mother who makes these meat things.'

Judith introduced him to me. 'This is Fred. A real Viennese gent. He's got something to celebrate, he was saying. Fred, this is Gerhard.'

He'd already celebrated thoroughly. Lurching and weaving cautiously like all drunks, he took himself off to the jukebox, propped himself up to select records as though there were nothing amiss, came back and sat down between Judith and myself. 'The boss, our Silvia, is from

Austria too. That's why I like celebrating my birthday at her pub. And take a look, I've got my birthday present.' He patted Judith's bottom with the flat of his hand.

'What do you do for a living, Fred?'

'Marble and red wine, import and export. And yourself?'

'I'm in the security business, property and personal security, bouncers, bodyguards, dog trainers, and whatnot. I could use a strong guy like you. You'd have to go easy on the alcohol, though.'

'Well, well, security.' He set down his glass. 'There's nothing more secure than a firm ass. Right, sweetheart?' He now used the hand that had been holding the glass to grope Frau Buchendorff's posterior. Judith's butt.

She turned round and slapped down hard on Fred's fingers, looking at him impishly. It hurt and he withdrew his hands, but he wasn't mad at her.

'And what are you doing here with your security?'

'I'm looking for people for a job. There's money in it, for me, for the people I find, and for the contractor I'm on the lookout for.'

Fred's face registered interest. Maybe because his hands weren't permitted to do anything with Judith's butt for the moment, he tapped my chest with a fleshy index finger. 'Isn't that a bit too big for you, gramps?'

I seized his hand, forced it down, twisting his finger in the process, and looking at him innocently all the while. 'How old are you today, Fred? You're not the man I'm looking for? Never mind, come on, I'll get you a drink.'

Fred's face was contorted with pain. I let go and he hesitated for a moment. Should he lay into me, or drink a beer with me? Then his eyes went to Judith and I knew what was coming.

His 'Fine, a beer' was an overture for the punch that caught me on the left side of my ribcage. But I'd already rammed my knee between his legs. He doubled up, cradling his testicles. When he straightened up, my right fist hit him in the middle of his nose. His hands flew up to shield his face, then he lowered them again and stared incredulously at the blood. I reached for his glass and emptied it over his head. 'Cheers, Fred.'

Judith had stepped to the side, the other clients kept their distance. Only the proprietress joined the battle on the front lines. 'Clear out, if it's trouble you want, clear out,' she said, already jostling me towards the exit.

'But sweetheart, can't you see, we're just having a bit of fun? We're getting on just fine, isn't that right, Fred?'

Fred wiped the blood from his lips. He nodded and looked around for Judith.

A quick survey of her pub convinced the proprietress that peace and order had been restored. 'Well, then, have a schnapps on the house,' she said soothingly. Her establishment was under control.

While she was pouring them, and Fred had slunk off to the toilet, Judith came over to me. She looked at me in concern. 'He was one of the ones at the War Cemetery. Is everything all right?' She spoke softly.

'He may have smashed my ribs, but if you'll call me Gerd, I'll get over it,' I replied. 'Then I'd simply call you Judith.'

She smiled. 'I think you're exploiting the situation, but I don't want to quibble. I was just picturing you in a trench coat.'

'And?'

'You don't need one,' she said.

Fred came back from the toilet. He'd put on a hang-dog expression in front of the mirror and even apologized.

'Not bad shape for your age. Sorry I got out of order. You know, basically it's not easy to grow old without a family and around my birthday I really feel it.'

Beneath Fred's friendly veneer, malice and the crooked charm of a Viennese pimp shone through.

'Sometimes something wild takes over, Fred. The thing with the beer wasn't necessary, but I can't undo it.' His hair was still damp and sticky. 'Don't hold it against me. I only get mad when women are involved.'

'What shall we do now?' asked Judith with an innocent blink of the eyes.

'First we'll take Fred home, then I'll take you home,' I ordained.

The proprietress jumped on the bandwagon. 'Right, Fred, you'll be taken home. You can collect your car tomorrow. Come in a taxi.'

We bundled Fred into my car. Judith followed us.

Fred claimed to live in Jungbusch, 'in Werftstrasse, just next to the old police station, you know', and wanted to be dropped off at the corner.

I couldn't care less where he didn't live. We drove over the bridge.

'That big story of yours, is there anything in it for me? I've done some security stuff before, for a big company round here too,' he said.

'We can talk about it. If you're looking for some action I'd be glad to have you. Just give me a call.'

I fished out a business card from my jacket pocket, a real one, and gave it to him. At the corner I let him out and he headed with a swaying gait towards the next pub. I still had Judith's car in the rear-view mirror. I drove via the Ring and turned round the Wasserturm into the Augusta-Anlage. I'd expected a farewell flash of her lights beyond the National Theatre and then to see nothing more of her. She followed me to Richard-Wagner-Strasse outside my front door and waited, motor running, as I parked.

I got out, locked up, and walked over to her. It was only

seven strides but I gave them everything about superior manliness that I'd picked up in my second youth. I leant down to her window, no rheumatic expense spared, and pointed to the next parking space with my left hand.

'You will come up for a cup of tea, won't you?'

11

Thanks for the tea

While I was making the tea, Judith paced the kitchen, smoking. She was still extremely worked up. 'What a twerp,' she said, 'what a twerp. And he put the fear of God in me at the War Cemetery.'

'He wasn't alone that time. And do you know, if I'd let him get going, I'd have been more frightened myself. He's beaten up quite a few people in his time.'

We took our tea into the sitting room. I thought back to breakfast with Brigitte and was glad that the dishes weren't lying in my kitchen now.

'I still don't know whether I can take on your case. But you should consider whether I really ought to take it on. I've investigated Peter Mischkey's affairs before. I turned him in for breaking into the RCW computer system, as a matter of fact.' I told her everything. She didn't interrupt. Her eyes were full of hurt and reproach. 'I can't accept the way you're looking at me. I did my job, and that sometimes means using people, exposing them, turning them in, even if they're likeable.'

'So what? Why the great confession then? Somehow you're seeking absolution from me.'

I spoke into her wounded, cold face. 'You are my client, and I like things to be straight between my clients and me. Why I didn't tell you the story right away, you might ask. I—'

'I might well ask. But actually I really don't want to

listen to the slick, cowardly falsehoods you might care to tell me. Thanks for the tea.' She grabbed her handbag and stood up. 'What do I owe you for your trouble? Send me a bill.'

I stood up, too. As she was about to open the door in the hallway, I pulled her hand away from the door handle. 'You mean a lot to me. And your interest in clearing up what happened to Mischkey isn't satisfied. Don't leave like this.'

While I'd been talking, she'd left her hand in mine. Now she withdrew it and left without a word.

I shut the door to the apartment. I took the olives out of the fridge and sat on the balcony. The sun was shining, and Turbo, who'd been roaming the rooftops, curled up purring on my lap. It was only because of the olives. I gave him a few. From the street I could hear Judith turning on the ignition of her Alfa. The motor roared, then petered out. Was she coming back? A few seconds later the motor was running again and she drove off.

I succeeded in not thinking about whether I had behaved correctly, and enjoyed every single olive. They were the black Greek ones that taste of musk, smoke, and rich earth.

After an hour on the balcony I went into the kitchen and prepared the herb butter for the snails we'd eat after the concert. It was five o'clock. I called Brigitte and let the phone ring ten times. As I did the ironing I listened to *La Wally* and looked forward to Wilhelmenia Fernandez. From the cellar I fetched a couple of bottles of Alsace Riesling and put them in the fridge.

12

Hare and Tortoise

The concert was in the Mozartsaal. Our seats were in the
sixth row, off to the left, so that our view of the singer
wasn't obscured by the conductor. Sitting down, I cast a
glance around. A pleasantly mixed audience, from elderly
ladies and gentlemen right down to kids you could easily
picture at a rock concert. Babs, Röschen, and Georg
arrived in a silly mood; mother and daughter sticking
their heads together and giggling, Georg sticking out
his chest and preening. I sat between Babs and Röschen,
patting the right knee of one and the left knee of the
other.

'I thought you were bringing a woman of your own to
pet, Uncle Gerd.' Röschen picked up my hand with the
tips of her fingers and let it drop next to her knee. She was
wearing a black lace glove that left the fingers free. The
gesture was crushing.

'Oh, Röschen, Röschen, when you were a little girl and
I rescued you from the Indians, you on my left arm, my
Colt in my right hand, you never spoke to me like that.'

'There aren't any Indians any more, Uncle Gerd.'

What had become of my sweet girl? I took a sideways
look at her, the postmodern angular haircut, and, hanging
down from her ear, the clenched silver fist with the
expressive thumb between the index and middle finger,
the flattish face she'd inherited from her mother, and the
somewhat too small, still childlike mouth.

The conductor was a slimy Mafioso, as short as he was fat. He bowed his permed head to us and drove the orchestra into a medley from *Gianni Schicchi*. The man was good. With the barest movements of his delicate baton he coaxed the most tender tones from the mighty orchestra. I also had to concede it was to his credit he'd placed an exquisite little female timpanist behind the kettledrums, in tails and dress trousers. Could I wait for her by the orchestra exit after the concert and offer my assistance in carrying her kettledrums home?

Then Wilhelmenia came on stage. She'd grown plumper since *Diva*, but looked enchanting in a glittering sequined evening gown. Best of all was *La Wally*. With her the concert ended, with her the diva conquered the audience. It was nice to see young and old united in applause. After two hard-fought-for encores, during which the small timpanist brilliantly made my heart turn somersaults again, we stepped lightly into the night.

'Shall we go on somewhere?' asked Georg.

'Back to my place, if you'd like. I've prepared snails and the Riesling is chilling.'

Babs glowed, Röschen moaned, 'Do we have to walk there?' and Georg said, 'I'll walk with Uncle Gerd, you can take the car.'

Georg is a serious young man. On the way he told me about his law studies where he was embarking upon his fifth term, about the grades he was getting and the criminal case he was working on at the moment. Environmental criminal law – that sounded interesting but it was just the usual camouflage for problems of perpetration, instigation, and being an accessory that I could have been asked forty years ago. Is it lawyers that have so little imagination, or reality?

Babs and Röschen were waiting by the front door. When I'd unlocked, it turned out that the lighting in the stairwell wasn't working. We felt our way up, with frequent stumbles and much laughter. Röschen was a bit afraid of the dark and pleasantly mute.

It turned into a nice evening. The snails were good and so was the wine. My performance was a complete success. When I took the cassette player with its small microphone that made pretty good recordings out of my inside pocket, opened it, and slipped the cassette into the tape deck on my stereo, Röschen recognized the reference immediately and clapped her hands. Georg got it when Wally started to sing. Babs looked at us questioningly. 'Mum, you'll have to check out *Diva* next time it's playing.'

We played Hare and Tortoise, the fashionable board game, and at half past midnight it was at a decisive stage and the wine all gone. I took my torch and went down to the cellar. I don't recall ever going down the main stairway without light before. But my legs had grown so used to the way over the long years that I felt quite secure. Until the second to last flight of stairs. Here the architect, perhaps to make the *belle étage* more impressive, and with higher ceilings, had built fourteen steps instead of the customary twelve. I'd never noticed, nor had my legs taken heed of this detail of the stairway, and after the twelfth step I took a large step out instead of a small step down. My legs buckled, I managed to hold on to the banister, but pain shot up my back. I straightened up, took a tentative next step, and turned on the torch. I got a terrible shock. The wall on the second to last section of stair has a mirror with a stucco frame, and in it I saw a man facing me, shining a beam of light right at me. It took just a fraction of a second for me to recognize myself. But the pain and the fright were enough to send me into the cellar with a hammering heart and unsteady step.

We played until two-thirty. When the taxi collected them and I'd mastered the dark stairs once more and cleaned up the dishes in the kitchen, I stood for the duration of a cigarette by the telephone. I felt an urge to call Brigitte. But the old school won.

13
Do you like it?

I frittered the morning away. In bed I leafed through Mischkey's file and thought again about why he had put it together, sipped at my coffee, and nibbled the pastries I'd bought yesterday in anticipation of Sunday. Then in *Die Zeit* I read a pastoral Op-Ed piece, a melodramatic political summary, the statesmanlike commentary from our ex-chancellor with the worldwide reputation, and the usual stuff from the owner. Once again I knew the lie of the land and so didn't feel the need to expose my mind to the food editor's review of a book on how to cook in a hot-air balloon. Then I smooched with Turbo. Brigitte still wasn't picking up. At half past ten Röschen rang the bell. She'd come to collect the car. I threw my dressing gown on over my nightshirt and offered her a sherry. Her brush-cut was in rack and ruin this morning.

At last I was weary of my pottering and drove over to the bridge between Eppelheim and Wieblingen where Mischkey had met his death. It was a sunny early autumn day; I drove through the villages, the mist was hanging over the Neckar, and although it was a Sunday, potatoes were being harvested, the first leaves were turning, and smoke rose from the inns' chimneys.

The bridge itself didn't tell me anything I didn't know from the police report. I looked down at the tracks that lay some five metres beneath me, and thought of the turned-over Citroën. A local train went by in the direction of

Edingen. When I walked across the car lanes and looked down on the other side I saw the old railway station. A beautiful sandstone building from the turn of the century with three floors, rounded bow windows on the second floor, and a little tower. The station café was apparently still open. I went in.

The room was gloomy, of the ten tables three were occupied, on the right-hand side was a jukebox, pinball, and two video games, on the counter, restored in the old German style, a stunted potted palm and in its shadow the landlady. I sat down at the free table at the window, with a view onto the platform and the railroad embankment, got a menu with *Wiener*, *Jäger* and *Zigeuner-schnitzel*, all served with fries, and asked the landlady what their special was, their *plat du jour*, to use Ostenteich's terms. She could offer *Sauerbraten* with dumplings and red cabbage, and broth with beef marrow. 'First rate,' I said, and ordered a wine from Wiesloch to go with it.

A young girl brought me the wine. She was around sixteen, with a lascivious voluptuousness that was more than the combination of too tight jeans, too tight a blouse, and too red lips. She'd have chatted up any man under fifty. Not me. 'Enjoy,' she said, bored.

When her mother brought me the soup I asked about the accident in September. 'Did you hear it at all?'

'I'd have to ask my husband about that.'

'And what would he say?'

'Well, we were already in bed, and then suddenly there was this smash. And shortly afterwards another. I said to my husband, "Something must have happened out there." He got up straight away and took the tear-gas gun with him, because our game machines are always being broken into. But this time it had nothing to do with the games machines, but with the bridge. Are you from the press?'

'I'm from insurance. Did your husband call the police?'

'My husband didn't know anything at that point. When he found nothing in the dining room he came back up and pulled some clothes on. Then he went out to the platform but he could already hear the ambulance siren. Who else could he have called?'

Her ample, blonde daughter brought the beef and listened attentively. Her mother sent her away to the kitchen.

'Your daughter didn't realize what was happening?' It was obvious they had a problem.

'She doesn't notice anything. Just stares at everything in trousers, if you know what I mean. I wasn't like that at her age.' Now it was too late for her. Her eyes were filled with hungry futility. 'Do you like it?'

'Just like home,' I said.

The bell in the kitchen rang, and she removed her willing flesh from my table. I wolfed down the *Sauerbraten* and the Wieslocher.

On the way to the car I heard quick steps behind me. 'Hey, you!' The kid from the station café was running after me breathlessly. 'You wanted to hear something about the accident. Is there a hundred in it for me?'

'Depends what you've got to say.' She was a hard-boiled little slut.

'Fifty upfront, and before that I don't even start talking.'

I wanted to know and pulled out two fifty notes from my wallet. One of them I gave to her, the other I rolled into a ball.

'So it was like this. That Thursday Struppi drove me home. When we came over the bridge, the delivery van was there. I wondered what it was doing on the bridge. Then Struppi and I, we, well, you know. And when the smash came I told Struppi to leave, as I was pretty sure my father would come any minute. My parents have something against Struppi because he's as good as married. But I love him. So what. Anyhow, I saw the delivery van drive off.'

I gave her the scrunched-up ball. 'What did the delivery van look like?'

'Strange, somehow. You don't see them round our way usually. But I can't tell any more. Its lights weren't on either.'

Her mother was peering out of the café doorway. 'Get over here, Dina. Leave the man in peace!'

'Okay, I'm coming.' Dina walked back at a provocatively slow pace.

Sympathy and curiosity prompted me to meet the man who'd been saddled with this wife and daughter. In the kitchen I came across a thin, sweating little guy juggling pots and pans and casseroles. He'd probably already made several attempts to kill himself with the tear-gas gun.

'Don't do it. The two of them aren't worth it.'

On the drive home I kept an eye open for delivery vans that aren't usually found round here. But I didn't see a thing, it was Sunday after all. If what Dina had told me was correct, there was, God knows, more to Mischkey's death than was contained in the police report.

When we met up in the evening at the Badische Weinstuben Philipp knew that Mischkey's blood group was AB. So it wasn't his blood I'd scraped off the side. What conclusions could be drawn?

Philipp ate his black pudding with relish. He told me about gingerbread hearts, heart transplants, and his new girlfriend, who shaved her pubic hair in the shape of a heart.

14

Let's stretch our legs

I'd spent half the Sunday with a case I didn't have a commission for any more. Private detectives don't do that, on principle.

I looked through the smoked glass out onto the Augusta-Anlage. Decided to decide at the tenth car how to proceed. The tenth car was a Beetle. I crawled behind my desk to write a closing report to Judith Buchendorff. Every end must have its form.

I took a writing pad and a pencil, and jotted down key points. What spoke against it being an accident? There was what Judith had told me, there were the two bangs that Dina's mother had heard, and above all there was Dina's observation. If I were continuing with the case, it was explosive enough to send me on an urgent hunt for the delivery van and its driver. Did the RCW have something to do with my case? Mischkey had done extensive research on it, with whatever intention, and it must be the large plant Fred had worked for once. Had Fred rained down punches that day in the War Cemetery on their behalf? Then I also had the traces of blood on the right side of Mischkey's convertible. And finally there was the feeling that something wasn't right, and various shreds of thought from the previous days. Judith, Mischkey, and a jealous, spurned rival? A different computer-hacking venture of Mischkey's, this time with deadly retaliation? An accident involving the delivery van, the driver of which committed a hit-and-run? I thought of the two bangs – an accident in which a third vehicle was also involved? Suicide? Had it all got too much for Mischkey?

It took me a long time to compose these half-baked things into a conclusive report. And I sat almost as long wondering whether I should write Judith an invoice and what should be in it. I rounded it off to a thousand marks and slapped on sales tax. When I'd typed the envelope, and stamped it and put in the letter and invoice and licked down the envelope, pulled on my coat and was ready to go and post it, I sat down again and poured myself a sambuca with three coffee beans.

It had all got fucked up. I'd miss the case, which had taken a stronger hold on me than work usually did. I'd miss Judith. Why not admit it?

When the letter was in the post box I turned to the case of Sergej Mencke. I called the National Theatre and made an appointment with the ballet director. I wrote to the Heidelberg Union Insurance asking if they'd be willing to foot the bill for a trip to the USA. The two best friends and colleagues of the self-mutilated ballet dancer, Joschka and Hanne, had both accepted engagements in Pittsburgh for the new season and had already left, and I'd never been to the States. I discovered that Sergej Mencke's parents lived in Tauberbischofsheim. The father was an army captain there. The mother said on the telephone I could look in at lunchtime. Captain Mencke ate lunch at home. I called Philipp and asked him whether in the annals of leg-breaks, self-induced breaks and breaks caused by a slammed car door were recorded at all. He offered to present his student with the problem as a dissertation theme. 'Three weeks okay for the results?' It was.

Then I set off for Tauberbischofsheim. I still had enough time to drive slowly through the Neckar valley and to stop for coffee in Amorbach. In front of the castle a school class was making a racket waiting for a guided tour. Can one really imbue children with a sense of the beautiful?

Herr Mencke was a bold man. He'd built himself a house, even though he might get relocated. He opened the door in uniform. 'Step right in, Herr Self. I don't have much time, I've got to head back in a minute.' We sat down in the living room. Jägermeister schnapps was offered, but no one drank.

Sergej was actually called Siegfried and had left his parents' house at the age of sixteen, much to his mother's distress. Father and son had broken ties with one another. The sporty son still wasn't forgiven for having evaded army service with a bogus spinal-chord injury. The path leading to ballet had also met with disapproval. 'Perhaps it's also got a good side, his not being able to dance any more,' his mother mused. 'When I visited him in hospital, he was just like my Sigi again.'

I asked how Siegfried had coped financially since then. There were apparently always some friends, or girlfriends, who supported him. Herr Mencke poured himself a Jägermeister after all.

'I'd have liked to give him something from Granny's inheritance. But you didn't want that.' She turned reproachful eyes on her husband. 'You've just driven him deeper into everything.'

'Leave it, Ella. That isn't of interest to the insurance man. I must be getting back. Come along, Herr Self, I'll see you out.' He stood in the doorway and watched me until I'd driven off.

On the journey home I stopped in at Adelsheim. The inn was full; a few business people, teachers from the boarding school, and at one table three gentlemen who gave me the feeling they were a judge, a prosecutor, and a defence lawyer from the Adelsheim local court, negotiating in peace and quiet without the bothersome presence of the accused. I remembered my days at court.

In Mannheim I met the rush-hour traffic and needed twenty minutes for the five hundred metres through the Augusta-Anlage. I opened the door to the office.

'Gerd,' someone called, and as I turned I saw Judith coming from the other side of the street through the parked cars. 'Can we talk for a moment?'

I locked the door again. 'Let's stretch our legs.'

We walked up Mollstrasse and along Richard-Wagner-Strasse. It took a while before she said anything. 'I overreacted on Saturday. I still don't think it's good you didn't tell me straight away on Wednesday about Peter and you. But somehow I can understand how you felt, and the way I acted as though you're not to be trusted, I'm sorry about that. I can get pretty hysterical since Peter's death.'

I needed a while, too. 'This morning I wrote you a final report. You'll find it along with an invoice in your mail, today or tomorrow. It was sad. It felt as though I was having to tear something out of my heart: you, Peter Mischkey, some better understanding of myself that I was getting from the case.'

'Then, you'll agree to continue? Just tell me what's in your report.'

We'd reached the art museum; a few drops were falling. We went in and, wandering through the nineteenth-century painting galleries, I told her what I'd discovered, my theories, and what I was pondering. In front of Feuerbach's painting of Iphigenia on Aulis she stopped. 'This is a beautiful painting. Do you know the story behind it?'

'I think Agamemnon, her father, has just deposited her as a sacrifice to the goddess Artemis so that a wind will

153

start to blow again and the Greek fleet can set sail for Troy. I love the painting.'

'I'd like to know who that lady was.'

'The model, you mean? Feuerbach loved her very much. Nanna, the wife of a cobbler from Rome. He quit smoking for her sake. Then she ran away from him and her husband with an Englishman.'

We walked to the exit and saw it was still raining. 'What do you plan to do next?' Judith asked.

'Tomorrow I want to talk to Grimm, Peter Mischkey's colleague in the Regional Computer Centre, and with a few people from RCW again.'

'Is there anything I can do?'

'If something comes to mind, I'll let you know. Does Firner actually know about you and Mischkey, and that you've hired me?'

'I haven't said anything to him. But why did he never actually tell me about Peter's involvement in our computer story? To begin with he always kept me up to date.'

'So you never realized that I'd tied up the case?'

'Well yes, a report from you crossed my desk. It was all very technical.'

'You only got the first part. Why, I would like to know. Do you think you can find out?'

She'd try. The rain had stopped, it had grown dark, and the first lights were coming on. The rain had brought the stench from the RCW with it. On the way to her car we didn't talk. There was weariness in Judith's step. As I said goodbye I could also see the deep tiredness in her eyes. She felt my eyes on her. 'I'm not looking good at the moment, right?'

'No, you should go away somewhere.'

'In recent years I've always gone on holiday with Peter. We met each other at Club Med, you know. We should be in Sicily now, we always travelled south in the late autumn.' She started to cry.

I put my arm round her shoulders. I didn't know what to say. She kept crying.

15

The guard still knew me

Grimm was barely recognizable. The safari suit had been exchanged for woollen flannel trousers and a leather jacket, his hair was cut short, his upper lip sported, resplendent, a carefully sculpted pencil moustache, and along with the new look there was a new confidence on display.

'Hello, Herr Self. Or should I say Selk? What brings you here?'

What was I to make of this? Mischkey wouldn't have told him about me. Who else then? Someone from the RCW. A coincidence? 'Good that you know. That makes my job simpler. I need to look at the files Mischkey worked on here. Would you show them to me, please?'

'What? I don't understand. There aren't any files of Peter's here any more.' He looked puzzled, and a shade mistrustful. 'Under whose mandate are you here, actually?'

'Two guesses. So you've deleted the files? Perhaps that's for the best. Tell me what you think of this.' I took the computer printout from my briefcase, the one I'd found in Mischkey's file.

He spread it in front of him on the table and leafed through it for quite a while. 'Where did you get this from? It's five weeks old, was printed here in the building, but has nothing to do with our stock.' He shook his head thoughtfully. 'I'd like to keep this here.' He glanced at his watch. 'I must be off to the meeting now.'

'I'll gladly bring you the printout again. I have to take it with me now.'

Grimm gave it to me, but it felt as though I were wrenching it from him. I put the obviously explosive contraband into my briefcase. 'Who took over Mischkey's responsibilities?'

Grimm looked at me in sheer alarm. He stood up. 'I don't understand, Herr Self ... Let's continue our discussion another time. I really must get to this meeting.' He escorted me to the door.

I stepped out of the building, saw a phone-box on Ebertplatz, and called Hemmelskopf immediately. 'Do you have anything at all at the credit bureau on a Jörg Grimm?'

'Grimm ... Grimm ... If we have something on him, it'll come up on the screen in a second. Just a moment ... There he is, Grimm, Jörg, born nineteenth November nineteen forty-eight, married, two children, resident of Heidelberg, in Furtwänglerstrasse, drives a red Escort, HD-S 735. He had debts once, seems to have made something of himself, though. Just around two weeks ago he paid back the loan at the Cooperative Bank. That was around 40,000 marks.'

I thanked him. That wasn't sufficient for Hemmelskopf, though. 'My wife is still waiting for that ficus tree you promised her in spring. When can you come by?'

I added Grimm to the list of suspects. Two people are involved with one another. One dies, the other gets rich, and the one who gets rich also knows too much – I didn't have a theory, but it seemed fishy.

The RCW had never asked me to return my entry pass. With it I had no problem finding a parking space. The guard still knew me and saluted. I went to the computer centre and sought out Tausendmilch without falling into the hands of Oelmüller. I'd have found it unpleasant having to explain to him what I was doing here. Tausendmilch was alert, keen, and quick on the uptake as ever. He whistled through his teeth.

'These are our data. A curious mixture. And the printout isn't from here. I thought everything was quiet again. Should I try to trace the printout?'

'Leave it. But could you tell me what these data are?'

Tausendmilch sat down at a computer and said, 'I'll have to flip through a bit.'

I waited patiently.

'Here we have a list of people on sick leave from spring and summer nineteen seventy-eight, then registers of our inventions and inventors' royalties, way back to before nineteen forty-five, and here's . . . I can't open it but the abbreviations might also stand for other chemical companies.' He turned the machine off. 'I wanted to thank you very much. Firner called me in and said you'd praised me in your report and that he had plans for me.'

I left a happy person behind. For a moment I could picture Tausendmilch, on whose right hand I'd spotted a wedding ring, coming home after work that day and telling his elegant wife, who had a martini ready for him and in her way was contributing to his rise, about his success today.

At security I sought out Thomas. On the wall of his office hung a half-finished plan of the course for security studies. 'I had something to do in the plant and wanted to discuss your kind offer of a teaching appointment. To what do I owe the honour?'

'I was impressed by how you solved our data-security problem. You taught us some things here, Oelmüller in particular. And it would be indispensable for the curriculum to have a freelancer involved.'

'What would be the subject?'

'The detective's work: from the practical to the ethical. With seminars and a final exam if that's not too much trouble. The whole thing should start in the winter term.'

'I see a problem there, Herr Thomas. According to your concept, and it also seems sensible to me, I can only teach the students by using my experience with real cases. But think of the business here at the Works we were just discussing. Even if I didn't mention any names and I went to lengths to disguise the whole thing a bit, it would be a case of the king's birthday suit.'

Thomas didn't get it. 'Do you mean Herr King in export coordination? But he doesn't have a birthday suit. And besides—'

'You still had some trouble with the case, Firner told me.'

'Yes, things were a bit tough with Mischkey.'

'Should I have been harsher?'

'He was rather uncooperative when you left him with us.'

'After everything I heard from Firner he was given the kid-glove treatment. No talk of police and court and prison – that would only encourage a lack of cooperation.'

'But Herr Self, we didn't tell him that. The problem lay elsewhere. He virtually tried to blackmail us. We never found out whether he really had something up his sleeve, but he made some noise.'

'With the same old stories?'

'Yes, with the same old stories. Threatening to go to the press, to the competition, to the union, to the plant authorities, to the Federal Antitrust Office. You know, it's tough to say this, and I'm sorry about Mischkey's death, but at the same time I'm happy not to be burdened with this problem any more.'

Danckelmann came in without knocking. 'Ah, Herr

Self, you've been the topic of conversation today already. Why are you still involved in this Mischkey business? The case is long since closed. Don't go rattling cages.'

Just as I had been when talking to Thomas, I was on thin ice with Danckelmann. Questions that were too direct could make it crack. But nothing ventured, nothing gained. 'Did Grimm call you?'

Danckelmann ignored my question. 'Seriously, Herr Self, keep your nose out of this story. We don't appreciate it.'

'For me, cases are only over when I know everything. Did you know, for example, that Mischkey took another stroll around your system?'

Thomas pricked up his ears and looked disconcerted. He was already regretting his offer of a teaching appointment.

Danckelmann controlled himself and his voice was tight. 'Curious notion you have of a job. It's over when the client says it's over. And Herr Mischkey isn't strolling anywhere any more. So please . . .'

I'd heard more than I'd dreamed possible and had no interest in a further escalation. Just one more wrong word and Danckelmann would remember my special ID. 'You're absolutely right, Herr Danckelmann. On the other hand, you certainly agree that when security is involved, things can't always be contained within the narrow limits of a job. And don't worry, being a freelancer, I can't afford to invest too much without a fee.'

Danckelmann left the room only partially appeased. Thomas was waiting impatiently for me to be gone. But I still had a treat for him. 'To return to what you were saying, Herr Thomas, I'm happy to accept the teaching appointment. I'll draw up a curriculum.'

'Thank you for your interest, Herr Self. We're around.'

I left security and found myself back in the courtyard

with Aristotle, Schwarz, Mendeleyev, and Kekulé. On the north side of the yard a sleepy autumn sun was shining. I sat down on the top step of a small staircase leading to a walled-up door. I had more than enough to think about.

16

Dad's dearest wish

More and more pieces of the jigsaw puzzle were fitting together. Yet they still didn't add up to a plausible picture. I now understood what Mischkey's file was: a collection of everything he could muster against the RCW. A wretched collection. He must have been playing high-stakes poker to impress Danckelmann and Thomas as much as he obviously had. But what did he want to achieve or prevent by this? The RCW hadn't told him to his face that they had no intention of instituting proceedings against him with the police, court, and prison. Why had they wanted to exert pressure? What were their intentions towards Mischkey, and what was he arming himself against with his feeble insinuations and threats?

My thoughts turned to Grimm. He'd come into money, he'd produced some strange reactions that morning, and I was fairly certain he had talked to Danckelmann. Was Grimm the RCW's man in the RCC? Had the RCW initially assigned this role to Mischkey? We won't go to the police, and you'll ensure our emissions data are always squeaky clean? Such a man would be valuable indeed. The monitoring system would be rendered obsolete and wouldn't interfere with production.

But none of this necessarily made the murder of Mischkey plausible. Grimm as the murderer, wanting to do business with the RCW and to have Mischkey out of the way? Or did Mischkey's material contain some other dynamite that had evaded me thus far, that had provoked the deadly reaction of the RCW? But then Danckelmann and Thomas could scarcely have overlooked such an act, and they wouldn't have spoken so openly to me about the conflict with Mischkey. And while Grimm might make a better impression than in his safari suit, even with his pencil moustache I couldn't picture him as a murderer. Was I looking in completely the wrong direction? Fred might have beaten up Mischkey under contract from the RCW, but also from any other employer, and he could have killed him for them. What did I know about all the ways Mischkey could have entangled himself through his confidence tricks? I'd have to talk to Fred again.

I took my leave of Aristotle. The courtyards of the old factory worked their magic again. I walked through the archway into the next courtyard, its walls glowing in the autumnal red of the Virginia creeper. No Richard playing with his ball. I rang the bell of the Schmalzes' work apartment. The elderly woman, whom I recognized by sight, opened the door. She was dressed in black.

'Frau Schmalz? Hello, the name is Self.'

'Hello, Herr Self. You're joining us for the funeral? The children will be collecting me any minute.'

Half an hour later I found myself in the crematorium of Ludwigshafen Cemetery. The family had included me in the mourning for Schmalz senior as though it were perfectly natural, and I didn't like to say that I'd stumbled upon the funeral preparations just by chance. Along with Frau Schmalz, the young married Schmalz couple, and their son Richard, I was driven to the cemetery, glad to be wearing my dark-blue raincoat and the muted suit. During the drive I learned that Schmalz senior had died of a heart attack four days ago.

'He looked so sprightly when I saw him a few weeks ago.'

163

The widow sobbed. My lisping friend told me about the circumstances that had led to his death. 'Dad kept on tinkering with old vans and trucks after retiring. He had a part of the old hangar by the Rhine where he could work. Lately he didn't take care. The cut in his hand didn't go that deep but according to the doctor he had heavy bleeding in the brain, too. After that Dad felt a tingling in the left part of the body all the time, he felt terribly unwell, and he didn't want to get out of bed. Then the heart attack.'

The RCW was well represented at the cemetery. Danckelmann gave a speech. 'His life was the Works' security and the Works' security was his life.' In the course of his speech he read out a personal farewell letter from Korten. The chairman of the RCW chess club, where Schmalz senior had played third board on the second team, asked Caissa's blessing on the deceased. The RCW orchestra played 'I Had a Comrade'. Schmalz was so moved, he forgot himself and lisped at me, 'Dad's dearest wish.' Then the flower-wreathed coffin glided into the furnace.

I couldn't get out of the funeral tea. I did manage, however, to avoid sitting next to Danckelmann or Thomas, although Schmalz junior had intended this seat of honour for me. I sat next to the chairman of the RCW chess club and we chatted to each other about the world championship. Over cognac we started a game in our heads. By the thirty-second move I lost my overview. We came round to the subject of the deceased.

'He was a decent player, Schmalz. Although he was a late starter. And you could depend on him in the club. He never missed a practice or a tournament.'

'How often do you practise?'

'Every Thursday. Three weeks ago was the first time Schmalz didn't come. The family said he'd over-exerted himself in the workshop. But you know, I believe the bleeding in the brain happened before then. Otherwise he wouldn't have been in the workshop, he'd have been at practice. He must already have been off-balance then.'

It was like any other funeral meal. It starts with the soft voices, the studied grief on the faces, and the stiff dignity in the bodies, lots of awkwardness, some embarrassment, and a general desire to get it over with as quickly as possible. And one hour later it's only the clothing that distinguishes mourners from any other gathering, not the appetite, nor the noise, nor, with a few exceptions, the expressions and gestures. I did grow a little thoughtful though. What would it be like at my own funeral? In the first row of the cemetery chapel, five or six figures, among them Eberhard, Philipp and Willy, Babs, perhaps Röschen and Georg. But it was possible no one at all would learn of my death and, apart from the priest and the four coffin-bearers, not a soul would accompany me to the grave. I could picture Turbo trotting behind the coffin, a mouse in his mouth. It had a bow tied round it: 'To my dear Gerd from his Turbo.'

17

Against the light

At five I was back in the office, slightly tipsy and in a bad mood.

Fred called. 'Hello there, Gerhard, do you remember me? I wanted to ask you again about the job. Do you already have someone?'

'I've a couple of candidates. But nothing's finalized yet. I can take another look at you. It would have to be straight away, though.'

'That suits me.'

I asked him to the office. Dusk was falling, I switched on the light and let the blinds down.

Fred came cheerfully and trustingly. It was underhand, but I got the first punch in immediately. At my age I can't afford a clean fight in such situations. I caught him in the stomach and didn't waste time removing his sunglasses before hitting his face. His hands flew up and I delivered another punch to his underbelly. When he ventured a half-hearted counterpunch with his right hand, I twisted his arm round behind his back, kicked the hollow of his knees and he sank to the ground. I kept my hold on him.

'Who contracted you to beat up a guy in the War Cemetery in August?'

'Hey, stop. You're hurting me. What's all this about? I don't know exactly, the boss doesn't tell me anything. I . . . aagh . . . let up . . .'

Bit by bit out it came. Fred worked for Hans who got

the jobs and made the arrangements, didn't name any names to Fred, just described the person, place, and time. Sometimes Fred had caught wind of something. 'I did some stuff for the wine king, and once for the union, and for the chemical guys . . . stop it, yes maybe that was it at the War Cemetery . . . stop it!'

'And for the chemical guys you killed him a few weeks later.'

'You're crazy. I never killed anyone. We messed him up a bit, nothing more. Stop, you're pulling my arm off, I swear.'

I didn't manage to hurt him so much that he'd prefer the consequences of an admission of murder to riding out the pain. Besides I found him credible. I let him go.

'Sorry I had to manhandle you, Fred. I can't afford to take anyone on who's mixed up in a murder. He's dead, the guy you took care of back then.'

Fred scrambled to his feet. I showed him the sink and poured him a sambuca. He gulped it down and was in a hurry to leave.

'That's fine,' he mumbled. 'But I've had enough, I'm out of here.' Maybe he found my behaviour acceptable from a professional point of view. But we'd never be best friends.

Another piece to fit in, but the picture was no less blurry. So the confrontation between the RCW and Mischkey had reached the stage of professional hit men. But from the warning beaten into him at the War Cemetery to murder was a huge step.

I sat down at my desk. The Sweet Afton had smoked itself and left nothing but its body of ash. The traffic raced by in the Augusta-Anlage. From the backyard I could hear the shrieks of playing children. There are days in autumn where there's a whiff of Christmas in the air. I wondered what I should decorate my tree with this year. Klärchen

167

loved the traditional way and decked the tree year in, year out with shiny silver baubles and tinsel. Since then I've tried everything from matchbox cars to cigarette packs. I've got a bit of a reputation for it among my friends, but I've also set standards I'm stuck with now. The universe doesn't have an endless supply of little objects that can be used as Christmas tree decorations. Cans of sardines, for example, would be ornamental, but are very heavy.

Philipp called and demanded I come and admire his new cabin cruiser. Brigitte asked what I was planning that evening. I invited her round to dinner, ran out and bought a fillet of pork, boiled ham, and endives.

We had braised pork, Italian style. Afterwards I put on *The Man Who Loved Women*. I knew the film already and was curious to see how Brigitte would react to it. When the womanizer, chasing after beautiful women's legs, ran in front of a car, she thought it served him right. She didn't particularly like the film. But when it was over she couldn't resist posing in front of the floor lamp, as if by accident, showing her legs off to advantage against the light.

18

A little story

I dropped Brigitte off at work at the Collini Centre and drank my second coffee at the Gmeiner. I didn't have a smoking gun in the Mischkey case. Naturally I could keep on looking for my stupid little jigsaw pieces, trying them helplessly this way and that, and combining them to make some picture or other. I was fed up with it. I felt young and dynamic after the night with Brigitte.

At the sales counter the boss was fighting with her son. 'The way you're carrying on makes me wonder if you really want to become a pastry cook.' Did I really want to follow my leads the way I was carrying on? I was timid about those that led to the RCW. Why? Was I afraid of discovering I had delivered Mischkey to his death? Had I messed up the trails deliberately out of consideration for myself and Korten and our friendship?

I drove to Heidelberg and the RCC. Grimm wanted to deal with me quickly, on his feet. I sat down and fetched Mischkey's computer printout from my briefcase.

'You wanted to take another look, Herr Grimm. I can leave it with you now. Mischkey really was a helluva guy, broke into the RCW system again although the connection was already cut. I suspect via telephone, or what do you think?'

'I don't know what you're talking about.' He was a bad liar.

'You're a bad liar, Herr Grimm. But that doesn't

169

matter. For what I've got to tell you it's not important whether you're a good one or a bad one.'

'What?'

He was still standing, looking at me helplessly. I made an inviting gesture. 'Wouldn't you care to take a seat?'

He shook his head.

'I don't have to tell you who the red Ford Escort HD–S 735 sitting in the parking lot down there belongs to. Exactly three weeks ago to the day on the bridge over the railroad between Eppelheim and Wieblingen, Mischkey plummeted in his car onto the tracks after being hit by a red Ford Escort. The witness I managed to unearth even saw that the number plate of the red Escort started with HD and ended with 735.'

'And why are you telling me this? You should go to the police.'

'Quite right, Herr Grimm. The witness should have gone to the police, too. I had to explain to him first that a jealous wife is no reason to cover up a murder. In the meantime he's ready to go to the police with me.'

'Yes, well then?' He folded his arms over his chest in a superior manner.

'The chances of finding another red Escort from Heidelberg with a number plate that fits the description are perhaps . . . Ah, work it out yourself. The damage to the red Escort appears to have been minimal and easy to repair. Tell me, Herr Grimm, was your car stolen three weeks ago, or did you lend it to someone?'

'No, of course not, what a lot of rubbish you talk.'

'I would have been surprised anyway. You'll certainly know that when a murder occurs you always ask, who benefits? What do you think, Herr Grimm? Who benefits from Mischkey's death?'

He snorted contemptuously.

'Then allow me to tell you a little story. No, no, don't

get impatient, it's an interesting little story. You still won't sit down? Well, once upon a time there was a large chemical plant and a Regional Computing Centre that was supposed to keep an eye on the chemical plant. It was in the chemical plant's interest that they didn't keep too careful an eye on it. Two people in the Regional Computer Centre were crucial for monitoring the chemical plant. An awful lot of money was at stake. If only they could buy off one of these supervisors! What wouldn't they give for that! But they would only buy off one because they only needed one. They sound out both. A little later one is dead and the other pays off his loan. Do you want to know how high the loan was?'

Now he did sit down. To compensate for this mistake he acted outraged. 'It's appalling what you're ascribing not only to me but to our most respected and venerable chemical enterprise. I'd best pass this on to them; they can defend themselves better than a minor employee like me.'

'I can well believe that what you'd most like to do is run to the RCW. But at the moment the story concerns only you, the police, myself, and my witness. The police will be interested in knowing your whereabouts at the time, and like most people, you too, three weeks *post festum*, won't be able to provide a solid alibi.'

If there'd been a visit with his poor wife and his doubtless disgusting children at his parents-in-laws' Grimm would have come out with that. Instead he said, 'There can't be a witness who saw me, because I wasn't there.'

I had him where I wanted him. I didn't feel any fairer than I had yesterday with Fred, but just as good. 'Right, Herr Grimm, nor is there a witness who saw you there. But I have someone who will say he saw you there. And what do you think will happen then? The police have a corpse, a crime, a culprit, a witness, and a motive. It may be that the witness finally cracks during the trial, but long before that you're finished. I don't know what they give you for taking bribes these days, but along with it comes detention awaiting trial for murder, suspension from work, disgrace for your wife and children, the contempt of society.'

Grimm had turned pale. 'What is this? What are you doing to me? What have I done to you?'

'I don't like the way you let yourself be bought. I can't stand you. Moreover there's something I want you to tell me. And if you don't want me to ruin you, you'd better play along.'

'What do you want?'

'When did the RCW contact you for the first time? Who recruited you, and who is, so to speak, the person who runs you? How much have you received from the RCW?'

He recounted the whole thing, from the initial contact Thomas had opened with him after Mischkey's death, to the negotiations over performance and pay, to the programmes, some of which were still only ideas and some of which he'd already written. And he told me about the suitcase with the crisp new notes.

'Stupidly, instead of paying back my loan bit by bit so as not to raise suspicion, I went to the bank straight away. I wanted to save on interest.' He took out a handkerchief and mopped away the sweat, and I asked him what he knew about Mischkey's death.

'So far as I could gather, they wanted to put him under pressure after you had turned him in. They wanted to have the cooperation they're now paying me for, but they wanted it for nothing, in exchange for keeping quiet about his hacking into the system. When he died they were somewhat disgruntled because then they had to pay. Me.'

He could have gone on talking for ever, probably wanted to justify himself, too. I'd heard enough.

'Thank you, that's plenty for now, Herr Grimm. In your place I'd keep our discussion confidential. If the RCW get wind of the fact that I know, you'll be useless to them. Should anything more about Mischkey's death come to mind, call me.' I gave him my card.

'Yes, but – don't you care about what's going on with the emissions control? Or are you going to go to the police anyway?'

I thought about the stink that so often caused me to shut the window. And about what was there, even though we couldn't smell it. Nonetheless it left me indifferent for the time being. I packed away Mischkey's printouts that were lying on Grimm's desk. When I turned to leave, Grimm stretched out his hand towards me. I didn't take it.

19

Energy and Stamina

In the afternoon I should have had my appointment with the ballet director. But I didn't feel like it and cancelled. At home I went to bed and didn't wake up until five. I almost never have a siesta. Because of my low blood pressure I find it difficult afterwards to get going again. I took a hot shower and made a strong coffee.

When I called Philipp at the station the nurse said, 'The doctor is already off to his new boat.' I drove through Neckarstadt to Luzenberg and parked in Gerwigstrasse. In the harbour I passed a lot of boats before finding Philipp's. I recognized it by the name. It was called *Faun 69*.

I know next to nothing about sailing. Philipp explained to me that he could sail to London in this boat or to Rome via France, just not venturing too far from the coast. There was water enough for ten showers, space enough in the fridge for forty bottles, and room enough in the bed for one Philipp and two women. After he'd shown me around he switched the stereo on, put on Hans Albers, and uncorked a bottle of Bordeaux.

'Do I get a test-drive, too?'

'Slowly does it, Gerd. Let's empty this little bottle first, and then we'll raise the anchor. I have radar and can set sail any time day or night.'

One bottle turned into two. First of all Philipp told me about his women. 'And what about you, Gerd, how's your love life?'

'Ah, what can I say?'

'Nothing on the go with smart traffic wardens or attractive secretaries, or whatever else you are involved in?'

'On a case I did get to know a woman recently who'd appeal to me, but it's difficult because her boyfriend isn't alive any more.'

'I beg your pardon, but where's the difficulty in that?'

'Oh, well, I can't flirt with a grieving widow, can I? Especially as I'm supposed to be finding out who murdered the boyfriend.'

'Why can't you? Is it your public prosecutor's code of honour, or are you simply afraid she'll turn you down?' He was laughing at me.

'No, no, you couldn't put it like that. And then there's somebody else – Brigitte. I like her too. I don't know what to do with two women.'

Philipp burst out laughing, loudly. 'You're a real philanderer. And what's stopping you from getting closer to Brigitte?'

'I am already . . . with her, I've even . . .'

'And now she's expecting a child by you?' Philipp could hardly contain his mirth. Then he noticed that I wasn't at all inclined to laugh, and enquired seriously about my situation. I told him.

'That's no reason to look so sad. You just need to be aware of what you want. If you're looking for someone to marry, then stay with Brigitte. They're not bad, these women around forty. They've seen everything, experienced everything, they're as sensual as a succubus if you know how to arouse them. And a masseuse, what's more, and you with your rheumatism. The other one sounds like stress. Is that what you want? *Amour fou*? A heaven of passion, then a hell of despair?'

'But I don't know what I want. Probably I want both,

the security and the thrill. At any rate sometimes I want one, sometimes the other.'

He could understand that. We identified with one other there. I'd worked out in the meantime where the Bordeaux was stored and fetched the third bottle. The smoke was thick in the cabin.

'Hey, landlubber, get to that galley and throw the fish from the fridge on the grill!' In the fridge was potato and sausage salad from Kaufhof and next to it deep-frozen fillets of fish. They just had to be popped into the microwave. Two minutes later I was able to return to the cabin with dinner. Philipp had set the table and put on Zarah Leander.

After eating we went up to the bridge, as Philipp called it. 'And where do you hoist the sail?' Philipp knew my silly jokes and didn't react. He also took my question as to whether he could still navigate as a bad joke. We were pretty tight by then.

We sailed under the bridge over the Altrhein and when we'd reached the Rhine we turned upstream. The river was black and silent. On the RCW premises many buildings were lit up, bright flames were shooting out of tall pipes, streetlamps cast a garish light. The motor chugged softly, the water slapped against the boat's side, and from the Works came an almighty, thunderous hissing. We glided past the RCW loading dock, past barges, piers, and container cranes, past railroad lines and warehouses. It was growing foggy and there was a chill in the air. In front of us I could make out the Kurt Schumacher Bridge. The RCW premises grew murky, beyond the tracks loomed old buildings, sparsely lit in the night sky.

Inspiration struck. 'Drive over to the right,' I said to Philipp.

'Do you mean I should dock? Now, there, next to the RCW? Whatever for?'

'I'd like to take a look at something. Can you park for half an hour and wait for me?'

'It's not called parking, it's dropping the anchor, we're on a boat. Are you aware that it's half past ten? I was thinking we'd turn by the castle, chug back, and then drink the fourth bottle in the Waldhof Basin.'

'I'll explain it all to you later over the fourth bottle. But now I have to go in. It has something to do with the case I mentioned earlier. And I'm not the least bit tipsy any more.'

Philipp gave me a searching look. 'I guess you know what you're doing.' He steered the boat to the right and sailed on with a serene concentration I wouldn't have thought him capable of at that point, moving slowly along the quay wall until he came to a ladder attached to it. 'Hang the fenders out.' He pointed to three white plastic, sausage-like objects. I threw them overboard, fortunately they were attached, and he tied the boat firmly to the ladder.

'I'd like to have you with me. But I'd rather know you're here, ready to start. Do you have a flashlight I can use?'

'Aye, aye, sir.'

I clambered up the ladder. I was shivering. The knitted jumper, some American label, I was wearing beneath the old leather jacket to match my new jeans didn't warm me. I peered over the quay wall.

In front of me, parallel to the banks of the Rhine, was a narrow road, behind it tracks with railway carriages. The buildings were in the brick style I was familiar with from the Security building and the Schmalzes' flat. The old plant was in front of me. Somewhere here was Schmalz's hangar.

I turned to the right where the old brick buildings were lower. I tried to walk with both caution and the necessary authority. I stuck to the shadows of the railway carriages.

They came without the Alsatian making a sound. One of them shone a torch in my face, the other asked me for my badge. I fetched the special pass from my wallet. 'Herr Self? What part of your special job brings you here?'

'I wouldn't require a special pass if I had to tell you that.'

But that neither calmed them nor intimidated them. They were two young lads, the sort you find these days in the riot police. In the old days you found them in the Waffen SS. That's certainly an impermissible comparison because these days we're dealing with a free democratic order, yet the mixture of zeal, earnestness, uncertainness, and servility in the faces is the same. They were wearing a kind of paramilitary uniform with the benzene ring on their collar patch.

'Hey, guys,' I said, 'let me finish my job, and you do yours. What are your names? I want to tell Danckelmann tomorrow that you can be relied on. Continue the good work!'

I don't remember their names; they were along the lines of Energy and Stamina. I didn't manage to get them clicking their heels. But one of them returned my pass and the other switched off his torch. The Alsatian had spent the whole time off to one side, indifferent.

When I couldn't see them any more and their steps had died away I went on. The low-slung buildings I'd seen seemed ramshackle. Some of the windows were smashed, some doors hung crooked from their hinges, here and there a roof was missing. The area was obviously earmarked for demolition. But one building had been rescued from decay. It, too, was a one-floor brick building, with Romanesque windows and barrel vaulting made of corrugated iron. If Schmalz's workshop was anywhere round here, then it had to be in this building.

My flashlight found the small service door in the large sliding gate. Both were locked, and the big one could only be opened from the inside. At first I didn't want to try the bank-card trick, but then I thought that on the evening in question, three weeks ago today, Schmalz might no longer have had the strength or the wit to think of details like padlocks. And indeed, using my special pass, I entered the hangar. Next second, I had to close the door. Energy and Stamina were coming round the corner.

I leaned against the cold iron door and took a deep breath. Now I was really sober. And still I knew it was a good idea to have come looking in the RCW grounds. The fact that on the day Mischkey had had his accident Schmalz had hurt his hand, had had a brain haemorrhage, and forgotten to play chess wasn't much in itself. And the fact that he tinkered with delivery vans and the girl at the station had seen a strange delivery van was hardly a hot lead. But I wanted to know.

Not much light shone through the windows. I could make out the outlines of three panel trucks. I turned on the flashlight and recognized an old Opel, an old Mercedes, and a Citroën. You certainly don't see many of those driving about round here. At the back of the hangar was a large workbench. I groped my way over. Amongst the tools were a set of keys, a cap, and a pack of cigarettes. I pocketed the keys.

Only the Citroën was roadworthy. On the Opel the windshield was missing, the Mercedes was up on blocks. I sat down in the Citroën and tried out the keys. One fitted and as I turned it the lights went on. There was old blood on the steering wheel and the cloth on the passenger's seat was bloodstained, too. I took it. As I was about to turn off the ignition, I touched a switch on the dashboard. Behind me I could hear the humming of an electric motor, and in the side-mirror I could see the loading doors open. I got out and went to the back.

20

Not just a silly womanizer

This time I didn't get such a fright. But the effect was still impressive. Now I knew what had happened on the bridge. Both inside surfaces of the rear doors of the delivery van, and the rear opening itself, had been covered with reflective foil. A deadly triptych. The foil was spread smooth, without creases or warps, and I could see myself in it like on Saturday in the mirror that hung in my stairwell. When Mischkey had driven onto the bridge, the delivery van had been parked there with its back doors open. Mischkey, confronted suddenly with the apparent headlights on his side of the road, had swerved to the left and then lost control of his vehicle. Now I recalled the cross on the right headlight on Mischkey's car. It wasn't Mischkey who'd stuck it on, it was old Schmalz, who'd thus been able to know, in the darkness, that he had to open the doors because his victim was coming.

I heard thumps on the door of the hangar. 'Open up, security!' Energy and Stamina must have noticed the beam from my flashlight. Apparently the hangar had been so much Schmalz's sole preserve that not even security had a key. I was glad that my two young colleagues didn't know the bank-card trick. Nonetheless I was sitting in a trap.

I took note of the number on the licence plate and saw that the plates themselves were tied on in a makeshift fashion with wire. I started the engine. Outside the door was being pounded with ever-increasing energy and stamina. I parked the vehicle just a metre from the door, its mirrored rear opened. Then I grabbed a long, heavy spanner from the table. One of my pursuers hurled himself against the door.

I pressed myself against the wall. Now what I needed was a lot of luck. When I estimated the next assault on the door would come, I pushed down the handle.

The door burst open, and the first security guard fell through it, landing on the ground. The second one stormed in after him with raised pistol and raked to a halt in fright in front of his own mirror image. The Alsatian had been trained to attack whoever was threatening his master with a raised weapon and leapt through the tearing foil. I could hear him howling in pain in the cargo area. The first security man lay dazed on the ground, the second hadn't cottoned on yet. I took advantage of the confusion, zipped out of the gate, and raced in the direction of the boat. I'd made it over the tracks and cleared maybe twenty metres down the road, when I heard Energy and Stamina in renewed pursuit: 'Stop or I'll shoot.' Their heavy boots beat out a fast rhythm on the cobblestones, the panting of the dog was getting closer and closer, and I had no desire to grow acquainted with the application of the regulations on usage of firearms on the plant's premises. The Rhine looked cold. But I had no choice, and jumped.

The dive from a headlong run had enough momentum to let me bob to the surface a good distance away. I turned my head and saw Energy and Stamina standing on the quay wall with the Alsatian, directing their flashlight at the water. My clothes were heavy, and the current of the Rhine is strong, and I could only make headway with difficulty.

'Gerd, Gerd!' Philipp let his boat drift downstream in the shadow of the quayside and called to me in a whisper.

'Here I am,' I whispered back. Then the boat was next to me. Philipp hoisted me up. At that moment Energy and Stamina saw us. I don't know what they planned to do. Fire at us? Philipp started the motor and with a spraying bow wave made for the middle of the Rhine. Exhausted and shivering with cold, I sat on the deck. I pulled the bloodstained cloth from my pocket. 'Could you do me another favour and test the blood group on this? I think I know, blood group O rhesus negative, but better safe than sorry.'

Philipp grinned. 'All that excitement over this damp cloth? But first things first. Go below, take a hot shower, and put on my bathrobe. As soon as we've made it past the water police I'll make you a grog.'

When I came out of the shower we'd reached safety. Neither the RCW nor the police had sent a gunboat after us and Philipp was just in the process of manoeuvring the boat back into the Altrhein channel by Sandhofen. Although the shower had warmed me, I was still shivering. It was all a bit much at my age. Philipp docked at the old mooring and entered the cabin. 'Jeezus,' he said. 'That was quite a fright you gave me. When I heard the guys hammering against the metal I thought something had gone wrong. I didn't know what to do. Then I saw you jump. Hats off!'

'Oh, you know, when you have a killer dog on your tail you don't stop to consider whether the water might be a little on the cold side. Much more important was that you did exactly the right thing at the right time. Without you I'd probably have drowned, with or without a bullet in my head. You saved my life. Boy, am I glad you're not just a silly womanizer.'

Embarrassed, Philipp clattered about in the galley. 'Maybe you want to tell me now what you'd lost at the RCW.'

'Nothing lost, but found some things. Apart from this disgusting wet cloth I found the murder weapon, probably the murderer, too. Which explains the wet cloth.' Over the steaming grog I told Philipp about the corrugated van and its surprising refit.

'But if it was as simple as that to chase your Mischkey off the bridge, what about the injuries to the veteran who was the Works' security guy?' Philipp asked when I was finished with my report.

'You should have become a private detective. You're quick on the uptake. I don't have any answers, unless . . .' I remembered what the owner's wife had told me at the railway restaurant. 'The woman at the old station heard two bangs, one right after the other. Now it's getting clear. Mischkey's car was hanging from the railings on the bridge, Schmalz senior, with a great deal of effort, managed to dislodge it, injuring himself in the process. And the effort killed him two weeks later. Yes, that's how it must have been.'

'One bang as it broke through the railings, the next as it crashed down onto the railroad bank. It all fits together medically, too. When old people strain themselves too much, it can happen that they haemorrhage a little in the brain. It goes unnoticed until the heart gives out.'

I was very tired all of a sudden. 'Still, there's a lot I'm hazy about. Schmalz senior himself didn't come up with the idea to kill Mischkey. And I still can't see a motive. Please take me home, Philipp. We'll have the Bordeaux some other time. I hope you won't get into any trouble on account of my escapades.'

As we turned from Gerwigstrasse into Sandhofenstrasse a patrol car complete with flashing light but without siren went tearing past us towards the harbour basin. I didn't even turn round.

21

Praying Hands

After a feverish night I called Brigitte. She came immediately, brought quinine for my temperature and nose drops, massaged my neck, hung up my clothes to dry that I'd dropped in the hallway the previous evening, prepared something in the kitchen that I was to heat up for lunch, set off, bought orange juice, glucose, and cigarettes, and fed Turbo. She was professional, industrious, and worried. When I wanted her to sit for a little on the edge of the bed, she had to leave.

I slept almost the whole day. Philipp called and confirmed the blood group, O, and the rhesus negative factor. Through the window a rumble of traffic from the Augusta-Anlage and the shouts of playing children drifted into the twilight of my room. I remembered back to sick days as a child, the desire to be outside playing with the other children, and simultaneously the pleasure in my own weakness and all the maternal pampering. In a feverish semi-sleep I kept running from the panting dog and Energy and Stamina. I was making up for the fear I hadn't felt yesterday where everything had happened too quickly. I had wild thoughts about Mischkey's murder and why Schmalz had done it.

Towards evening I was feeling better. My temperature had gone down and I was weak, but I felt like eating the beef broth with pasta and vegetables that Brigitte had prepared, and smoking a Sweet Afton afterwards. How should work on the case proceed? Murder belonged in police hands, and even if the RCW, as I could well imagine, pulled a veil of oblivion over yesterday's incident I'd never find out anything more from anyone in the Works. I called Nägelsbach. He and his wife had finished dinner and were in the studio.

'Of course you can come by. You can listen to *Hedda Gabler*, too, we're in the third act just now.'

I stuck a note on the front door, to reassure Brigitte in case she came to check on me again. The drive to Heidelberg was bad. My own slowness and the quickness of the car made uneasy companions.

The Nägelsbachs live in one of the Pfaffengrunder settlement houses of the twenties. Nägelsbach had turned the shed, originally meant for chickens and rabbits, into a studio with a large window and bright lamps. The evening was cool and the Swedish wood-burning stove held a few crackling logs. Nägelsbach was sitting on his high stool, at the big table on which Dürer's *Praying Hands* were taking shape in matchstick form. His wife was reading aloud in the armchair by the stove. It was a perfect idyll that met my eyes when I came through the garden gate straight to the studio and looked through the window before knocking.

'My word, what a sight you are!' Frau Nägelsbach vacated the armchair for me and took another stool for herself.

'You must really have something on your mind to come here in this state,' was Nägelsbach's greeting. 'Do you mind if my wife stays? I tell her everything, work-wise, too. The rules of confidentiality don't apply to childless couples who only have one another.'

As I recounted my tale, Nägelsbach worked on. He didn't interrupt me. At the end of my narration he was silent for a little while, then he switched off the lamp above his workplace, turned his high stool towards us, and said to his wife: 'Tell him.'

'With what you've just told us, maybe the police will get a search warrant for the old hangar. Maybe they'll find the Citroën still there. But there'll be nothing remarkable or suspicious about it. No reflective foil, no deadly triptych. That was pretty, by the way, how you described that. Right, and then the police can interrogate a few of the security people and the widow Schmalz and whoever else you named, but what is it going to achieve?'

'That's it, and of course I could prime Herzog in particular about the case, and he can try to use his contacts with security, only it won't change a thing. But you know all that yourself, Herr Self.'

'Yes, that's where my thinking has brought me too. Nonetheless I thought you might have an idea of something the police could do, that . . . oh, I don't know what I thought. I haven't been able to resign myself to the case ending like this.'

'Do you have any idea of a motive?' Frau Nägelsbach turned to her husband. 'Couldn't we get further that way?'

'I can only imagine from what I know thus far that something went wrong. Just like that story you read to me recently. The RCW is having trouble with Mischkey, and it's getting more and more bothersome, and then someone in control says, "That's enough," and his subordinate gets a fright and in his turn passes the baton: "See to it Mischkey is quietened down, exert yourself," and the person this is said to wants to show his dedication and prods and encourages his own subordinate to think of something, and it can be unusual, and at the end of this long chain someone believes he's supposed to knock off Mischkey.'

'But old Schmalz was a pensioner and not even part of the chain any more,' his wife offered.

'Hard to say. How many policemen do I know who still feel like policemen after retirement?'

'Dear God,' she interrupted him, 'you're not going to—'

'No, I won't. Perhaps Schmalz senior was one of those who still thought of himself as being in service. What I mean is there needn't be a motive for murder in the classical sense here. The murderer is simply the instrument without a motive, and whoever had the motive wasn't necessarily thinking about murder. That's the effect, and indeed the purpose, of commanding hierarchies. We know that in the police, too, and in the army.'

'Do you think more could be done if old Schmalz were still alive?'

'Well, to begin with, Herr Self wouldn't have got as far. He wouldn't have found out at all about Schmalz's injury, wouldn't have looked in the hangar, and certainly wouldn't have found the murder vehicle. All traces would have been removed long before. But, all right, let's imagine we'd come by this knowledge in a different way. No, I don't think we'd have got anything out of old Schmalz. He must have been a tough old nut.'

'But this just isn't okay, Rudolf. Listening to you, the only person you can get in this chain of command is the last link. And the others are all supposedly innocent?'

'Whether they're innocent is one question and whether you can get them is another. Look, Reni, I don't know of course whether something really went wrong, or whether it's not the case that the chain was so well oiled that everyone knew what was meant without it being spoken out loud. But if it was oiled like that, it certainly can't be proved.'

'Should Herr Self be advised to talk to one of the big cheeses at the RCW? To get a sense of how that person conducts himself?'

'So far as prosecution goes, that won't help either. But you're right, it's the only remaining thing he can do.'

It was good to watch the pair of them, in this question-and-answer game, making sense of what I was too groggy to work out for myself. So what was left for me was a talk with Korten.

Frau Nägelsbach made some verbena tea and we talked about art. Nägelsbach told me what appealed to him in his reproduction of *Praying Hands*. He found the usual sculpture reproductions no less sickly sweet than I. And that very fact made him want to achieve the sublime sobriety of Dürer's original through the rigorous simplicity of the matches.

As I left he promised to check up on the licence plate of Schmalz's Citroën.

The note for Brigitte was still hanging on the door. When I was lying in bed she called. 'Are you feeling better? Sorry I couldn't come round to see you again. I just didn't manage it. How's your weekend looking? Do you think you'll feel up to coming to dinner tomorrow?' Something wasn't right. Her cheerfulness sounded forced.

22

Tea in the loggia

On Saturday morning I found one message from Nägels-bach on the answering machine and one from Korten. The number on the licence plate on old Schmalz's Citroën had been allotted to a Heidelberg postal worker for his VW Beetle five years ago. Presumably the licence plate I saw originated from this scrapped predecessor. Korten asked whether I wouldn't like to visit them in Ludolf-Krehl-Strasse. I should call him back.

'My dear Self, good to hear you. This afternoon, tea in the loggia? You whipped up quite a storm for us, I hear. And you sound as though you have a cold. It doesn't surprise me, ha ha. Your level of fitness, I'm full of respect.'

At four o'clock I was in Ludolf-Krehl-Strasse. For Inge, if it was still Inge, I had brought an autumn bouquet. I marvelled at the entrance gate, the video camera, and the intercom system. It consisted of a telephone receiver on a long cable that the chauffeur could pick up and pass on to the good ladies and gentlemen in the rear. Just as I wanted to sit back in my car with the receiver I heard Korten with the tortured patience you use for a naughty child. 'Don't be silly, Self! The cable car is on its way for you.'

On the ride up I had a view from Neuenheim over the Rhine plain to the Palatinate Forest. It was a clear day and I could make out the chimneys of the RCW. Their white smoke merged innocently with the blue sky.

Korten, in cords, checked shirt, and a casual cardigan, greeted me heartily. Two dachshunds were leaping around him. 'I've had a table set in the loggia, it won't be too cold for you, will it? You can always have one of my cardigans, Helga knits me one after the other.'

We stood enjoying the view. 'Is that your church down there?'

'The Johanneskirche? No, we belong to the Friedenskirche parish in Handschuhsheim. I've become an Elder. Nice job.'

Helga came with a coffee pot and I unloaded my flowers. I'd only known Inge fleetingly and didn't know whether she'd died, divorced, or simply left. Helga, new wife or new lover, resembled her. The same cheerfulness, the same false modesty, the same delight over my bouquet. She stayed to have a first slice of apple cake with us. Then: 'You men certainly want to talk among yourselves.' As was right and proper we contradicted her. And as was right and proper she went anyway.

'May I have another slice of apple cake? It's delicious.'

Korten leant back in his armchair. 'I am sure you had good reason for frightening security on Thursday evening. If you don't mind I'd like to know what it was. I was the one who recently introduced you to the Works, if you like, and I'm the one to get all the puzzled looks when your escapades became known.'

'How well did you know Schmalz senior? A personal message from you was read out at his funeral.'

'You weren't looking for the answer to that question in the shed. But fine, I knew him better and liked him better than all the other men in security. Back in the dark years we grew close to some of the simple employees in a way that is no longer possible today.'

'He killed Mischkey. And in the hangar I found proof, the thing that killed him.'

'Old Schmalz? He wouldn't hurt a fly. What are you talking yourself into, my dear Self.'

Without mentioning Judith or going into detail, I reported what had happened. 'And if you ask me what any of this has to do with me then I'll remind you of our last talk. I ask you to go gently on Mischkey and shortly afterwards he's dead.'

'And where do you see a reason, a motive, for such action on the part of old Schmalz?'

'We can come back to that in a minute. First I'd like to know if you have any questions about the order of events.'

Korten got up and prowled back and forth heavily. 'Why didn't you call me first thing yesterday morning? Then we might still have discovered something more about what went on in Schmalz's hangar. Now it's too late. It was planned for weeks – yesterday the building complex, along with the old hangar, was demolished. That was also the reason I spoke to old Schmalz myself four weeks ago. We had a little schnapps and I tried to break the news to him that we, unfortunately, couldn't keep the old hangar, nor his apartment.'

'You were round at Schmalz senior's?'

'No, I asked him to come and see me. Naturally I don't usually deliver such messages. But he's always reminded me of the old days. And you know how sentimental I am deep down.'

'And what happened to the delivery van?'

'No idea. The son will have taken care of it. But once again, where do you see a motive?'

'I actually thought you'd be able to tell me.'

'What makes you say that?' Korten's steps slowed. He stood still, turned, and scrutinized me.

'That Schmalz senior personally had no reason to kill Mischkey is clear. But the plant did have some trouble with him, put him under pressure, even had him beaten up; and he did show resistance. And he could have blown your deal with Grimm. You're not going to tell me you knew nothing about all this?'

No, Korten wasn't. He had been aware of the trouble and also of the deal with Grimm. But that was surely not the stuff of murder. 'Unless . . .' he removed his glasses, 'unless old Schmalz misinterpreted something. You know, he was the sort of man who still imagined himself in service, and if his son or another security man told him about the trouble with Mischkey, he might have seen himself as obliged to act as saviour of the Works.'

'What could Schmalz senior have misunderstood with such serious repercussions?'

'I don't know what his son or anyone else might have told him. Or if anyone just plain incited him? I'll get to the bottom of it. It's unbearable to think that my good old Schmalz ended up being exploited like this. And what a tragic end. His great love for the Works and a silly little misunderstanding led him to take a life senselessly and unnecessarily, and also to sacrifice his own.'

'What's the matter with you? Giving life, taking life, tragedy, exploitation – I'm thinking: "It's not reprehensible to use people, it's just tactless to let them notice".'

'You're right, let's get back to the matter at hand. Should we bring in the police?'

That was it? An over-eager veteran of security had killed Mischkey, and Korten didn't even turn a hair. Could the prospect of having the police in the Works frighten him? I tried it out.

Korten weighed up the pros and cons. 'It's not only the fact that it's always unpleasant to have the police in the Works. I feel sorry for the Schmalz family. To lose a husband and father and then to discover he had made a lethal mistake – can we take on the responsibility for that? There's nothing left to atone, he paid with his life. But I'm thinking about reparation. Do you know whether Misch-key had parents he looked after, or other obligations, or whether he has a decent gravestone? Did he leave anyone behind we could do something for? Would you be willing to take care of it?'

I assumed that Judith wouldn't particularly care to have anything of the sort done for her.

'I've investigated plenty in Mischkey's case. If you're serious, Frau Schlemihl can find out what you need to know with a couple of phone calls.'

'You're always so sensitive. You did wonderful work on Mischkey's case. I'm also grateful that you kept going with the second part of the investigation. I need to be aware of such things. May I extend my original contract belatedly and ask you to send a bill?'

He was welcome to the bill.

'Ah, and another thing,' said Korten, 'while we're talking business. You forgot to enclose your special pass with your report last time. Please do pop it in the envelope with the bill this time.'

I took the pass out of my wallet. 'You can have it right now. And I'll be on my way.'

Helga came onto the loggia as though she'd been eavesdropping behind the door, and had picked up the signal for saying goodbye. 'The flowers are truly delight-ful, would you like to see where I've put them, Herr Self?'

'Ah, children, drop the formalities. Self is my oldest friend.' Korten put an arm round both our shoulders.

I wanted out. Instead, I followed the two of them into the sitting room, admired my bouquet on the grand piano, listened to the popping of the champagne cork, and clinked glasses with Helga, over the dropping of formal-ities.

'Why haven't we seen you here more often?' she asked in all innocence.

'Yes, we must change that,' said Korten, before I could respond at all. 'What are your plans for New Year's Eve?'

I thought about Brigitte. 'I'm not sure yet.'

'That's wonderful, my dear Self. Then we'll be in touch with each other again soon.'

23

Do you have a tissue?

Brigitte had prepared beef stroganoff with fresh mush-rooms and rice. It tasted delicious, the wine was at a perfect temperature, and the table was lovingly set. Brigitte was chattering. I'd brought her Elton John's *Greatest Hits* and he was singing of love and suffering, hope and separation.

She held forth on reflexology, acupressure, and Rolfing. She told me about patients, health insurers, and col-leagues. She didn't care in the least whether it interested me, or how I was.

'What's going on today? This afternoon I scarcely recognize Korten, and now I'm sitting here with you and the only thing you have in common with the Brigitte I like is the scar on your earlobe.'

She laid down her fork, put her elbows on the table, rested her head on her hands, and began to weep. I went round the table to her, she nuzzled her head into my belly, and just cried all the more.

'What's wrong?' I stroked her hair.

'I . . . oh . . . I, it's enough to drive me to tears. I'm going away tomorrow.'

'Why the tears about that?'

'It's for so terribly long. And so far.' She raised her face.

'How long, then, and how far?'

'Oh . . . I . . .' She pulled herself together. 'Do you have a tissue? I'm going to Brazil for six months. To see my son.'

I sat down. Now I felt ready to weep, too. At the same time I felt angry. 'Why didn't you tell me before?'

'I didn't know things would turn out so nice between us.'

'I don't understand.'

She took my hand. 'Juan and I had intended to take the six months to see whether we couldn't be together after all. Manuel misses his mother all the time. And with you I thought it would just be a short episode and over anyway by the time I left for Brazil.'

'What do you mean, you thought it would be over anyway when you left for Brazil? Postcards from Sugar Loaf Mountain won't change a thing.' I was quite bleak with sadness. She said nothing and stared into space. After a while I withdrew my hand from hers and got up. 'I'd better go now.' She nodded mutely.

In the hallway she leaned against me for one last moment. 'You see, I can't go on being the raven mother that you never liked anyway.'

24

She'd hunched her shoulders

The night was dreamless. I woke up at six o'clock, knew I had to talk to Judith today and thought about what I should tell her. Everything? How would she be able to continue working at RCW and hold on to her old life? But that was a problem I couldn't solve for her.

At nine o'clock I phoned her. 'I've wrapped up the case, Judith. Shall we take a walk by the harbour and I'll fill you in?'

'You don't sound good. What have you found out?'

'I'll pick you up at ten.'

I put coffee on, took the butter out of the fridge, and the eggs and smoked ham, chopped onions and chives, warmed up milk for Turbo, squeezed three oranges for juice, set the table, and made myself two fried eggs on ham and lightly sweated onions. When the eggs were just right I sprinkled them with chives. The coffee was ready.

I sat for a long time over my breakfast without touching it. Just before ten I took a couple of gulps of coffee. I set down the eggs for Turbo and left.

When I rang the bell, Judith came down straight away. She looked pretty in her loden coat with its collar turned up, as pretty as only an unhappy person can be.

We parked the car by the harbour office and walked between the rail tracks and the old warehouses along Rheinkaistrasse. Beneath the grey September sky it all had the peacefulness of a Sunday. The John Deere tractors were parked as though they were waiting for a field chaplain to begin the service.

'Will you please finally start to tell me?'

'Didn't Firner mention my run-in with plant security on Thursday night?'

'No. I think he'd gathered I was with Peter.'

I started with the talk I'd had with Korten yesterday, lingered over the question of whether old Schmalz was the last link of a well-functioning chain of command, had crazily set himself up as the saviour of the plant, or had been used, nor did I spare the details of the murder on the bridge. I made it clear that what I knew, and what could be proved, were leagues apart.

Judith strode along firmly beside me. She'd hunched her shoulders and was holding the collar of her coat closed with her left hand against the north wind. She hadn't interrupted me. But now she said with a small laugh that cut me even further to the quick than her tears would have done: 'Do you know, Gerhard, it's so absurd. When I took you on to find out the truth I thought it would help me. But now I feel more at a loss than ever.'

I envied Judith the purity of her grief. My sadness was pervaded by a sense of weakness, of guilt, because I'd delivered Mischkey to the dogs, albeit unwittingly, a feeling that I'd been used, and a strange pride at having come so far. It also saddened me that the case had initially connected Judith and myself then entangled us so much with one another that we'd never be able to grow closer without a sense of awkwardness.

'You'll send me the bill?'

She hadn't understood that Korten wanted to pay for my investigation. As I explained this to her, she retreated even further into herself and said: 'That fits perfectly. It would also fit if I were to be promoted to Korten's personal assistant. It's all so repulsive.'

Between warehouse number seventeen and number nineteen we turned left and came to the Rhine. Opposite lay the RCW skyscraper. The Rhine flowed past, wide and tranquil.

'What do I do now?'

I had no answers. If she managed tomorrow to lay the folder of letters in front of Firner to sign, as though nothing had happened, she'd come to terms with it.

'And the terrible thing is that Peter is already so far away, inside. I've cleared out everything at home that reminded me of him, because it hurt so much. But now my loneliness feels tidied away, too, and I'm getting cold.'

We walked along the Rhine, following it downstream. Suddenly she turned to me, seized me by the coat, shook me and said: 'We can't just let them get away with it!' With her right arm she made a sweeping gesture encapsulating the Works opposite. 'They shouldn't be let off the hook.'

'No, they shouldn't be, but they will be. Since the beginning of time, people with power have got away with it. And here perhaps it wasn't even the people with power, it was a megalomaniac, Schmalz.'

'But that's exactly what power is, not having to act yourself, but getting some megalomaniac to do it. That can't excuse them.'

I tried to explain to her that I didn't want to excuse anyone, but that I simply couldn't pursue the investigation.

'Then you're just one of the somebodies who does the dirty work for those people with power. Leave me alone now, I'll find my own way back.'

I suppressed the impulse to leave her there, and said instead: 'That's mad, the secretary of the director of the RCW reproaching the detective who carried out a contract for the RCW, for working for the RCW. That's rich.'

We walked on. After a while she put an arm through mine. 'In the old days, if something bad happened, I always had the feeling it would all be okay again. Life, I mean. Even after my divorce. Now I know nothing will ever be the same again. Do you recognize that?'

I nodded.

'Listen, it really would be best if I go on walking here on my own for a bit. You needn't look so worried, I won't do anything silly.'

From Rheinkaistrasse I looked back. She hadn't moved. She was looking over to the RCW at the levelled ground of the old factory. The wind blew an empty cement sack over the street.

Part Three

I

A milestone in jurisprudence

After a long, golden Indian summer, winter started abruptly. I can't remember a colder November.

I wasn't working much then. The investigation in the Sergej Mencke affair advanced at a crawl. The insurance company was hemming and hawing about sending me to America. The meeting with the ballet director had taken place on the sidelines of a rehearsal, and had taught me about Indian dance, which was being rehearsed, but otherwise only revealed that some people liked Sergej, others didn't, and the ballet director belonged to the latter category. For two weeks I was plagued by rheumatism so that I wasn't fit for anything except getting through the bare necessities. Beyond that I went on plenty of walks, frequented the sauna and the cinema, finished reading *Green Henry* – I'd laid it aside in the summer – and listened to Turbo's winter coat grow. One Saturday I bumped into Judith at the market. She was no longer working at RCW, was living off her unemployment money, and helping out at the women's bookshop Xanthippe. We promised to get together, but neither of us made the first move. With Eberhard I re-enacted the matches of the world chess championship. As we were sitting over the last game, Brigitte called from Rio. There was a buzzing and crackling in the line; I could barely make her out. I think she said she was missing me. I didn't know what to do with that.

December began with unexpected days of sultry wind. On 2 December the Federal Constitutional Court pronounced as unconstitutional the direct emissions data gathering introduced by statute in Baden-Württemberg and the Rhineland-Palatinate.

It censured the violation of constitutional rights of business data privacy and establishment and practice of a commercial enterprise, but eventually the statute was annulled for lack of legislative authority. The well-known columnist of the *Frankfurter Allgemeine Zeitung* celebrated the decision as a milestone in jurisprudence because, at last, data privacy had broken free of the shackles of mere civil rights protection and was elevated to the rank of entrepreneurial rights. Only now was the true grandeur of the court's judgment regarding data protection revealed.

I wondered what would become of Grimm's lucrative sideline. Would the RCW continue to pay him a fee, for keeping quiet? I also wondered whether Judith would read the news from Karlsruhe, and what would go through her head as she did. This decision half a year earlier would have meant that Mischkey and the RCW wouldn't have locked horns.

That same day there was a letter from San Francisco in the mail. Vera Müller was a former resident of Mannheim, had emigrated to the USA in 1936, and had taught European literature at various Californian colleges. She'd been retired for some years now and out of a sense of nostalgia read the *Mannheimer Morgen*. She'd been surprised not to hear anything back about her first letter to Mischkey. She'd responded to the advertisement because the fate of her Jewish friend in the Third Reich was sadly interwoven with the RCW. She thought it a period of recent history that should be more widely researched and published, and she was willing to broker contact with Frau Hirsch. But she didn't want to cause her friend any unnecessary excitement and would only establish contact if the research project was both academically sound and fruitful from the aspect of coming to terms with the past. She asked for assurances on this score.

It was the letter of an educated lady, rendered in lovely, old-fashioned German, and written in sloping, austere handwriting. Sometimes in the summer I see elderly American tourists in Heidelberg with a blue tint in their white hair, bright-pink frames on their spectacles, and garish make-up on their wrinkled skin. This willingness to present oneself as a caricature had always alienated me as an expression of cultural despair. Reading Vera Müller's letter I could suddenly imagine such a lady being interesting and fascinating and recognize the wise weariness of completely forgotten peoples in that cultural despair. I wrote to her saying I'd try to visit her soon.

I called the Heidelberg Union Insurance company. I made it clear that without the trip to America all I could do was write a final report and prepare an invoice. An hour later the clerk in charge called to give me the go-ahead.

So, I was back on the Mischkey case. I didn't know what there was left for me to find out. But there it was, this trail that had vanished and had now re-emerged. And with the green light from the Heidelberg Union Insurance I could pursue it so effortlessly that I didn't have to think too deeply about the why and wherefore.

It was three o'clock in the afternoon and I figured out from my diary that it was 9 a.m. in Pittsburgh. I'd discovered from the ballet director that Sergej Mencke's friends were at the Pittsburgh State Ballet, and International Information divulged its telephone number. The girl from the exchange was jovial. 'You want to give the little lady from *Flashdance* a call?' I didn't know the film. 'Is the movie worth seeing? Should I take a look?' She'd seen it three times. With my dreadful English the long-distance call to Pittsburgh was a torture. At least I found out from the ballet's secretary that both dancers would be in Pittsburgh throughout December.

I came to an understanding with my travel agency that I'd receive an invoice for a Lufthansa flight Frankfurt–Pittsburgh, but would actually be booked on a cheap flight from Brussels to San Francisco with a stopover in New York and a side trip to Pittsburgh. At the beginning of December there wasn't much going on over the Atlantic. I got a flight for Thursday morning.

Towards evening I gave Vera Müller a call in San Francisco. I told her I'd written, but that rather suddenly a convenient opportunity had arisen to come to the USA, and I'd be in San Francisco by the weekend. She said she'd announce my visit to Frau Hirsch; she herself was out of town over the weekend but would be glad to see me on Monday. I noted down Frau Hirsch's address: 410 Connecticut Street, Potrero Hill.

2

A crackle, and the picture came up

From the old films I had visions in my mind of ships steaming into New York, past the Statue of Liberty and on past the skyscrapers, and I'd imagined seeing the same, not from the deck of a liner, but through the small window on my left. However, the airport was way out of the city, it was cold and dirty, and I was glad when I'd transferred and was sitting in the plane to San Francisco. The rows of seats were so squashed together that it was only bearable to be in them with the seat reclined. During the meal you had to put your seat-back up; presumably the airline only served a meal so that you would be happy afterwards when you could recline again.

I arrived at midnight. A cab took me into the city via an eight-lane motorway, and to a hotel. I was feeling wretched after the storm the airplane had flown through. The porter who'd carried my suitcase to the room turned on the television; there was a crackle, and the picture came up. A man was talking with obscene pushiness. I realized later he was a preacher.

The next morning the porter called me a cab, and I stepped out into the street. The window of my room looked out onto the wall of a neighbouring building, and in the room the morning had been grey and quiet. Now the colours and noises of the city exploded around me, beneath a clear, blue sky. The drive over the hills of the town, on streets that led upwards and swooped down again straight as an arrow, the smacking jolts of the cab's worn-out suspension when we crossed a junction, the views of skyscrapers, bridges, and a large bay made me feel dizzy.

The house was situated in a peaceful street. Like all the houses it was made of wood. Steps led to the front door. Up I went and rang the bell. An old man opened the door. 'Mr Hirsch?'

'My husband's been dead for six years,' she said in rusty German. 'You needn't apologize, I'm often taken for a man and I'm used to it. You're the German Vera was telling me about, right?'

Perhaps it was the confusion or the flight or the cab ride – I must have fainted and came to when the old woman threw a glass of water at my face.

'You're lucky you didn't fall down the steps. When you're ready, come and I'll give you a whisky.'

The whisky burned inside me. The room was musty and smelt of age, of old flesh and old food. The same smell had suffused my grandparents' house, I suddenly recalled, and just as suddenly I was seized by the fear of growing old that I'm continuously suppressing.

The woman was perched opposite, and scrutinizing me. Shafts of sunlight shone through the blinds onto her. She was completely bald. 'You want to talk to me about Weinstein, my husband. Vera thinks it's important that what happened is told. But it's not a good story. My husband tried to forget it.'

I didn't realize straight away who Karl Weinstein was. But as she started to talk I remembered. She didn't realize she was not only telling his story but also touching upon my own past.

She spoke in an oddly monotonous voice. Weinstein had been professor of organic chemistry in Breslau until 1933. In 1941, when he was put in a concentration camp, his former assistant Tyberg put in a request for him for the RCW laboratories, which was granted. Weinstein was even quite pleased that he could work in his field again and that he was working with someone who appreciated him as a scientist, addressed him as Professor, and politely said goodbye in the evening when he was taken back to the camp along with the other forced labourers of the Works. 'My husband didn't cope well with life, nor was he very brave. He had no idea, or didn't want to know, what was happening around him and what was coming for him, too.'

'Did you go through this time at the RCW as well?'

'I met Karl on the transport to Auschwitz in nineteen forty-one. And then again only after the war. I'm Flemish, you know, and could hide in Brussels to begin with, until they caught me. I was a beautiful woman. They conducted medical experiments on my scalp. I think that saved my life. But in nineteen forty-five I was old and bald. I was twenty-three.'

One day they'd come to Weinstein, someone from the Works and someone from the SS. They'd told him how he must testify before the police, the prosecutor, and the judge. It was a matter of sabotage, a manuscript that he'd supposedly found in Tyberg's desk, a conversation between Tyberg and a co-worker that he'd supposedly overheard.

I could picture Weinstein, as he was led into my office, in his prisoner's clothes, and gave his testimony.

'He hadn't wanted to at first. It was all false and Tyberg hadn't been bad to him. But they showed him they would crush him. They didn't even promise him his life, only that he could survive a little longer. Can you imagine that? Then my husband was transferred and simply forgotten in the other camp. We'd arranged where we would meet should the whole thing ever be over. In Brussels on the Grand Place. I came there simply by chance in the spring of nineteen forty-six, not thinking of him any more. He'd been waiting there for me since the summer of nineteen forty-five. He recognized me immediately although I'd become this bald, old lady. Quite irresistible!' She laughed.

I couldn't bring myself to tell her that I was the one Weinstein had delivered his testimony to. I also couldn't tell her why it was so important to me. But I had to know. And so I asked, 'Are you certain that the testimony your husband gave was false?'

'I don't understand. I've told you what he told me.' Her face turned cold. 'Get out,' she said, 'get out.'

3
Do not disturb

I walked down the hill and came to the docks and warehouses by the bay. Far and wide I could see neither cab nor bus, nor subway station. I wasn't even sure if San Francisco had a subway. I set off in the direction of the skyscrapers. The street didn't have a name, just a number. In front of me a heavy, black Cadillac was crawling along. Every few steps it drew to a standstill, a black man in a pink silk suit got out, trampled a beer or coke can flat, and dropped it into a large blue plastic sack. A few hundred metres ahead I saw a store. As I came closer I saw it was barred like a fortress. I went in looking for a sandwich and a packet of Sweet Aftons. The goods were behind grating and the checkout reminded me of a counter at the bank. I didn't get a sandwich and no one knew what Sweet Aftons were, and I felt guilty even though I hadn't done anything. As I was leaving the store with a carton of Chesterfields, a freight train rattled past me in the middle of the street.

On the piers I came across a car rental and rented a Chevrolet. I was taken by the one-piece front seating. It reminded me of the Horch on whose front seat I was initiated into love by the wife of my Latin teacher. Together with the car I got a town plan with the 49 Mile Drive highlighted. I followed it without trouble, thanks to the signs everywhere. By the cliffs I found a restaurant. At the entrance I had to edge forward in a line before being led to a seat by the window. Mist was curling over the

Pacific. The show captivated me, as though, beyond the rents in the fog, Japan's coast would come into view any second. I ate a tuna steak, potato in aluminum foil, and iceberg lettuce salad. The beer was called Anchor Steam and tasted almost like a smoked beer in the Bamberg Schlenkerla. The waitress was attentive, kept refilling my coffee cup without my having to ask, enquired after my health and where I was from. She knew Germany, too; she'd visited her boyfriend at the US base in Baumholder once.

After the meal I stretched my legs, clambered around on the cliffs, and suddenly saw before me, more beautiful than I remembered it from films, the Golden Gate Bridge. I took off my coat, folded it, put it on a rock, and sat on it. The coast fell away steeply, beneath me bright sailing boats were criss-crossing, and a freight ship ploughed its gentle path.

I had planned to live at peace with my past. Guilt, atonement, enthusiasm and blindness, pride and anger, morality and resignation – I'd brought it all together in an elaborate balance. The past had achieved abstraction. Now reality had caught up with me and was threatening that balance. Of course I'd let myself be manipulated as a prosecutor, I'd learned that much after 1945. One may question whether there is better manipulation and worse. Nevertheless, I didn't think it was the same thing to be guilty of having served a putative great, bad cause, or to be used by someone as a pawn on the chessboard of a small, shabby intrigue I didn't yet understand.

The stuff Frau Hirsch had told me, what did it amount to exactly? Tyberg and Dohmke, whom I'd investigated, had been convicted purely on the strength of Weinstein's false testimony. By any standard, even the National Socialist one, the judgment was a miscarriage of justice and my investigation was wrong. I'd been taken in by a plot made to trap Tyberg and Dohmke. My memory of it started to come back. In Tyberg's desk hidden documents had been found that revealed a promising plan, essential to the war effort, initially pursued by Tyberg and his research group, then apparently abandoned. The accused repeatedly stressed to me and to the court that they couldn't have followed two promising paths of research at the same time. They had only put the other one on a backburner, to return to later. The whole thing was under the strictest secrecy and their discovery had been so exciting that they'd safeguarded it with the jealousy of the scientist. That had been the only reason for the cache in the desk. That might have got them off, but Weinstein reported a conversation between Dohmke and Tyberg in which both agreed to suppress the discovery to bring about a quick end to the war, even at the price of a German defeat. And now this conversation had never actually taken place.

The sabotage story had unleashed outrage at the time. The second charge of racial defilement hadn't convinced me, even then: my investigation hadn't produced any evidence that Tyberg had had intercourse with a Jewish forced labourer. He was sentenced to death on that account, too. I pondered who from the SS and who from the economic side back then could have set up the conspiracy.

There was a constant flow of traffic over the Golden Gate Bridge. Where did everyone want to get to? I drove to the approach, parked my car beneath the monument to the architect, and walked to the middle of the bridge. I was the only pedestrian. I gazed down onto the metallic gleaming Pacific. Behind me limousines whizzed by with a callous regularity. A cold wind blew round the suspension cables. I was freezing.

With some trouble I found the hotel again. It soon

215

turned dark. I asked the porter where I could get a bottle of sambuca. He sent me along to a liquor store two streets away. I scanned the shelves in vain. The proprietor regretted he didn't have sambuca, but he did have something similar, wouldn't I like to try Southern Comfort? He packed the bottle in a brown paper bag for me, and twisted the paper shut round the neck. On the way back to the hotel I bought a hamburger. With my trench coat, the brown paper bag in one hand, and the burger in the other I felt like an extra in a second-rate American cop film.

Back in the hotel room I lay down on the bed and switched on the TV. My toothbrush glass was wrapped in cellophane, I tore it off and poured myself a shot. Southern Comfort really doesn't bear the slightest resemblance to sambuca. Still, it tasted pleasant and trickled quite naturally down my throat. Nor did the football on TV have the faintest in common with our football. But I understood the principle and followed the match with increasing excitement.

After a while I applauded when my team had made decent headway with the ball. Finally I must have whooped when my team won, because there came a knocking through the wall. I tried to get up and thump back, but the bed kept tipping up at the side I was trying to get out of. It wasn't that important. Main thing was that topping up the glass still went smoothly. I left the last gulp in the bottle for the flight back.

In the middle of the night I woke up. Now I felt drunk. I was lying fully clothed on the bed, the TV was spitting out images. When I switched it off, my head imploded. I managed to take off my jacket before falling asleep again.

When I woke up, for a brief moment I didn't know where I was. My room was cleaned and tidied, the ashtray empty, and the toothbrush glass back in cellophane. My watch said half past two. I sat on the toilet for a long time, clutching my head. When I washed my hands I avoided looking in the mirror. I found a packet of aspirin in my toilet bag, and twenty minutes later the headache was gone. But with every movement the brain fluid slapped hard against the walls of my skull, and my stomach was crying out for food while telling me it wouldn't keep it down. At home I'd have made a camomile tea, but I didn't know the American word, nor where I'd find it, nor how I'd boil the water.

I took a shower, first hot, then cold. In the hotel's Tea Room I got a black coffee and toast. I took a few steps out onto the street. The way led me to the liquor store. It was still open. I didn't begrudge the Southern Comfort the previous night, I'm not one to nurse a grudge. To make this clear I bought another bottle. The proprietor said: 'Better than any of your sambuca, hey?' I didn't want to contradict him.

This time I intended to get drunk systematically. I got undressed, hung the 'Do not disturb' sign outside my door and my suit over the clothes stand. I stuffed my worn undershirt into a plastic bag provided for the purpose and left it out in the corridor. I added my shoes and hoped that I'd find everything in a decent state the next morning. I locked the door from the inside, drew the curtains, turned on the TV, slipped into my pyjamas, poured my first glass, placed bottle and ashtray within reach on the bedside table, laid my cigarettes and folder of matches next to them, and myself in bed. *Red River* was on TV. I pulled the covers up to my chin, smoked, and drank.

After a while the images of the courtroom I'd appeared in, of the hangings I'd had to attend, of green and grey and black uniforms, and of my wife in her League of German Girls outfit began to fade. I could no longer hear the echo of boots in long corridors, no Führer's speeches on the

People's Receiver, no sirens. John Wayne was drinking whisky, I was drinking Southern Comfort, and as he set off to tidy things up I was with him all the way.

By the following midday, the return to sobriety had become a ritual. At the same time it was clear the drinking was over. I drove to the Golden Gate Park and walked for two hours. In the evening I found Perry's, an Italian restaurant I felt almost as comfortable in as the Kleiner Rosengarten. I slept deeply and dreamlessly, and on Monday morning I discovered the American breakfast. At nine o'clock I gave Vera Müller a call. She would expect me for lunch.

At half past twelve I was standing in front of her house on Telegraph Hill with a bouquet of yellow roses. She wasn't the blue-rinsed caricature I'd envisaged. She was around my age and if I had aged as a man as she had as a woman, I'd have had reason to be content. She was tall, slim, angular, wore her grey hair piled high, over her jeans a Russian smock, her spectacles were hanging from a chain, and there was a mocking expression hovering round her grey eyes and thin mouth. She wore two wedding rings on her left hand.

'Yes, I'm a widow.' She had noticed my glance. 'My husband died three years ago. You remind me of him.' She led me into the sitting room through the windows of which I could see Alcatraz. 'Do you take Pastis as an aperitif? Help yourself, I'll just pop the pizza into the oven.'

When she returned I had poured two glasses. 'I had to confess something to you. I'm not a historian from Hamburg, I'm a private detective from Mannheim. The man whose advertisement you answered, not a Hamburg historian either, was murdered and I'm trying to find out why.'

'Do you already know by whom?'

'Yes and no.' I told my story.

'Did you mention your connection to the Tyberg affair to Frau Hirsch?'

'No, I didn't dare.'

'You really do remind me of my husband. He was a journalist, a famous raging reporter, but each time he wrote a piece, he was afraid. It's good, by the way, you didn't tell her. It would have upset her too much, because of her relationship with Karl, too. Did you know, he had an amazing career again, in Stanford? Sarah never adapted to that world. She stayed with him because she thought she owed it to him for his having waited so long. And at the same time he only lived with her out of a sense of loyalty. The two of them never married.'

She led me out onto the kitchen balcony and fetched the pizza. 'One thing I do like about growing older is that principles develop holes. I never thought I'd be able to eat with an old Nazi prosecutor without choking on my pizza. Are you still a Nazi?'

I choked on my pizza.

'All right, all right. You don't look like one to me. Do you sometimes have problems with your past?'

'At least two bottles of Southern Comfort's worth.' I told her how the weekend had been spent.

At six o'clock we were still sitting together. She told me about her start in America. At the Olympic Games in Berlin she'd met her husband and moved with him to Los Angeles. 'Do you know what I found most difficult? Wearing my bathing suit in the sauna.'

Then she had to leave for her night shift with the help line. I went back to Perry's and merely took a six-pack of beer to bed with me. The next morning I wrote Vera Müller a postcard over breakfast, settled the bill, and drove to the airport. In the evening I was in Pittsburgh. There was snow on the ground.

4

Demolishing Sergej

The cabs that took me to the hotel in the evening and to the ballet the next morning were every bit as yellow as those in San Francisco. It was nine, the ensemble was already in the midst of a rehearsal, at ten they took a break and I was directed to the Mannheimers. They were standing in tights and leotards next to the radiators, yoghurt in hand.

When I introduced myself and the subject of my visit, they could hardly believe I'd come all this way just for them.

'Did you know about Sergej?' Hanne turned to Joschka. 'Hey, I mean, I feel just devastated.'

Joschka was startled, too. 'If we can help Sergej in any way . . . I'll have a word with the boss. It should be fine for us to start again at eleven o'clock. That way we can sit down together in the canteen and talk.'

The canteen was empty. Through the window I looked onto a park with tall, bare trees. Mothers were out with their children, Eskimos in padded overalls, romping around in the snow.

'All right, I mean, it's really important for me to share what I know about Sergej. I'd find it, like, absolutely awful, if someone thought . . . if someone got the wrong . . . Sergej, he's so incredibly sensitive. And he's so vulnerable, not at all macho. You see, that's why he couldn't have done it for starters, he was always terribly afraid of injuries.'

Joschka wasn't so sure. He stirred the contents of his Styrofoam cup with a little plastic stick, contemplatively. 'Herr Self, I don't think Sergej maimed himself either. I just can't imagine anyone doing that. But if anyone . . . You know, Sergej was always having crackpot ideas.'

'How can you say such mean stuff?' Hanne interrupted him. 'I thought you were his friend. No way, that makes me, like, really sad.'

Joschka placed his hand on her arm. 'But, Hanne, don't you remember the evening we were entertaining the dancers from Ghana? He told us how, when he was a boy scout, he deliberately cut his hand with the potato peeler to get out of kitchen duty. We all laughed about it, you too.'

'But you got it completely wrong. He only pretended he'd cut himself and wrapped a large bandage around it. If you're going to, like, distort the truth like that . . . I mean, really, Joschka . . .'

Joschka didn't appear convinced, but didn't want to quarrel with Hanne. I enquired about the shape, and mood, Sergej was in during the last few months of the season.

'Exactly,' said Hanne. 'That doesn't fit with your strange suspicion either. He believed completely in himself, he absolutely wanted to add flamenco to his repertoire, and tried to get a scholarship to Madrid.'

'But, Hanne, he didn't get the scholarship, that's the thing.'

'But don't you get it, the fact he applied for it, that had so much power somehow. And his relationship, that was finally going well in the summer with his German professor. You know, Sergej, he isn't gay, but he can also love men. He's absolutely fantastic that way, I think. And not just something brief, sexual, but like, really deep. It's impossible not to like him. He's so . . .'

'Sweet?' I suggested.

'Yeah, sweet. Do you actually know him, Herr Self?'

'Uh, could you tell me who the German professor is you mentioned?'

'Was it really German, not law?' Joschka frowned.

'Oh, crap, you're demolishing Sergej. He was a Germanist, such a cuddly guy. But his name . . . I don't know if I should tell you.'

'Hanne, the two of them hardly made a secret of it considering how they carried on round town. It's Fritz Kirchenberg from Heidelberg. Maybe it's a good idea for you to talk to him.'

I asked them about Sergej's qualities as a dancer. Hanne answered first.

'But that's beside the point. Even if you're not a good dancer you don't have to hack your leg off. I'm not even going to discuss it. And I'm still convinced you're wrong.'

'I don't have any concrete opinion as yet, Frau Fischer. And I'd like to point out that Herr Mencke hasn't lost his leg, merely broken it.'

'I don't know what sort of knowledge you have of ballet, Herr Self,' said Joschka. 'At the end of the day, it's the same with us as it is everywhere else. There are the stars, and the ones who will be stars one day, and then there's the solid middle rank of the ones who've let go of their daydreams of glory but don't have to worry about earning a living. And then there are the rest – the ones who have to live in constant fear of whether there'll be a next engagement, for whom it's certainly over when they start to get older. Sergej belongs to the third group.'

Hanne didn't contradict. She let her defiant expression show how completely out of order she felt this conversation was. 'I thought you wanted to find out something about Sergej, the person. You men have nothing in your heads beyond careers, really.'

'How did Herr Mencke envisage his future?'

'On the side he'd always done ballroom dancing and he told me once he'd like to start a dance school, a perfectly conventional one, for fifteen- and sixteen-year-olds.'

'That also proves he couldn't have done anything to himself. Think it through, Joschka. How's he supposed to become a dance teacher minus a leg?'

'Did you also know about his dancing school plans, Frau Fischer?'

'Sergej played around with lots of ideas. He's so brilliantly creative and has an incredible imagination. He could also imagine doing something completely different, breeding sheep in Provence, or something.'

They had to get back to rehearsal. They gave me their telephone numbers in case other questions came to me, asked whether I had plans for the evening, and promised to set aside a complimentary ticket for me at the door. I watched them go. Joschka moved with concentration and there was a spring in his step, Hanne trod lightly, as though walking on air. Admittedly, she'd talked, like, a lot of nonsense, but she walked with conviction, and I'd have liked to watch her dance that evening. But Pittsburgh was far too cold. I had a car take me to the airport, flew to New York, and got a return flight that same evening to Frankfurt. I think I'm too old for America.

5

So whose goose are you cooking?

Over brunch in Café Gmeiner I drew up a programme for the rest of the week. Outside, the snow was falling in thick flakes. I'd have to root out the scoutmaster of the troop Mencke had belonged to, and speak to Professor Kirchenberg. And I wanted to talk to the judge who'd sentenced Tyberg and Dohmke to death. I had to know whether the sentence had been influenced from above.

Judge Beufer had been elevated to the Appellate Court in Karlsruhe after the war. At the main post office I found his name in the Karlsruhe telephone directory. His voice sounded astonishingly young, and he remembered my name. 'Master Self,' he crooned in his Swabian accent. 'Whatever became of him?' He was willing to have me round for a talk that afternoon.

He lived in Durlach in a house on the hillside with a view of Karlsruhe. I could see the large gasometer with its welcoming inscription 'Karlsruhe'. Judge Beufer opened the door in person. He had a soldier's upright posture, was wearing a grey suit, beneath it a white shirt and a red tie with a silver tie pin. The collar of his shirt had become too large for the old, scraggy neck. Beufer was bald and his face had a heavy downward pull, bags under the eyes, jowls, chin. We'd always joked about his sticking-out ears in the public prosecutor's office. They were more impressive than ever. He looked ill. He must be well over eighty.

'So, he's become a private detective. Isn't he ashamed? He was a good lawyer, after all, a sharp prosecutor. I expected to see him back with us when the worst of it was over.'

We sat in his study and sipped sherry. He still read the *New Legal Weekly*. 'Master Self hasn't simply come to pay his old judge a visit.' His little piggy eyes were twinkling shrewdly.

'Do you remember the case of Tyberg and Dohmke? End of nineteen forty-three, beginning of forty-four. I was leading the investigation, Södelknecht was the prosecutor. And you were presiding over court.'

'Tyberg and Dohmke . . .' He spoke the names softly to himself a few times. 'Yes, of course. They were sentenced to death and Dohmke was executed. Tyberg escaped. He went a long way, that man. And was a true gentleman, or is he still alive? Bumped into him once at a reception in Solitude, joked about old times. He certainly understood we all had to do our duty back then.'

'What I'd like to know – was the court given signals from above regarding the outcome, or was it a perfectly normal trial?'

'Why does that interest him? Whose goose is he cooking, that Master Self?'

The question was bound to come. I told him about a coincidental connection to Frau Müller and my meeting with Frau Hirsch. 'I simply want to know what happened back then, and what role I played.'

'To reopen the trial, what the lady told you is nowhere near enough. If Weinstein were still alive . . . but he isn't. I don't believe it anyway. A lawyer has his gut feeling, and the more clearly I remember, the more certain I am the verdict was right.'

'And were there signals from above? I'm sure you won't misunderstand me, Herr Beufer. We both know that

German judges knew how to preserve their independence even under extraordinary conditions. Nevertheless, now and then some interested party would try to exert influence, and I'd like to know whether there was an interested party in this trial.'

'Oh, Self, why won't he let sleeping dogs lie? But if it's essential for his peace of mind . . . Weismüller called me a few times back then, the former general director. His focus was to clear it out of the way and stop people gossiping about RCW. Perhaps the sentencing of Tyberg and Dohmke met with his approval, simply for that reaon. Nothing clears up a case quite so effectively as a quick hanging. Whether there were other reasons he wanted the sentence . . . No idea, I don't think so, though.'

'That was it?'

'Weismüller also had some business with Södelknecht. Tyberg's defence counsel had brought forward someone from the RCW as a witness who talked himself blue in the face on the witness stand, and Weismüller intervened on his behalf. Hang on, that man also went a long way, yes, Korten is the name, the current general director. There we have them, the whole merry crew of general directors.' He laughed.

How could I have forgotten? I had been glad not to have to bring my friend and brother-in-law into it myself, but then the defence had hauled him in. I'd been glad because Korten had worked so closely together with Tyberg that his participation in the trial could have cast suspicion on him, or damaged his career at least. 'Was it known at court then that Korten and I are brothers-in-law?'

'My word. I'd never have thought it. But you advised your brother-in-law badly. He spoke out so strongly for Tyberg that Södelknecht almost arrested him on the spot at the hearing. Very decent, too decent. It didn't help Tyberg one bit. It smells just a little fishy when a witness for the defence has nothing to say about the deed and only spouts friendly platitudes about the accused.'

There was nothing left to ask Beufer. I drank the second sherry he poured me, and chatted about colleagues we'd both known. Then I took my leave.

'Master Self, now he's off to follow that sniffing nose again. The quest for justice won't let go of him, eh? Will he show his face again at old Beufer's? Be delighted.'

On top of my car were ten centimetres of fresh snow. I swept it off, was glad to make it safely down the hill, onto the autobahn. And once I was on that, I drove north in the wake of a snowplough. It had turned dark. The car radio reported traffic jams and played hits from the sixties.

6

Potatoes, cabbage, and hot black pudding

In the thick snow I missed the turn-off to Mannheim at the Walldorf intersection. Then the snowplough drove into a parking lot, and I was lost. I made it as far as the Hardtwald service area.

At the stand-up snack bar I waited with my coffee for the driving snow to stop. I stared into the swirling flakes. All at once pictures from the past came vividly alive.

It was on an evening in August or September, 1943. Klara and I had to leave our apartment in Werderstrasse, and had just completed the move to Bahnhofstrasse. Korten was over for dinner. There were potatoes, cabbage, and hot black pudding. He enthused about our new apartment, praised Klara for the meal, and this annoyed me, because he knew what a pitiful cook Klärchen was and it couldn't have escaped him that the potatoes were over-salted and the cabbage burnt. Then Klara left us men with our cigars for a bit of male conversation.

At that time the Tyberg and Dohmke file had just reached my desk. I wasn't convinced by the results of the police investigation. Tyberg was from a good family, had volunteered for the front, and it was only against his will, as his research work was essential to the war effort, that he'd been left behind at the RCW. I couldn't picture him as a saboteur.

'You know Tyberg, don't you? What do you think of him?'

'A man beyond reproach. We were all horrified that he and Dohmke were arrested at work, without anyone knowing why. Member of the national German hockey team in nineteen thirty-six, winner of the Professor Demel Medal, a gifted chemist, esteemed colleague and respected superior – no, I really don't understand what you people at the police and prosecutors are thinking.'

I explained to him that an arrest wasn't a conviction and that in a German court no one was sentenced unless the necessary evidence was at hand. This was an old theme of ours from our student days. Korten had come across a book at a bookstall about famous miscarriages of justice and argued for nights on end with me whether human justice can avoid miscarriages. That was my contention, Korten's position being the opposite, that one has to accept they occur.

A winter evening during our student days in Berlin came to my mind. Klara and I were tobogganing on the Kreuzberg, and were expected back at the Korten household for supper. Klara was seventeen, I'd encountered her and overlooked her, thousands of times, as Ferdinand's little sister. I'd only taken the brat tobogganing with me because she'd begged so. Actually, I was hoping to meet Pauline on the toboggan run, help her up after a fall or protect her from the ghastly Kreuzberg street urchins. Was Pauline there? At any rate, all of a sudden I only had eyes for Klara. She was wearing a fur jacket and a bright scarf, and her blonde curls were flying, and snowflakes melting upon her glowing cheeks. On the way home we kissed for the first time. Klara had to persuade me into going up to supper. I didn't know how to behave towards her in front of her parents and brother.

When I left later she found some pretext to bring me to the front door and gave me a secret kiss.

I caught myself smiling out of the window. In the parking lot a military convoy stopped, also unable to make headway in the snow. My car was swathed in another thick layer. At the counter I fetched a coffee refill and a sandwich. I took up my place at the window again.

Korten and I had also come round to talking about Weinstein that time. An irreproachable man as the accused and a Jew as the prosecution witness – I wondered whether I shouldn't drop the investigation. I couldn't tell Korten about Weinstein's significance, nor could I let the opportunity of learning something about Weinstein slip by.

'What do you actually think about using Jews at the Works?'

'You know, Gerd, that we've always thought differently about the Jewish question. I've never had any truck with anti-Semitism. I find it difficult having forced labourers in the plant, but whether they're Jews or Frenchmen or Germans is all the same. In our laboratory we have Professor Weinstein working with us and it's a crying shame that the man can't be behind a lectern or in his own laboratory. His service to us is invaluable, and if you go by his appearance and cast of mind, you couldn't find anyone more German. A professor of the old school, up until nineteen thirty-three he had a chair in organic chemistry at Breslau. Everything that Tyberg is as a chemist he owes, as his pupil and assistant, to Weinstein. The loveable, scatterbrained academic type.'

'And if I were to tell you that he's the one accusing Tyberg?'

'My God, Gerd. And with Weinstein so fond of his student Tyberg . . . I really don't know what to say.'

A snowplough made its way to the parking lot. The

driver got down and came into the snack bar. I asked him how I could get to Mannheim.

'A colleague has just set off for the Heidelberg intersection. Get going quickly before the lane is blocked again.'

It was seven. At a quarter to eight I was at the Heidelberg intersection and at nine in Mannheim. I had to stretch my legs and revelled in the deep snow. I'd have liked to have driven a troika through Mannheim.

7

What exactly are you investigating now?

At eight I awoke, but I didn't manage to get up. It had all been too much, the night flight from New York, the trip to Karlsruhe, the discussion with Beufer, the memories, and the odyssey along the snow-covered autobahn.

At eleven Philipp called. 'Wow, caught you at last? Where have you been gadding off to? Your dissertation is ready.'

'Dissertation?' I didn't know what he was talking about.

'Door-induced fractures. A contribution to the morphology of auto-aggression. You did commission it.'

'Oh, yes. And now there's a scientific treatise? When can I have it?'

'Anytime. Just come by the hospital and pick it up.'

I got up and made some coffee. The sky was still heavy with snow. Turbo came in from the balcony, powdered white.

My refrigerator was empty and I went shopping. It's nice that they go easier than they used to on sprinkling salt in towns. Instead of wading through brown slush, I walked on crunchy, tightly packed fresh snow. Children were building snowmen and having snowball fights. In the bakery at the Wasserturm I bumped into Judith.

'Isn't it a splendid day?' Her eyes were sparkling. 'Before, when I still had to go to work, the snow always irritated me. Clear the windshield, car doesn't start, drive slowly, get stuck. I was really missing out on something!'

'Come on,' I said, 'let's have a winter walk to the Kleiner Rosengarten. You're invited.'

This time she didn't say no. I felt somewhat old-fashioned next to her; she in her padded jacket, trousers, and high boots that are probably a spin-off of space technology, me in my overcoat and galoshes. On the way I told her about my investigations in the Mencke case and the snow in Pittsburgh. She also asked straight away whether I'd seen the little lady from *Flashdance*. I was getting curious about the film.

Giovanni was wide-eyed. When Judith had gone to the restroom he came up to our table. 'Old lady notsa good? New lady better? Next time you getta Italian lady from me, then you have peace.'

'German man don't needa the peace, need lotsa, lotsa, ladies.'

'Then it's lotsa good food you need.' He recommended the steak pizzaiola preceded by the chicken soup. 'The chef slaughtered the chicken himself this morning.' I ordered the same for Judith and a bottle of Chianti Classico to go with it.

'I was in America for another reason, Judith. The Mischkey case won't leave me in peace. I haven't made any progress. But the trip confronted me with my own past.'

She listened attentively to my report.

'What exactly are you investigating now? And why?'

'I don't know. I'd like to talk with Tyberg, if he's still alive.'

'Oh, he's alive all right. I often wrote letters to him, sent him business reports or birthday presents. He lives on Lake Maggiore, in Monti sopra Locarno.'

'Then I'd also like to speak to Korten again.'

'And what does he have to do with Peter's death?'

'I don't know, Judith. What wouldn't I give to be able

to get to the bottom of it? At least Mischkey has got me working on the past. Have you had any further thoughts about the murder?'

She'd considered taking the story to the press. 'I find it simply unbearable for the whole thing to end like this.'

'Do you mean not knowing? It won't improve by going to the press.'

'No. I believe the RCW hasn't really paid. Regardless of the way things went with old Schmalz, it does fall under their responsibility somehow. And besides, perhaps we'll discover more if the press stirs up a hornets' nest.'

Giovanni brought the steaks. We ate for a while in silence. I couldn't warm to the idea of going to the press. After all, I had been commissioned by the RCW to find Mischkey, at least the RCW had paid me for it. All that Judith knew and could go to the papers with she knew from me. My professional loyalty was at stake. I was annoyed I'd accepted Korten's money. Otherwise I'd be free now.

I explained my concern to her. 'I need to consider whether I can change my spots, but I'd prefer you to wait.'

'All right then. I was perfectly happy back then not to have to foot your bill, but I should have known straight away it would come at a price.'

We were finished with dinner. Giovanni brought two sambucas. 'With the compliments of the house.' Judith told me about her life as an unemployed person. To begin with she had enjoyed the freedom, but slowly the problems began. She couldn't expect the Unemployment Office to find her another comparable job. She'd have to get going herself. At the same time she wasn't sure if she wanted to embark on a life as an executive assistant again.

'Do you know Tyberg personally? I last saw him forty years ago and I don't know if I'd recognize him again.'

'Yes, at the RCW centenary, I was assigned as his Girl Friday, to look after him. Why?'

'Would you like to come with me if I visit him in Locarno? I'd like that.'

'So you really want to know. How do you propose to make contact with him?'

I pondered.

'Leave it to me,' she said. 'I'll set it up somehow. When do we go?'

'How soon could you organize a meeting with Tyberg?'

'Sunday? Monday? I can't say. Maybe he's in the Bahamas.'

'Set the date for as soon as possible.'

8

On the Scheffel Terrace

Professor Kirchenberg was willing to see me straight away when he heard it had to do with Sergej. 'The poor boy, and you want to help him. Then come round right now. I'm in the Palais Boisserée all afternoon.'

From the press coverage of a trial involving the German department, I knew it was housed in the Palais Boisserée. The professors considered themselves rightful descendants of the early princely residents. When rebellious students had profaned the palais, an example had been made of them with the help of the law.

Kirchenberg was particularly princely in his professorial manner. He had thinning hair, contact lenses, a gorged, pink face, and, in spite of his tendency to corpulence, he moved with a light-footed elegance. As a greeting he clasped my hand in both of his. 'Isn't it simply shocking what has befallen Sergej?'

I replied with my queries about Sergej's state of mind, career plans, finances.

He leaned back in his armchair. 'Serjoscha has been shaped by his difficult youth. The years between eight and fourteen in Roth, a bigoted garrison town in Franken, were sheer martyrdom for the child. A father who could only live out his homoeroticism in military power postures, a mother as busy as a bee, good-hearted, utterly weak-willed. And the tramp, tramp, tramp,' he drummed his knuckles on the desktop, 'of soldiers marching in and out every day. Listen hard.' With one hand he made a gesture commanding my silence, with the other he kept up the drumming. Slowly the hand grew still. Kirchenberg sighed. 'It's only with me that he's been able to work through those years.'

When I broached the suspicion of self-mutilation, Kirchenberg was beside himself. 'That's so laughable, it's ridiculous. Sergej has a very loving relationship with his body, almost narcissistic. Amid all the prejudices doing the rounds about us gays, surely this much at least is understood, that we take better care of our bodies than the average heterosexual. We are our body, Herr Self.'

'Was Sergej Mencke really gay, then?'

'Such prejudice in your questions,' said Kirchenberg, almost pityingly. 'You've never sat on the Scheffel Terrace reading Stefan George. Do it sometime. Then perhaps you'll feel that homoeroticism isn't a question of being, but rather of becoming. Sergej isn't, he's becoming.'

I took my leave from Professor Kirchenberg and passed Mischkey's apartment on the way to the castle. And I did spend a little time on the Scheffel Terrace. I was cold. Or was I becoming cold? There was no becoming going on, perhaps I couldn't expect it without Stefan George.

In Café Gundel their special Christmas cookies, embossed with local sights, were on display already. I purchased a bagful, intending to surprise Judith with them on the journey to Locarno.

Back in the office everything ran like clockwork. From Information I obtained the telephone number of the Catholic priest's office in Roth; the chaplain was only too happy to interrupt his sermon preparation to inform me that the leader of the Catholic Scout troop in Roth since time immemorial had been Joseph Maria Jungbluth, senior teacher. I reached Senior Teacher Jungbluth immediately thereafter. He said he'd be glad to meet me the next day in the early afternoon to talk about little Siegfried.

Judith had fixed a date with Tyberg for Sunday afternoon, and we decided to travel on Saturday. 'Tyberg looks forward to meeting you.'

9

And then there were three

Mannheim to Nürnberg on the new autobahn should take two hours. The Schwabach/Roth exit comes thirty kilometres before Nürnberg. One day Roth will lie on the Augsburg–Nürnberg autobahn. I won't be around then.

Fresh snow had fallen in the night. On the journey I had the choice of two open lanes, a well-worn one on the right and a narrow one for overtaking. Passing a truck was a lurching adventure. Three and a half hours later, I arrived. In Roth there are a couple of half-timbered houses, a few sandstone buildings, the Evangelical and the Catholic churches, pubs that have adapted themselves to military needs, and lots of barracks. Not even a local patriot could describe Roth as the Pearl of Franken. It was just before one and I picked an inn. In the Roter Hirsch, which had resisted the trend for fast food and had even retained its old furnishings, the proprietor did the cooking himself. I asked the waitress for a typically Bavarian dish. She didn't understand my request. 'Bavarian? We're in Franken.' So I asked her to recommend a typical dish from Franken. 'Everything,' she said. 'Our entire menu is Frankish. Including the coffee.' Helpful breed of folk here. Pot luck. I ordered *Saure Zipfel* with fried potatoes, and a dark beer.

Saure Zipfel are bratwurst, but they're not fried, they're heated up in a stock of vinegar, onions, and spices. And they taste like it, too. The fried potatoes were deliciously crispy. The waitress softened enough to point out the way to Allersberger Strasse where Senior Teacher Jungbluth lived.

Jungbluth opened the door in civilian clothes. In my mind's eye I'd pictured him in long socks, knee-length brown trousers, blue neckerchief, and a wide-brimmed scout's hat. He couldn't recall the scout camp at which the young Mencke wore a real or pretend bandage to shirk washing-up duty. But he remembered other incidents.

'Siegfried liked getting out of chores. In school, as well, where he was in my class in the first and second year. You know, he was a frightened child – and a cringing one. I don't understand much about medicine, beyond first aid, of course, which I need as senior teacher and scoutmaster. But I would think you need a certain level of courage for self-mutilation, and I can't imagine Siegfried having that courage. Now his father, on the other hand, he's made of different stuff.'

He was showing me to the door when he remembered something else. 'Would you like to see some photos?' The pictures in the album were of various combinations of scouts, tents, campfires, bicycles. I saw children singing, laughing, and fooling around, but I could also see in their eyes that the snapshots were engineered by Senior Teacher Jungbluth. 'That's Siegfried.' He pointed to a rather frail blond boy with a reticent look on his face. A few photos later I came across him again. 'What's wrong with his leg?' His left leg was in plaster. 'Right,' said Senior Teacher Jungbluth. 'An unpleasant story. For six months the accident insurance tried to stick me with negligence. But Siegfried just had a careless fall when we were in the stalagmite caves in Pottenstein, and broke his leg. I can't be everywhere at once.' He looked at me seeking agreement. I was glad to concur.

On the way home, I took stock. Not much remained to

be done on the Sergej Mencke case. I still wanted to take a look at Philipp's young scholar's thesis, and I'd saved my visit to Sergej in the hospital for last. I was tired of them all, the senior teachers, the army captains, the gay German professors, the whole ballet scene, and Sergej too, even before I'd seen him. Had I grown weary of my profession? In the Mischkey case I'd already let my professional standards drop, and as for my distaste for the Mencke case, it wouldn't have been there before. Should I call it quits? Did I want to live beyond eighty anyway? I could get my life insurance paid out, that would feed me for twelve years. I decided to talk to my tax adviser and insurance agent in the new year.

I drove westwards, into the setting sun. As far as my eye could see the snow gleamed in a rosy hue. The sky was tinted the blue of pale porcelain. In the Franken villages and small towns I drove past, smoke unfurled from the chimneys. The homely light in the windows rekindled old desires for security. Homesick for Nowhere.

Philipp was still on duty when I looked him up in the station at seven. 'Willy is dead,' he greeted me dejectedly. 'The idiot. To die of a burst appendix these days is just ridiculous. I don't understand why he didn't call me; he must have been in terrible pain.'

'You know, Philipp, I've often had the impression in the years since Hilde's death that he didn't actually have the will to live.'

'These silly husbands and widowers. If he'd just said the word, I know women who'd make him forget any number of Hildes. What's become of your Brigitte, by the way?'

'She's running around in Rio. When's the funeral?'

'A week from today. Two p.m. at the main cemetery in Ludwigshafen. I had to see to it all. There's no one else. Would a red sandstone gravestone with a screech owl on it meet with your approval? We'll pool resources, you, Eberhard, and me, so that he gets planted decently.'

'Have you thought of the announcements? And we'll have to inform the dean of his old faculty. Could your secretary do that?'

'That's fine. I wish I could join you to have a bite to eat. But I can't get away. Don't forget the dissertation.'

And then there were three. I went home and opened a can of sardines. I wanted to try empty sardine cans on my Christmas tree this year and had to start collecting them. It was almost too late to get enough together before Christmas. Should I invite Philipp and Eberhard next Friday for a funeral feast of sardines in oil?

'Door-Induced Fractures' was fifty pages long. The system underlying the work emerged as a combination of doors and breaks. The introduction contained a diagram, the horizontal of which depicted the various fracture-inducing doors, and the vertical the door-induced fractures. Most of the 196 squares contained figures revealing how often the corresponding constellation had cropped up at the city hospital in the last twenty years.

I looked for the line 'car door' and the column 'tibia fracture'. At the point they met I found the number 2 and afterwards in the text the respective case histories. Although all names had been removed I recognized Sergej's in one. The other dated back to 1972. A nervous cavalier, while helping his lady into the car, had shut the door too swiftly. The study could only cite one case of self-mutilation. A failed goldsmith had hoped to gain heaps of gold with his insured, and broken, right thumb. In the furnace cellar he had placed his right hand in the frame of the iron door and slammed it shut with his left. The affair only came apart because, with the insurance money already paid, he had bragged about his coup. He told the police that as a child he'd attached his wobbly milk-teeth to the door handle with a thread and pulled them out. That's what had given him the idea.

The decision to call Frau Mencke and enquire about young Siegfried's methods of tooth extraction was one I put on ice.

Yesterday I'd been too tired to stay up to watch *Flashdance*, borrowed from the video rental on Seckenheimer Strasse. Now I slid in the cassette. Afterwards I danced under the shower. Why hadn't I stayed longer in Pittsburgh?

In Basle Judith and I took our first break. We drove off the autobahn into town and parked on Münster-Platz. It was covered in snow and was free of aggravating Christmas decorations. We walked a few steps to Café Spielmann, found a table by the window, and had a view over the Rhine and the bridge with the small chapel in the middle.

'Now tell me in detail how you set this up with Tyberg,' I asked Judith over a bowl of muesli, which was particularly delicious here, with lots of cream and without an overabundance of oat flakes.

'During the centenary when I was assigned to him he invited me to look him up if I was ever in Locarno. I mentioned this and said I had to chauffeur my elderly uncle,' she placed a soothing hand on mine, 'to look for a holiday home there. I added that he knew this elderly uncle from the war years.' Judith was proud of her diplomatic move. I was concerned.

'Won't Tyberg throw me out on the spot when he recognizes me as the former Nazi prosecutor? Wouldn't it have been better to have told him straight out?'

'I did consider it, but then perhaps he wouldn't even have let the former Nazi prosecutor over his threshold.'

'And why elderly uncle, actually, and not elderly friend?'

'That smacks of lover. I think Tyberg was interested in me as a woman, and perhaps he wouldn't see me if he thought I was firmly attached to someone else, especially if I brought this someone with me. You are a sensitive private detective.'

'Yes. I'm perfectly willing to face up to the responsibility of having been Tyberg's prosecutor. But should I confess to him in one fell swoop that I'm your lover, not your uncle?'

'Are you asking me?' She said it abruptly yet playfully, and got out her knitting as though settling down to a longer discussion.

I lit a cigarette. 'You've interested me as a woman time and again, and now I wonder whether I was just an old dodderer to you, avuncular and sexless.'

'What are you after now? "You've interested me as a woman time and again." If you were interested in me in the past then leave it. If you're interested in the present then say so. You always prefer taking responsibility for the past rather than for the present.' Knit two, purl two.

'I don't have a problem saying I'm interested in you, Judith.'

'Listen, Gerd, of course I see you as a man, and I like you as a man. It never went far enough for me to make the first move. And certainly not in the past few weeks. But what sort of agonized first move is this, or isn't it one? "I don't have a problem saying I'm interested in you" when you obviously have an enormous problem just squeezing that roundabout, cautious sentence out. Come on, let's get going.' She wrapped the started pullover sleeve round the needles and wound more wool round it.

My mind went blank. I felt humiliated. We didn't exchange a word all the way to Olten.

Judith had found Dvořák's Cello Concerto on the radio and was knitting.

What had actually humiliated me? Judith had only hit me around the head with what I'd felt myself in recent months: the lack of clarity in my feelings towards her. But she'd done it so unkindly by quoting myself back at me that I felt exposed and skewered. I told her so near Zofingen.

She let her knitting sink to her lap and stared out in front of her at the road for a long while.

'When I was an executive assistant I so often encountered men who wanted something from me, but didn't put themselves on the line. They'd like to have something going with me, but at the same time they'd pretend they didn't. They'd arrange things so they could immediately retreat without getting really involved. It seemed to me that was the lie of the land with you, as well. You make the first move, but perhaps it isn't really one, a gesture that costs you nothing and has no risk attached. You talk about humiliation . . . I didn't want to humiliate you. Oh, shit, why are the only little wounds you notice your own?' She turned her head away. It sounded as if she was crying. But I couldn't see.

By Lucerne it was getting dark. When we reached Wassen I didn't want to drive any further. The autobahn was cleared, but it had started snowing. I knew the Hotel des Alpes from earlier Adriatic expeditions. There, still, in Reception was the cage with the Indian mynah bird. When it saw us, it squawked, 'Stop thief, stop thief.'

At dinner we had the creamy *Zürcher Geschnetzeltes* and diced roast potatoes. During the drive we had started to argue about whether success inevitably leads an artist to despise his audience. Röschen had once told me about a concert of Serge Gainsbourg's in Paris where the more contemptuously Gainsbourg treated the audience, the more appreciatively they applauded. Since then this question has preoccupied me, and expanded in my mind into the larger problem of whether one can grow old without despising people either. Judith put up a lengthy resistance to this argument about the link between artistic success and scorn of others. Over the third glass of Fendant she gave in. 'You're right, Beethoven went deaf, after all. Deafness is the perfect expression of contempt for one's environment.'

In my monastic single room I slept a sound, deep sleep. We set off early for Locarno. When we drove out of the Gotthard tunnel, winter was over.

I I

Suite in B minor

We arrived towards midday, took rooms in a hotel by the lake, and lunched in the glassed-in veranda, looking out at the colourful boats. The sun beat warmly through the panes. I was nervous thinking about tea at Tyberg's house. From Locarno a blue cable car goes up to Monti. At the halfway point, where the ascending cabin meets the descending one, there's a station, Madonna del Sasso, a famous pilgrimage church, not beautiful to look at, but in a beautiful location. We walked that far on the Way of the Cross, strewn with large round pebbles. And then we took the cable car to save ourselves the rest of the climb.

We followed the curving street to Tyberg's house on the small square with the post office. We were standing in front of a wall at least three metres high that came down to the street, with cast-iron railings running along it. The pavilion on the corner, and the trees and bushes behind the railings, underscored the elevated situation of the house and garden. We rang the bell, opened the heavy door, went up the steps to the front garden, and there facing us was a simple, red-painted, two-level house. Next to the entrance we saw a garden table and chairs, like the ones in beer-gardens. The table was awash with books and manuscripts. Tyberg unwrapped himself from a camel-hair blanket and came towards us, tall, with a slightly bent forward gait, a full head of white hair, a neat, short-trimmed grey beard, and bushy eyebrows. He was wearing a pair of half-spectacles, over the top of which he was now looking at us with curious brown eyes.

'Dear Frau Buchendorff, lovely that you thought of me. And this is your good uncle. You are also welcome to Villa Sempreverde. We've met before, your niece tells me. No, wait,' he deflected me as I was about to start talking, 'I'll work it out on my own. I'm working on my memoirs at the moment,' he indicated the table, 'and like to practise jogging my memory.'

He led us through the house to the back garden. 'Shall we walk a little? The butler will make tea.'

The garden path followed the mountain upwards. Tyberg enquired after Judith's health, her plans, her work at the RCW. He had a quiet, pleasant manner of putting his questions, and showing his interest to Judith by small observations. Nonetheless I was amazed at how openly Judith, albeit not mentioning my name or role in it all, recounted her departure from the RCW. And just as amazed at Tyberg's reaction. He was neither sceptical regarding Judith's picture of events, nor enraged by any of the participants, from Mischkey to Korten, nor did he express condolence or regret. He simply registered Judith's account attentively.

With tea the butler brought us pastries. We sat in a large chamber with a grand piano that Tyberg referred to as the music room. Discussion had turned to the economic situation. Judith juggled with capital and labour, input and output, the balance of trade, and the gross national product. Tyberg and I connected over the notion of the Balkanization of the Federal Republic of Germany. He agreed so swiftly that to begin with I feared he'd misunderstood me and thought I meant there were too many Turks. But his mind, too, was on the decrease in the number of trains and in their punctuality, and how the post office worked less and continuously less reliably, and the police were getting more shameless by the day.

'Yes,' he said thoughtfully. 'Also there are so many regulations that not even the bureaucrats themselves take them seriously any more, instead they apply them either rigidly or sloppily entirely by whim, and sometimes don't apply them at all. I often wonder what sort of industrial society is going to grow out of all this. Post-democratic feudal bureaucracy?'

I love discussions like this. Unfortunately, although he may read a book now and again, Philipp's sole interest is women, and Eberhard's horizon doesn't go beyond the sixty-four squares. Willy had thought in grand evolutionary perspectives and toyed with the idea that the world, or what humans leave of it, will be taken over by birds in the next millennium.

Tyberg scrutinized me for a long time. 'Of course. Being Frau Buchendorff's uncle doesn't mean you have to be called Buchendorff. You are the retired public prosecutor Doctor Self.'

'Not retired, dropped out in nineteen forty-five.'

'Made to drop out, I bet,' said Tyberg.

I didn't want to explain myself. Judith noticed and jumped in. 'Just leaving doesn't mean much. Most of them went back. Uncle Gerd didn't, not because he couldn't, but because he no longer wanted to.'

Tyberg continued to look at me probingly. I felt ill at ease. What do you say to someone sitting opposite you whom you almost sent to the gallows due to an erroneous investigation? Tyberg wanted to know more. 'So you didn't want to remain a public prosecutor after nineteen forty-five. That's interesting. What were your reasons?'

'When I tried to explain it to Judith once she found my reasons to be more aesthetic than moral. I was disgusted by the attitude of my colleagues during and after their re-employment, the lack of any awareness of their own guilt. All right, I could have got involved again if I'd had a different attitude and kept the guilt in mind. But I'd have felt like an outsider, and so I preferred to stay properly outside.'

'The longer you sit there facing me, the clearer I see you as the young prosecutor. Of course you've changed. But there's still that sparkle in your eyes, more mischievous now, and that cleft in your chin was already a dimple back then. What were you thinking of, to wipe the floor with Dohmke and me like that? I've just been working on the trial in my memoirs.'

'The trial came up again for me recently, as well. That's why I'm glad to be able to talk to you. In San Francisco I met the partner of the late prosecution witness Professor Weinstein and discovered his testimony was false. Someone from the Works and an SS officer put pressure on him. Do you have any idea, or do you even know who could have had an interest in your and Dohmke's disappearance? I hate to have been used as the tool of unknown interests.'

Tyberg rang a bell, the butler appeared, tidied up, and served sherry. Tyberg sat there, frowning, staring into space. 'I started pondering this in prison while I was awaiting trial, and to this day I have found no answer. Time and again I've thought of Weismüller. That was also the reason I didn't want to return to RCW immediately after the war. But I've no confirmation for this notion. I've also been preoccupied for a long time by how Weinstein could have given that testimony. That he made it to my desk, found the manuscript in the drawer, misinterpreted it, and reported me, I found devastating enough. But his testimony about a conversation between Dohmke and myself that never took place was even more devastating. I wondered if it was all for a few advantages at the camp.

Now I hear he was forced. It must have been terrible for him. Did his partner know and tell you that he tried to contact me after the war, and I refused? I was too hurt and he must have been too proud to tell me in his letter about the pressure he'd been under.'

'What happened to your research at the RCW, Herr Tyberg?'

'Korten kept going with it. It was the result anyway of close cooperation between Korten, Dohmke, and myself. The three of us had also made the decision together that we would only pursue the one path to begin with, and put the other on the backburner. The whole thing was our baby, you see, that we jealously hatched and tended and didn't let anyone near. We didn't even let Weinstein into our confidence although he was an important part of our team, scientifically almost on equal footing. But you wanted to know what happened to our research. Since the oil crisis I wonder sometimes if it won't become highly topical again all of a sudden. Fuel synthesis. We'd gone at it a different way from Bergius, Tropsch, and Fischer because from the outset we attributed great significance to the cost factor. Korten continued the development of our process with great dedication, and readied it for production. That work was, quite rightly, the basis of his swift ascent in the RCW even though after the end of the war the process itself was no longer of importance. Korten, I believe, had it patented, though, as the Dohmke-Korten-Tyberg process.'

'I don't know if you realize how dreadful I feel that Dohmke was hanged; and equally how happy I am that you managed to escape. It's mere curiosity, of course, but would you mind telling me how you did it?'

'That's sort of a long story. I want to tell you, but . . . you will stay for dinner, won't you? How about afterwards? I'll just let them know so the butler can prepare the food and make a fire. And until then . . . Do you play an instrument, Herr Self?'

'The flute, but I haven't had any time to play all summer and autumn.'

He stood up, fetched a flute case from the Biedermeier cupboard and had me open it. 'Do you think you can play this?' It was a Buffet. I put it together and played a few scales. It had a wonderfully soft, yet clear tone, jubilant in the high reaches, in spite of my bad intonation after the long break. 'Do you like Bach? How about the Suite in B minor?'

We played until dinner, after the Suite in B minor, Mozart's Concerto in D major. He played the piano confidently and with great expression. I had to bluff my way through some of the fast passages. At the end of the pieces Judith laid her knitting aside and clapped.

We ate duck with chestnut stuffing, dumplings, and red cabbage. The wine was new to me, a fruity Merlot from Tessin. By the fire, Tyberg asked us to keep his story to ourselves. It would be made public soon, but until then discretion would be appreciated. 'I was in Bruchsal Penitentiary, in the death cell waiting for my execution.' He described the cell, the everyday routine on death row, knocking on the wall to communicate with Dohmke in the neighbouring cell, the morning Dohmke was taken away. 'A few days later I was also taken, in the middle of the night. Two members of the SS were demanding my transfer to a concentration camp. And then I realized one of the SS officers was Korten.' That same night he had been taken over the border beyond Lörrach by Korten and the other SS man. On the other side two gentlemen from Hoffmann La Roche were waiting for him. 'The next morning I was drinking chocolate and eating croissants, as though it were the middle of peacetime.'

He could tell a good story. Judith and I listened,

captivated. Korten. Again and again he filled me with amazement, or even admiration. 'But why couldn't this be made public?'

'Korten is more modest than he appears. He emphatically asked me to hush up his role in my escape. I've always respected that, not only as a modest, but also as a wise gesture. The deed wouldn't have sat well with the image of a top industrialist that he was fashioning then. It was only this summer that I revealed the secret. Korten's standing is universally recognized these days, and I think he'll be happy if the story appears in the portrait that *Die Zeit* wants to do next spring when he turns seventy. That's why I told the reporter who was here doing research for the portrait some months ago.'

He put another log on the fire. It was eleven o'clock.

'One other question, Frau Buchendorff, before the evening's over. Would you care to work for me? Since I've been writing my memoirs I've been looking for someone to conduct research for me in the RCW archive, in other archives and in libraries, someone who'll read things over with a critical eye, who'll get used to my handwriting and type the final manuscript. I'd be happy if you could start on the first of January. You would be based mostly in Mannheim, and be here for an occasional week or two. The pay wouldn't be worse than before. Think it over until tomorrow afternoon, give me a call, and if you say yes, we can discuss details tomorrow.'

He escorted us to the garden gate. The butler was waiting with the Jaguar to take us back to the hotel. Judith and Tyberg said goodbye with a kiss to the left and right cheek. When I shook his hand he smiled at me and winked. 'Will we meet again, Uncle Gerd?'

12

Champagne and sardines on my own

At breakfast Judith asked what I thought of Tyberg's proposal.

'I liked him,' I began.

'I'm sure you did. You were quite a number, you two. When the prosecutor and his victim adjourned for chamber music, I couldn't believe my ears. It's all very well that you like him, so do I, but what do you think of his proposal?'

'Accept it, Judith. I don't believe a better thing could come along for you.'

'And that I interest him as a woman doesn't make the job difficult?'

'But that can happen in any workplace, you'll be able to deal with it. And Tyberg is a gentleman, he won't grope you under your skirt during dictation.'

'What will I do when he's finished with his memoirs?'

'I'll come back to that in a minute.' I stood, went over to the breakfast buffet, and, as a finale, helped myself to a crisp-bread with honey. Well, well, I thought. What kind of security is she after? Back at the table I said, 'He'll find you something. That should be the last of your worries.'

'I'll think it over again on a walk along the lake. Shall we meet for lunch?'

I knew how things would unfold. She'd accept the job, call Tyberg at four, and discuss details with him into the evening. I decided to look for my holiday home, left Judith a message wishing her luck in her negotiations with Tyberg, and drove off along the lake to Brissago, where I was transported by boat to Isola Bella and ate lunch. Afterwards I turned towards the mountains and drove in a wide sweep that took me down by Ascona to the lake once more. There was an abundance of holiday homes, that I could see. But then to reduce my life expectancy so drastically to be able to buy one from my life insurance, no, that didn't appeal to me. Perhaps Tyberg would invite me to stay for the next vacation anyway.

When darkness fell I was back in Locarno, strolling through the festively decorated town. I was looking for sardine cans for my Christmas tree. In a delicatessen beneath the arcades I came across some Portuguese vintage sardines. I took two recent tins, one from last year in glowing greens and reds, the other from two years ago in simple white with gold lettering.

Back at the hotel reception a message was waiting from Tyberg. He'd like to have me picked up for dinner. Instead of calling him and having myself picked up I went to the hotel sauna, spent three pleasant hours there, and lay down in bed. Before falling asleep I wrote Tyberg a short letter, thanking him.

At eleven-thirty Judith knocked at my door. I opened up. She complimented me on my nightshirt, and we agreed on a departure time of eight o'clock.

'Are you content with your decision?' I asked.

'Yes. The work on the memoirs will last two years, and Tyberg has already been giving some thought to afterwards.'

'Wonderful. Then sleep well.'

I'd forgotten to open the window and was awakened by my dream. I was sleeping with Judith who, however, was the daughter I'd never had and was wearing a ridiculous red hula skirt. When I opened a can of sardines for the two

256

of us, Tyberg came out, growing bigger and bigger, until he filled the whole room. I felt stifled and woke up.

I couldn't go back to sleep and was glad when it was time for breakfast, even gladder when we were on the road at last. Beyond the Gotthard tunnel, winter began again, and it took us seven hours to reach Mannheim. I'd actually intended to visit Sergej that day, in hospital after a repeat operation, but I wasn't up to it now. I invited Judith in for some champagne to celebrate her new job, but she had a headache.

So I had champagne and sardines on my own.

13

Can't you see how Sergej is suffering?

Sergej Mencke was lying in a double room in the Oststadt Hospital on the garden side. The other bed was currently unoccupied. His leg was suspended from a kind of pulley and held in place at the correct slant by a metal frame and screw system. He'd spent the last three months, with the exception of a few weeks, in hospital and looked correspondingly miserable. Nonetheless I could clearly see that he was a handsome man. Light, blond hair, a longish, English face with a prominent chin, dark eyes, and a vulnerable, arrogant cast to the lips. Unfortunately his voice was petulant, maybe just as a result of the past months.

'Wouldn't it have been right to come and see me first, instead of bothering my entire social world?'

So he was one of those. A whiner. 'And what would you have told me?'

'That your suspicions are pure fantasy, they're the product of a sick brain. Can you imagine mutilating your own leg like this?'

'Oh, Herr Mencke.' I pulled the chair to his bed. 'There's a lot I wouldn't do myself. I could never cut open my thumb to avoid washing up. And what I, as a ballet dancer without a future, would do to make a million, I really couldn't say.'

'That silly story from scout camp. Where did you dredge that one up from?'

258

'From bothering your social world. What was the story with the thumb again?'

'That was a completely normal accident. I was carving tent pegs with my pocket knife. Yes, I know what you want to say. I've told the story differently, but only because it's such a nice one, and my youth doesn't provide many stories. And as for my future as a ballet dancer . . . Listen. You don't exactly give the impression of a particularly rosy future yourself, but you wouldn't go breaking a limb because of it.'

'Tell me, Herr Mencke, how did you plan to finance the dance school you've talked about so often?'

'Frederik was going to support me, *Fritz* Kirchenberg, I mean. He has stacks of money. If I'd wanted to cheat the insurance company I'd have thought up something a little cleverer.'

'The car door isn't that silly. But what would have been cleverer?'

'I have no desire to discuss it with you. I only said *if* I'd wanted to cheat the insurance people.'

'Would you be willing to undergo a psychiatric examination? That would really facilitate the insurance company's decision.'

'Absolutely not. I'm not going to have them tag me as mad. If they don't pay up right away, I'm going to a lawyer.'

'If you go to trial you won't be able to avoid a psychiatric examination.'

'Let's wait and see.'

The nurse came in carrying a little dish with brightly coloured tablets. 'The two red ones now, the yellow one before and the blue one after your meal. How are we today?'

Sergej had tears in his eyes as he looked at the nurse. 'I can't go on, Katrin. Nothing but pain and no dancing ever

259

again. And now this gentleman from the insurance company wants to make me out to be a cheat.'

Nurse Katrin laid her hand on his forehead and glowered at me. 'Can't you see how Sergej is suffering? You should be ashamed of yourself! Leave him in peace. It's always the same with insurance companies; first they make you pay through the nose and then they torture you because they don't want to cough up.'

I couldn't add anything to this conversation and fled. Over lunch I noted down keywords for my report to the Heidelberg Union Insurance. My conclusion was neither that of deliberate self-mutilation, nor mere accident. I could only gather together the points that spoke for one or the other. Should the insurance not wish to pay they wouldn't have a bad case.

As I was crossing the street, a car spattered me from head to toe in slushy snow. I was already in a foul mood when I reached my office and the work on the report made me all the more morose. By the evening I'd laboriously dictated two cassettes that I took round to Tattersallstrasse to be typed up. On the way home it struck me I'd wanted to ask Frau Mencke about little Siegfried's tooth-extraction methods. But now I couldn't care less.

14

Matthew 6, verse 26

It was a small huddle of mourners that gathered at the Ludwigshafen Cemetery at 2 p.m. on Friday. Eberhard, Philipp, the vice-dean of the Heidelberg faculty for the sciences, Willy's cleaning lady, and myself. The vice-dean had prepared a speech, which, due to the low turnout, he delivered gracelessly. We discovered that Willy had been an internationally recognized authority in the field of screech owl research. And this with heart and soul: in the war, as an adjunct lecturer at Hamburg at the time, he had rescued the entire family of distraught screech owls from the burning aviary in Hagenbeck Zoo. The minister spoke about Matthew 6, verse 26, about all the birds beneath the heavens. Beneath blue heavens and on crunchy snow we walked from the chapel to the grave. Philipp and I were first behind the coffin. He whispered to me, 'I must show you the photo sometime. I came across it when I was tidying up. Willy and the rescued owls, with singed hair, or feathers respectively, six pairs of eyes looking exhaustedly but happily into the camera. It warmed my aching heart.'

Then we stood by the deep hole. It's like eena, meena, mina, mo. According to age, Eberhard is next, and then it's my turn. For a long time now when someone I'm fond of dies, I've stopped thinking, 'Oh, if only I'd done this or that more often.' And when a contemporary dies it's as though he's just gone on ahead, even if I can't say where to. The minister recited the Lord's Prayer and we all joined in; even Philipp, the most hard-boiled atheist I know, said it aloud. Then each of us cast a small shovelful of earth into the grave, and the minister shook our hands, one by one. A young guy, but convinced, and convincing. Philipp had to return to work straight away.

'You will come by this evening for a funeral meal, won't you?' Yesterday in town I'd bought another twelve little sardine cans and laid the tiny fish in an Escabeche marinade. To go with it there'd be white bread and Rioja. We settled on eight o'clock.

Philipp strode off like a Fury, Eberhard did the honours with the vice-dean, and the cleaning lady, still emitting heartrending sobs, was led gently on the arm of the minister to the exit. I had time and slowly wandered along the cemetery paths. If Klara had been buried here I'd have wanted to visit her now, and commune a bit.

'Herr Self!' I turned around and recognized Frau Schmalz, complete with small trowel and watering can. 'I'm just on my way to the family grave, where Heinrich's urn is at rest now, too. It's looking nice, the grave. Will you come and see?' She looked at me shyly from her narrow, careworn face. She was wearing an old-fashioned black winter coat, black button-up boots, a black fur hat over her grey hair pinned in a bun, and was carrying an imitation-leather handbag that made one wince with pity. In my generation there are female figures, the sight of whom rouses in me a belief in all the pronouncements of all the prophets of the women's lib movement. Not that I've ever read them.

'Are you still living in the old compound at the Works?' I asked her on the way.

'No, I had to get out, it's all torn down. The Works found me somewhere on Pfingstweide. The apartment's fine and everything, very modern, but you know, it is hard after so many years. It takes me a full hour to get to the grave of my Heinrich. Later today my son, thank God, will pick me up in his car.'

We were standing in front of the family grave. It was heaped high with snow. The ribbon from the wreath bequeathed by the Works, and long since decomposed, was fixed to a cane and rose up like a standard by the gravestone. Widow Schmalz put down the watering can and let the trowel drop. 'I can't do anything today with this load of snow.' We stood there, both thinking of old Schmalz. 'These days I hardly get to see my little Richard either. I live too far out. What do you think, is it right that the Works . . . Oh God, now that Heinrich's no longer around I'm always thinking such things. He never let me, never let anybody question the Works.'

'How much warning did you have that you had to leave?'

'A good six months. They wrote to us. But then everything went so quickly.'

'Didn't Korten make a point of talking to your husband four weeks before your move, so that it wouldn't be too hard on you?'

'Did he? He never told me about it. He did have a close relationship with the general, you know. From the war, when the SS assigned him to the Works. Since then it was right what they said at the funeral, the Works was his life. He didn't get much out of it, but I was never allowed to say that either. Whether SS officer or security officer, the fight goes on, he used to say.'

'What became of his workshop?'

'He set it up with such love. And he really cared for those vans and trucks. Then it was all got rid of very quickly during the demolition, my son could scarcely retrieve a thing. I think they scrapped it all. I didn't think that was right either. Oh, God.' She bit her lips and made

263

a face as though she'd committed a mortal sin. 'Forgive me, I didn't mean to say anything bad about the Works.' She grasped my arm appeasingly. She held on tightly for a while, staring at the grave. Thoughtfully, she continued, 'But perhaps at the end Heinrich himself didn't think it was right the way the Works was treating us. On his deathbed he wanted to say something to the general about the garage and the vans. I couldn't understand him properly.'

'You'll permit an old man a question, Frau Schmalz. Were you happy in your marriage with Heinrich?'

She gathered up the watering can and trowel. 'That's the sort of thing people ask nowadays. I never thought about it. He was my husband.'

We walked to the parking lot. Young Schmalz was pulling in. He was happy to see me. 'The good doctor. Met your mum at your dad's grave.' I told him about my friend's funeral.

'I'm grieved to hear that. Painful, taking leave of a friend. I've been there too. I remain grateful for your help with our little Richard. And one day my wife and I would like to have that coffee with you. Mum can come along, too. Any particular cake your favourite?'

'My absolute favourite is sweet damson shortcake.' I didn't say it to be mean. It really is my favourite cake.

Schmalz handled it well. 'Ah, plum with floury-butter crumble. My wife can bake it like no other woman. Coffee maybe in the quiet lull between the impending holiday and New Year?'

I said yes. We'd telephone regarding the exact date.

The evening with Philipp and Eberhard was one of melancholic gaiety. We remembered our last Doppelkopf evening with Willy. We'd joked then about what would come of our games circle if one of us were to die. 'No,' said Eberhard, 'we're not going to look for someone new to make up the four. From now on it's Skat.'

'And then chess, and the last one will meet himself twice a year to play solitaire,' said Philipp.

'It's all very well for you to laugh, you're the youngest.'

'It's nothing to laugh about. Solitaire? I'd rather be dead.'

15

And the race is on

Ever since I moved from Berlin to Heidelberg I've been buying my Christmas trees at the Tiefburg in Handschuhs-heim. It's been a long time since they were any different from those elsewhere. But I like the small square in front of the ruined castle with its moat. The tram used to turn around here on squealing tracks; this was the end of the line and Klärchen and I often set off on our walks on the Heiligenberg from here. These days Handschuhsheim has turned trendy and everyone who thinks of themselves as having a modicum of cultural and intellectual flair gathers at the weekly market. The day will come when the only authentic neighbourhoods are places like the suburban slums of the sixties.

I'm particularly fond of silver firs. But so far as my sardine cans went, I felt a Douglas spruce would be more appropriate. I found a beautiful, evenly grown, ceiling-height, bushy tree. Stretching from the right-hand corner on the passenger side to the back left-hand corner, it fitted in neatly over the reclined front seat and the folded-down back seat of my Opel. I found a space in the parking garage by the town hall. I'd made a little list for my Christmas shopping.

All hell was loose on the main street. I battled my way through to Welsch the jeweller and bought earrings for Babs. It'll never happen, but I'd like to have a beer with Welsch one day. He has the same taste as me. For

Röschen and Georg, from the selection at one of those all-pervading gift shops, I chose two of those disposable watches, currently modern among our postmodern youth, made of see-through plastic with a quartz movement and a heat-sealed face. Then I was exhausted. In Café Schafheutle I bumped into Thomas with his wife and three puberty-ridden daughters.

'Isn't a security man supposed to make a gift of sons to his Works?'

'In the security field there's an increasingly attractive range of jobs for women. For our course we're estimating around thirty per cent female participants. Incidentally the conference of Ministers of Culture and Education is going to support us as a pilot project, and so the technical college has decided to establish a separate department for internal security. That means I can introduce myself today as the designated founding dean. I'm leaving the RCW on the first of January.'

I congratulated the right honourable dean on his office, the honour, the prestige, and the title. 'What's Danckelmann going to do without you?'

'It will be difficult for him in the next few years until he retires. But I would like the department to provide consultation too, so he can buy advice from us. You'll remember the curriculum you wanted to send me, Herr Self?'

Evidently Thomas already felt emancipated from RCW and was adapting to his new role. He invited me to join them at their table where the daughters were giggling and the mother was blinking nervously. I looked at my watch, excused myself, and dashed off to Café Scheu.

Then I embarked on round two of checking off my list. What do you give a virile man in his late fifties? A set of tiger-print underwear? Royal jelly? The erotic stories of Anaïs Nin? Finally I bought Philipp a cocktail shaker for his boat bar. Then revulsion for the Christmas din and commercialism swamped me. I was filled with immense discontent with the people and with myself. It would take me hours to shake it off at home. Why on earth had I launched myself into the Christmas mêlée? Why did I make the same mistake every year? Haven't I learned anything in my life? What is the point of the whole thing?

The Opel smelled pleasantly of fir forest. When I'd fought my way through the traffic to the autobahn I heaved a sigh of relief. I shoved in a tape, fished out from way down the pile, as I'd heard the others too often on the journey to and from Locarno. But no music came.

A telephone was picked up, the dialling tone sounded, a number was dialled, and the recipient's phone rang. He answered. It was Korten.

'Hello, Herr Korten. Mischkey here. I'm warning you. If your people don't leave me alone your past is going to explode around your ears. I won't be pressured like this any longer, and I certainly won't be beaten up again.'

'I'd imagined you'd be more intelligent from Self's report. First you break into our system and now you threaten blackmail. I have nothing to say.' Actually Korten should have hung up that very second. But the second came and went, and Mischkey talked on.

'The times are over, Herr Korten, where all it takes is an SS contact and an SS uniform to move people from here to there, to Switzerland and to the gallows.' Mischkey hung up. I heard him take a deep gulp of air, then the click of the tape recorder. Music began. 'And the race is on and it looks like heartache and the winner loses all.'

I turned off the player and pulled over to the hard shoulder. The tape from Mischkey's Citroën. I had simply forgotten it.

16

Anything for one's career?

I couldn't sleep that night. At six o'clock I gave up and busied myself setting up and decorating my Christmas tree. I'd listened to Mischkey's tape over and over. On Saturday I'd been in no state to think and make order in my mind.

I put the thirty empty sardine cans that I had accumulated into the sink of water. They shouldn't still smell of fish on the Christmas tree. I looked at them, my elbows on the edge of the sink, as they sank to the bottom. The lids of some of them had been torn off as they were opened. I'd stick them back on.

Was it Korten, then, who'd made Weinstein discover the hidden documents in Tyberg's desk and report him? I should have thought of it when Tyberg told us that only he, Dohmke, and Korten knew about the stash. No, Weinstein hadn't come across them by accident as Tyberg supposed. They'd ordered him to find the documents in the desk. That was what Frau Hirsch had said. And perhaps Weinstein had never even seen the documents; the important thing was the statement, not the find.

When it started growing light outside I went out onto the balcony and fitted the Christmas tree to the stand. I had to saw and use the hatchet. Its top was too high. I trimmed it in such a way that the tip could be reattached to the trunk with a needle. Then I moved the tree to its place in the sitting room.

Why? Anything for one's career? Yes. Korten couldn't have made such a mark if Tyberg and Dohmke had still been around. Tyberg had spoken of the years following the trial as the basis for his ascendancy. And Tyberg's liberation had been Korten's reinsurance. It had certainly paid off. When Tyberg became general director of the RCW Korten was catapulted to dizzying heights.

The plot – with me as the dupe. Set up and executed by my friend and brother-in-law. And I'd been happy not to have to drag him into the trial. He'd used me with contemptuous calculation. I thought back to the conversation after our move to Bahnhofstrasse. I also thought of the last conversations we'd had, in the Blue Salon and on the terrace of his house. Me, the sweetheart.

My cigarettes had run out. That hadn't happened to me in years. I pulled on my winter coat and galoshes, pocketed the St Christopher that I'd taken from Mischkey's car and only remembered yesterday, walked to the train station, then dropped by to see Judith. It was mid-morning now. She came to the front door in a dressing gown.

'What's the matter with you, Gerd?' She looked at me aghast. 'Come on up, I've just put some coffee on.'

'Do I look that bad? No, I won't come up, I'm in the middle of decorating my tree. Wanted to bring you the St Christopher. I needn't tell you where it's from, I'd completely forgotten it, and I just found it again.'

She took the St Christopher and supported herself against the doorpost. She was fighting back tears.

'Tell me something, Judith, do you remember if Peter went away for two or three days in the weeks in between the War Cemetery and his death?'

'What?' She hadn't been listening, and I repeated my question. 'Away? Yes, how do you know?'

'Do you know where to?'

'South, he said. To recover because it had all been too much for him. Why do you ask?'

'I'm wondering whether he went to Tyberg pretending to be a journalist from *Die Zeit*.'

'You mean looking for material to use against the RCW?' She considered this. 'I wouldn't put it past him. But according to what Tyberg said about the visit, there wasn't anything to unearth.' Shivering, she pulled the dressing gown more tightly around her. 'Are you sure you won't have a coffee?'

'You'll be hearing from me, Judith.' I walked home.

It all fitted together. A despairing Mischkey had attempted to use Tyberg's grand aria about decency and resistance for his own ends against Korten. Intuitively he had recognized the dissonances better than all of us, the connection to the SS, the rescue of Tyberg, not that of Dohmke. He didn't realize how close to the truth he was and how threatening that must have sounded to Korten. Not just sounded – was really, thanks to his dogged research.

Why hadn't I thought of it? If it was so easy to save Tyberg, why, then, hadn't Korten rescued both of them two days earlier while Dohmke was still alive? One was sufficient as reinsurance and Tyberg, the head of the research group, was more interesting than his co-worker Dohmke.

I removed my galoshes and clapped them against each other until all the snow had dropped off. The stairwell smelled of *Sauerbraten*. Yesterday I hadn't bought anything else to eat and I could only make myself two fried eggs. The third egg I whisked over Turbo's food. He'd been driven to distraction in recent days by the sardine odour in the apartment.

The SS man who'd helped Korten to liberate Tyberg had been Schmalz. Together with Schmalz Korten had

271

exerted pressure on Weinstein. Schmalz had killed Misch-key for Korten.

I rinsed the sardine cans clean with hot water and dried them off. Where the lids were missing, I glued them back on. I chose green wool to hang them and threaded it through the curl of the rolled-back lid, or through the ring-pull, or around the hinge where an open lid was attached to its can. As soon as a can was ready I looked for its proper place on the tree; the big ones lower down, the small ones higher up.

I couldn't fool myself. I didn't give a damn about my Christmas tree. Why had Korten allowed his accessory Weinstein to survive? I suppose he hadn't had any influence over the SS, only over Schmalz, the SS officer in the Works, whom he'd seduced and conquered. He couldn't steer things so that Weinstein would be killed back in the concentration camp. But he could safely assume it. And after the war? Even if Korten were to discover that Weinstein had survived the camp, he could count on the fact that anyone who'd had to play a role such as Weinstein's would prefer not to go public.

Now the final words made sense, too, the ones the widow Schmalz repeated from her husband's deathbed. He must have tried to warn his lord and master about the trail he himself hadn't been able to remove, given his physical state. How well Korten had known how to make this man depend on him! The young academic from a good home, the SS officer from a modest background, great challenges and tasks, two men in the service of the Works, each in his place. I could imagine the course of things between them. Who knew better than I how convincing and winning Korten could be?

The Christmas tree was ready. Thirty sardine cans were hanging, thirty white candles were erect. One of the vertically hanging sardine cans was oval and reminded me of the garland of light you get in depictions of the Virgin Mary. I went to the basement, found the cardboard box with Klärchen's Christmas tree decorations and in amongst them the small, willowy Madonna in a blue cloak. She fitted into the can.

17

I knew what I had to do

The next night I couldn't sleep either. Sometimes I dozed off and dreamed of Dohmke's hanging and Korten's performance in court, my leap into the Rhine that I didn't resurface from in my dream, Judith in her dressing gown, fighting back her tears at the doorpost, old, square-set, stout Schmalz climbing down from the statue pedestal in the Heidelberg Bismarckgarten and coming towards me, the tennis match with Mischkey, at which a small boy with Korten's face and an SS uniform threw us the balls, my interrogation of Weinstein, and again and again Korten laughing at me, saying, 'Self, you sweetheart, you sweetheart, you sweetheart . . .'

At five I made a cup of camomile tea and tried to read, but my thoughts wouldn't leave me alone. They kept circling. How could Korten have done it? Why had I been blind enough to let myself be used by him? What should happen now? Was Korten afraid? Did I owe anyone anything? Was there anyone I could tell everything to? Nägelsbach? Tyberg? Judith? Should I go to the media? What was I to do with my guilt?

For a long time the thoughts circled in my mind, faster and faster. As they were accelerating into craziness, they flew apart and formed themselves into a completely new picture. I knew what I had to do.

At nine o'clock I called Frau Schlemihl. Korten had left on vacation at the weekend to his house in Brittany where he and his wife spent Christmas every year. I found the card he'd sent me last Christmas. It showed a magnificent estate of grey stone with a slanting roof and red shutters, the crossbars of which formed an inverted Z. Next to it was a high windmill, and beyond it stretched the sea. I checked the timetable and found a train that would get me in to Paris-Est at five o'clock in the afternoon. I'd have to hurry. I prepared a fresh litter-tray for Turbo, shook an abundant amount of cat food into his dish, and packed my travel bag. I ran to the station, changed money, and bought a ticket, second class. The train was full. Noisy soldiers on home-leave over Christmas, students, late businessmen.

The snow of the last weeks had thawed completely. Dirty greenish-brown countryside whipped by. The sky was grey, and sometimes the sun was visible as a faded disk behind the clouds. I thought about why Korten had feared Mischkey's disclosures. He could, indeed, be prosecuted for Dohmke's murder, which was not subject to a statute of limitations. And even if he went free due to lack of evidence, his comfortable life and the legend he'd become would be destroyed.

There was a car rental in the Gare de l'Est and I took a standard-class car, one of those where every make looks much the same as every other. I left the car at the rental and went out into the hectic evening pulse of the city. In front of the station was an enormous Christmas tree that exuded about as much Christmas spirit as the Eiffel Tower. It was half past five, I was hungry. Most of the restaurants were still closed. I found a brasserie I liked the look of that was bustling in spite of what time it was. I was shown to a small table by the headwaiter and found myself in a row of five other uncommonly early diners. They were all eating *Sauerkraut* with boiled pork and sausages and I chose the same. And with it a half-bottle of Alsace

Riesling. In the twinkling of an eye, a steaming plate, a bottle in a cooler with condensation on its sides, and a basket of white bread were in front of me. When I'm in the mood I like the atmosphere of brasseries, beer-cellars, and pubs. Not today. I finished quickly. At the nearest hotel I took a room and asked to be woken in four hours.

I slept like a stone. When I was roused at eleven by the ringing of the phone I didn't know where I was. I hadn't opened the shutters and the noise of the traffic from the boulevard only made a muffled echo in my room. I showered, brushed my teeth, shaved, and paid. On the way to the Gare de l'Est I drank a double espresso. I had a further five poured into my thermos flask. My Sweet Aftons were running out. I bought a carton of Chesterfield once again.

I had reckoned on six hours for the journey to Trefeuntec. But it took an hour just to get out of Paris and onto the highway to Rennes. There was little traffic, and the driving was monotonous. It was only then that it struck me how mild it was. A green Christmas means a cold Easter. Every so often I'd pass a toll booth and never knew if I should be paying or getting a ticket. Once I pulled off the road to fill up and was astounded by the price of petrol. The lights of the villages were growing sparser. I wondered whether it was because of the late hour or because the country was emptier. To begin with I was happy to have a radio in the car. But then there was only clear reception to one station and after I'd heard the song about the angel walking through the room for the third time, I switched it off. Sometimes the road surface would change and the tyres would sing a new song. At three, just after Rennes, I almost fell asleep, or at least I was hallucinating that there were people running all over the highway. I opened the window, drove to the next rest area, drained my thermos flask, and did ten sit-ups.

As the journey continued, my thoughts turned to Korten's performance at the trial. He had been playing for high stakes. His statement mustn't save Dohmke and Tyberg, yet it had to sound as though that was just what he wanted, without seriously damaging him in the process. Södelknecht had almost had him arrested. How had Korten felt then? Secure and superior because he knew how to pull the wool over everybody's eyes? No, he wouldn't have suffered any twinges of conscience. From my colleagues in the law I knew that there were two means of dealing with the past: cynicism, and a feeling of having always been right and only doing one's duty. In retrospect had the Tyberg affair served the greater glory of the RCW for Korten?

When the houses of Carhaix-Plouguer were behind me, I looked in the rear-view mirror and saw the first streak of dawn. Another seventy kilometres to Trefeuntec. In Plonévez-Porzay the bar and the bakery were already open and I ate two croissants along with my milky coffee. At a quarter to eight I reached the bay of Trefeuntec. I drove the car onto the beach, still wet and firm from the tide. Beneath a grey sky the grey sea rolled in. It crashed against the high coast to the right and left of the bay with dirty white crests. It was even milder than Paris in spite of the strong westerly wind that drove the clouds before it. Shrieking gulls were swept aloft on its current before they dropped in a plummeting dive to the water.

I began the search for Korten's house. I drove a little inland and came to a field-track on the craggy northerly coast. With its bays and cliffs rising from the shore it stretched as far as the eye could see. In the distance I could make out a silhouette, it could be anything under the sun, from a water tower to the large windmill. I left the car behind a wind-buffeted hut and made for the tower.

Before I saw Korten, his two dachshunds saw me. They rollicked towards me, yapping. Then he emerged from a dip. We weren't far from one another but between us was a bay that we each headed round. Along the narrow path that ran along the cliff top, we walked towards one another.

18

Old friends like you and me

'You look terrible, my dear Self. A few days' rest here will do you a world of good. I hadn't expected you yet. Let's walk a bit. Helga's preparing breakfast for nine. She'll be glad to see you.' Korten linked his arm through mine and prepared to continue. He was wearing a light loden coat and looked relaxed.

'I know everything,' I said, stepping away.

Korten looked at me enquiringly. He understood immediately.

'It's not easy for you, Gerd. It wasn't easy for me either, and I was happy not to have to burden anyone with it.'

I stared at him speechlessly. He stepped up to me once more, took my arm, and nudged me along the path. 'You think it had to do with my career. No, in the whole mess of those last years of the war what mattered most was sorting out real responsibility and making clean decisions. Things wouldn't have gone well for our research group. Dohmke consigning himself to the sidelines that way – I was sorry back then. But so many people, better people, lost their lives. Mischkey had his choice too, and dug himself deeper and deeper into trouble.' He stood still and grabbed my shoulders. 'You have to understand, Gerd. The Works needed me to be the way I became in those difficult years. I always had great respect for old Schmalz. He was simple but he could understand these tricky connections.'

'You must be crazy. You murdered two men and you talk about it as though . . . as though . . .'

'Oh, those are big words. Did I murder them? Or was it the judge or the hangman? Old Schmalz? And who headed the investigation against Tyberg and Dohmke? Who set the trap for Mischkey and let it snap shut? We're all entangled in it, all of us, and we have to recognize that and bear it, and do our duty.'

I broke loose from his hold. 'Entangled? Perhaps we all are, but you pulled the strings!' I was shouting into his placid face.

He stood still, too. 'That's just child's stuff – "he did it, he did it." And even when we were children we never really believed it; we knew perfectly well that we were all involved when a teacher was being goaded, or one of our classmates bullied, or the other side in the game was being fouled.' He spoke with utter concentration, patiently, didactically, and my head was dazed and confused. It was true, that's how my sense of guilt had eroded, year by year.

Korten was still talking. 'But, please – I did it. If that's what you need – yes, I did it: What do you think would have happened had Mischkey gone to the press? That sort of thing doesn't end with an old boss being replaced by a new one, and everything goes on as before. I needn't tell you the play his story would have got in the USA, and England and France, or talk about what it would do when we're fighting our competition inch by inch, or about how many jobs would be destroyed, and what unemployment means today. The RCW is a large, heavy ship going at breakneck speed through the drift-ice despite its bulk and if the captain leaves and the steering is loose, it will run aground and be wrecked. That's why I say yes, I did it.'

'Murder?'

'Could I have bribed him? The risk was too high. And

don't tell me that no risk is too high when it's about saving a life. It's not true. Think of road deaths, accidents in the workplace, police who shoot to kill. Think of the fight against terrorism: the police have shot as many people by accident as the terrorists have intentionally – is that a reason to give up?'

'And Dohmke?' I suddenly felt empty inside. I could see us standing there, talking, as though a film were running without a soundtrack. Beneath the grey clouds, a craggy coastline, a mist of dirty spray, a narrow path and the fields beyond, and two older men in heated discussion – hands gesticulating, mouths moving – but the scene is mute. I wished I wasn't there.

'Dohmke? Actually I don't have to comment on that. The years between nineteen thirty-three and nineteen forty-five are supposed to remain a blank – that's the foundation on which our state is built. Fine, we had to – still have to – produce some theatre with trials and verdicts. But in nineteen forty-five there was no Night of the Long Knives, and that would have been the only chance of retribution. Then the foundation was set. You're not satisfied? Okay then, Dohmke couldn't be trusted; he was unpredictable, a talented chemist maybe, but an amateur in everything else. He wouldn't have lasted two minutes at the front.'

We walked on. He hadn't needed to link arms with me again; when he continued I'd stuck by his side.

'Fate may talk that way, Ferdinand, but not you. Steamships that set a course, solid foundations, entanglements in which we're all mere puppets – you can tell me all about the powers and forces in life but none of it alters the fact that you, Ferdinand Korten, and only you—'

'Fate?' Now he was furious. 'We are our own fate, and I don't offload anything on powers and forces. You're the one who never sees things through to the end, nor leaves them well and truly alone. Get Dohmke and Mischkey in a mess, yes, but when what inevitably happens next does, you find your scruples and you don't want to have seen it or been it. My God, Gerd, grow up at last.'

He stumped on. The path had narrowed and I walked behind him, cliffs to the left, a wall to the right. Beyond it, the fields.

'Why did you come?' He turned round. 'To see whether I'd kill you, too? Push you over?' Fifty metres below the sea seethed. He laughed, as though it were a joke. Then he read it in my eyes before I said the words.

'I've come to kill you.'

'To bring them back to life?' he mocked. 'Because you ... because the perpetrator wants to play judge? Do you feel innocent and exploited? What would you have been without me, without my sister and my parents, before nineteen forty-five, and all my help afterwards? Jump yourself if you can't deal with it.'

His voice cracked. I stared at him. Then that grin came to his face, the one I'd known, and liked, since we were young. It had charmed me into shared escapades and out of fatal situations, understanding, winning, superior.

'Hey, Gerd, this is crazy. Two old friends like you and me ... Come on, let's have breakfast. I can smell the coffee already.' He whistled to the dogs.

'No, Ferdinand.'

He looked at me with an expression of utter incredulity as I shoved against his chest with both hands. He lost his balance and plummeted down, his coat billowing. I didn't hear a cry. He thudded against a rock before the sea took him with it.

19

A package from Rio

The dogs followed me to the car and frolicked alongside, yapping, until I turned off the field-track, onto the road. My whole body was trembling and yet I felt lighter than I had in a long time. On the road a tractor came towards me. The farmer stared at me. Had he been high enough to see me as I pushed Korten to his death? I hadn't even thought about witnesses. I looked back; another tractor was ploughing its furrows in a field and two children were out on bikes. I drove west. At Point-du-Raz I considered staying – an anonymous Christmas abroad. But I couldn't find a hotel, and the cliff line looked just like Trefeuntec. I was going home. At Quimper I came to a police roadblock. I could tell myself a thousand times that it was an unlikely spot to be searching for Korten's murderer, but I was scared as I waited in the queue for the police to wave me on.

In Paris I made the eleven o'clock night train. It was empty and I had no trouble getting a sleeping car. On Christmas Day towards eight o'clock I was back in my apartment. Turbo greeted me sulkily. Frau Weiland had laid my Christmas mail on the desk. Along with all the commercial Christmas greetings I found a Christmas card from Vera Müller, an invitation from Korten to spend New Year's Eve with him and Helga in Brittany, and from Brigitte a package from Rio with an Indian tunic. I took it as a nightshirt, and went to bed. At half past eleven the telephone rang.

'Merry Christmas, Gerd. Where are you hiding?'

'Brigitte! Merry Christmas.' I was happy, but I could hardly see for weariness and exhaustion.

'You grouch, aren't you pleased? I'm back.'

I made an effort. 'You're kidding. That's really great. Since when?'

'I arrived yesterday morning and I've been trying to reach you ever since. Where have you been hiding?' There was reproach in her voice.

'I didn't want to be here on Christmas Eve. I felt very claustrophobic.'

'Would you like to eat *Tafelspitz* with us? It's already on the stove.'

'Yes . . . who else is coming?'

'I've brought Manu with me. I can't wait to see you.' She blew a kiss down the telephone.

'Me too.' I returned the kiss.

I lay in bed, and felt my way back to the present. To my world in which fate doesn't control steamships or puppets, where no foundations are laid and no history gets made.

The Christmas edition of the *Süddeutsche* lay on the bed. It gave an annual balance sheet of toxic incidents in the chemical industry. I soon laid the paper aside.

The world wasn't a better place for Korten's death. What had I done? Come to terms with my past? Wiped my hands of it?

I arrived far too late for lunch.

20

Come with the Wind!

Christmas Day brought no news of Korten's death, nor did the next. Sometimes I was fearful. Whenever the doorbell rang, I was frightened and assumed the police had arrived to storm the apartment. When I was relaxing happily in Brigitte's arms, alive with her sweet kisses, occasionally I wondered anxiously if this might be our last time together. At times I imagined the scene with Herzog, telling him everything. Or would I prefer to give my statement in front of Nägelsbach?

Most of the time I was easy in myself, fatalistic, and enjoyed the last days of the year, including coffee and plum-with-floury-butter-crumble-cake at the younger Schmalzes'. I liked little Manuel. He tried valiantly to speak German, accepted my morning presence in the bathroom without jealousy, and hoped staunchly for snow. To begin with the three of us went on our expeditions together, visiting the fairytale park on Königstuhl and the planetarium. Then he and I set out on our own. He liked going to the cinema as much as I did. When we came out of *Witness* we both had to fight our tears. In *Splash* he didn't understand why the mermaid loved the guy although he was so mean to her – I didn't tell him that's always the way. In the Kleiner Rosengarten he figured out the game Giovanni and I played, and played along. There was no teaching him a sensible German sentence after that. On the way back from ice skating he took my hand and said, 'You always with us when I come back?'

Brigitte and Juan had decided Manuel should go to high school in Mannheim, starting next autumn. Would I be in prison next autumn? And if not – would Brigitte and I stay together?

'I don't know yet, Manuel. But we'll certainly go to the cinema together.'

The days passed without Korten hitting the headlines, either dead or missing. There were moments when I wished things would come to an end, no matter how. Then once again I was grateful for the time gained. On the 27th Philipp called. He complained he hadn't caught a glimpse of my Christmas tree yet this year. 'And where have you been these last few days?'

That's when I got the idea about a party. 'I have something to celebrate,' I said. 'Come round on New Year's Eve, I'm having a party.'

'Should I bring you round a squeezable little Taiwanese something?'

'No need, Brigitte is back.'

'A-ha, Come with the Wind! But may I bring a little something for me to the party?'

Brigitte had followed the phone call. 'Party? What party?'

'We're celebrating New Year's Eve with your friends and mine. Who would you like to invite?'

On Saturday afternoon I dropped by to see Judith. I caught her in the midst of packing. She was planning to travel to Locarno on Sunday. Tyberg wanted to introduce her to Tessin society in Ascona on New Year's Eve. 'It's nice of you to come round, Gerd, but I'm in a terrible rush. Is it important, can't it wait? I'll be back at the end of January.' She indicated the open suitcases, and the packed ones, two large moving cartons, and a wild confusion of clothes. I recognized the silk blouse that she'd worn when she'd shown me to Firner's office. The button was still missing. 'I can tell you the truth about Mischkey's death now.'

She sat down on a suitcase and lit a cigarette. 'Yes?'

She listened without interrupting. When I'd finished she asked: 'And what happens to Korten now?'

It was the question I had dreaded. I had racked my brains over whether I should only go to Judith once Korten's death was public knowledge. But I mustn't make my actions dependent upon Korten's murder, and without it there was no reason to hush up the solving of the case any longer. 'I'll try to put him on the spot. He'll be back from Brittany at the beginning of January.'

'Oh, Gerd, you can't believe that Korten will break down in mid-sentence and confess?'

I didn't answer. I was reluctant to enter into a discussion about what should happen to Korten.

Judith took another cigarette from the pack and rolled it between the fingertips of both hands. She looked sad, worn out by all the to-ing and fro-ing that had accompanied Peter's murder, also aggravated, as if she wanted finally, finally, to put the whole thing behind her. 'I'll talk to Tyberg. You don't mind, do you?'

That night I dreamed that Herzog was interrogating me. 'Why didn't you go to the police?'

'What could the police have done?'

'Oh, we have impressive possibilities these days. Come on, I'll show you.' Through long corridors, via many stairs, we came to a room that I recognized from castles of the Middle Ages, with pincers, irons, masks, chains, whips, straps, and needles. A hellfire was burning in the grate. Herzog pointed to the rack. 'We'd have made Korten talk on that. Why didn't you trust the police? Now you'll have to go on it yourself.' I didn't struggle and was strapped to it. When I couldn't move, panic surged through me. I must have cried out before I woke. Brigitte had switched on the bedside lamp and turned to me with concern.

'Everything's fine, Gerd. No one's hurting you.'

I kicked myself free of the sheets that were stifling me. 'My God, what a dream.'

'Tell me, then you'll feel better.'

I didn't want to and she was hurt. 'I keep noticing, Gerd, that something's wrong with you. Sometimes you're hardly there.'

I snuggled into her arms. 'It'll pass, Brigitte. It has nothing to do with you. Have patience with an old man.'

It was only on New Year's Eve that Korten's death was reported. A tragic accident at his holiday home in Brittany on the morning of Christmas Eve had caused him to fall from the cliffs into the sea while out walking. The information gathered by the press and radio for Korten's seventieth birthday was now used for obituaries and eulogies. With Korten an epoch had ended, the epoch of the great men of Germany's era of reconstruction. The funeral was to take place at the beginning of January, attended by the president, the chancellor, the economics minister, as well as the complete cabinet of Rhineland-Palatinate. Scarcely anything better could have happened for his son's career. As his brother-in-law I'd be invited, but I wouldn't go. Nor would I send condolences to his wife.

I didn't envy him his glory. Nor did I forgive him. Murder means never having to say you forgive.

21

I'm sorry, Herr Self

Babs, Röschen, and Georg arrived at seven. Brigitte and I had just been putting the finishing touches to the party preparations, had lit the Christmas tree candles, and were sitting on the sofa with Manuel.

'Here she is, then!' Babs looked at Brigitte with kindly curiosity and gave her a kiss.

'Hats off, Uncle Gerd,' said Röschen. 'And the Christmas tree looks really cool.'

I gave them their presents.

'But Gerd,' said Babs reproachfully, 'I thought we'd decided against Christmas presents this year,' and took out her package. 'This is from the three of us.'

Babs and Röschen had knitted a wine-red sweater to which Georg had attached, at the appropriate spot, an electric circuit with eight lamps in the shape of a heart. When I pulled on the sweater the lamps started to flash to the rhythm of my heartbeat.

Then Herr and Frau Nägelsbach arrived. He was wearing a black suit, complete with stiff wing-collar and bow tie, a pince-nez on his nose, and was the spitting image of Karl Kraus. She was wearing a fin-de-siècle dress. 'Hedda Gabler?' I greeted her cautiously. She gave a curtsy and joined the ladies. He looked at the Christmas tree with disapproval. 'Bourgeois nonsense.'

The doorbell didn't stop ringing. Eberhard arrived with a little suitcase. 'I've come with a few magic tricks.'

Philipp brought Füruzan, a feisty, voluptuous Turkish nurse. 'Fuzzy can belly-dance!' Hadwig, a friend of Brigitte's, had her fourteen-year-old son Jan with her, who immediately took charge of Manuel.

Everyone streamed into the kitchen for the cold buffet. Dusty Springfield's 'I Close My Eyes and Count to Ten' played unnoticed in the living room. Philipp had put on *Hits of the 1960s*.

My study was empty. The telephone rang. I shut the door behind me. Only muffled jollity from the party reached my ears. All my friends were here – who could be calling?

'Uncle Gerd?' It was Tyberg. 'A Happy New Year! Judith told me and I read the newspaper. It appears you've solved the Korten case.'

'Hello, Herr Tyberg. All the best to you for the New Year, too. Will you still write the chapter about the trial?'

'I'll show it to you when you come to visit. Springtime is very nice at Lake Maggiore.'

'I'll be there. Until then.'

Tyberg had understood. It helped to have a secret ally who wouldn't call me to account.

The door burst open and my guests were asking for me. 'Where are you hiding, Gerd? Füruzan is going to do a belly dance for us.'

We cleared the dance floor and Philipp screwed a red lightbulb into the lamp. Füruzan entered from the bathroom in a veil and sequined bikini. Manuel and Jan's eyes popped out of their heads. The music began, supplicating and slow, and Füruzan's first movements were of a gentle, languorous fluidity. Then the tempo of the music increased and with it the rhythm of the dance. Röschen started to clap, everyone joined in. Füruzan discarded the veil, and let a tassel attached to her belly button circle wildly. The floor shook. When the music died away Füruzan ended with a triumphant pose and flung herself into Philipp's arms.

'This is the love of the Turks,' Philipp laughed.

'Laugh all you like. I'll get you. You don't play around with Turkish women,' she said, looking him haughtily in the eye.

I brought her my dressing gown.

'Stop,' called Eberhard as the audience was ready to disperse. 'I invite you to the breathtaking show by the great magician Ebus Erus Hardabakus.' And he made rings spin and link together and come apart again, and yellow scarves turn to red; he conjured up coins and made them disappear again, and Manuel was allowed to check that everything was above board. The trick with the white mouse went wrong. At the sight of it, Turbo leapt onto the table, knocked over the top hat it had supposedly disappeared into, chased it round the apartment, and playfully broke its neck behind the fridge before any of us could intervene. In response Eberhard wanted to break Turbo's neck, but luckily Röschen stopped him.

It was Jan's turn. He recited 'The Feet in the Fire' by Conrad Ferdinand Meyer. Next to me sat an anxious Hadwig, silently mouthing the poem with him. 'Mine is the revenge, saith the Lord,' thundered Jan at the end.

'Fill your glasses and plates and come back,' called Babs. 'It's on with the show.' She whispered with Röschen and Georg and the three of them pushed tables and chairs to the side and the dance floor became a small stage. Charades. Babs puffed out her cheeks and blew, and Röschen and Georg ran off.

'*Gone with the Wind*,' called Nägelsbach.

Then Georg and Röschen slapped one another until Babs stepped between them, took their hands, and joined them together. 'Kemal Atatürk in War and Peace!'

'Too Turkish, Fuzzy,' said Philipp and patted her thigh. 'But isn't she clever?'

It was half past eleven and I went to check there was plenty of champagne on ice. In the living room Röschen and Georg had taken over the stereo and were feeding old records onto the turntable: Tom Waits was singing 'Waltzing Matilda', and Philipp tried to waltz Babs down the narrow corridor. The children were playing tag with the cat. In the bathroom Füruzan was showering away the sweat of her belly dance. Brigitte came through to the kitchen and gave me a kiss. 'A lovely party.'

I almost didn't hear the doorbell. I pressed the buzzer for the front door, but then saw the green silhouette through the frosted glass of the apartment door and knew the visitor was already upstairs. I opened up. In front of me stood Herzog in uniform.

'I'm sorry, Herr Self . . .'

So this was the end. They say it happens just before you're hanged, but now the pictures of the past weeks went shooting through my mind, as if in a film. Korten's last look, my arrival in Mannheim on Christmas morning, Manuel's hand in mine, the nights with Brigitte, our happy group round the Christmas tree. I wanted to say something. I couldn't make a sound.

Herzog went ahead of me into the apartment. I heard the music being turned down. But our friends kept laughing and chattering cheerfully. When I had control of myself again, and went into the sitting room, Herzog had a glass of wine in his hand, and Röschen, a little tipsy, was fiddling with the buttons on his uniform.

'I was just on my way home, Herr Self, when the complaint about your party came through on the radio. I took it upon myself to look in on you.'

'Hurry up,' called Brigitte, 'two minutes to go.' Enough

time to distribute the champagne glasses and pop the corks.

Now we're standing on the balcony, Philipp and Eberhard let off the fireworks, from all the churches comes the ringing of bells, we clink glasses.

'Happy New Year.'